Trees of Heaven

JESSE STUART

Trees of Heaven

With a Foreword by
Wade Hall

THE UNIVERSITY PRESS OF KENTUCKY

Dedicated
to
Naomi Norris Stuart

Foreword by Wade Hall copyright © 1980 by The University Press of Kentucky

Scholarly publisher for the Commonwealth,
serving Bellarmine College, Berea College, Centre
College of Kentucky, Eastern Kentucky University,
The Filson Club, Georgetown College, Kentucky
Historical Society, Kentucky State University,
Morehead State University, Murray State University,
Northern Kentucky University, Transylvania University,
University of Kentucky, University of Louisville,
and Western Kentucky University.

Editorial and Sales Offices: The University Press of Kentucky
663 South Limestone Street, Lexington, Kentucky 40508-4008

The Library of Congress has cataloged the first printing of this title as follows:

Stuart, Jesse, 1907-
 Trees of heaven / Jesse Stuart ; with a foreword by Wade Hall.
— Lexington, Ky. : University Press of Kentucky, c1980.

 340 p. : ill. ; 23 cm.

 Reprint of the 1940 ed. published by E.P. Dutton, New York.
 ISBN 0-8131-1446-2. ISBN 0-8131-0150-6 (pbk.)

 I. Title
PS3537.T92516T7   1980   813'.52—dc19   80-51020
                                                   MARC

This book is printed on acid-free recycled paper meeting
the requirements of the American National Standard
for Permanence of Paper for Printed Library Materials.
☉ ⊛
Manufactured in the United States of America

CONTENTS

FOREWORD

In July of 1938 when Jesse Stuart returned from a Guggenheim-sponsored year in Scotland, he heard some startling news. Over forty years later he recalled vividly his disbelief: "I discovered that E.P. Dutton, my publisher then, had put out publicity that I had gone to Europe to write my first novel. The fact was that I had *not* been in Europe writing a novel! But with all the publicity out about me, I thought I'd better write one. So I wrote *Trees of Heaven.*"

It was to be his fifth book. He began writing on August 8, 1939—his thirty-second birthday—and completed the novel seventy-two days later. It was published on April 22, 1940. In the meantime—on October 14, 1939—he had married Naomi Deane Norris of nearby Greenup, Kentucky. It was a period of new frontiers in the young writer's life.

Stuart has given some of the credit for his first novel to another Kentucky novelist: "Earlier I had met Elizabeth Madox Roberts in Louisville. She asked me why I hadn't written a novel. I said, 'I just can't manage it. I can't bring it through.' Then she gave me some good advice. 'You do short stories well. Let your stories be your stepping stones or low ridges and the novel be your main long ridge.' So when I started *Trees of Heaven*, I put together two story ideas. One story is about Anse Bushman, who is a composite of my father and another man, Forrest King, my second father with whom I boarded when I taught at McKell High School. Both men were hard workers and made everybody around them work too. The other story is about a man who used to live in W-Hollow in a little lean-to which has since burned down. I call him Boliver Tussie in the novel. He was shiftless, lazy, carefree and wouldn't work. And I loved him. He enjoyed life."

Indeed, with these two stories Stuart had the outline for *Trees of Heaven*. Set in Stuart's native Greenup County, Kentucky—here called Greenwood—the novel examines man's right relationship with the land. The theme is explored in the conflict between two men and their opposing life-styles. Anse Bushman is a hard-working, acquisitive landowner. Boliver Tussie is a hard-drinking, happy-go-lucky squatter who works only enough to provide himself and his family with bare necessities. Boliver cares nothing for deed ownership of the land. On the other hand, Anse has spent most of his seventy-one years "gettin ahead." He has almost killed his wife with work. His rough life has driven off, killed, or alienated ten of his eleven children. His youngest son, eighteen-year-old Tarvin, is still at home but is beginning to wonder if there may not be a better way to live. After he meets Boliver Tussie and his pretty daughter Subrinea, Tarvin sees an alternative to his father's back-breaking life of labor and land greed. The developing love between Tarvin and Subrinea is a Romeo-Juliet counterpart to the enmity between their parents.

To Anse Bushman the Boliver Tussies are trashy poor whites who choose to live little better than hogs. In fact, Stuart paints Boliver at the start in bold strokes as a Kentucky hillbilly cousin of Erskine Caldwell's Georgia cracker, Jeeter Lester. Boliver, one feels, would be at home on Tobacco Road or in the rural slums of Dogpatch. When Tarvin first meets him, he is sprawled out drunk on his front porch in a pair of ragged, sweaty overalls, his bare feet hanging over the edge and flies crawling over his body. He is a cartoon caricature of the hillbilly at his unsavory worst. As Boliver's full portrait emerges, however, Stuart gives him many redeeming qualities, and it is toward Boliver's view of life that the novel moves. He is the kind of man of whom Stuart was to say forty years later, "I loved him." But the moral gauge does not move all the way to the Tussie side. Before the novel ends, a more balanced view of life is suggested by the union of Tarvin and Subrinea. To the new family Tarvin will bring the Bushman virtues of work and responsibility, and Subrinea will contribute her family's gift of joy and leisure. In truth, though, Stuart suggests that all men are but short-lived squatters on the land—till they are received back into the earth.

Soon after they met, Subrinea took Tarvin to see the squatter graveyard where her ancestors have been resting for generations. It is surrounded by wilderness and covered by ailanthus trees, the trees of heaven. Later, Tarvin muses on the dead Tussies: "They didn't waste their lives away buyin land and more land and working like brutes to pay fer land like Pa has. They didn't work their wives like Pa has worked Ma. They took life easier and I don't know but it was better. . . . They lived while they lived." Indeed, "Live while you live" is a simple way to state what this novel is about.

When Stuart published *Trees of Heaven* in 1940, he had already staked out his claim to a rich literary lode of eastern Kentucky hill country. His territory was familiar to the thousands of people who had read his four previous books. *Harvest of Youth* (1930) and *Man with a Bull-tongue Plow* (1934) contained poetic renderings of his land and its people. In *Head o' W-Hollow* (1936) he expressed himself in short stories. *Beyond Dark Hills* (1938) was an autobiographical narrative. His single poems and stories had been read by additional thousands of people in such magazines as *Scribner's, Esquire, Saturday Review of Literature, Harper's, New Republic, American Mercury,* and *Collier's.*

When *Trees of Heaven* appeared, Stuart was already regarded as an important literary voice of the Kentucky hill people. The novel added scope and depth to his voice. It also prefigured the dimensions of his fictional country. Set principally in Ragweed Hollow, the story opens out to include other landmarks and place-names thoroughly explored in subsequent Stuart works. More important, it demonstrated that Stuart could sustain a novel-length narrative and revealed in great depth an insider's knowledge of his country's rich folklife and humor. On the large canvas of the novel, he unfolded a colorful panorama of life in the Kentucky hills: timber cutting, tobacco growing, hog killing, molasses making, and a people who love, dispense justice, fight, and frolic. His characters sometimes play rough and talk rough. They are not the cleaned-up, refined back-country personages prepared fifty or more years before by a John Fox, Jr., or a Mary Noailles Murfree for exhibit in a folk museum. Stuart's people speak and behave like real people, with sheep dung on their shoes and tobacco spittle running down their mouths. Above all, they live with zest and energy.

In *Trees of Heaven* Stuart used a simple declarative style that he was to develop into a hallmark of his fiction. Indeed, the novel contains some of his most skillful writing—a spare, sinewy prose that can be as direct as a twelve-gauge shotgun or as lyrical as August corn tassels blowing in the warm wind. Somewhat less successful is young Stuart's experiment with narration in the present tense, a technique that sometimes produces only a strained immediacy.

Jesse Stuart would tighten and strengthen his narrative style in later novels and stories. He would flesh out his characters with finer strokes and greater deftness. He would plot his fiction with more unity. But he would never write any more accurately of the country he had known since birth. Nor would he ever introduce a more enduring contribution to the literature of the American poor white than the Tussies, a family whose kin ranges from A.B. Longstreet's antebellum Ransy Sniffle to William Faulkner's Flem Snopes. And he would seldom stray very far from the rich lode that he mined on a grand scale for the first time in *Trees of Heaven*.

WADE HALL
Bellarmine College

Part I

1.

"TARVIN, YOU aint takin that gun out agin," says Fronnie. "I'm gittin tired of seein that gun leave this house every time your Pa gits away. You take the gun and go. You never bring back any game. What is the matter? Has your eyes failed you? Don't you know your Pa comes to the house and furses with me every time you go out with the gun?"

"No, Ma, I didn't know it," says Tarvin. "Haf to stay here and work from daylight until dark all the time. I like to have a little fun. If I'd listen to Pa, I wouldn't do anything in my life but work. That is all he does. I never intend to kill myself workin like Pa has. I intend to slip out with the gun when I can."

Fronnie stands in the kitchen door and watches Tarvin clean

the gun. Fronnie is a tall mountain woman, her once crow-wing black hair is streaked with silvery streaks of gray; her eagle-gray eyes are being dimmed by time. Time, hard work on the farm and in the house, and childbirth have not bent her tall body. She stands straight as a poplar sapling in the kitchen door and watches Tarvin. Her long arms hang limp at her sides. With the calloused long slim fingers of her left hand she fingers at her apron pocket. She is crumbling the home-grown bright burley leaf into finer tobacco crumbs to put in her long-stemmed brown clay pipe.

"Gun's rusted," says Tarvin. "There must be a leak in the house. Look at the red rust on this gun barrel. It's shore hard to take off'n here, Ma. I've rubbed and rubbed on this gun barrel. This is a harder job than hoein corn."

Tarvin rubs the meat rind up and down the gun barrel. He bends over the gun barrel and bears down with the weight of his shoulders and tries to make the meat rind cut the rust. He takes a rag and rubs over where the meat rind has been. There is a blue glint coming to the shotgun barrel. Tarvin takes another meat rind, tied to a sea-grass string on one end and a tenpenny nail on the other. He drops the nail down the twelve-gauge shotgun barrel and pulls the clump of oily meat rind through the gun barrel. He does this over and over again. Fronnie stands in the kitchen door and watches him. She takes her pipe from her blue-checked apron pocket, holds it in her right hand and puts pinches of fine sand-colored burley tobacco crumbs into her pipe. She fills her pipe without looking at it. Her eyes are watching what Tarvin is doing to the family shotgun. Fronnie loads her pipe and puts it in her mouth. She fingers a match from the tobacco crumbs in her apron pocket, strikes it on the kitchen door-facing and cups her left hand over the bright blaze to keep the lazy August wind from blowing it out. She lights her pipe and big blue clouds of smoke roll from her lips.

"You're usin all my meat rinds, Tarvin," says Fronnie, taking her pipe from her mouth and holding it in her right hand. "I won't have enough left to grease the bread pans if you clean that gun a few more times. You know the corn pone sticks in the bottom of the pan when I don't grease the bottom of the pan with a meat rind. Your Pa will furse with me over your usin so many meat rinds."

"Yes, Ma," says Tarvin, "but Pa allus said he'd rather be buried without an oakboard coffin as to hunt with a dirty gun. He said that of all that he wanted clean was a gun. Said he'd rather have his ears full of dirt until he couldn't hear, his neck, feet, and hands scaly with dirt as to be caught in the woods with a dirty gun. I don't like the way Pa does things and I don't take atter Pa—but I am like Pa when it comes to a gun. Since my gun's rusted I'm goin to fix the leak in the roof, so help me God. I aint goin to stand this. When I go to the woods I like to have my gun bright and shiny. There aint anything purtier than a clean gun—one bright and shiny, so when the sun shines on the barrel you can see yourself like in a lookin-glass."

Tarvin sits on the upheaved root of the poplar tree in the kitchen yard. His long overall-covered legs are crossed and his bare feet shift in a little pile of sand where water has run across the kitchen yard toward the well-gum. His toes wriggle in the warm sand when he bears down on the rag, pressing down with all the weight of his broad shoulders, giving the blue shotgun barrel the final polish to make it have a looking-glass finish. The wind rustles the dry poplar leaves above him and specks of sun filter down among the canopy of soft-bellied poplar leaves—making light and dark spots over his gray-checked gingham homemade shirt.

"Got it cleaned, Ma," says Tarvin, "but I'm hot as a roasted tater. Lord, but that sun is hot when a body is snug back in the shade. I know the barrel is clean. I can see myself in the gun barrel now."

Tarvin gets up and stands beside the trunk of the tree. His

tall bean-pole body reaches to the low limbs on the poplar tree and half his head is hidden among the leaves. He stands six feet and five inches barefooted. The shotgun stock is resting on his bare foot and the muzzle is pointed upward toward the poplar leaves, reaching just a little above Tarvin's knees.

"Eight years ago," says Fronnie, blowing clouds of smoke from her pipe, "when you was jest a little shaver ten years old, you ust to take that very gun to the woods and bring back as many as twelve squirrels. Now you air a man eighteen years old and you go out every time your Pa is gone and you don't bring back nothin. No wonder your Pa gits riled at you. You must be huntin another kind of game. You aint found a purty gal over there amongst the timber squatters, have you?"

"Aint the squirrels here they ust to be, Ma," says Tarvin. "You know that. The timber is about all gone. All that aint gone is goin fast. You can't have squirrels if you don't have timber. That is a cinch. The squirrels don't have any place to make their nests. You know they won't nest on the ground like a ground spar. They've got to have tall trees with knot-holes in 'em. They've got to have tall trees with wild grape-vines runnin up amongst them when they build a nest out in the open. Squirrels like knotholes and hollow trees."

Tarvin puts the shotgun across his shoulder. He walks across the kitchen yard and around the corner of the house to the front-yard gate. Fronnie follows him to the front yard. She smokes her pipe and watches Tarvin walk over the yellow clay bank. She watches his tall body move slowly down the hill, under the hot August sun. She can see the heat glimmer in the sultry air—jerky traces in the wind that hurts her eyes. She can hear the grasshoppers flying from bunch grass to bunch grass making sizzling noises with their wings like bacon frying in a pan. It reminds Fronnie of the clean bodies of squirrels in the big skillet over the kitchen fire.

"Bring back a half dozen squirrels, Tarvin," Fronnie reminds him. "You know how your Pa likes squirrel broth this

hot weather when rough grub don't set well with his stummick." Fronnie holds her pipe in her hand and watches him
as he walks deeper down into the deep hollow below the house.
Tarvin does not hear. He does not answer Fronnie. Maybe it is
the thickness of the glimmering heat that has muffled her
words to him; maybe the rock walls that enclose the hollow
have batted back her words to her; perhaps Tarvin is thinking
only about the rough cattle road that leads to Cat's Fork where
a family of squatters live.

2.

THE AUGUST sun looks down upon a tall boy as he wends his
way along a tiny path with a gun across his shoulder, the
barrel bright and shiny and glistening like a September sassafras leaf in the hazy autumn sunlight. The August sun plays
in the torrid sky above him, plays like an agate marble in an
arch of void. The earth below is a wilted mass of smelly vegetation. The earth below is a smelly earth, an earth fragrant
with many odors; odors that pierce the nostrils and inflame the
brain and bring tears to the eyes. There is the smell of resin
from the pine trees on the rocky slopes; sweet smelling odors
from the red and golden fine-haired cornsilks growing from
the shooting ears of corn; and there are odors from the locust
leaves, the sassafras sprouts, jimson weeds, shoe-lace, smart-
weed and wild phlox, growing on the creekside banks. There is
a mixed smell of pleasant odors going to Tarvin's nostrils as he
walks lazily under the August sun down Ragweed Hollow.

He turns to his right, takes the path up Cat's Fork, a narrow
path where the yokes of oxen have snaked the giant logs down
the creek to the sawmill. The path is the color of a copperhead's belly, for the ends of the logs have skimmed away the
black loamy surface of rotted leaves down to a reddish clay,
and down even in places to a clay that is duck-bill yellow.
Tarvin's bare feet walk over this hot mulched earth, so hot that

it stings his bare toes. On the left and right of this path are heaps of treetops, massed in places thirty feet high, with leaves still clinging to their boughs. These trees were cut while they were green and the leaves didn't fall from their boughs—pale green mountains of withered leaves, still clinging to sapless boughs—waiting for a spark of fire, and all the earth will be barren again, and all life that can't fly away, crawl fast enough or run fast enough will return to white wisps of ashes. Even the tiny ravines that are flooded each spring with blue mountain water leaping from rock to rock, are now smoothed as if they had never been, with wreckage of these trees.

"I can tell Ma," Tarvin thinks, as he looks at this waste of life, "that they aint no squirrels. I can tell her they aint a tree left fer the squirrels on Cat's Fork. I can tell her I didn't smoke all the time I was in the woods fer I was afraid to strike a match. If the woods got on fire I'd be burned to death, fer I couldn't outrun the fire."

Tarvin walks up the path, his heart beating faster, but not because he has exerted his long lean muscular frame by over-walking. He will soon be in sight of a squatter's shack on Cat's Fork. If it were not for the shack ahead of him, he would prowl into the undergrowth. He would find a hickory tree where the squirrels are cutting on green hickory nuts. He would lie down flat on his back under the tree, and as the shade of evening drew across the land the squirrels would come to get their suppers. He would lie under the tree and shoot them out of the hickory treetop as fast as they came. He would shoot half a dozen before he would get up from his bed on the ground. Tarvin, with the gray eyes of an eagle, would not miss a shot. He would make every shell count; because he had to steal out hens' eggs from the nests to buy his shells and he knows how hard that is to do. Anse Bushman, his father, is too tight to buy shotgun shells; besides, Anse has other places to put his money. Anse has dreams of his own. Wouldn't the big Sexton Land Tract be sold as soon as the timber was cut, sawed and hauled away? It would go cheap, too, for there wouldn't be anything left but sawdust piles, slab piles, stumps, treetops and squatter shacks. He can buy it for five dollars an acre. And he will be ready to buy it, for it joins his farm. Anse, like his father before him, loves the land. He will have hundreds of acres of land to live on and he will have the freedom that his father had before him. Anse doesn't want people moving close to him, their dogs hunting over his land and killing his game; their chickens meeting his chickens in the woods and mating with them, ruining his gray game chickens; and the ugly smoke rising in dirty gray-green clouds from their chimneys. The smoke from a neighbor's chimney was always ugly to Anse if the neighbor lived close enough for Anse to see the smoke. He will not have it. He will buy the land. He will be ready. He isn't going to buy Tarvin's shotgun shells no matter if he does like squirrel broth when victuals don't set well on his stomach. He would rather die of stomach trouble than to be smothered to death by neighbors living too close.

3.

"GEE CHRIST," says Tarvin, "this sun is hot. August here, nights cool and days hot. Corn growin so fast you can't reach the tassels with a ten-foot pole."

Tarvin take his index finger and wipes the sweat from his forehead, flings it in a tiny circle on the hot dry sand in the road. He is below the squatter's shack now. The shack is up on the hillside in a little flat. It stands like a big brown dirt-colored box in the sunlight. There is not a shade around it. There is a small place cleared away from around the house so if the woods catch on fire the flames cannot reach the shack. The clear spot around the house is planted in corn and garden truck. There is a bright path, worn slick as a path from a ground-hog hole, over the hill to the creek. The path leads to a spring beside a sycamore stump, shaded by clumps of jimson weeds and pokeberry shoots where the family gets water to drink and to use for cooking. There is another path that leads down to the oxen road the way that Tarvin has just come. These are the only paths that leave the shack. Behind it are mountains of green vegetation back to where the timber once stood. Beginning where the timber once stood are mountains of brown wreckage with an occasional oxen road dividing these mountains of wreckage as tiny ravines and streamlets cut and scar across mountains of badlands in winter.

"I can't hep it," thinks Tarvin, "what Pa will say if he ever finds out that I come here. I don't care what he says if he ever finds out. I'm as big as Pa and I believe I'd have a purty good chance at 'im in a fair fist fight. I don't want to haf to fight 'im but if I do haf to fight 'im I'll fight to whop Pa. What would he say if he's ever to find me here? But Pa won't be here unless he happens to be lookin over this land. He won't bother with squatters. I'd like to know why Pa hates a squatter worse than a copperhead."

"And you have come," says a tall barefooted girl running down the hot dry path to meet Tarvin. A golden shock of long hair falls over her shoulders. It is not combed any more than a patch of love-vines growing among briars and sprouts. Her long brown arms are flung high in the air as she runs down the path toward Tarvin. Her brown strong muscular legs move

like pistons in perfect rhythm and her thin blue-checked gingham dress is caught above her knees as she runs.

"Yes, Subrinea," says Tarvin. "I had a time gittin away, but
I got here. Pa had plenty of work laid out fer me to do but I
polished my gun and told Ma I's goin squirrel huntin. Ma
didn't say much. Said I wasn't the hunter I ust to be. I think
I'm a better hunter than I ust to be, don't you?"

"Yes," says Subrinea smilingly, and showing two rows of
white teeth pretty as two rows of fresh-husked autumn corn.
"I hope you air a better hunter. I hope you like the game
you've found."

Subrinea takes Tarvin by the hand. They walk up to the
shack under the boiling August sun. They walk up to the little
porch that Subrinea's father has made of slabs that he has
carried on his back up the hill from the sawmill. The slabs are
rough and full of knotholes and their edges are covered with
rough strips of bark. The house is made of slabs and covered
with clapboards. The chimney is made of rocks picked up from
the hillside. It is a rough stone chimney, the color of sand.

"Howdy, Tarvin," says Subrinea's father. "Dog my cats if
it aint old Anse Bushman's baby boy. You can't fool an old
squatter like Boliver Tussie—dang my hide, tallow and liver
if you can!"

Boliver slaps his bare legs and laughs. He lies on the porch
floor with his shoes for a pillow. His pants legs are rolled
nearly to his knees. He does not wear a shirt and his overall
suspenders are all that cover his shoulders. Subrinea's mother
is sitting on the porch fanning with a bundle of spicewood
sprouts when she doesn't fight the flies with her fan. Subrinea's three small sisters are lying on the porch floor with
only one piece of clothing girded about their hips. Her two
brothers are lying out on the grass under the shade of a rosebush. One is strumming the strings of an old dilapidated-
looking guitar while both of them sing:

Darlin Cora, Darlin Cora,
Come lay your hand in mine,
You'll live a lady's life
Long as the sun may shine.

I wrote Darlin Cora a letter,
And in this letter ran,
I've got me another woman,
You can get you another man.

Yonder stands Darlin Cora,
With the mud up to her knees,
Drinkin' down her troubles
And courtin' whoever she pleases.

I told little Cora a secret,
A secret fer to keep,
She told it to her Mammie,
A-talkin' in her sleep.

Some say whiskey will run a man crazy,
Some say it will effect his head;

But if whiskey will run 'im crazy,
Purty wimmen will kill 'im dead.

The last time I saw Darlin Cora
She was sittin' on the bank by the sea
With a big forty-four around her waist
And a banjer on her knee.

They do not have shoes on their feet, nor shirts on their backs. They wear ragged pants that barely hide their nakedness from their waists to their knees. Subrinea's largest sister sits beside her mother on a block of wood. She fans with a bundle of spicewood sprouts and fights the flies. Subrinea's mother has a small baby in her lap. He is as naked as a picked chicken. Tarvin holds Subrinea's hand and they stand silently on the porch and listen to her brothers sing and play "Darlin Cora" on the guitar. There is a sad wailing sound coming from the muted strings of the guitar.

"Crissie, that is old Anse Bushman's boy," says Boliver. "He may be my son-in-law. He's been comin here a lot. I can see 'im makin goo-goo eyes at Subrinea and I've seen her castin sheep eyes at 'im. When you get goo-goo eyes and sheep eyes together, you've got love."

"Shet your trap, Boliver," says Crissie. "I'll get a stick of wood and brain you if you don't."

"Pay Pap no minds, Tarvin," says Subrinea. "You know what's the matter with Pap. If Ma aint there to git his money on Saturday, he gits it and the moonshiners wait fer it. Then he gits drunk as a owl and lays on the porch every Saturday afternoon and Sunday. When I come around, Pap jest tries to show hisself!"

"Show hisself," Boliver repeats. "Show hisself." He slaps his thighs with his big red hairy hands and laughs. He slaps his thighs again with his big hands and he laughs and laughs. The flies alight on his bare arms, his shoulders and the bald dome on his head, but he wriggles his body and shoos them off. He brushes them from his hairy arms with his hands. When Crissie shoos the flies from herself with the spicewood sprouts they fly down and alight on Boliver. Tarvin does not sit down on the porch. He stands and looks down at Boliver lying drunk on the rough slab porch. He sees the sweat stream from his body and mix with the dust on the floor.

"How could I ever put up with 'im?" Tarvin thinks. "What if Pa was to catch me here? He would take a withe and try to whop me all the way home. How could Pa stand all this dirt in this little slab-built shack without a shade tree around it and drinkin water from a spring that is open to the gnats, frogs, lizards, snakes, turtles and the sunlight. Looks like water warm as dishwater from a shallow spring that would make 'em all sick."

Tarvin looks in at the open kitchen door. He sees the flies swarm in and out in a long black line. He sees a dishpan filled with dirty dishes sitting on the table. The flies alight on the dishpan, stay awhile and then fly back out at the hole sawed in the wall of slabs for a window. There isn't a windowpane nor a windowsash in the house; just holes sawed in the slabs for windows.

"No use to lay around and fight the flies with spicewood sprouts," thinks Tarvin, "when there's not a winderpane in the whole house. No use to shoo 'em out'n the house when you leave the dishes on the table fer 'em to clean. It is a lot as Pa says. The squatters air a dirty lot and they air a triflin lot. They live like hogs. But amongst families that live like hogs there is often a purty girl. And when you love a girl you don't haf to love the family, and when you marry a girl you don't haf to marry the family."

Tarvin holds to Subrinea's hand. He looks down at her loose-flung uncontrolled shock of golden wheat-straw-colored hair. Her head comes even with his shoulders. Her cat-green eyes look up toward Tarvin's brown face. He looks at her strong shapely body, the outline of her full bosom beneath her thin dress and her strong brown muscular legs. She is a wild phlox in beauty for him to look at, and she is the ripe fruit ready to be plucked. He squeezes her long shapely calloused hand with his big fire-shovel calloused hand.

"Don't you know people call us squatters, young man," says Boliver Tussie, "but we've been in this county long as some of you damn good people and I don't mind tellin you. I've jest got enough rot-gut licker in me to speak my mind fer me—to speak the things I've allus wanted to speak and I couldn't get the words out nohow. My people have been in this county since the old iron-furnace days. They come here from God knows where. They've been here ever since. They hepped to cut cordwood over all these hills fer the iron furnaces that ust to be in this county. Atter the ore played out and the furnaces went down, they squatted on the land. Many of 'em moved away. Now we've hepped to cut timber and make crossties all over this county. It's hard fer me to rent a farm in this county. I'm a good crosstie maker and timber-cutter and I'm a good squatter. And young man, you're in love with my Subrinea and when old Anse knows it he's goin to raise hell and you know it."

"Boliver, you air a-doin too much talkin," says Crissie. "You don't know nothin about Anse Bushman. He aint somewhere sprawled on the floor drunk as a swine. I know that much about 'im. You make a dollar a day fer five days a week and a half-dollar on Saturday and you try to drink that up. If it wasn't fer our garden and truck patches and the wild berries in the fields I don't know how we'd live. Anse Bushman is a good provider fer his family and you know that."

"I aint sayin he aint a good provider" says Boliver, slapping at the flies on his chin with his big fire-shovel hands. "I'm tryin to say that he aint our kind. He aint no squatter. And when a man aint a squatter hisself, he looks down on squatters. Our families don't mix. His boy is coming to see my gal.

I think it's better fer 'im to spark his own kind o' gals instead of a squatter's gal. It will save a lot of trouble in the end."

"I think you're like a lot of other old cusses," says Tarvin, looking down at Boliver with a frown on his face and fire dancing in his eyes. "I think the sooner you kick up your heels your family will be better off. It aint none of your damn business who Subrinea sparks. You married the gal you wanted, now you air tryin to choose fer Subrinea. You aint tellin me what to do."

Tarvin looks at Subrinea. Subrinea looks at Tarvin.

"And you aint tellin Subrinea what to do, either," Tarvin adds.

Crissie giggles when Tarvin says these words to Boliver. She looks at Tarvin admiringly. She looks at his long slender body with his head against the slabs on the porch roof. She looks at Subrinea standing beside Tarvin, her own daughter standing there holding the hand of Anse Bushman's boy. That is something for a squatter's girl to do. She is proud that Subrinea is doing this.

"Sometimes I think I'll take the ax," says Crissie, "when Boliver gits on his week-end drunk, and take the double bitt and split his goddamn head wide open. I git so tired of this life. I've allus wanted to escape it and live as other people live. I see how other people live. I see 'em livin beside the roads that lead to town. I see 'em laughin and talkin and havin a good time. I see 'em walkin from painted houses and drivin big fine cars. They pass me when I come from town carryin a load of grub fer my children big enough to break my back. I think back of my family of seven dirty-faced youngins and my shack allus in the head of Cat's Fork without a wagon road leadin to it. Jest a fox path, a hunter's path or the road the oxen make is the way you'll allus walk to my shack. And we don't know how long we git to stay here. Soon as the timber is worked out, we'll haf to be movin on."

"Hmmm," says Boliver, spitting ambeer on the porch floor

among the flies, "you aint goin to git old Boliver asleep to split his brains out with a double-bitted ax. He aint takin no chance on you. He's watched you fer a long time. If I didn't have me a little snort from the jug every Saturday life wouldn't be worth livin. Jest a little snort from the jug on Saturday and fox huntin two nights out'n the week and something to eat three times a day, good homemade twist to chaw, and old Boliver can git along in this world."

Crissie takes her pipe from her pocket. She fills it with dark tobacco leaves and tamps the tobacco down with her index finger into the stone clay pipe. She takes a match from her apron pocket, strikes it on the porch floor and lights her pipe. She puffs tiny clouds of smoke from her pipe. She rocks the naked baby in her lap on the rockerless chair and hums "Darlin Cora" to it to get it to sleep. There is a soft wail of guitar music coming from the guitar down by the rosebush. Her boys are singing "Darlin Cora" again.

"I aint fer my gal sparkin nobody but her own kin," says Boliver, "and I don't keer what you say about it. She's as much my gal as she is yourn. We had her in partnership and I aim fer her to listen to her old Pap a little. You know I want to do all I can fer my own gal."

"Do all you can, huh!" says Crissie. "Let her sweep out the lumberjacks cabins fer thirty-five cents a week. You let her go amongst them men and work and clean up their old dirty shacks fer thirty-five cents. You know she is good to look at and they aint no wimmen around here. They try to make love to her and you know it. Then you do all you can fer your own gal! You don't do it and you know you don't. Look at the money that goes down your long rusty bull-neck."

"Stop quarrelin at 'im, Ma," says Subrinea. "You know he's full of rotgut moonshine licker. Leave Pa alone and let 'im go to sleep."

"So Crissie can split my brains out with the double-bitted ax," says Boliver. "Nope, old Boliver if he goes to sleep will sleep like a snake—with both eyes wide open. I've been layin here thinkin about that ax."

"And I'm settin here wonderin where we're goin when this timber job is finished," says Crissie. "We'll haf to light some place. We'll haf to leave here. This land will be sold soon as the last tree is cut. I know somebody is jest waitin with the money to buy it."

Tarvin does not speak. He looks at Crissie and then he looks at Boliver lying sprawled on the porch floor with the flies covering his body. All the clothing Boliver has on his body is a pair of ragged overalls. They are damp with sweat and loud with smell. The fumes from the wilted spicewood leaves are nauseating the house flies and that is why Crissie uses them. The mixed odors from Boliver's body and the hot breaths from the children are unpleasant for Tarvin to smell.

"Let's git out and go to the spring," says Tarvin. "I haf to have a drink o' water."

"All right," says Subrinea, "we'll git a drink o' water. I want a drink o' water too."

4.

"DAMN THE FLIES to hell nohow," says Boliver; "they won't let a body rest in peace. Atter a week cuttin timber a body likes to rest." Boliver slaps at the flies that have covered his face and are working their way up closer and closer to his lips. Boliver cranes his neck up to watch the young couple walk down the path toward the spring. He bends only his neck and leaves his body lying relaxed on the hard slab floor.

"I don't like it," says Boliver; "damned if I do. I'd ruther see Subrinea go with a lumberjack. I'd ruther see her go with a squatter. She'll never be happy livin the life like the Bushmans live. You can't tell me that Bushman boy aint atter Subrinea. I saw the color come to his face when you told him about Subrinea sweepin out the lumberjacks' shacks fer thirty-five cents a week. He didn't like it. No siree, he didn't like it one bit."

"You'd ruther Subrinea would do like our people has done," says Crissie. "Look at the Tussies! They couldn't find squatters to marry and they've married one another. Uncles have married nieces and first cousins have married first cousins, and grandpas have married granddaughters. I don't know what it does to people but I know what it does to hogs. I know the stock in hogs will run out when you breed cousins to cousins and uncles to nieces and aunts to nephews and grandpas to granddaughters. And I know the stock has about run out'n the Tussies. Look at Uncle Greenwood's boy Lonnie! Look at his long neck and his little head. He can't git a cap small enough fer 'im, his head is so little. I aint a Tussie and look at our children. All got good health, good pluck and good minds!"

"I still don't like the Bushmans," says Boliver, "and I don't want to see Subrinea go with that big tall brown-faced Bushman boy. He looks all right but his people will look down on us. I don't like it. I like my way of livin better than I like their ways of livin. They have plenty to eat and wear, and they have a big white-painted house on the hill—and money in the bank I 'spect, but Crissie, they aint no happier than we air, fer they worry all the time. We don't worry a lot about things. We let every day provide fer itself and God send Sunday."

5.

SUBRINEA TAKES the gourd dipper from a nail on the sycamore stump. She pushes the gnats from the surface of the water and dips the gourd deep into the spring. She bends down on her knees and leans out over the spring. Tarvin looks at her curved body with her dress pressed tightly against her, her golden hair in the fading sunlight streaming across her shoulders and her muscular brown legs on the grass and her feet with hard calluses on the bottoms. Tarvin watches her use the gourd, dipping deep into the bottom of the spring to get cool water from the seep that comes from under the sycamore roots.

"You air shore purty, Subrinea," he says. "I could love you forever."

"Have a drink," says Subrinea, getting up from the spring and handing Tarvin the gourd filled with fresh water.

"Drink first," says Tarvin.

"I won't do it," she says. "I'm gittin you a drink."

Subrinea curves her lips and smiles. She looks at Tarvin as he takes the dipper. He holds it in his hand and looks at her. Slowly he puts the dipper to his mouth. He looks at the girl who gave him the water. "Gurgle-gurgle-gurgle."

"It's good and cool," says Tarvin, handing Subrinea the dipper. "I didn't think the water would be cool from a spring that's left open."

"I dipped down deep to git water fer you," she says. "I got it from the fresh runnin-water seep in the bottom of the spring. I wanted you to have a cool drink o' water."

"Thank you," says Tarvin. "You let me dip you a drink o' water."

"Thank you," says Subrinea, "but I'd better do it. This is a funny spring. You've got to know jest how to dip the water out without stirrin up the sand in the bottom."

She bends over the spring and dips deep into the spring

water. She carefully lifts the dipper from the spring and rises
to her knees, then to full standing position. She drinks from
the dipper and looks at Tarvin. The August sun is slowly
moving beyond the cornfield back of the shack on the hill.
Shadows are lengthening over a mountain of green and brown.
Insects are making whirring noises in the grass; a whippoorwill
calls from the hilltop.

"It's time fer me to be goin," says Tarvin. "Pa will be out
huntin me if he comes in and finds out that I haven't done
any work and that I haven't killed any squirrels. I want to
leave in time to git a squirrel. I know where I can git one fer
Pa, out'n a hickory above the road. I passed there the other
day and I saw where squirrels were cuttin on the green hickory
nuts."

"I'll go with you a piece," says Subrinea, "if you don't mind.
I'll walk down the hollow to the trees of Heaven. I want to be
with you a little while longer. I looked fer you all day yesterday and you didn't come."

"It's hard fer me to git away," says Tarvin. "I've done an
awful lot of squirrel huntin this summer and a lot of berry
pickin; and, anymore I never kill many squirrels and I never
find many wild berries. I've been berry pickin and squirrel
huntin every day since I met you at the dance. I didn't know
there was a girl in the world as purty as you."

They walk down the path below the spring toward the path
that Tarvin followed up the hollow. Tarvin puts his right arm
around her waist and she puts her left arm around Tarvin's
waist. He holds her right hand with his left hand and the two
mountain lovers walk down the narrow trail to the oxen road.
Tarvin glances once more toward the shack and he sees
Boliver's bare feet sticking over the porch. He can see him
wiggling his ugly toes.

"Pa is really drunk when he gits like that," says Subrinea.
"If it wasn't fer Ma he'd stay drunk like that fer days. He
would sprawl out on the porch and never move atter he scooted

down fur enough to git his feet over the edge of the porch. Jest lay there and wiggle his toes, and when you try to wake him he hollers that he's fallin over a cliff and a tree is about to fall on 'im.''

"Was he ever hit by a tree?" Tarvin asks.

"Not exactly," says Subrinea, "but he was nearly hit by one once. If it had a-hit Pa there wouldn't a-been a greasy spot left of 'im. He's had nightmares about it ever since. He was a-heppin cut a tall poplar that growed down in the hollow. It was sixty feet to the first limb. If they had cut it low against the ground the tree would a-fell over the cliff and broke to pieces. They cut the tops down on two trees that stood beside of it and made scaffolds up in the air. They climb up the tree scaffolds and took their saw, ax, wedge and sledge. They sawed the tree off thirty feet above the ground and it didn't fall right. Pa had to jump to keep the tree from crashin over him and pinnin him under it on the ground. That's why he thinks he's allus fallin."

"He hates me," says Tarvin. "He jest had enough moonshine in 'im to make him talk today. I know how he feels."

Tarvin looks at the road ahead of him. He looks at the mountain of wrecked treetops and the bright tops of stumps where the trees have been cut. The two walk down the oxen road, their bare feet making tracks in the sand over a road where the cattle have strained beneath the rawhide whips to pull the giant logs down the hollow to the mill. The sand is cool and soft to their feet now, but it wouldn't matter whether the dirt beneath their feet was hard or soft, rocks or briars, for the skin is calloused and hard enough to serve their feet like shoe leather.

"I must git my gun, Subrinea," says Tarvin.

"All right, Honey," she says.

He lets loose of her hand and takes his arm from around her. He walks up the bank from the road under a clump of poplar trees. Subrinea stands in the road and waits for him.

Tarvin walks back from under the poplars carrying the twelve-gauge shotgun across his shoulder. He walks down the bank into the road beside Subrinea. He lifts the gun from his shoulder, pulls his shirttail from under his overalls and begins to wipe the gun barrel.

"What air you doin?" Subrinea asks.

"Wipin the dew from my gun barrel," says Tarvin. "I don't want a speck of rust on it. I had a time gittin it cleaned this atternoon before I started. A drap of dew means a speck of rust."

"Here, Honey," says Subrinea, "use my dresstail instead of your shirttail. You'll have more rags to work with."

Subrinea stands close to Tarvin and he puts his shirttail back in place. He takes her skirt and wipes his gun barrel. He rubs the gun barrel dry. Subrinea stands close with her hand on Tarvin's shoulder while he dries the dew from his gun. He drops her dress and spreads out the wrinkles with his long straight hands. He stands beside her and draws her close to him. Her brown face against his brown face, his lips meet her lips in strong embrace. The two young people stand in the oxen road unmindful of night slipping upon them, unmindful of the squirrels that are cutting green hickory nuts and waiting to be killed by Tarvin's gun. They stand with their strong youthful bodies pressed close to each other, thrilled to ecstasy with youthful passion and love.

"It's good to be here again," says Tarvin. "It's good to smell the leaves of the trees of Heaven. I love that loud sweet smell."

"The only trees that escaped the ax," says Subrinea. "These trees of Heaven have stood here since cordwood days. My people are buried beneath them."

"The only reason they aint been cut down," says Tarvin. "They air in a graveyard. They aint no count fer timber nohow, but the lumberjacks would have cut 'em fer wood to feed the sawmill biler."

The grove of trees stands deep-rooted in a loamy ravine on

the left-hand side of Cat's Fork when you come down the creek. In the twilight of evening, their long branches with their big calf-ear-shaped leaves look like the long green-robed arms of ghosts tiptoeing behind one. They stand silently under the evening sky, save for a slight rustle of the evening wind and a whippoorwill that alights in one of the limbs to sing. The two lovers stand in the shadow of the trees of Heaven, the green oasis of timber amid the vast desert of broken bodies, wreckage and stumps.

"I'm glad they couldn't cut the trees of Heaven," says Subrinea. "We have met so many times under 'em. We have parted here so many nights."

"And we have told each other so many things here," says Tarvin.

"You first told me that you loved me at this very spot," says Subrinea.

"Last spring when the trees begun to leaf, we sat here under the shadder of these trees," says Tarvin. "We watched a white cloud float over their fan-shaped tops. We watched the moon go under the white cloud. Do you remember?"

"Yes, I remember."

"And do you remember how we'd slipped away from your shack?"

"Yes, I remember."

"What is a tree of Heaven good fer?"

"Nothin, but it's good to smell and it's purty to look at. Its roots air to hide the dust of my people."

Subrinea stands beside Tarvin. He has his arms around her. The two young lovers stand beneath the ailanthus trees, looking toward a robin's-egg-blue sky. The sweet smell from the ailanthus leaves sweetens the air about them. A gray owl flies above their dewy tops, his great wings' spread cutting the twilight wind; silently, majestically, he skims over the treetops and disappears beyond the mountains of brown wasteland that lies beyond.

"Tell me," says Tarvin, "about them shacks you swept fer the lumberjacks. Tell me about the men, Subrinea."

"I don't keer fer 'em," says Subrinea. "They don't mean nothin to me."

"I want to know what they said to you," says Tarvin.

"Jerome Tussie," says Subrinea, "wanted me to marry 'im. I wouldn't do it."

"He did, huh," says Tarvin.

"Then he wanted to pay me to live with 'im."

Tarvin releases Subrinea of his tight embrace. He looks her in the face. His face is covered with a frown.

"He's your uncle, too," says Tarvin, his face reddening like an autumn red-oak leaf. "A nice uncle."

"He's Pa's brother," she says.

"He ought to be shot at sunset between the eyes with a hog rifle."

"Eif Tussie wanted me to marry 'im, too."

"And he's your cousin, aint he?" Tarvin asks.

"Yes, he is."

"Your kin people don't mind marryin you, do they?" he asks. "They must want to keep you in the family."

"They've allus married among themselves," says Subrinea.

"Hogs," says Tarvin.

"Worse than that," says Subrinea. "I jest hate that my name is Tussie."

"We'll change that name someday," says Tarvin. "You'll be one Tussie that aint goin to marry a Tussie."

"That Bollie Beaver," says Subrinea, "aint no Tussie and he tried to marry me."

"He did!" says Tarvin. "The first time I saw 'im I didn't like 'im. We aint made to git along. What did he say to you?"

"I wouldn't marry 'im, I told 'im," says Subrinea. "He follered me all over the shack when I's sweepin it. The rest of the men was out in the yard. He tried to kiss me. I wouldn't let 'im. Then he told me he'd give me more money than I's gittin if I'd do what he ast me. He offered me five dollars."

"I'll haf to fight 'im someday," says Tarvin. "I've got to git vengeance on 'im. We'll meet again."

"You ast me to tell you," says Subrinea. "If I'd a-knowed you's goin to have trouble I wouldn't a-told you. Bollie Beaver is a mean man. The lumberjacks air afraid of Bollie. He can whop any of 'em. He'll kill you, Tarvin."

"He'll haf to eat a lot more corn bread before he can kill me," says Tarvin. "He might be tough out there cuttin down big trees and standin upon their tops and choppin down through 'em with an ax, but Bollie is stiff. I can go in and throw 'im to the ground and beat his face into a jelly. And I'll do it."

"No use jumpin on 'im," says Subrinea. "Nothin aint happened to me. I aint gone out with none of the men in the timber shacks. I aint goin out with none of 'em. I don't care how much money they offer me. Ma hit Bollie over the head with a tree limb and nearly busted his brains out. Bollie was laid out fer two weeks."

"She oughta kilt 'im," says Tarvin. "He's a viper."

"He insulted Ma," says Subrinea. "Pa don't know it. If Pa's to find it out he'd go atter Bollie with a knife. Pa will knife. He wouldn't say a word either until he got near Bollie and he'd let his open knife fall from his sleeve—he'd jump a-straddle of Bollie and cut his throat."

"I don't want you ever to go back to them shacks," says Tarvin. "I want you to stay away from there. You know I love you or I wouldn't talk like this."

He pulls Subrinea close to him in a strong embrace. He kisses her beneath the rush of wind in the ailanthus leaves.

"I must go," says Tarvin, relaxing his arm around her shoulder. "I must be goin. You must be gittin back to the house. Your Pa will be atter you."

"He'll never be atter me tonight, Honey," says Subrinea. "He's still stretched out with his feet hangin over the porch."

"And I love my little squatter gal," says Tarvin, "and I allus will love you. I've loved you from the first time I danced all night with you without stoppin. Do you remember?"

"I remember."

"Remember we wore our shoes that night and when I brought you home how we pulled our shoes off and waded the mud?"

"I'll never fergit it. I remember how I hated fer you to bring me down the hill to our shack that mornin, but you come anyway. I didn't want you to see where we lived. I'd heerd you lived in a big white house on the hill!"

"It's jest a log house under that weather-boardin and white paint," says Tarvin. "It's jest like we all air. We air all human beins under the skin. You didn't want me to find out you's a squatter, but I have found it out and what does it matter? You air purtier than any gal I've ever seen. I love you and you love me and that is all that matters!"

Tarvin holds Subrinea in his arms. He kisses her again. They part and Tarvin walks down the road. Subrinea runs up the road like a rabbit. Tarvin turns to see her running up the crooked road like a long thin ghost in the twilight. Her thin dress skirt is floating behind her as she runs against the wind, her legs and arms in perfect rhythm, and like a ghost she disappears around a sharp turn in the road and fades into the twilight.

6.

TARVIN HURRIES down the road to a little path that leads from the oxen road upon a rocky bluff to the big hickory tree. Quietly he walks, stealthily he climbs the bluff with his shotgun in his hand, pulling his way up the path by holding to the sprouts. He can hear himself getting his breath. He stops to slow his wind so the squirrels won't hear him if there are any in the tree this late. He stops, holds his breath and listens.

He hears the drip-drip of the green hickory-nut hulls down through the leaves from the top of the tree. The green hickory-nut hulls fall from the tree and hit him on top of the head. He looks carefully up among the green leaves. He raises his gun, aims; steadily he holds the gun, and slowly he squeezes the trigger. There is a flash of fire. The squirrel tumbles from the tree. Tarvin reloads and aims at a squirrel jumping from the hickory tree to a tall persimmon tree beside it. His aim is true, for the squirrel falls from midair. Tarvin kills it on the jump. He picks up the two squirrels and slips down the bluff the way he came to the oxen road. He hurries down Cat's Fork to Ragweed Hollow that leads him home.

7.

THE WHIPPOORWILLS are calling everywhere. There are a million insect sounds coming from the dew-covered bunches of bull grass, the saw-briar clumps and the sprout thickets. A bull-bat flies above Tarvin's head, its black wings beating the twilight wind over the dark hollow, and its terrifying screams penetrating his eardrums, almost making him scream. Summer night in Kentucky, when all life stirs, when the insects awake to music, singing their farewell songs for a summer soon to pass—singing from the dewy weeds, the briars, sprouts and stalks of stalwart shooting corn.

There is a loneliness that comes to Tarvin that makes him want to cry. He walks up Ragweed Hollow with two dead gray squirrels in his overall pockets and his trusty shotgun across his shoulder. He hears the song of the insects and the whippoorwills, but only the shrill screaming of the bull-bat can arouse his thoughts. He thinks not of the rugged slopes, the pastures and the corn, but he remembers her hair, golden as the shooting cornsilks in August; and he remembers the clean sweet smell of her hair, sweet-smelling as August corn tassels streaming in the wind; and he remembers her strong legs brown as a pawpaw leaf in September. He remembers her ghostlike body, tall as a sapling, swift as a ground sparrow, and timid as a wild rabbit, slipping back to a shack.

"I can't hep it," he thinks, "I can't hep it. Why was she ever put on earth? Why was I ever born? What will I ever do with old Boliver if I marry Subrinea and he comes to visit me? Where will I fix 'im a porch to sleep on and stick his feet over? What will I ever do with all her sisters and brothers? How can I buy terbacker fer all of 'em?"

Tarvin walks up the path and these thoughts flash through his mind. All he can see is Subrinea. He can feel her in his arms. She will not go away. She has knocked at the door of his brain and she has entered. The pounding of his heart against the panels of his ribs is Subrinea knocking, knocking to escape the life in the dirty shack, the insults from the lumberjacks, her drunken father—trying to escape from a world of squatters that have intermarried their own blood kin for years, trying to escape the doomed living for the happiness Tarvin can offer her.

Under the blue sky studded with twinkling stars he walks, in the velvety twilight of evening, wading the stilly wind saturated with dew and pleasant odors of corn, phlox, briar and sprout; he walks with his heart beating high and proud with joy of living. Tarvin is now mindful that the songs of the whippoorwills are the sweetest he has ever heard, and the drowsy lull of the beetles reminds him of water pouring over rocks on an April night, something he never thought comparable before this night; he is mindful that the katydids were singing love songs in the dewy corn and the songs of the cicadas in the smartweeds, strong, piercing and beautiful to hear—just those trifling little insects singing songs that arouse him as they have never aroused him before. Tarvin takes the dead squirrels from his pocket and walks up the yellow clay bank in front of the house, turning to glance once more at the hills of slaughtered timber.

8.

"SON, I'VE been tellin your Ma," says Anse, "there aint nothin in the world like good squirrel broth when a man's sick at his stummick. When a man gits so he can't eat squirrel broth he is liable to kick the bucket. He's about ready to journey to the Great Beyond."

"I thought about that, Pa," says Tarvin. "I hunted the hills over fer you a squirrel and I couldn't find one. I waited under that hickory tree on the left-hand slope of Cat's Fork. I waited until the squirrels come to git their supper."

"I've kilt a-many a squirrel in that tree, son," says Anse. "I kilt 'em there when I's a boy."

Anse leans back in his chair at the breakfast table. He wipes his long red beard with his right hand. He takes a cigar from his vest pocket, cuts the end from it with a case knife, strikes a match on his corduroy pants leg and lights his cigar. He puffs a stream of smoke over the breakfast table. Tarvin has got up late and he is eating while Anse is smoking. He is looking at Fronnie. She has finished her breakfast and she is smoking her pipe, blowing blue swirls of smoke across the table to meet the clouds of smoke that Anse puffs from his cigar. The two clouds of smoke intermingle and go upward toward the ceiling. The smoke ascends, thins to a grayish red-oak-sap color and gradually disappears on the kitchen loft.

"Squirrels air gittin scarce in this country," says Tarvin.

"Yes," says Anse, "the timber is goin fast. You haf to have timber if you have squirrels."

"That's what I told Ma yesterday," says Tarvin.

"But he's been goin so much lately to the woods," says Fronnie, "and he never brings back nothin."

"It's hard to git game when they aint no game to git," says Anse, reared back in his chair, smoking his long cigar and playing with his long red beard. "I know Tarvin's a good shot. If there is game in the woods, Tarvin will find it."

"He's usin too many of my meat rinds to clean his gun," says Fronnie. "When you come in and find the good brown crust torn from the corn bread you'll know the reason. You know if you'll run a meat rind over the bottom of the bread pan the bread won't stick. I've tried both lard and butter and I know a meat rind's the best."

"Be savin, son, with your Ma's meat rinds," says Anse. "We want to make every edge cut that will. Your Ma is usin butter instead of lard now. Butter is cheaper than lard and we can sell lard when we render the meat this fall. We'll git a good price fer it and we'll do our seasonin o' grub with butter. We've got somethin ahead of us. We need more land."

"We don't want a lot of squatters stuck in shacks around us when that land is sold," says Fronnie. "We don't want squatters fer neighbors."

"I'd soon be in hell with my back broke," says Anse, "as to have 'em around me. I know 'em. Pap ust to warn us about 'em. They ust to throng this county. They lived here and there in a little shack stuck on some poor pint. Somehow, atter the timber was cut and the treetops and saplins cut into cordwood, a lot of 'em stayed on and dug a livin out'n the ground until second-growth timber got big enough to cut agin. I don't want 'em near me."

"We'd better git out and git the cows milked," says Fronnie. "If Anse goes to talkin about squatters he'll be talkin all day. He'll preach a Sunday sermon about 'em."

Fronnie knocks the ashes from her pipe onto her plate. Anse takes his index finger and knocks the long white ash from his cigar onto his plate. He takes his left hand and gently strokes his long beard, clean and glistening and autumn persimmon-leaf red.

"Yep," says Anse, "I guess we'd better git out and git the work done. It's nearly seven o'clock."

"Cows up?" Tarvin asks.

"Yep," says Anse.

"Who got 'em up?" Tarvin asks.

"I got 'em up," says Anse. "I went out and got 'em at four o'clock this mornin while you's still in bed."

Anse carries two big buckets of slop to the barn for the fattening hogs. Tarvin carries two buckets filled with clabbered milk for the shoats. Fronnie walks behind, barefooted, smoking her pipe and carrying empty milk buckets. They walk out the path from the house to the barn.

"Pig-o-wee, pig-o-wee, pig-o-wee, piggie, piggie, pig, pig, pig," Anse calls.

The white hogs and the red shoats come running down the hill under the trees in the oak grove. Anse pours the slop into a chute that carries it into the trough. The white hogs come and start drinking. Tarvin pours his two buckets of clabbered milk into a chute that carries the milk into a long trough for fifteen red shoats. The white hogs know their trough and they run in the same hog pasture.

"I'd ruther watch hogs eat," says Anse, "as to eat myself. It's religion to me to take time on Sunday mornins and watch my hogs eat and to throw salt on the cows' backs and watch 'em lick the salt off. Watch them white hogs try to lay down in the trough, won't you? I like to see 'em greedy like that. I like to see a person eat like a hog. I'm jealous of a man that can eat more than I can. It's my stummick that holds me back. I've allus had a appetite like a hog fer I've allus worked like a brute."

"When you git through watchin the hogs eat," says Fronnie, "come down and hep me milk these cows. Remember we have nine cows to milk."

"We're comin," says Anse. "Jest give us a little more time."

They watch the shoats and the hogs lick the troughs as clean as if they had been scrubbed. They watch the red shoats with puffed sides waddle slowly to the shade of the oak trees in the grove and lie down in a heap. The white hogs lie down by their troughs. One lies down in the trough.

Fronnie sits on a stool and milks two streams of milk into the three-gallon zinc bucket while the cows stand contentedly eating wheat bran from the feed box. Anse had saved it from the wheat that he raised and had ground.

"I figured with the miller," says Anse, "it was cheaper in the long run fer me to save my wheat bran and my middlins and pay hard cash fer the grindin."

Anse pours feed into the cow's box, sits down on a stool and milks with both hands, fast streams of milk into the big bucket. They zigzag and crisscross and pound the tin walls of the bucket like rain on a tin roof. Tarvin feeds his cow and milks two streams of milk into a big bucket.

"I hate to see people a-settin all humped up beside a cow," says Fronnie, "milkin with one hand. I've allus said that it took a lazy person to do that. Anybody with one eye and half sense knows that if you milk two teats at once that you can milk two cows while a person milkin with one hand can milk one. I'll tell you there's been a lot of times when I would have loved to 've had three hands. That was last summer when you's so busy in the crops and I had all nine cows to milk in the mornin."

They soon milk three cows each. Anse and Tarvin carry two big buckets of milk each to the cellar under the smoke-house. Each walks back to the barn and takes two more to the cellar. Fronnie carries the empty slop buckets to the house. The cows walk slowly down the path by the barn, through the barn-lot gate to the cool shade of the tall timber. Beyond the timber is the grass, grass knee-deep on the slopes and overflowing.

"It takes grass to make cows give milk," says Anse as he walks beside Tarvin carrying the two buckets of milk. "Don't tell me these hills won't raise grass. When I give three hundred dollars fer my first fifty acres here my neighbors said I'd starve to death. We aint been scarce o' grub yit, have we? I've raised eleven children on this farm. I've saved money and added more acres."

Tarvin does not speak. He walks beside Anse along the path toward the cellar. His gray eagle eyes look toward the rugged slopes where the timber has fallen in ruinous heaps, where a sawmill has been moved seven times to more convenient places for the cattle to pull the big logs to the mill. He looks toward the new-made barn on the far ridge where twenty yoke of cattle lie under the shade and rest this Sunday —weary from the great strain on their tremendous bodies and their giant necks, their strong forelegs, their tough briskets, their cloven roofs. Tarvin looks toward the bright August wind that hovers over Cat's Fork; he looks to the hills beyond him and he doesn't speak. There is little for him to say.

"Tomorrow," says Anse, "we will go to the fur field and cut sprouts from the grass. If we want cows that will milk we must see that they git grass and not sprouts. We must clean the grass of sprouts, green briars, saw briars and wild grapevines.

"Here, Fronnie, 's the rest of the milk," says Anse as they walk down the cellar doorsteps. Anse hands Fronnie the two buckets of milk. She takes one at a time and sets the buckets on the cold concrete floor. Tarvin carries two buckets of milk and reaches them to his mother.

"I'll tell you, Anse," Fronnie says, "this cream separator has been a lifesaver. I don't haf to fill up every crock, waterbucket, pan and utensil on the place to let the milk set over night so I can skim the cream with a spoon. We pour it in the separator and in a few minutes we pour the cream in the cans to ship to Cincinnati."

"And the cows paid fer that," says Anse stroking his red beard and getting his breath hard.

"We ought to be thankful to the cows, the way we like milk," says Tarvin.

Tarvin walks out the path from the cellar. Anse turns the separator and watches the skimmed milk shoot over into the bucket and the rich flow of yellow cream slowly drip into the cream can.

"Where air you goin, Tarvin?" Anse asks.

"Think I'll take my gun," says Tarvin, "and kill a couple of squirrels. Today is Sunday and I aint got nothin to do."

"Will you be home fer dinner?" Fronnie asks.

"If I'm not home fer dinner," says Tarvin, "you go on and eat. I'll be in when I git a mess of squirrels fer Pa."

"What air you goin to hunt," Anse asks, "when squirrel season is over?"

"Birds and rabbits," says Tarvin, walking down the path below the house with the shotgun across his shoulder.

"Don't git in too late," Anse reminds him. "Remember we haf to git in the sprout field by daylight in the mornin. Haf to have the cows milked and the work done up by that time. If we cut the sprouts in dog days, they won't sprout any more. We must make haste while dog days air here."

"All right, Pa," says Tarvin, his long body moving slowly down the path on the yellow clay bank below the house, his gun barrel glistening across his shoulder in the August agate sunlight.

9.

"THIS IS the time of mornin a body must git out," says Anse, "if he wants to do a day's work. He must git out soon as he can see to cut sprouts. When you see a man gittin out to work on a farm at eight and nine o'clock, you can jest beware—that man aint no good."

"Yes, Pa," says Tarvin. He lifts his sprouting hoe into the morning twilight wind. He lets his hoe fall easily with the dignity of a man that has cut tough hickory sprouts, persimmon sprouts and pawpaw sprouts on the stubborn pasture slopes. His long muscular arms swing the hoe above his shoulder again and again, and each time the hoe falls a sprout kicks up its heels to wither when the sun gets higher in the sky.

"It's a shame cows won't eat persimmon sprouts," says Anse. "They won't touch a pawpaw sprout, ner a hickory sprout, nohow. They'll eat oak sprouts when the grass gits short in dry weather. They'll eat 'em when they haf to. And when they haf to eat sprouts, they fail givin milk."

Anse works as if he is digging yellow-jackets' nests from the ground. He is short and thick through the shoulders. He has a barrel body with short thick arms, hairy wrists and big gnarled hands like roots on an ancient tree where the dirt has slipped away. Tarvin works without clothing from his knees down and his waist up. His body is brown as an autumn oak leaf. The sun has tanned his broad shoulders to a deep brown darkness and when he swings the hoe the muscles ripple in his arms and shoulders; and knots of muscles contract and relax across his stomach and his bony ribs. There is not an ounce of fat on Tarvin's body. He is muscle and bone.

"By the time dog days air over," says Anse, "we'll be walkin over the last pasture. The sprouts will all be down and the grass will have a new start in the spring."

Anse wipes the sweat from his beardy face with a big red bandanna. His homemade striped gingham shirt is opened at the collar and the sweat trickles down the heavy red beard on his Adam's apple. His shirt and overalls are as wet as if he had jumped into the river for a swim with his clothes on. Tarvin's overall knee-pants are as wet with sweat as if they have been soused in the wash-tub. The two men work steadily, with ease; yet they work hard, for cutting sprouts from persimmon stools and hickory sprouts from hickory stools under the earth and pawpaw sprouts from wiry stringy soft roots under the earth is hard work. When they find a clump of green briars and a patch of blackberry briars they use the briar scythe and scythe them to earth, leaving them in heaps all over the pasture slope.

"I jest think sometimes," says Anse, standing by his briar scythe where he has scythed a patch of blackberry briars to the earth, standing wiping the sweat with his bandanna and getting his breath hard, "about all my children. Raised 'em in a good nest; but they went away like a wild bunch of quails. Here I'm left with all this land and I want more. It was the war that hurt me."

Anse swings the scythe and stops again.

"Bert and Elmer kilt in France," he says softly, nodding his head like the wind slowly nods the tops of the tough hickory sprouts. "Jest heerd about the war and about fightin. Enlisted and went fer the trip. Never got back. Steve and Joe went to Akron durin the war when they's a-payin sicha big wages. They come back a few times; but they married in Ohio and they live there today. Never even as much as git a card once a year from 'em now. Ust to git one at Christmas times. The fever kilt Tom and Willie. John fit all his life and was stabbed in the back and kilt at a square dance on Laurel. Murt and Ethel married and air livin up on Big Sandy. They never come home and they aint but fifty miles between us. I jest got you left. I've been thinkin about you goin to school and learnin all you can about farmin."

"I don't know, Pa," says Tarvin.

"You'd haf to miss a lot of huntin," says Anse, "and a lot of hard work."

"That's it," says Tarvin. "I'd hate to miss the huntin. You can't take a gun off to school with you, I'm told. I'd miss the feel of my gun. I like to git it out and hold it in my hands and feel it, rub it and caress it, when I aint huntin with it. I love a gun."

"Son, you'll haf a lot of land here someday when I'm gone," says Anse, "and I couldn't sleep in my grave if I thought you's lettin the fence fall and the gullies wash the land."

The sprouts lie thick upon the pasture slope. Briar stools lie in mats upon the grass. The sun like a molten ball of fire climbs high into the sky. The leaves wilt on the sprouts and briars. There is a smell of autumn in the wilting leaves, a good clean smell of wind. It is a lazy wind that molests the purple tops of the ironweeds and the sweet-scented blossoms of the wild phlox growing in the deep ravines and in the cool recesses around rotting logs and stumps left to decay and fertilize the pasture earth.

"I'm jest waitin fer all that timber land to be sold," says Anse. "I've got the money and I'm jest waitin. I've got my mind made up what I aim to do soon as I git that land. I aim to conquer it as I have conquered this. Look at this land, Tarvin. Look how purty it is to the fur hilltop yander beyond the house! Fifteen years ago this was all a wilderness; the brush was so thick you couldn't see to shoot a rabbit here. You'd haf to git down on your knees and feel your way on your all-fours to git through this wilderness. Now look at it."

Tarvin can remember the great thickets of briars and wild grapevines and the thickets of sassafras sprouts that the rabbits peeled each winter. He can remember seeing his father work winter days in the clearing when the ground was frozen and thin patches of blue snow lay blotched over the hills like the white spots on an English pointer's back. Tarvin can remember the cattle his father used to work to a giant cutter plow to tear the newground stumps from the earth. He can remember the great prolific growth of corn in summer, the fine-haired silking corn, the sweet smells of corn, and the insects' calling. He can remember the pumpkins that lay scattered over the field, holding to the dead pumpkin vines after the frost had fallen and the corn was cut. He can remember the great clusters of corn-field beans and his mother picking beans to fill a pickling barrel—picking beans in her apron and the colored bean leaves clinging to her apron and her shawl. Something goes back like thin gossamer lines of cobwebs roping oak tree to oak tree. It is a dream that goes back as he looks at the grass fields on his father's farm and the kind of land it was when he bought it.

"I'll haf to hunt renters next year," says Anse. "I'm goin to have too much land to tend. I'll haf to lease a lot of land and rent a lot. I want to git that big timber tract in shape if I buy it. I want to put it in shape as the last job I do on this earth. I don't want to lose a lot of time and do it by parts. I want to do it soon as I can, fer my years air not as many as they have been."

"It'll bring good corn," says Tarvin, "fer I saw a good field of corn over on Cat's Fork. It was rank and dark and long-eared and purty."

"Who's farmin there?" Anse asks, leaning on his hoe handle and talking to Tarvin across a ravine of blackberry briars.

"Boliver Tussie," says Tarvin. "He's cuttin timber there. He aint doin much farmin but his wife and youngins raised it."

"Good people to work?" Anse asks.

"Guess so," says Tarvin. "They've got the finest corn I've seen any place this season. Corn is over twelve foot tall. Big ears sag down from the stalks. The Tussies air good farmers."

"But they air squatters," says Anse. "How can they be good to work? How can they grow good corn? I aint heard that much good of a squatter yet."

"Boliver's raised better corn than we have raised," says Tarvin, as if to say a squatter can raise good corn same as any of the old settlers. "Go over there and see fer yourself. I passed through it the other evenin when I was squirrel huntin and honest, Pa, I was surprised. I've never seen sicha corn grow out'n the earth."

"He might make a good renter," says Anse, "but a man would haf to bind him up mighty tight with a ar-tickle. Can't let 'im have the advantage. I aint never rented my land. I've allus farmed it myself but if that man shows that he will work and his family will work, I might rent fifty acres of land to 'im."

"Boliver Tussie's allus lived on that timber tract," says Tarvin. "That land is his flesh and the water in the creeks is his blood. When the land is sold, he won't have no place to go."

Tarvin swings his hoe over his shoulder and lets it fall hard on a hickory sprout. Anse gives short licks and knocks the sprouts as he comes to them. He is a veteran with a sprouting hoe. His short thick body is tougher than the hickory sprouts.

"Think it's gittin time fer beans," says Anse. "I can step on the head of my shadder and there's a gnawin in my stummick."

Anse lays his hoe by a tall clump of sprouts. He hangs the briar scythe in a locust tree so that in case of rain the water will run off the blade and prevent its rusting. Tarvin drops his hoe beside Anse's hoe. The two walk away where the intense August heat glimmers over the pasture land. There is the musty smell of ironweeds, milkweeds, silkweeds, clusters of smartweeds, jimson weeds, and bull grass on the lazy wind— a mixture of smells that is pleasing to the nostrils.

There is singing of the grasshoppers and katydids. There is the singing from the jarflies among the soapy poplar leaves. Summer is here with all of her farewell sounds; summer with her luxurious growth, now matured and passing slowly into oblivion. Summer with her high skies and her great white mountains of thunder clouds rolling over the pine tops in the timber patches.

Anse and Tarvin walk around the path toward the big barn. Soon they are out of sight, immersed in the grove of pines by the hog lot. They walk toward the white house on the hill.

Dog days pass, and the songs of the beetle, the katydids,

cicadas and whippoorwills grow weaker with the passing of summer days. The great white thunder clouds roll across the sky and occasional showers splinter down their soft splashes on the thirsting grass. August showers feed the thirsting throats of the white corn roots and the budding ears are filled with large full grains.

Days pass in single file; days keep earth replenished with the sun's hot rays and crops grow into maturity. There is the lazy passing of the days and the music of the wind in the corn —music of the flutes among the dying love-vines on the paling fences; music of the cymbals among the coloring sycamore leaves when they beat together, and there are the shrill weird notes of the viols in the dead grasses on the slopes. There is the music of the harp strings plucking among the oak limbs and the pine boughs. Summer is passing and Anse and Tarvin are working in the sprout fields to get the sprouting finished.

Farewell-to-summer is blooming on the cliffs in purple and white masses. Blackbirds gather and fly over the pasture lands and above the fields of buff-coloring corn, flying to the south. Life is changing in the procession of passing days. The multi-colored butterflies flit slowly on fragile wings above the blooming elders beside the creeks and above the rooster-combed pods of shoe-make berries.

10.

"TARVIN, AUTUMN is upon us," says Anse. "We've got our corn to cut, terbacker to cut and hang in the barn, and we've got taters to dig, cane to strip and lasses to make. We've got our late hay to cut and haul to the barn. This is a good harvest and our barns will be full. They will be full and overflowin. We won't have room fer all that we've raised. We must harvest before frost. Frost must not bite the juices in our cane and ruin our cane fodder blades. We'll haf to cut the corn first."

Anse and Tarvin walk upon a slope where the buff-colored fodder blades rattle in the wind. They walk between two rows of corn, bend four stalks across the balk and loop their tops together every twelve-hills' length. They cut four rows of corn through the field, place the stalks around these riders and tie with a middle band. They cut four rows more on each side of this shock row and carry and place the corn stalks around these middle bands; then they tie two bands around the shocks.

"This is the way I like to railroad corn," says Anse.

They work all night long when the moon shines. They work as long as the moon is in the sky to give them light. They go home, get their breakfasts, come back to the cornfields and work until the dew dries from the fodder. After the dew dries, the fodder gets brittle and rakes the tough leather-brown skin on their faces like the blade of a knife. When the sun is in the sky and the fodder is dry, Anse and Tarvin sleep.

When Anse and Tarvin cut corn, they can hear the giant trees lumbering earthward on the Sexton Timber Tract. They can see the top of a tree weave against the sky, slowly move and then tumble earthward, riding the small saplings to the earth, stripping them of limbs, peeling their bark and breaking their bodies. There is a cloud of dust and dry leaves ascending where the giant tree falls; then they hear a crash like thunder —a heavy swish against the earth. Another tree has left its place near the heavens and there is another open space there now. There is a tombstone stump left to mark the tree's pass-ing. It will stand two years, five years or maybe ten years, and then it will rot and leave a hole in the earth. The tree will not be any more.

"I hate to see 'em fall," says Anse, "but the sooner they fall, the sooner I'll know what I aim to do. It will all be over by February. Atter the timber is cut it won't be a month until that land will be sold under the hammer. I've heard the Sexton heirs will haf to sell it to pay their debts. I'll have my crops sold and I'll be ready."

"Pa, it's better to dig taters with a pitchfork," says Tarvin. "We can fork 'em from the loamy ridges and not cut any of the taters."

"Yes," says Anse, "if we plow 'em out'n the ground we miss so many taters. We missed a lot last year. That's why we had only sixty-five bushels to sell above our usins."

They drive the mules and sled between the rows, fork the potatoes from the earth, clean every little clod of dirt from them and throw them in the straw-lined sled bed. "Straw keeps from bruisin the taters," says Anse.

They fill a bin in the cellar for their own use. They dig holes in the garden and line the holes with oak leaves. They heap the potatoes into the holes and cover them with cone-shaped hills of dirt. They dig ditches around each mound to drain the water. They will leave them until spring comes back to the hills. They will be sweet to dig out and eat; they will be fresh to plant in the fresh spring dirt for another season.

"Cuttin terbacker is the job," says Anse. "Frost will soon be on us. We must work hard and fast to keep ahead of the seasons."

Anse and Tarvin take their tobacco knives and slit the tobacco stalks downward toward the root. Then they hack the stalk off with a knife, put four and five tobacco stalks on one tobacco stick and they stick the sharpened stick into the earth, leaving the stalks in the sun to dry. There is the smell of green tobacco and dying tobacco on the loamy slopes. The crab-grass is dying and the seeds gather in the eyes of their shoes as they walk along the crab-grass-carpeted balks and split the giant tobacco stalks. "Terbacker's good this year," says Anse. "It's damned good terbacker. I can throw my hat in the patch any place and it can't reach the ground. It's over a man's head. It's hard to handle. It will be tough gittin it on the tier poles in the barn. When a man's clothes git so stiff with the green terbacker glue that they stand alone, then it's time a man has his terbacker in the barn."

Tarvin stands upright in the long tobacco row. He has been bent down cutting the big tobacco stalks until his back aches. He turns his brown face and his blue eyes toward the autumn skies. He can see the wild geese flying high above the yellow-turning tobacco field. They look like specks against the sky. Tarvin can hear their honking cries sounding over the autumn-colored world. He is filled with loneliness to hear the cries of the wild geese above a changing world. He is so lonely amid the smells of the gluey tobacco, the carpets of dead crab-grass, and flying leaves that tears come to his eyes. He thinks of Subrinea when he hears the wild geese honking over the lonely land. He thinks of the times they have stood silently beneath the trees of Heaven and watched the wild geese flying over and listened to their lonely cries. The dark loamy productive earth puts a mood in him. The wind and the cries of the wild geese make him want to cry. When he sees his father getting farther and farther away with his row of tobacco, Tarvin bends over again and starts cutting tobacco.

They take the mules and sled and go around the slopes of the ten-acre tobacco field, gather the sticks of tobacco, lay them flatwise on the sled bed and the sled runners glide easily over the soft loamy earth to the tobacco barn. Brown heaps of tobacco reach the barn, a barn without sides, where the wind passes freely among the sticks of tobacco hanging with their tips pointing downward. Anse rolls cigars out of the brown curing burley and smokes them as he works, blowing great clouds of smoke from his red-bearded face. Anse chews the ends of his cigars and spits bright ambeer into the autumn wind. He takes the brightest leaves home for Fronnie to smoke in her pipe. Tarvin smokes the bright new leaves in his pipe and carries a bundle away to Cat's Fork when he takes the gun to shoot squirrels.

Their overalls get stiff enough with green tobacco glue to stand alone. Tobacco-cutting season has ended. When the rainy days come the brown leaves will grow damp. The tobacco will be in cases. Anse, Tarvin and Fronnie will pull the leaves from the stalks and tie them in hands ready for market.

In the autumn moonlight when the dew is on the flour-sprinkled stalks of cane, Anse and Tarvin take paddles and walk along the cane rows, beating the cane blades down to the earth. They take row by row, Anse leading Tarvin up and down the bottom cane ground, their paddles beating a swish-swish in the bright autumn moonlight. They leave green puddles of blades at the roots of the cane stalks. They work all night long. They sleep while the morning is cool. When the sun rises and dries away the dew, Anse and Tarvin walk along each row, tie the cane blades into bundles and stack them into heaps. "Best fodder in the world," says Anse, "and if you leave the blades on the stalks the sorghum will have a greenish color. By strippin the blades we have purtier sorghum molasses and we have more roughness fer the stock."

They take corn knives and cut the bladeless stalks, pile them in heaps. They cut the bright red pods of seeds from the cane tops and pile them in heaps. They take the mules and sled, haul the cane blades to the barn. They haul the cane seeds to the granary. "Good chicken feed," says Anse. "Feed the chickens cane seed and save the corn."

11.

"ALL THE WORK done now," says Tarvin, "but the sorghum makin. When we make the sorghum, we ought to invite the neighbor boys and girls in fer a frolic."

"It's all right with me," says Anse; "soon as the last gallon of sorghum is run from the pan, you can have a shindig if you want it. Young folks like to have a little fun and we old folks will like to watch you. It will remind us of the days gone by. We have worked hard to beat the frost. If it had come it would have whopped us. Now we air ahead of the frost. It can't hurt us now. The cane is cut and in a stack at the mill. We air ready to make sorghum and to frolic."

The Barney mule is hitched to a long sweep, he walks steadily around a circular path that is covered with ground cane stalks. His bridle rein is tied to a shaft that is fastened to the sweep that leads him on as the sweep moves. He plods slowly until he becomes dizzy going round and round the circle; then he is taken out and his mate, Jack, is hitched to the sweep to relieve him. Fronnie sits at the mill and pokes the green stalks of cane between the huge steel burrs. The burrs squeeze the stalks into a flat juiceless pulp. A green stream of cane juice flows from the burrs to the sorghum pan.

Anse stands at the pan and stirs the juice from one division of the pan to another, starting the raw juice at the end of the pan where it is piped from the burrs. By the time the green cane juice gets across the pan, it is a bright honey-colored thick sorghum molasses ready to be poured into barrels. Tarvin feeds cane wood into the furnace and carries away the sapless cane stalks and throws them in a heap beyond the circular path where the mule walks.

Anse, Tarvin and Fronnie work the day long, go home to milk the cows and feed the hogs. They get their supper and go back to work by moonlight until far into the night. They fill five barrels with sorghum molasses. They roll the barrels over by the high pile of sapless cane stalks. They throw cane stalks over the barrels to hide them. "You can't tell," says Anse, "somebody might haul off a barrel. I jest don't take a chance on strangers passin through these parts."

"What's the matter with you, Tarvin?" Fronnie asks. "You act like you air tired. You won't be able fer the dance. Jest one more night, you know."

Tarvin staggers as he carries loads of cane stalks to the heap.

"I'm all pooped out, Ma," says Tarvin. "I'm gittin tired. Pa has nearly worked me to death."

"I've worked this way all my life," says Fronnie, "to have what we have. The people here that makes a little more than the rest air old long before their time to git old and they die before their time to die. The squatters and the rest of the no-count people don't work so hard and they enjoy life. They can't live as long as they should live, fer they don't have enough to live on. It's about the same either way you look at it, starve to death or die workin yourself to death. We have these two kinds of people among these hills."

"Yes," says Tarvin, "Pa puts his money into the land. He puts my work into the land. All of my strength goes back into the land. The land is all. All the fun I git out'n life is square dancin and squirrel huntin on Cat's Fork."

Tarvin staggers across the mule path with a load of cane stalks. His long body swaggers like a drunken man as he carries the big armload of stalks. Tarvin is not a drunken man; Tarvin is a tired man. His bones and muscles in his youthful body are not seasoned to hard work like the bones and muscles in the bodies of his mother and father. But the sorghum is about made. All the barrels are about filled. "We'll jest about have seven barrels," says Tarvin. "Thank God, it will be all over then."

"Did I hear somebody callin me?" Anse asks, climbing up the bank by the green cane-stalk pile with his molasses stir in his hand.

"Did you think you heerd somebody?" Fronnie laughs.

"Yes," says Anse, " 'peared like I heerd somebody usin my name."

"Maybe it was the spirits, Pa," says Tarvin. Tarvin laughs and Fronnie laughs. Anse wipes the sweat from his beard. He takes the molasses stir and walks back down the bank to the boiling cane juice in the molasses pan. He dips the green foam with a long dipper and throws it into the skimming hole. Anse smokes cigars and makes the bright amber-colored sorghum molasses.

"If you ever marry, Tarvin," says Fronnie, "don't you ever let your wife work like I haf to work. I've had to work like this and carry you youngins. I've worked like this up to a week before one of you was born. I've throwed my hoe down in the cornfield and went to the house to have my baby. Young man, you wasn't born in the house. You was born in the cornfield. I couldn't git to the house in time."

"I'll never let my wife work like you have worked, Ma," says Tarvin. "I'll never let my children work like we have had to work. Guess I'd a-been seven feet tall if Pa hadn't stunted my growth workin me. I'm gittin weak, Ma, I'm doin too much. No wonder Pa can't hire hep. He says people won't work nowadays. They can't stand to work fer Pa. They try to do as much work as he does and it will kill a man to work with Pa. The lumberjacks couldn't stand to work with Pa."

"Let's quit fer tonight," Anse hollers to Fronnie and Tarvin. "We'll jest have a little work fer tomorrow and tomorrow night. We got to leave some juice to run off tomorrow night and let everybody have a good bait of lasses foam."

"Suits me, Pa," says Tarvin. "I'm about all pooped out nohow."

"My bones air gittin all weary hunkered down feedin this

mill," says Fronnie. "I'm ready to go home and go to bed fer rest."

Anse stops Jack and unhitches his trace chains from the sweep. Fronnie leaves the mill, climbs on Jack's back and rides up the hollow. Anse unties Barney from a black-jack sapling and climbs on his back. Fronnie lights her pipe and smokes as she rides the mule up the hollow. Anse smokes a cigar as he rides. Tarvin walks behind the mules.

"Son," says Anse, "you can go around tomorrow and norate that we're goin to have a little shindig to celebrate a good harvest. Norate it to everybody that you want to come."

"There'll be a lot here I don't ast to come," says Tarvin. "You know how it is. People aint got a lot of places to go around here. That's the reason they come to celebrate. I'll ast a lot of people."

"I'll git the platform ready fer the dance," says Anse. "I'll do that tomorrow atternoon while you air out noratin the word."

"We'll have enough cane left fer to run off the last batch of sorghum before the dance," says Fronnie. "The young and the old can git around the sorghum pan with their sticks and lick the foam from the pan. We ust to do that when we's girls. Lord, I can remember the good times we had! We didn't mind the work when we made sorghum molasses. We thought about the good time we's goin to have when we finished makin the molasses."

"I'll invite Subrinea," thinks Tarvin. "I'll invite her. Pa don't know her and Ma don't know her. They'll never think about her bein from a squatter family. They'll see she's a purty gal. They'll see a gal purty as a angel when they see Subrinea."

Fronnie and Anse, tired as fox hounds, ride the tired mules home in the moonlight. The sound of the beetle is low in the dying grass; the robust song of the cicadas is silent as stone; and the whippoorwills cannot be heard. The katydids have ceased to sing their love songs in the cornfields. Only the corn stubble now remains and the long rows of wigwam'd fodder-shocks. The sky is bright blue and is filled with twinkling stars. These bright eyes fastened in the roof of the sky look far away tonight into the illimitable blue spaces. The tired mules bearing Fronnie and Anse walk beneath this blue sky with its covering of stars. Their hoofs lightly touch the path. You cannot hear Tarvin's big bare feet walking behind them on the path. Tarvin's feet can feel a coldness in the earth and his flesh can feel a sharpness in the eternal wind that makes his blood tingle.

"We're jest gittin done in time," thinks Tarvin. "Frost is on its way to us."

Morning brings a world covered with a gossamer sheet of frost. The mists rise above the yellowing hills and the frost quilt disappears on the clean blue autumn air. It is an air that makes one breathe deeply. It makes one draw breaths of wind deeply into the lungs to feel the clean air, the pure air, the autumn-scented air.

Tarvin rides the mule down Ragweed Hollow to norate the word to be at the shindig tonight. There are two white clouds of air coming from the Barney mule's nostrils and thinning on the blue air as vapor in the sunlight. Anse takes the Jack mule, hitches him to the one-mule express wagon and hauls planks and posts to make a platform for the dance.

Fronnie works in the house, cleaning dirty dishes, sweeping floors and washing clothes. She is doing work that has been left undone in the house while the rush of harvest was on to finish before frost.

12.

THE MULE walks around the well-worn path, pulling the long cane mill sweep. Fronnie sits at the burrs and pokes the long green stalks of cane into the mill. Fronnie has her once crow-black hair, now streaked with gray, combed over her head and twisted in a round knot. Anse has his long red beard washed clean and his thinning red hair hangs in loose locks below the brim of his big black umbrella hat. He is wearing his powder-blue, double-breasted, peg-legged suit that he has kept for years to wear on special occasions. Tarvin is wearing a pair of blue serge pants, white shirt, necktie and low-cut slippers.

"Now Tarvin," says Anse, "don't git your good clothes stained with cane stalks. Remember you jest got a few more armloads to carry out. It will all be over then. The sorghum makin will be done and you can frolic until the frost falls in the mornin."

"I'm watchin, Pa," says Tarvin. "I aint gitten my clothes messed up. There's goin to be a lot of people here tonight. There will be plenty of music. I've got the Braden Band."

"I feel like your Ma and me can go through with a couple of sets tonight," says Anse. "I feel young agin."

"Aint you tired atter the way you've worked?" Tarvin asks.

"Lord, no!" says Anse. "I aint been workin hard. I've jest been playin along. I've jest been foolin; makin sorghum molasses allus rests me."

"Ma's been complainin o' bein mighty tired here lately," says Tarvin. "Says she's about all pooped out. Says workin all day and half o' the night's been about to git the best of her."

"But when that music starts," says Anse, "your Ma's feet will begin workin like they ust to when she's a pert young gal. I know her."

"Is that right, Ma?" Tarvin hollers to Fronnie.

"Is what right?" Fronnie asks. "What air you talkin about?"

"Pa said your feet would start workin when you heerd the music tonight."

"Guess he's right," says Fronnie. "When I hear music, I want to dance. I haf to dance. I can't hep how tired I am. I was born to dance, to bear children and to work, I guess."

Fronnie laughs and feeds another armload of cane stalks

to the mill. While the burrs slowly pull the stalks between them, pressing the juice from the stalks and sending a stream of green juice down the chute to the pan, Fronnie pulls her pipe from her apron pocket, fills it with dry crumbs of burley and strikes a match on the sole of her shoe. She puts the yellow flame, glowing in the twilight, to the pipe of tobacco crumbs. She draws on the long stem and a cloud of smoke rolls from her lips.

"One good thing about terbacker smoke at night," says Fronnie, "it shoos away the mosquitoes. They quit hangin around a body."

"Son, you'd better light the lanterns," says Anse, "and hang 'em on the posts by the platform. The crowd will soon be here."

"All right, Pa."

Tarvin picks up four lanterns by the cane mill. He carries them over a few steps from the mill to the platform that Anse has built. He takes a match, lifts each globe and lights the wick. He lowers the globes to keep the slow-moving wind from blowing out the flames. He carries the lanterns out, hangs each lantern on a post set at each corner of the platform. The platform is a floor of oak planks nailed down to six logs that lie on the earth for sleepers. The lanterns give a dim light over the platform. Beside the platform is the cane-stalk pile, juiceless and dry.

"Pa, you built a good platform," says Tarvin, walking over it. "It's good and solid."

"I've built enough of 'em in my days, Son," says Anse, "to know how to build a good one. When we ust to be at home, we had a platform already built. We jest hauled it out'n the barn and set it up every time we wanted a dance."

"I hear 'em comin," says Fronnie. "Listen! 'Pears like the whole country has turned out. Hear the music! Hear 'em singin as they come."

Fronnie gets up from her hunkered position by the cane-mill

burrs. She stands silently under the starry dome of night and listens. Anse puffs his cigar and stands by the sorghum pan with the skimming dipper in his big hand and listens. Tarvin leans against a platform post and listens. The mule stops his beat around the path, wriggles his ears and listens as if something strange has happened in the hollow. It is not the buzzing insects that he hears.

> Down in the valley, valley so low,
> Hang your head over, hear the wind blow;
> Hear the wind blow, Love, hear the wind blow;
> Hang your head over, hear the wind blow.
>
> Down in the valley, down on my knees,
> Praying to heaven to give my heart ease;
> Give my heart ease, Love, give my heart ease,
> Praying to Heaven to give my heart ease.

"Listen to that banjer in there," says Anse. "That's shore purty music."

"And listen to them guitars," says Tarvin.

They stand and listen to the volume of music coming down the hollow. It is carried by the slow moving wind that is rustling the coloring autumn leaves.

"I love to hear a violean," says Fronnie. "It shore makes purty music."

"The way they sing it seems like there must be a whole army of singin, dancin and fun-lovin people," says Anse.

The song continues:

> Down in the meadow, the mocking bird sings,
> Telling my story, here's what she sings:
> Roses love sunshine, violets love dew,
> Angels in Heaven, know I love you;
> Know I love you, Dear, know I love you,
> Angels in Heaven know I love you.

Write me a letter, send it by mail,
Send it in care of Greenupsburg jail;
Greenupsburg jail, Love, Greenupsburg jail,
Send it in care of the Greenupsburg jail.

The great procession of people walk down Ragweed Hollow. They walk down the mule road to the cane mill. They walk straight toward the lantern light on the posts by the platform.

"Great day," says Anse as he sees the crowd of people. "It's the biggest crowd of people I ever saw at a gatherin here. Bigger than I ever saw come to a funeral when a good man dies at Plum Grove."

"You must-a norated the word to everybody in these parts," says Fronnie to Tarvin.

"Not to that many," says Tarvin, "but I'm glad they've come. People like to go places here and they aint many places fer a body to go. They jest heerd people talkin about comin and they've come too."

"The platform's big enough," says Anse. "Ten sets of people can dance on that platform."

"Yep, Pa," says Tarvin, "we'll have plenty of room."

The crowd of people move toward the cane mill. Boys carrying guitars, fiddles and a banjo walk in front, and the great procession of people dressed in their finest clothes follow them. Many of the small children are barefooted. The old men are dressed in their blue serge suits. They wear brogan shoes that will crack on the hard platform planks. They will not be dancing unless their feet knock on the hard planks the tune that the music is playing.

"Come on in, all of you," says Anse. "Come right in and make yourself at home. You air welcome as the October leaves on the trees, every blessed one of you."

Anse walks away from the pan where the cane juice is boiling in big blubbers and white heaps of foam. He holds his skimming dipper with one hand and he shakes hands with the men. Tarvin walks among the girls and boys and shakes hands with them. Fronnie shakes hands with the mothers of the boys and girls. There are mixing and mingling in the crowd; there are sounds of laughter and words are spoken freely. They are pleasant words, happy words, ringing on the freedom of the night wind. They are happy people getting together for a night of laughter, dancing, loving, drinking; a night to break the monotony of hard farm work; a night that will be remembered in Ragweed Hollow and talked of for years to come.

"Now, boys and girls," says Anse, "I've got to git back to the sorghum pan before the juice sticks. Git your paddles and git around the pan. We'll soon have the last run off and it will be the last fer the season. No more gittin foam from sorghum juice in this holler until next year."

The crowd begins to gather around the sorghum pan. Young men stand beside their sweethearts, tall lean men with brown faces and muscular bodies. Their hands are hardened with work on their farms. Young girls, blossoming in the spring of young womanhood, gather beside their lovers and talk idle talk, laugh and rake their paddles into the white sweet foam on the sorghum pan. The young girls' faces are brown where they have worked in the cornfields and the tobacco patches with hoes alongside the men.

"Only one time to be young," says Anse, "and that's when you air young. Now you young people laugh a lot. Have a good time. We'll have plenty of foam fer you to sop."

Anse rubs his big hairy hand over his long red beard. He holds his cigar in his mouth and puffs smoke to the night wind. He skims the green scum from the pan with the dipper and throws it into the skimming hole, a hole dug waist-deep by Tarvin into the earth where the green scum is thrown from the pan. When the mill is moved away the hole will be covered with the earth. The green scum is sticky and it ruins the clothes where it touches them. It is terrible to smell.

"Watch the skimmin hole, children," says Fronnie. "Don't one of you fall into it."

"We'll watch it," says a big red-faced boy in the crowd, putting foam into his girl's mouth with his paddle. She feeds him white drippings of foam from her paddle. That is the way all the young couples are acting around the pan. Tarvin is standing by Subrinea. She is feeding Tarvin foam from her paddle and he is feeding her foam from his paddle. They eat foam and laugh and talk. Bollie Beaver is on the other side of the sorghum pan looking across at Tarvin and Subrinea. He does not have a girl. Bollie is not good to look at. His long horse teeth are broken and discolored in front and his ears hang over like a mule's ears. He twists his ears like a mule that is listening, to get every word that is said. Bollie's eyes are black as the night. He wears a light blue faded work-shirt, and a black bow tie that works up and down on his Adam's apple as he eats foam from his own paddle. Bollie wears a peg-legged, double-breasted, powder-blue serge suit like Anse wears. He has a bouquet of farewell-to-summer in his coat lapel.

Tarvin looks across the pan at Bollie. Bollie will not look at Tarvin when Tarvin looks at Bollie. He looks down at the foam surging over the bottom of the pan, foam circulating in little streamlets from one division of the pan to another—moving forward all the time toward the hole where the plug is taken out and the golden sorghum runs out into the barrel. When Tarvin looks at Subrinea, Bollie watches him with his midnight-black searching eyes. He will not let Tarvin see that he is watching him. Tarvin glances from the corner of his eye to see that Bollie is eyeing him every time he has the chance.

"I'll fool 'im if he ever tries to start anything with me," thinks Tarvin. "I'm quick as a cat. If the good Lord ever put anything in my brain it was somethin that warns me when danger is near. I'll git 'im before he ever has time to draw a gun on me if he's in my reach. I'll knock 'im cold as a cucumber. I'll salivate 'im."

The old mix and mingle. They talk about crops, chickens, cattle, hogs and next year's crops. The young mix and mingle and talk about love, and they don't talk about anything much. They feed each other foam and laugh. They slap each other on the back and laugh and the boys slap the girls little light love licks, and take them by the arms and fondle them lightly.

"Dad, let me do a little sorghum makin there fer you," says a man with red beard on his face. "I ust to make sorghum molasses. Let me try my hand on this last run and spell you a little."

"Don't mind if you do, my friend," says Anse. "I'm gittin a little restless jest now since the neighbors have drapped in. Here's my stir and dipper."

Anse steps aside and the red-bearded man with hard calloused hands takes over the dipper and stir. Anse goes among the neighbor men, shaking their hands, asking them about their crops, hogs, cattle, land and next year's farming. Anse looks like the patriarch of the men in his neighborhood. His long red beard, clean as a hound dog's tooth, falling down to his waist, gives Anse the dignity of a patriarch. Anse is proud of his beard because he has the longest beard of any man in the neighborhood. When he talks to a neighbor he plays with his beard and smokes a cigar. He stands solid as an oak tree in front of the men when he talks. Sometimes he talks loudly. He speaks the words with his mouth and directs them with his hands. He is so commanding that the men around him remain silent and listen to all Anse has to say.

Fronnie tells the neighbor women about how hard she has had to work to get the harvest done before frost. She tells them about the Big Baptist Association that she and Anse attended at Mountain Chapel. She tells them about this Baptist preacher and that Baptist preacher and how long each preached and she can tell a few things that each said in his two-, three- and four-hour sermons. Fronnie is dressed in a new gingham dress. She wears a neatly ironed apron with a pocket on the corner to hold her pipe, matches and tobacco. Her apron is tied behind with a neat little bow. Fronnie is tall, thin and hand- some despite the years of hard labor, dancing and childbearing. Her graying hair gives her the dignity of a woman for her years. She is commanding among other women in the neigh- borhood, but she is not commanding with her husband. He is the patriarch, the man that cannot make a mistake in the com- munity, the man whose words everybody must listen to; the man whose big farm and whose reputation for hard work and thrift have earned for him an enviable place in the community.

"I ust to make these old lasses," says the red-headed man that took Anse's place. "Believe I can beat Mr. Bushman at his own job. Watch me run 'em around, boys, over the pan. Haf to git done here. We got to dance soon as this pan of sorghum is done. Eat foam while you can, youngins."

"Listen at Pa," says Subrinea to Tarvin. "He'll make Mr. Bushman mad talkin like he is. Mr. Bushman won't like fer a man to say he can make better sorghum that he can before a crowd of people!"

"Now, little gal," says Anse, circling back among the crowd and shaking hands, "if a man can make better sorghum molasses than I can, I'll be honest enough to tell 'im so. Let me see what my new friend is doin."

Anse walks down to the pan where the young and old are dipping foam from the pan. He bends over the pan and looks down at the boiling sorghum. He holds his beard in his hand to keep it from getting in the boiling sticky sorghum. If it should catch Anse by the beard, it would hold him there until someone took a pocketknife and released him. Then there would be the whole pan of sorghum molasses wasted because it would have Anse's beard in it. Anse could not bear the thought of losing a pan of sorghum molasses just because he'd been careless enough to let his long beard fall into it. He wouldn't be the same man either if he got his beard cut off. The loss of his beard would weaken his superiority among men.

"My Lord!" says Anse. "Friend, what is your name?"

Anse rises from the pan and looks at the stranger dipping the green scum from the pan with a dipper and shoving the bright amber-colored fluid through the divisions of the pan with a stir and talking and laughing with the young and old at the same time.

"My name is Boliver Tussie," he says.

"That's the purtiest sorghum molasses I ever put my peepers on, Boliver Tussie," says Anse. "How did you do it?"

"I aint trying to tell you how to make sorghum lasses," says Boliver, "but you let your juice stay too long in each division to git the right colorin and the right sweetness. You want to keep it movin. You don't make it move fast enough."

"I've never had anybody to tell me that before," says Anse.

"Where do you live, Mr. Tussie?" Anse asks. " 'Peared like I've heerd that name before."

"I live up on Cat's Fork," says Boliver, lifting his dipper of green skimmings from the pan, flinging it across his shoulder, not looking and hitting the skimming-hole center as true as the heart in a hickory tree. Anse looks at him with more surprise. Boliver goes on skimming the green scum from the pan and stirring the sorghum and talking to Anse at the same time. "I'm a squatter. You've heerd of the squatter Tussies, aint you?"

"Yes, I have," says Anse, "but I didn't think one of 'em knowed how to make sorghum molasses."

"Lots of things we know how to make," says Boliver.

Anse does not say a word. He watches Boliver run the sorghum through the divisions of the pan, chasing the golden currents of sorghum with his stir, laughing and talking as he does it. Subrinea and Tarvin do not pay their fathers any attention. They are very busy feeding each other, laughing and talking to one another and watching Bollie Beaver. He is still on the other side of the pan watching Tarvin with his midnight-black searching eyes when Tarvin is not watching him.

"I'm ready to run off this last batch," says Boliver. "Git your barrel ready."

Anse shifts the barrel under the plug, lifts the plug from the hole and the golden sorghum runs down in a golden twisted stream into the barrel.

The crowd of people around the pan with their foam paddles step back with their stomachs filled as the last molasses flows from the pan, carrying with it white streams of foam. Anse and Boliver lift a washing tub filled with water and pour into the pan so the furnace fire beneath it will not cause the pan-bottom to scorch.

"It's all over, children," says Anse. "The harvest is ended. Now to the dance. Now fer the all-night frolic. Kick up yer heels and God bless you!"

The Braden boys walk up on the platform. They sit down on a log split in two and resting on blocks of wood at each end. They start tuning their instruments and the crowd of people surge toward the platform. Bollie walks on one side of Subrinea and Tarvin walks on the other side.

"How about me whirly-giggin with you fer a couple of rounds, Subrinea?" Bollie asks.

He looks up at Subrinea so as to avoid Tarvin's glance. He is shorter than Subrinea and looks up toward her face.

"I'll answer fer her," says Tarvin. "I'll say 'No'!"

"A nice way fer you to treat your guests," says Bollie.

"You aint my guest," says Tarvin. "You jest come here. You aint even been invited. You followed like a dog."

"You aint runnin this place," says Bollie. "I'll tell you that right now."

Bollie starts to reach into his bulging pocket. Before he gets his hand into his pocket, Tarvin, quick as a cat, squares himself, draws back his long muscular arm and sends a haymaker to Bollie's chin, laying him out flat on the ground. Bollie falls as if shot between the eyes with a hog rifle. He lies on the cane stalks with his hand on the butt of his pistol.

"I got you, old boy, before the draw," says Tarvin. "You aint offerin Subrinea money now. Every time I think about that my face burns. You low-down viper!"

Tarvin stands above Bollie's limp body. Tarvin is shaking like a winter oak in the wind with madness.

"What's the matter here, boys?" Anse asks. "Can't have no trouble here."

"No trouble," says Tarvin. "Jest two licks struck. I struck 'im and he struck the ground. A boy can't come around and insult a girl when I'm with 'er."

Anse walks over and sees Bollie lying on the cane-stalk pile with his mouth and nose bleeding. Boliver Tussie walks over and looks at him.

"He's been follerin me around all atternoon," says Subrinea. "I can't git shet of 'im."

"He aint no good, Mr. Bushman," says Boliver. "I know 'im. He's a bad man. You'd better take that gun off'n 'im while he's knocked out cold. When he comes to he'll pull his pistol and start shootin up the place."

Tarvin bends over and takes Bollie's arm. He pulls Bollie's hand from his pocket. He holds a death grip on his .32 Smith and Wesson pistol though he is knocked cold as a cucumber.

"Look at this pistol," says Tarvin, wresting it from his grip. "It has three notches on it."

"My God!" says Anse. "I'm glad he didn't make the fourth notch with your pelt."

"Better see if he's got a knife," says Boliver. "He's a bad'n to knife."

Tarvin searches his pockets and brings out a long hook-bladed barlow knife.

"Durned if it aint notched once," says Tarvin. "He believes in keepin account of his deeds."

"Never heard of a man notchin a knife," says an old man in the crowd with a beard nearly as long as Anse's beard. "That beats all I ever seed in my life."

"I'll take care of these," says Tarvin.

Tarvin puts the knife in his pocket. He hands the pistol to Anse.

"Take care of it, Pa," he says. "We've had a little trouble before. I don't want him with a gun. Hep me throw 'im over here on the cane-stalk pile, Boliver."

Boliver takes Bollie by the hands and Tarvin grabs his legs. They throw him over on the stalk pile as they would throw a sack of corn. Bollie lies there, moaning and groaning like a stuck hog, and the music goes on mindless of a little fight. Fights have happened before at square dances and no one minds a little fight. They love the excitement of it. The crowd looks at Bollie and laughs.

"That tall boy tamed that bully, didn't he?" says the old bearded man. "Reminds me of the old days. People aint lost the color of their blood yit." He laughs with a big hee-haw and wipes his beard. "Lord, he hit 'im a deadner! I heard the lick pop plum over here. Bollie Beaver was the bully among the lumberjacks. He aint no more. Who was that boy that hit Bollie nohow?"

"My boy," says Anse. "Tarvin Bushman. I didn't larn 'im to fight but I'd beat 'im to death if he didn't take his part when another fellar picks at 'im. A man that won't fight fer his woman aint got the right color of blood in his veins. That's all I got to say. Come on and let's dance! Fill up the floor!"

"Who can call fer this dance?" Willie Hillman asks.

No one answers.

"Let Subrinea call," says Tarvin. "She can call."

"There's others here that can call," says Subrinea. "Let a man call. His voice will be louder. It's a man's place to call."

"You don't mind, do you, Honey?" Tarvin asks.

"Go on and call, Subrinea," says Boliver.

"All right," she nods.

"Everybody git your couples and fill up the floor."

The young couples walk onto the platform floor. Old men walk out with their wives. Anse walks onto the floor with Fronnie. Boliver walks onto the floor with Crissie. Couples follow until there are thirty-two couples on the platform under the lantern light and the stars in the blue dome of the night sky.

"Four couples to a set," says Subrinea. "We have enough fer eight sets."

The dancers couple off into groups of four couples.

"Let's have 'Birdie,' boys," says Anse, "the best dance tune that ever come from a mountain fiddle."

"And let's dance 'Cage the Bird,' " says Boliver. "It's the purtiest dance of them all."

"Don't matter so we dance," says Mary Spriggs. "My feet feel the music."

The fiddles, guitars and banjo start playing the tune, "Birdie." Subrinea stands in the middle of the dance floor beside Tarvin. She is taller than the girls about her. Her golden hair is clasped in a long braid and falls over her shoulder. She wears slippers tonight and a long neatly fitting blue gingham dress. Her legs are bare and brown. Her body is supple and she moves to the rhythm of the music. Subrinea calls while she dances.

"First couple out and circle," Subrinea says. Her voice is musical as a mocking bird's singing. The first couple leads out in each set, their shoes clicking on the oak-plank floor.

"Cage that bird, that purty little bird."

Now the heels are clicking and the boys and girls of each set have caught hands and they are circling around a girl that stands in the middle of each circle.

"Bird hops out and the crow hops in,
All hands up and gone again.

"Move, children, move! Move, children, move!
Too slow that step you're in!
Move, children, move! Move, children, move!

"Change left-hand lady, left hand around,
Partner by the right and go whirly-giggin 'round."

"Lord," says Anse, "this is hotter work than makin sorghum molasses."

Anse swings Fronnie as lively as any young couple on the floor.

Subrinea's long lithe body is graceful on the dance floor. Other women envy her skill on the dance floor and the young men envy Tarvin because he dances with her.

"You swing yours and I'll swing mine,
El mend your left—

Meet your Honey and go right and left—
Sift the meal and save the bran,
I'm goin' home with Sally Ann—"

Subrinea goes through with the dance call as each couple dances. The sweat pours from the young couples' brown faces and it runs and drips from the old men's beards. The music is lively and there are laughter, talking and squeals from the dancing couples as the music gets fast and furious. Anse steps lively in his big brogan shoes; sparks fly from the hobnails on his shoe soles when he leaps in the air and comes down on the hard planks. When Anse leaps in the air and comes back to the floor he lets out a big "Whoopee." The harvest is over and Anse is celebrating a rich harvest before the approaching winter. When each couple goes through with their part of the

dance, the music comes to a halt and the dancers stop to mop
the sweat from their brows.

"Air you all cooled enough," Subrinea asks, "so we can go
on with the next dance?"

"I'm hot as a roasted tater," says Jeff LeMasters, "but it
won't keep me from kickin a weaked toe. Come on with the
dance!"

"It's shore like work," says Anse, mopping his heavy beard
with a big red bandanna. "How air you feelin, Fronnie?"

"I feel like dancin another set," she says.

"What do you want to dance, Mrs. Bushman?" Subrinea
asks.

"Grapevine Twist," says Fronnie.

"It's a hard dance on us old'ns," says Murt Horsley.

"Let the music go, boys," says Subrinea. "Couples, git your
partners and git on the floor."

The Bradens start the music. There is a wild swirl of couples, mingling and mixing for the second dance. The winds
blow over the platform. The stars shine down on the dancers.
The mules stand and prance, hitched to their posts. There is a
smell of cane stalks permeating the air. There is a smell of
molasses, a sweet smell mixed with the sour smell of cane
stalks. Children romp over the cane-stalk pile and play. They
play over Bollie Beaver's limp body.

"Jine hands and circle down south,
Git that sunshine in your mouth."

The shoes and slippers crack on the hardwood floor as the
dancers start to dance.

"Chickens in the barnyard pickin up corn,
The Devil's goin to git you shore's you're born."

The old men swing their partners and the boys lift their

partners off the floor when they swing them. Tarvin lifts
Subrinea high into the air as he swings her and as they
promenade around he holds her lithe body close. Her lips move
quickly as she calls.

"Turn them corners, turn them slow,
Maybe the last time, I don't know.
Ho by-gosh and ho by-joe!
First couple out and lady in the lead,
Gent falls through and takes the lead.
Lady falls through the old side door,
Swing in the center and tie up four,
You tie up four in the center of the floor.
Left-hand lady and left-hand dough,
Partner to the right and go waltz the floor."

"All right, boys," says Mort Flannigan, "let's move. Let's
move, children. Let's move!"

Mort stands in the corner and claps his hands on his knees.
The crowd is going wild. The dance grows faster and more
furious as the fiddlers bend over their fiddles and the guitar
players pick faster on the strings.

"Listen to that banjer talk, won't you, boys," says Amos
Skaggs. "That Percy Braden is shore a banjer-pickin fool if I
ever heerd one. He makes that banjer talk."

"Swing the one that stole the sheep.
Now swing the one that stole the meat,
Now the one that gnawed the bone,
Now the one you left at home.

"Everybody swing!

"Swing and balance two,
Git that lady behind you!
All home and dance your best.
What air you goin to do,
With your elbow left?
Watch 'em come and watch 'em go,
And watch 'em shake that calico!

"Meet your partner and promenade!
Everybody swing!
Circle four in the middle of the floor,
Left-hand lady go left hand around,
Meet your Honey as she comes round,
Around behind and swing when you meet,
Back to the center, and oh, how sweet!

"Everybody swing!"

The men swing their partners and the music stops. It is the end of another dance.

"Now let me git you somethin to revive your spirits, boys," says Anse.

Anse walks over to the cane-stalk pile. He takes a pitchfork and throws aside a few forkfuls of juiceless cane stalks. He removes the cane stalks from four white two-gallon jugs with brown necks.

"Hep yourself, boys," says Anse. "It's good moonshine. It won't pizen you. It is the kind that makes you love your neigh-

bor as you love yourself. It will make you kick your heels high.
Don't take too much of it now if you want to dance until
mornin."

The men walk over and keep four jugs going at one time.
They hike and spit and drink. The women talk to one another
on the platform. The children play, fight and scream on the
cane-stalk pile. The night is getting young and the crowd is
getting happy.

"Now, a man that would pull a gun in a good crowd like
this," says Pat Flannigan, "ought to be run home. Knocked out
yet. Wonder if he's hurt. Might be Tarvin hit 'im harder than
he thought."

Pat takes Bollie Beaver by the heels. He drags him off the
cane-stalk pile. The men pass the jug and make remarks about
Bollie. They laugh as Pat drags him by the heels and his coat
slips back over his shoulders showing his berry-stained blue
shirt.

"We need water to throw on 'im," says Pat. "Cold water
will bring 'im to. Old Bollie don't know what fun he's missin."

"There's a skimmin hole over there," says Brady Smith.
"Dump 'im in it."

Pat drags Bollie to the skimming hole. He puts his feet in
first and then he takes Bollie by the shoulders and stands him
up in the skimming hole.

Bollie opens his eyes. He looks around. His face is nearly
even with the ground, he is so short and the hole so deep.

"My God, what has happened to me?" Bollie asks. "Am I
sinkin? Where am I?"

"In the skimmin hole," Pat says. Pat rears back and laughs
and all the men on the cane pile laugh. The children laugh
and the women laugh. The men pass the jugs and laugh. They
bend over and hit their knees and laugh. They slap each
other on the back and laugh.

The green cane-juice scum sloshes up and down under
Bollie's chin.

"Hep me," says Bollie. "I feel like I'm sinkin and sinkin."

"If we take you out," says Pat, "you got to go home."

"Hell," says Bollie, "I aint stayin in this damned place. I want to git out'n here. Nice way to treat guests the way I've been treated. There'll come another time. Git me out'n this damned hole."

Pat and Anse take Bollie's arms and lift him from the skimming hole. Bollie comes up with the green scum stringing from his blue serge suit. The green foam is running off in rope-size sluices from his hands. He is awful to look at.

"Looks like the frogs has been roostin on 'im," says Mort Hargis, "durned if it don't. Bollie, it won't pay you to pull a pistol in this crowd and start to kill somebody. You'd better git home while there's life still left in your body."

Bollie staggers up the road the way he came with great streams of cane-juice skimmings running down his wet soggy blue serge suit. The women laugh as he passes the platform.

"I feel like goin, Subrinea," says Boliver. "Give us that good old 'Figure Eight' dance. It's got life in it."

"Start your music, boys, says Subrinea. "Boys, git your partners and git on the floor."

The men leave their jugs on the cane pile. They walk quickly to the floor and grab their partners.

> "First couple out—change and swing.
> Croquet waltz and croquet swing.
> Change right back to the same old thing,
> Croquet waltz and croquet swing.
> Circle four, left-hand lady and left-hand dough,
> Partner by the right and waltz the floor."

The men are hollering as they swing. Anse is dancing as he has never danced before. The sweat breaks from the men's faces.

"Jump up high and come down straight.
Sixteen hands and circle eight,
Circle eight when you git straight.
Knock down Sall and pick up Kate.

"Everybody swing!

"Move, children, move!
Move, children, move!

"She went up the new cut road,
And I come down the lane,
Stuck my toe in a holler log
And out jumped Lizzie Jane.

"Meet your Honey with a double hook-on,
And promenade your own."

The music goes on and the dance goes on through the morning hours. The small children lie sleeping on the cane-stalk pile. Many of the old women and old men sit on the cane-stalk pile and smoke their pipes and clap their hands while the younger dancers dance. Fronnie and Anse are standing the dance. Boliver and Crissie are dancing equal to the young dancers. The boys hug the girls tight and kiss them on the dance floor.

"This holler aint seen a dance like this since I've been livin here," says Anse, "and I've lived here all my life."

"We need more of these good dances," says Boliver, "and people would be a lot happier. I ust to think, Anse Bushman, that you's a old sour-puss but now I know that you aint. You air a man next to my heart. I've allus loved a good dance and good spirits to drink. It runs in my people. It's in our blood, Mr. Bushman."

"Yes," says Anse, "it's in the blood and there's power in the blood."

Anse jumps high in the air and cracks his feet together twice.

"I'm still a young man," he hollers.

"That aint enough yit," says Boliver. "Watch me."

Boliver jumps into the air and cracks his brogan shoes together three times before he hits the dance floor. The crowd clap their hands when Boliver does this.

"Aint a young man in the crowd can beat me," he says.

"I can do it as many times as you can, Pa," says Subrinea.

Subrinea jumps up and cracks her slippers together three times before she lightly sets her feet back on the platform.

"Stars air leavin the sky," says Mort Hargis. "I've got to git home and feed and milk this mornin. I've got a hard day's work ahead of me today."

"I 'spect we'd all better be goin," says Willie Hillman; "by the time we git home it will be broad daylight. A lot of us have a fur piece to go."

"Yes," says Boliver, "we've got to git up Cat's Fork tonight and I've got to cut timber tomorrow."

"Then if it's partin," says Anse, "I'm glad to have had you fer my guests. I hope you've all had a good time. Now we can go to our homes and go to work. When we work we can remember one night of frolic and fun."

The crowd hollers as Anse gets through talking. They holler and scream. They do not holler because of the words Anse said. They holler because they want to holler and because the moonshine is telling the men to holler and scream.

The crowd starts up the hollow. The musicians are in front playing their guitars, fiddles and the banjo. The crowd walks behind, many of the men stagger from one side of the road to the other. Anse rides the Barney mule and smokes a cigar. Fronnie rides the Jack mule and smokes her pipe. The procession moves up the hollow—everybody singing and hollering as they move along.

Down in the valley, valley so low,
Hang your head over, hear that wind blow;
Hear that wind blow, Love, hear that wind blow,
Hang your head over, hear that wind blow.

The women hold their screaming children's hands. The children are sleepy and cry because they have been awakened in the early morning hours. The men and women and their children leave on every road that comes into the Ragweed Hollow road. They go out on every path to the hilltops. The crowd starts dwindling as the procession moves along. They are singing, swearing, laughing and talking as they journey along toward their homes.

Anse and Fronnie see Tarvin with his arm around Subrinea and her arm around him, walk up Cat's Fork with Crissie and Boliver. They do not say anything, for Tarvin and Subrinea are singing as the stars fade into the early morning sky. There is all the work to do and Anse and Fronnie will have to do it without Tarvin's help, but this is a night of rejoicing and festivity.

PART II

1.

EARTH IS arid now. Avalanches of leaves sweep over the fallow lying land. Giant sycamore leaves clang in the air like rustling cymbals, tumbling and turning earthward. Leaves are strewn on the meadow and along the rocky ravines. The milkweed furze is flying on Anse Bushman's pasture fields like the soft down picked from geese and let go to a light blowing wind. The purple ironweeds are dying along the pasture creek banks. The powdery purple blossoms of silkweeds are falling—drifting over the fallow land with the leaves. Boneset and queen of the meadow are dying—leaving their dead stems upon the fallow land.

"A changin world," Anse meditates, as he carries a bag of salt out to salt the cattle. "Strange about the seasons. We know when to plant and when to reap. We know our earth and the seasons that go with our earth."

Anse walks down from the knoll that faces the white house on the hill. He sees his nine cows picking brown frosted grass along Ragweed Creek. Anse calls, "Swookie, swookie, cows! Swookie, swookie, cows!" The cows come to his call. He dips salt from the bag with his big hand, throws it on each cow's back. She bends her neck to lick the salt from her back with her long grainy tongue.

"Killin two birds with one stone," thinks Anse, "fer salt on a cow's back will kill the 'wobbles' that git into her back and I save a lot of salt by puttin it on the cow's back. I make 'em work to git their salt."

Anse walks the point toward the sheep barn. "I'll allus find the sheep on the highest pint up amongst the cliffs," thinks Anse. "They round up there late in the evenings to sleep. They love high places and rocks. They keep their hoofs whetted off on the rocks. Saves me a lot of labor trimmin their feet."

Anse puffs as he walks up the steep hill. Streams of his white breath go out from his nostrils like two streams of escaping steam. His big body weaves to and fro but moves briskly along. Anse does not use a walking stalk. He walks straight up the point of the high hill, pulling his body up occasionally by holding to a sprout, or by bracing his foot and placing the other foot securely above him before he steps.

Anse reaches the hilltop, blows a sigh of relief, flings the bag of salt from his shoulder to the ground. He pulls a cigar from his coat pocket, strikes a match on his pants leg and lights his cigar. Anse smokes his cigar, wipes the sweat from his forehead with his red bandanna handkerchief. "Sheepie, sheepie, sheepie," he calls. His voice re-echoes on the distant hill near his house.

The sheep come running from all directions. Three hundred sheep come from under the trees and among the rocks. Anse takes the seventy-five-pound bag of salt that has had a few pounds taken out for the cows. He spreads the salt like a thin layer of snow over the rocks. The sheep baa to each other and put their little noses to the big salt rock. The lichen moss is worn off the rocks where the sheep have licked so much salt.

"Sheep air purty things," Anse thinks. "Watch the little fellars nibble their salt." The sheep look at Anse from their innocent gray eyes as he stands among them, master and owner of the flock. "Can't hep themselves. A body hast to hep 'em. See a dog among 'em and up-end 'im with a rifle at three hundred yards. Still have the eyes of an eagle and nerves steady as steel. Allus give the dogs nice burials somewhere they won't be heard of agin."

Anse looks over the ewes, checking this one and that one that is with lamb.

"Daub tar on my buck's forelegs," says Anse, "and I'll find tar on the yowe's hips. A lot of my yowes air heavy with lamb. I'll have a time right in cold weather this year. Yowes will be drappin their lambs in January."

Anse pats his ewes on the head. He knows this ewe and that ewe personally out of the whole flock. He remembers all of the ewes that have borne twin lambs, and the three ewes that have borne triplets are Anse's pets. Anse cares little for the cull ewes that will not bear lambs. He pats the old ewe the copperhead bit on the sack and caused it to wither away. He does not consider her a cull.

Anse walks down the path toward the cove where Tarvin is cutting wood. He can hear two voices. He stops and puts his cupped hand above his ear. "A woman's voice," says Anse. "What's a woman doin down there?"

The sound of the ax stops echoing against the bluffs. Anse walks closer, peeping from the brush as he goes. He walks softly, placing his big brogan shoes carefully on the leaves so as not to make any noise. "I'll jest see who she is," thinks Anse. "I'll see what a woman is doin where Tarvin is cuttin wood."

Anse gets closer, parts the brush again. He can see the open spot among the brush down on a little fork of Ragweed Hollow. He can see the girl. She is the tall girl he saw Tarvin dancing with at the cane mill. She is Subrinea Tussie. She has one end of the crosscut saw. She is sawing wood with Tarvin. He can see her long brown arms moving like pistons. She is sawing wood and laughing and talking as she saws. He can see her loose-flung hair falling over her shoulders like frosted autumn grass bending down to the earth after the frost has first struck it and the sun beams upon it. He can see her bare feet when the stick of wood falls from the sawhorse as she walks around to get her ax and split the block of wood into sticks of stove wood.

"That gal is a good worker," thinks Anse. "Fronnie's done a lot of hard work but she aint no account with the ax. Fronnie can't use the ax like a man. She's a good gal to git out and work that way with a man! But somethin might come of this! They aint married! It's hard to see a boy of mine marry into that squatter set even if the woman is good to work. That frolickin, drinkin, pilferin and no-countness is in their blood.'"

Anse sits on a rock. He sits silently. He does not move his feet to rustle the leaves. He does not even smoke so they will smell the smoke. Anse wants to see what is going on here. He holds the empty salt sack on his lap and watches his tall son and the tall girl saw wood. He watches them split the blocks into white shiny sticks and carry them to the rick. They work like machines. Anse can only see movements of strong youthful bodies and youthful muscles toiling in the woods—laughing as they work with the clean sweet-smelling wood. He watches them until they put their tools away. He watches Subrinea turn and run up the hollow like a rabbit—around the path and over the gap at the Coon Den Hollow toward Cat's Fork. Tarvin watches her as she goes. When she is out of sight, Tarvin picks up his ax and walks down the creek to Ragweed Hollow and up the path home.

"No wonder he can put up three cords of wood some days," says Anse. "I didn't think he was still that much better man than I was." Anse picks up his empty salt bag and walks down the hill to the hollow.

2.

"OCTOBER NEARLY gone," says Anse, "and hog-killin time is here. Weather's gettin too cold to put much more meat on the hogs. It will take too much corn. The corn will be worth more than the meat. We need another good man to hep us butcher— and two wimmen to hep Fronnie render the lard."

"I know where we can git 'em," says Tarvin. "There aint a better butcher in this county than Boliver Tussie. He knows how to stick hogs, too, without runnin the knife in the shoulders and ruinin the good meat. His wife, Crissie, and his girl Subrinea, can hep Ma render the lard. They know what they air doin when it comes to handlin hogs. Everybody in the county tries to git 'em. Can't git 'em only on Saturdays, fer Boliver works in the timber woods until Saturday at noon."

"Go see 'em," says Anse. "See if you can git 'em and while you do that I'll git everything ready. We'll butcher tomorrow. The weather is cold enough now fer the meat to keep. We must git butcherin done fer our year's supply of lard is runnin slim. We don't have but one ham and a middlin of meat left in the smokehouse."

Tarvin catches Barney, bridles him, leaps astride bareback and rides away. Anse takes Jack, hitches him in the sled, and drives to the woods back of the barn. He cuts little dead locust poles that are dry as powder. He loads them on the sled and hauls them to the twin hickory trees back of the house. He puts washing tubs on the sled, drives to the creek, and dips the tubs full of water. He hauls the water to the hickory trees back of the house and pours it into the big barrels. He gets all the kettles, tubs and buckets on the spot for the next day's killing.

"It will take lots of wood and lots of water," says Anse, "fer we have twenty hogs to butcher."

"We'll have a lot of lard to render tomorrow," says Fronnie. "The hogs air powerfully fat. We'll have a hundred and fifty gallons of lard."

Anse rises from bed long before daylight. When the light streaks the east, the cows have been milked and turned into the pasture. Fronnie has washed the breakfast dishes, swept the floors and dusted the furniture. It is butchering day and it is always a hard day at Anse Bushman's house. It is a full day's work. Tarvin has his long hog rifle, bright and shiny, and a box of long cartridges.

As daylight dawns on the frost-covered fields, Boliver walks out to the barn where Tarvin and Anse are standing. Subrinea and Crissie walk under the trellis of leafless vines where Fronnie is standing in the yard smoking her pipe.

"I put fire under the kettles," says Anse, "when I first got up this mornin. The water is bilin and ready. The mules air hitched to the sled and ready. We air ready to begin work."

"How many do you haf to kill?" Boliver asks.

"Twenty."

"Then we'd better kill ten at a time," says Boliver.

"A good idear," says Anse.

Anse takes a hammer, knocks a board from the fence. The hogs are hanging around the trough to be fed. They file through the hole in the fence one by one—heavy-jowled hogs, sagging with fat and eyes set far back in their heads. When they get out of the pen and have their freedom, they start rooting up the dirt. Tarvin takes his rifle, levels the barrel at the center spot between the eyes. He squeezes the trigger. "Spink" goes the rifle. The hog falls kicking. It never squeals. Boliver takes a long knife, sticks the hog in the throat to the artery to bleed it. Again the "spink" of the rifle, the fall of the hog and the big long knife stuck into its throat, until ten are lying dead on the ground with puddles of red blood gathered about their slashed throats. Anse drives the mules beside the hogs. Anse, Tarvin and Boliver lift the big hogs by legs and ears onto the sled. They haul five at a load to the twin hickory trees back of the house.

They dip water from the kettles into the scalding barrel set under the hickory trees. They fasten the rope from the block and tackle, fastened to a big limb on the hickory tree, to the hind legs of the hog. They lift the hog from the sled. The three men hold the rope. They lift the hog up and let it fall back into the barrel of hot scalding water. They jostle the hog up and down—splashing the water until the hair slips. They lift the hog from the barrel and scald another hog and then another until the five hogs are scalded. Anse drives the mules back to haul the next five hogs. They scald these five and lay them on the planks. Then they pour more water into the kettles on the fire and chuck the firebrands under the kettle. They put dry sticks of wood around the kettle to heat more water. There are ten hogs yet to kill.

Fronnie, Subrinea and Crissie take their hands and slip the hair from the scalded hogs. They leave piles of hair on the planks. If there is a place on the hog where the hair will not slip, one dips a bucket of hot water from the kettle and pours it over the spot until the hair does slip. While the rifle cracks out at the barn and the long knife stabs the throat artery, the women clean the hogs. The sun peeps over the east range of Ragweed Hollow hills and ten cleaned hogs lie stretched on the plank floor.

At eleven o'clock Fronnie goes to the kitchen to get dinner for the workers. There are ten more hogs, cleaned, shiny and white, lying beside the other ten hogs, waiting to be hung on the scaffold, to be split open and the entrails removed. There is a long hickory sapling resting in the forks of the twin hickories on one end, with its other end suspended in the air by two saplings set in the earth, each with a fork on its end lifting up the other end of the hickory sapling.

"That hickory will hold fifty hogs," says Anse, "if we had 'em to hang on it. Aint no danger of it fallin."

They cut the flesh around the leaders in the hogs' hind legs, put the ends of the sharpened stick behind each leader. The stick spreads their legs apart and as the block and tackle lift them in the air, their legs pull inward on the stick, holding them securely when they are tied to the scaffold. When Fronnie says dinner is ready, there are twenty cleaned hogs tied to the scaffold, ready to be gutted, drained, pulled from the scaffold and cut apart, and the meat trimmed of its fat.

After dinner Fronnie, Anse, Boliver and Crissie sit in the house and smoke. Anse and Boliver smoke cigars and Fronnie and Crissie smoke their pipes. They talk about hogs, meat and lard. They talk about corn in the shock this time of year and the mice being so plentiful to eat the corn. They talk about sheep, and wonder why a buzzard can always tell when a sheep is dead or even when it is going to die.

"Buzzards air smart things," says Anse, blowing smoke from his basket of beard.

"I've jest wondered if one could smell," says Boliver. "I can see 'em flyin over your sheep pasture ever once in a while."

"Yes," says Anse, "when we see the buzzards flyin we take our guns, our sheep medicine jugs and we go. We know a sheep has died, 'r has been kilt—'r a sheep is sick and is goin to die. I wouldn't have a buzzard kilt on my farm fer love ner money."

"When I got sick once," says Boliver, "—Crissie can tell you there about it—the buzzards flew over my house all day. Got so close the children could throw rocks up amongst 'em. It plagued me to death——"

"It larnt Boliver a lesson," says Crissie. "He watches the moonshine he drinks now. He got a-holt of some pizen moonshine. Boliver might' nigh kicked the bucket."

"It's time," says Boliver, "that we git back to cuttin up hogs. It's a right smart job to cut up twenty hogs and trim the fat from the meat."

"It is that," says Anse, getting up and following Boliver from the room. Tarvin and Subrinea sit in the room and listen to the old people talk. Tarvin smokes his pipe. The room is filled with tobacco smoke as the workers get up and leave the room. Fronnie leaves her dishes on the table. She goes out to work with the rest. After all, this is butchering day and the butchering must be done in a day.

Boliver guts the hogs, Fronnie and Crissie trim the fat from their intestines. They put the fat in the kettles over the fire. Subrinea and Tarvin stir the rendering fat into lard in the two big kettles. Anse throws a bucket of clean water onto the hogs and washes them clean after Boliver takes away the entrails. The clean bodies of the hogs are cooled on the scaffold. The October air is clean, clear, crisp and fine. It makes one want to breathe deeply and feel the air going into the lungs. There is the clean sweet smell of butchered hogs and the savory greasy smell of lard rendering in the kettles. Subrinea stands near the kettle, the steam comes from the lard and covers her white face—blows away and leaves her face oily with grease.

"Allus put a bucket of cold lard in the kettle," says Fronnie, "before you put your fat from the entrails in the kettle. That makes good lard."

Anse and Boliver lower the cleaned cooled hogs to the table. They cut them into middlings, shoulders, hams, heads and jowls. "Fat meat aint good meat to eat," says Anse. "Take all the fat from the meat you can find." The women trim piles of fat meat from the clean hogs. They carry the piles of fat and put them in the lard kettles. Anse and Boliver carry hams, shoulders and middlings to the big wooden table in the smokehouse. They cover them with layers of salt and put them in stacks.

"How much lard will we have, Tarvin?" Fronnie asks.

"I believe we'll have nearly two hundred gallons, Ma," says Tarvin.

All afternoon the kettles boil. Tarvin has a kettle, Fronnie has a kettle, and Subrinea has a kettle. Crissie dips lard from the kettles and puts it into the cans. She carries the fat from the wooden table to the kettles. "I never could stand the smell of renderin lard," says Crissie. " 'Pears like the fumes allus put a swimmin in my head."

As the sun goes down over the range of hills on the west of Ragweed Hollow, Tarvin, Anse and Boliver carry thirty-one seven-gallon lard cans to the smokehouse and stack them against the wall. "That's some lard," says Boliver.

There is the heap of white meat stacked in piles on the big table in the smokehouse. There are stacks of backbone, ribs, heads, livers, spleens, hoofs and hearts. "Now hep yourselves to all the fresh meat you can carry home," Anse says as he hands a dollar to Boliver, a dollar to Subrinea and a dollar to Crissie. They take all the fresh meat that they can carry. They walk down the path as the sun goes over the range of hills leaving a path of red behind on the blue October sky. Anse and Tarvin take brooms and sweep up the hog hairs and pile them on the embers of a kettle-fire. They sweep the planks clean, lower the scaffold and put the tubs, barrels and buckets back in their places. They clean up the hog-killing mess. The day is over and the meat and lard are in the smokehouse for winter use and to sell.

"That Boliver is shore a handy man," says Anse, "when it comes to butcherin hogs. I can't understand why a body can have sich a purty gal with sich a ugly Pa and Ma. I jest looked at her today. She's a purty thing! Actually she is!"

"Glad you think so, Pa," says Tarvin. "I think she's right purty myself."

3.

WIND SINGS loud and lonesome, whipping the remaining leaves from the poplars, sycamores, elms and sugar maples. Wind sings loud and lonesome over the fallow earth—over the stubbled fields—sings loud and lonesome among the leafless briars whose thorns jab into the wind as it blows by. One would know November by the wind whipping the barren branches of the trees and rustling the clusters of tough-butted white-oak leaves that cling stubbornly to the boughs; leaves that will not leave the trees until sap comes in the spring and new blood in the veins of the white oaks compels these oaks to shed their leaves. A new life is born and the old is cast aside—the way of life.

The flowers have gone. All that marks where they have stood is the barren stems, falling to the earth to rot and decay. The murky clouds float over the gray earth and there is a cool damp feel of snow. The November days are here when trees look desolate. Their bodies are stripped of leaves. Life has left the hills. The trees have gone into the sleep of death—that sleep of an awaited resurrection, that long sleep when the ground hog licks his paw and the hard-working bees live in a cozy hollow tree eating honey. Anse Bushman lives from the toil he has given to the land, the hard work that the land has taken from him but has repaid him many fold.

"All we haf to do now," says Anse, "is to shuck our corn. We've got a lot of cornshocks yit to shuck. Now is the time to shuck the corn so we won't tear up the fodder. It is damp now—even if the November rains aint started yet. Fodder is allus like the wind about it. When the wind is damp, the fodder is damp. When the wind is dry, the fodder is dry. Now is the time to gather the corn, fer atter the November rains the bad weather comes.

Anse and Tarvin walk up to a shock of corn. Tarvin takes hold of the top, pulls it to the ground. Tarvin pulls the bright fodder from the shock. Don, the collie, runs under the shock to catch the mice. Anse gets on one side of the shock, Tarvin gets on the other. They husk the big white ears of corn. They throw them in a heap where the fodder shock has stood. They tie the fodder in bundles. "A bundle is a mess of roughness fer a cow," says Anse.

When they shuck every ear of corn and pile it in a heap, they throw the fodder bundles over the heap of corn. "You can't tell what night it might snow," says Anse, "and it would be hard to find white ears of corn in the snow. Better to play safe than to be sorry."

When the fodder shocks have all been pulled down and the corn shucked, heaped in piles and covered, Anse and Tarvin take the mules and sled and follow the corn rows. They remove the fodder, load the corn in the sled bed and haul it off the steep loamy hills to the corncrib. They scoop it from the sled bed into the crib.

When the corn is hauled to the crib and the big cribs have been filled, Anse and Tarvin go over the cornfields, carry the bundles of fodder and stack them against the bodies of large trees that have been girdled in the cornfield. Sometimes they put fifteen fodder shocks into one big shock. Tarvin takes one end of a wild grapevine and Anse takes the other end. They go around the big shock. They met each other and pull the grapevine as tight as they can. They twist its ends over each other. They leave the fodder stacked in the field awaiting a snowfall. The sled will be easy to pull then and they can load on enough fodder to break down a sled. The mules can pull it with ease. The cornfields stand with giant shocks of fodder around the girdled trees. The cornstubble, bright and glistening, stands in curved rows around the steep hill slopes.

November passes as a mist of autumnal rain hanging in the dark and desolate valley. Great white sheets of mist climb the mountainside like gossamer threads the spiders spin among the dewy summer weeds. November passes with a shrill whistle of wind among barren branches of trees and the green tops of wild ferns looking from the ledges of rocks. There is a smell of wet earth soured by rain among the November hills. The rocks are washed clean by the rain and the blotches of occasional sunlight beam on the lichen stones, cleansed to purplish gray.

As Tarvin walks through the sloppy mud around the barn-yard, milks the cows, feeds the hogs, and throws hay from the barnloft to the mangers below, he can see Subrinea. He can see the trees of Heaven, tall against the sky, and he can remember the nights they have stood beneath these trees and the words they have said. He can remember the times he held her close to his tall body and the times he embraced her fondly. He cannot forget her.

November passes into oblivion. December comes, a white blanket of snow covering the hills. The sheep are driven from the high hills to the sheep barn. December comes, with long trains of crows flying over the white mounds of hills. They fly down to the ragweed patches and the giant shocks of fodder. They scratch among the fodder blades for loose grains of corn. Crows fly over the sheep field looking for a dead sheep. Crows fly over the cow pasture looking for a dead cow or a dead calf.

"It looks like life preys upon life here," thinks Tarvin as he stands by the window watching the crows alight in a tree. He watches the crows fly down from the tree to the ground while two crows sit in the tree and caw-caw down to the fussy crows in the snow. "Crows have found a dead sheep. Look how smart they air to keep guards in the tree. Crows air smart birds."

Tarvin stands by the window and watches more crows come to the tree until the limbs are bending with the weight of the crows. These birds fly down. He can hear them fussing with the crows on the ground. Soon it seems that all the crows in the county have found this spot. There are chattering and caw-caws among the crows. Their strong harsh voices sound above the snow-covered silent land. "A sheep has died in the snow," thinks Tarvin. He stands by the window a few minutes longer and he sees the great swarm of crows leave the spot silently. Silently they fly over the pine grove. Their strong wings beat against the tyrannous wind. Soon the long black train of crows has gone. Tarvin walks out of the house. He makes his way through the deep snow to the spot. He finds the snow padded down hard by crow tracks. A sheep's skeleton is lying on the snow. The bones have been picked clean and the wind whistles among them. "Maybe it was a yowe heavy with lamb," thinks Tarvin. "If I could have only been here to have seen."

4.

"FEED HEAVY, Tarvin, through the month of December," says Anse. "Give the cattle plenty of hay, corn and fodder. This is the month and this is the time they need plenty of heat fer their bodies. This is a rough December. When you go to the sheep barn, don't fail to throw down plenty of hay and shell plenty of corn in the troughs fer the yowes. They start drappin lambs next month. It is in January when our jobs begin."

"Yes, Pa," says Tarvin, "when I go to the sheep barn I'll look atter the sheep. I'll either git 'em in the barn 'r I'll git 'em in the windbreak. I'll take care of 'em, Pa. I'll see that they can git water too. I'll look atter 'em same as if you's along."

Anse keeps his cattle and mules in the barn by the house. He keeps the hogs in a pen near the house. He keeps the sheep at a barn on the ridge-top on the west side of the farm. "I can move the sheep to the feed," says Anse, "quicker than I can move the feed to the sheep. The barn at the house won't hold all the livestock. I haf to use the big barn on the ridge fer ter-backer barn in the falltime and a sheep barn in winter."

Anse has a little house built beside the big barn where he can sleep at night when the ewes are lambing. He can carry the lambs into this little house and warm them by the fire until life comes to them and they are strong enough to suckle their mammies. The little house has only one room. It has a table, a coffeepot, a few dishes, a small safe with food supplies, and a heating stove. He uses this house in the autumn for a tobacco-stripping room and in the winter he often stays here during the night when the ewes are dropping lambs. He keeps bottles filled with cow's milk, with nipples on the bottles for the lambs to suckle when the ewes won't own their lambs. He keeps a flashlight, an automatic rifle and an automatic twelve-gauge shotgun in this room beside the cot where he often lies down for a nap of sleep.

"I've got the place sorty fixed up fer lambin season," says Anse. "And when lambin season is over I move the guns, cookin utensils and the cot from the house and lock the doors. It's a handy sheep shanty."

It is a good place for Tarvin to warm himself after he has fed the sheep. Tarvin looks over the ewes in their stalls. He looks to see if there is a lamb. After he feeds the sheep grain and hay, he goes back to the sheep shanty and makes a boiler of coffee. He fries a skillet of flapjacks, drinks coffee and eats flapjacks with sorghum molasses. He waits awhile and then he goes back to the barn and looks about the sheep. He stays until midnight and then returns to the big house on the hill. "Aint so dangerous through December," says Anse. "A lamb might come. It is January when the lambs start comin—from January until February."

December with blustery winds drives the snow into drifts. Snowdrifts in the ravines are up to Tarvin's waist. The cornstalks stand with tops above the snow. The rabbits gnaw the frozen bark from the sassafras sprouts. "They'll gnaw the bark up high as the snow will be deep," says Anse. "We aint had the deep snow yit. The rabbits never lie. We'll have a real deep snow about January."

Water pours over the rocks and down the rugged cliffs. Icicles hang over the rocks. Crows fly over the barn in swarms, pilfering to find a loose grain of corn or a dead sheep. Snowbirds gather in the giant fodder-shock tops to roost on evenings when the stilly chill covers the land and the frozen snow crunches beneath one's feet. December goes as the yellow leaves of autumn went; December is passing into pages of past seasons as bright October with cool frosty nights passed into pages of the past; December goes into oblivion as rainy November with her sullen skies and her icy wind went into eternity.

5.

"TARVIN," says Anse, "I've jest been out to the sheep barn. You can't guess what I found?"

"Yes, I can," says Tarvin. "You found a lamb."

"Right."

"Is it alive?"

"Yes, he's a healthy fine lamb over there now sucklin his mammie."

"Sign of good luck fer the whole season to save the first lamb."

"That's a purty shore sign."

"I've been thinkin it over, Pa," says Tarvin. "Why can't I stay over at the barn at night and you stay durin the day until lambin season is over? It will save a lot of work and a lot of lambs."

"I've been thinkin about the same thing," says Anse. "We can't both sit up all the time. One hast to rest while the other works. I'll stay durin the day atter I git the work done up here."

"And I'll stay at night," says Tarvin.

On the night of January seventh, a snow falls on top of the snow that lies already on the ground. It falls deep enough to hide the top scars made on the sassafras sprouts by the rabbits. "I told you," says Anse, "that the heavy snow was yit to come. The rabbits don't lie. I've lived too many years and checked it too many times. The rabbits aint fooled me yit."

Anse puts on his mackinaw coat and gloves his hands. He starts over the deep snow for the sheep barn. Tarvin and Fronnie watch Anse walking up the snow-covered pasture hill with a long stick in his hand. Over Anse's head are sullen gray clouds that float across the sky like gaunt-bellied greyhounds. Don follows Anse up the hill. Soon the sullen clouds float away and the sky becomes clear. The cold wind blows and the snow falls from the limbs of the trees. Snow drifts into the fence corners, ditches and ravines.

Anse walks down the snow-covered hill breaking a new path in the snow. He walks across the pasture back of the house. He plows slowly along over the snowed-under path, pushing his big boots through the snowdrift down along the pasture creek.

Anse waves his mittened hands beside him in the icy wind as he moves along. His mackinaw coat is white with snow. His big umbrella hat is spotted with snow, and snow is clodded under his boot straps. Icicles are hanging from his long red beard. His ears are red as sassafras leaves in autumn and his breath comes in two white strips of vapor from his nostrils. Slowly he walks to the house, kicks the loose snow from his boots, opens the front door and walks into the front room.

"It's terrible weather," says Anse. "Durned if I've seen weather this bad since the winter of '17. Yowes drappin their lambs in a time like this! It's awful! Lost eight lambs today and saved four. 'Pears like every cold spell is when the yowes drap their lambs."

"That's too bad, Pa," says Tarvin. "You mean to tell me you've lost eight lambs! That's more than we've ever lost in a whole season before."

"Yes, I mean to tell you I've lost eight lambs today," says Anse, pulling a cigar from his coat pocket and lighting it with a stick of kindling from the red blaze of the wood fire. "I mean to tell you I have done well to save four lambs today. I've never seen sicha weather. The tracks I made to the lambin pens this mornin were snowed under by this afternoon. The wind riz about noon today, atter the blasts of snow, and turned so cold that I thought I'd freeze to death."

"You have wood in the sheep shanty, don't you, Pa?" Tarvin asks.

"Yes," says Anse. "and I had a fire. But the fire didn't do me much good. I had a time keepin fire in the shanty and seein about the yowes in the barn. I had to look atter every lambin pen. If I didn't see a lamb soon as it was born, it soon froze to death. I wropped 'em in blankets and I saved only four. I buried eight under the snow. The ground was too hard to dig a hole to bury 'em in. You'll hear the foxes fightin over 'em tonight."

"Yes," says Tarvin. "It will be lonely and cold there on that ridge tonight. I dread workin there tonight. I've done the feedin fer you, Pa. You can git in wood and git up water."

"That's good of you to do that, Son," says Anse, "fer I'm about all pooped out. Workin with sheep gits me. It's almost like keerin fer babies when a man keers fer young lambs!"

" 'Spect I'd better go out there and stay with Tarvin tonight," Fronnie says. Fronnie smokes her pipe and looks at Anse. Her hawk-gray eyes are dimmed by time. The wrinkles look like crow tracks around Fronnie's eyes.

"No, Mother," says Anse softly, "it aint no place fer a woman. I jest said a woman could keer fer lambs better than a man. Lambs air so much like young babies. I never had sicha day in all my life as I had today. Do you think I'd let you walk through a mile of snow to that sheep barn and sit up all night and work with lambin yowes? I wouldn't think about it. We can live the rest of our days if we do lose a few lambs."

"But we aint goin to lose no lambs," Tarvin breaks in. "We aint goin to lose no lambs. We can't let 'em stay out there and die jest because this is a cold spell. I'm goin out there and take keer of the lambs. I'll stay until broad daylight and take keer of the lambs. You come out to the barn about eight or nine in the mornin. Daylight comes late now since the winter days air so short."

"That's the way I like to hear you talk, Son," says Anse. "I plan to make this a big sheep farm some day. I expect to have five hundred sheep on this farm when I git more land and git it conquered and in grass. You'll be here to run it, Son. You'd better be gettin ust to sheep. It's a man's job and you'll see that it is. Now don't lose a yowe if you can hep it."

"All right, Pa," says Tarvin, putting on his heavy sheep-lined coat. Tarvin pulls a wool cap over his ears. He puts heavy mittens on his hands. He puffs blue clouds of smoke from his pipe.

"Be shore," says Anse, "that you make regular trips from

the sheep shanty to the barn. Take the lantern and look in every lambin pen."

Anse puffs smoke from his cigar. He stands in front of the blazing log fire and holds to the mantel above, sticking the toe of first one boot and then the other over the fire. His beard has lost its dampness now. The icicles have melted and the water has run and dripped from his beard to the hearth. It evaporated into tiny streams of mist. His beard is clean and fluffy red.

"I'm leavin, Pa," says Tarvin. "Be shore to relieve me at eight or nine in the mornin." Tarvin walks toward the door.

"I'll be uneasy about you, Son," says Anse, "out there on a night like this. I know what you haf to go through with. I've jest been through with it."

"Don't worry about me, Pa," says Tarvin. "I'll do the work. Don't you worry, I'll save the lambs. We'll never have a worse night than this all the winter long."

"You're right, Tarvin," says Fronnie; "weather can't git worse. I aint seen sicha weather in all my lifetime as we're havin right now."

"Good night," says Tarvin.

"Good night," says Fronnie.

"Good night," says Anse.

Anse and Fronnie watch Tarvin as he opens the door, and walks out into the flying fields of frost. A white mist flies in at the door with a puff of wind as Tarvin walks out. Anse and Fronnie look from the window as their son moves clumsily down the bank, across the cow pasture—and is soon out of sight in a frost storm that is falling on top of the heavy snow.

"That takes nerve," says Anse. "It takes nerve to go out on a night like this. I'll tell you, old Tarvin is changin a lot. He's gittin a man's ways about 'im and that is somethin fer a boy of his age." Anse puffs his cigar and walks back over to the fire—now that Tarvin has disappeared in the frosty mists. He catches hold of the mantel, sticking one boot-toe over the fire and then the other.

"Wouldn't surprise me nary bit if I aint frostbit my toes," says Anse. "They're achin an awful lot."

Tarvin walks over the old tracks the way Anse came from the barn. When he gets to the hollow, he wades snow above his boots. He can feel the frozen steely grains of snow working down under the tops of his boots. He can feel the blood rush to his face. He can feel the biting winds against his cheeks. Tarvin pushes through the drift, walks on undaunted through the snow, boot-top deep, measured on his long legs. He reaches the hill. The path is snowed under—there isn't a path. There is only a mass of snow and barren sassafras sprouts sticking above the snow. There are hickory sprouts and oak sprouts sprinkled among the sassafras sprouts. There are large trees, frosted white, creaking in the winter blasts. Tarvin zigzags up the hill, wading the deep frozen corn-meal snow. Tarvin holds to the frozen sprouts. Often a sprout breaks like an icicle, for it is frozen and brittle. He can feel the snap of the sprout when it breaks in his hand through his heavy sheep-lined mittens. He can feel the little jar up his arm to his elbow as if his hands and arms were dry pieces of boards catching sounds.

As Tarvin walks midway up the hill, sweat breaks from his forehead. He wipes the sweat from his face with his heavy mittens. He can see a thin one-quarter moon racing above the mists across the January sky. He can see vaguely through the frosty mists the big dipper, the little dipper and the milky way. Tarvin stands for a minute, blowing the huge puffs of warm air from his nostrils like two flour sacks filled with mists. He looks at the frozen sprouts about him, and the frozen trees in their midst—sleeping the sleep of death.

"Their resurrection," thinks Tarvin, "will be in the spring. They will leaf again and blossoms will come to their boughs. Green leaves will wave in the wind, feel the warm clean air and the sunshine. Their blossoms and their leaves will drink the sunshine and the rain. Even they will mate again as if they had never been through a winter and their lives will go on and on. All of my youth has been winter. When I met Subrinea it was spring. It has allus been spring fer me since I first saw her. Life means a lot to me now. It doesn't matter. I'll take keer of the sheep."

Tarvin starts again toward the hilltop. "I must hurry," he thinks. "Two hours have passed since Pa was here. There'll be more lambs when I git there and a lamb can't live over an hour in sicha weather." The howl of the winter winds sweeping around the high snow-covered slope is lonely to Tarvin's ears. They seem to sing too mournfully the song of death for the sleeping trees. Tarvin wonders if it is a dream that he is so heavily dressed in sheep-lined clothes going to a sheep barn on a night like this. He kicks a bunch of bull grass with the top of his boot as he steps up higher on the slope. Two birds fly into the icy air—chirruping plaintively, fluttering as they fly, their wings hitting the barren limbs of brush—out in this zero night.

"Sorry I run 'em out'n their warm bed," thinks Tarvin. "I'm afeared they'll not be able to find another roostin place and they'll freeze to death. If they only knowed to fly across the holler to my left where we have the big fodder shocks around the dead newground trees. But this is night. They won't know." Tarvin moves on—shifting his path from the brown tops of bull grass that stick above the snow.

"Now the woods," thinks Tarvin, "the thick path of woods, and the moon is dim. It cannot make enough light through the mists. I'd better light my lantern." Tarvin removes the mitten on his right hand and holds it with his left hand. He reaches his bare warm hand into his corduroy pants pocket. He gets a match. He squats down on the snow with his back to the wind. He lifts the lantern globe with the lantern catch. He holds it with his left hand. He strikes a match. He holds the tiny tender blaze to the lantern wick. The blaze catches the wick. He lowers the globe with the catch. He moves on into the dark woods where the snow has drifted under the pines. There is not a path here. He must depend upon his sense of direction. Now the moon is wholly obscured by mists. The big dipper, the little dipper and the milky way have disappeared from sight. Tarvin stumbles on into the dark pine woods.

"I can't be lost on this farm," thinks Tarvin, "but I ought to be at the sheep barn by now. I'm not gittin anywhere." Then he thinks: "In the strangeness of night a body is often lost when he is on a path that he knows like he does his ABC's. Night makes all the difference in the world. Jest somethin about night that makes a body feel different. He feels lost when he is on the right road. Night is so strange and a man gits tangled on mountain paths at night like a wild grapevine gits tangled in the tops of trees. There air three spurs that leave this ridge path that leads me to the sheep barn. Don't suppose I'm off on a spur that leads me from the barn. I've been bearin to my right too much. I'll cut across this little holler and it'll take me to the barn."

Tarvin starts down the hill. He slips, slides, waves the lantern while he is in motion. He catches hold of trees as he moves down the hill slope—he holds the lantern to his shoulder and over his head when he can stand for a minute. He throws the lantern light as far as he can. He looks for cliffs below him—places where there are jump-offs into snow-covered space. He catches hold of briars and vines. He is unmindful now about the tops of dead bull grass. He doesn't care how many wild birds he shoos into the night storm. He wanders to the foot of the hill slope in the hollow.

"Now it must be on this hilltop where the barn is," thinks Tarvin. "I know my sense of direction won't bear me too fur to the right side of the barn." Tarvin looks toward the hilltop. He starts to ascend. He cannot see the bulk of a barn against the sullen gray-coated winter sky. He moves along, the sweat pouring from his brow. He pulls by sassafras sprouts toward the hilltop. He pulls until he feels as if his muscles will pull in two like a worn well-rope. He holds to trees—rests behind trees where he can plant his boot securely without sliding back down the hill. He walks slowly, for he doesn't take a chance now. His boots are rapidly filling with snow. He finally makes his way to the top of the hill.

"Not any barn here," he says; "nothin but stumps kivered with snow. And here are deadened trees. It must be a cornfield. The snow is too deep fer me to tell. If the snow was jest off fer an hour, I could find my way." He waves his lantern over his head. He stands where the wind hits him fairer than it did in the pine woods. He waves his lantern now and wonders.

"I'll bear back to my left," Tarvin thinks. "I've come too fur to my right. The lambs will die. I must hurry. I must reach the barn. I must git there. I haf to do it. I'll do it if it takes all night. I'll do it 'r I'll freeze to death tryin. I'm lost. I can't find the barn and I can't git back home. I can't track myself back, fer the frost has kivered my tracks."

"Air you lost?" shouts a voice from the hilltop back at Tarvin's right. It is a woman's voice. "Come this way to the sheep barn! Come this way!"

"A voice," thinks Tarvin, "on a night like this! It is sweeter than gittin a good cold drink of water atter a body gits home from plowin in the newground. A voice like this on a winter night! It sounded like Subrinea's voice. It can't be her. What would she be doin at the sheep barn on a night like this? She didn't know that I was comin to the barn—"

These thoughts flash through Tarvin's brain like lightning flashes over a dark field of newground corn when the earth is hot and dry and wanting water to drink and there isn't any water.

"Yes, I'm lost," Tarvin shouts, above the sound of the January wind. "Air you at Bushmans' barn?"

"Yes," says the woman's voice.

"That is Subrinea's voice. Subrinea is here. I must git to her!"

Tarvin cannot see a light. He cannot see a barn. He can only see the mists before him. He can feel the heavy drag of snow at his feet. He can feel his heavy wool boot socks getting soggy wet with melted snow that has gone down his boots when he was slipping and sliding on the bluffs and wading through the drifts. Tarvin moves along among the snow-covered stumps. He sees now a dim light as he moves toward the beckoning voice.

"There's the dim bulk of a barn right out there," Tarvin says. "I've been in our cornfield and didn't know it. I come out the left spur back yander on the ridge instead of the right. If I'd gone over the hill I would a-been among the Artner woods and cliffs—in a wild country and God knows how I'd 've ever got out alive. Maybe I'd a-been a mess fer the hungry crows, the buzzards and the foxes. Thank God, I'm here at the barn at last."

"This way, Tarvin," says Subrinea, "right out here and warm yourself! I've got a good fire!"

"My God, Honey, what air you doin here?" Tarvin asks.

"Don't ast me that. Warm yourself and I'll tell you."

Subrinea is standing between the sheep shanty and the barn. Tarvin walks past the barn toward the sheep shanty. The snow has been trampled by the feet of many sheep. It is packed solidly against the earth. Tarvin walks faster now over the packed snow. He walks up to the bulk of a woman dressed in a heavy coat with a white glare of frost covering it.

"How on earth—"

"Don't ast me now, Tarvin," says Subrinea. "Git into the sheep shanty. See what I've got!"

Subrinea and Tarvin walk side by side swinging their lanterns. Their white streams of breath go out on the night air. Their heavy bulks of clothes wrapping their tall bodies are frost-covered. They walk through the yard gate to the sheep shanty.

Subrinea opens the door. Tarvin knocks the snow clods from his boots on the doorstep. He brushes his coat with his mittens. He brushes his pants legs and enters the sheep-shanty door. Tarvin squints his eyes as he enters, for there is a bright lamp-light.

"Pull off your boots, Honey, and warm your feet," says Subrinea, "fer I know your feet air cold!"

"Jest wet."

"Well, they'll soon be cold."

"Jest so they don't frostbite."

Subrinea opens the stove door and punches the fire with a poker. She punches the living coals down to a mass of red ember. She picks up dry sticks of wood from the corner of the big pile of sawed wood in the sheep shanty. She carries an arm-load of sticks and feeds them to the gaping mouth of the stove. Tarvin unstraps his boots and unlaces the buckskin strings. He pulls the boots from his feet. He holds them up and pours the dirty melted-snow water from his boots. It makes dark puddles on the floor. His heavy socks are wet as water can make them.

"Hold your feet before the fire, Honey!"

"All right."

Tarvin holds one foot before the red-hot stove for a minute; then he changes and holds the other foot. He keeps alternating his feet before the fire and the steam rises from his wet socks. Tarvin's cheeks are flushed rose-petal red. It looks as if the blood will burst from his cheeks any minute.

"You come in one gittin lost."

"Yes, I did."

"And you would a-froze to death."

" 'Spect I would on a night like this."

"I thought somethin would happen tonight."

"How did you git here?"

"Your Pappie talked to my Pa."

"Did you hear 'em talkin?"

"No, Pa was cuttin wood. Your Pappie passed. He told Pa

that this would be a bad night. Said you'd be at the barn alone. He said it was a job to handle lambs. Said they's jest like babies. So I come tonight. I thought I'd better come."

Subrinea stands with cat-green eyes filled with tears looking at Tarvin. Her cheeks are red as the skin on a Roman Beauty apple in autumn. Tarvin sits on a stool chair drying his socks. He does not look at Subrinea. He looks at the heating stove with its round belly reddening. His socks get drier and drier.

"How did you git away from home, Subrinea?"

"I slipped out the winder."

"Your Pa will find out."

"I walked up the road the way he drug wood to the house."

"That will be frosted under with flyin frost by mornin."

"I'll go home before the frost stops flyin and my tracks will be kivered over again."

"What's that over there movin under the blankets?"

"Walk over and see."

Tarvin gets up from his stool chair and walks over to the cot in his sock feet. He lifts the blankets from the bed. He sees four lambs stretched out, moving their legs and showing life.

"Can you beat that!"

"But they would a-died. Soon as Pa went to bed I slipped out. Pa goes to bed with the chickens. If I hadn't come up here when I did the lambs would a-been dead."

"What air the tags doin around their necks?"

"Out of three hundred yowes, how could I know their mammies?"

"Have you got them tagged too?"

"No, but I got their pens marked."

"You know how to do things. I believe you can do anything."

"Your Pappie said they's like babies."

"They air jest like 'em."

"Aint you been where a baby was born?"

"Gee Christ, no, I aint been where no baby was born. What would I be doin there?"

"See that pan of water over there?"

"Yes."

"I put the lambs in milk-warm water. I washed 'em. I worked their legs and necks. I brought life back to 'em. Sometimes I had to shake the breath into one. I saved 'em all, though."

"And you saved me."

"Yes."

Tarvin begins to laugh as he looks at the lambs in bed. He spreads the blanket back over them as they begin to kick with their long legs.

"What air you laughin about?"

"I never saw a lamb in bed before. We allus warmed one and took 'im back to his mother."

"You lost a lot of lambs, too."

"Yes, eight died today."

"I could a-saved 'em."

"You could!"

"Yes."

"Yip-yip-yip-yip—"

"Grrrrrrr—grrrrrrr—"

"Listen, Subrinea! Foxes atter the lambs Pa buried in the snow."

Tarvin grabs the gun from the corner. He slips across the floor in his sock-feet. He opens the door. Subrinea holds the door to keep the blasts of wind from blowing it wide open. She leaves just enough space for Tarvin to shoot from. Tarvin levels the gun toward the growling foxes. He pulls the trigger on his automatic. There is a sluice of fire from the automatic. Fire flashes into the mists. The growling stops. The foxes flee.

"Don't know whether I kilt one 'r not," says Tarvin. "I know they've scattered. One might be kickin on the snow."

Tarvin walks back across the sheep-shanty floor. He puts the gun back in the corner. Subrinea closes the door.

"When air you goin to feed these lambs, Subrinea?" Tarvin asks.

"Atter while I aim to let their mammies feed 'em."

"Good!"

"It's time now fer more lambs in the barn. Git your boots on and let's go look."

"All right."

Tarvin walks back over to the stove. He picks up his boots where he has their tops turned toward the heat from the stove so they will dry. He slips his dried socks into the boots, fastens the straps, sits down on his chair, buckles the straps, and laces the buckskin strings through the eyes and around the hooks.

"Where did you git the water in this pan?"

"I melted snow in the teakettle. That's how I got it."

"I never thought about that."

"Your Pappie said wimmen would know more about lambs than men."

"Yep, he told Ma that. Ma wanted to come out here whether 'r not. Pa wouldn't let 'er. I'm glad she didn't come."

"I am too."

"We jest need one lantern, Honey."

Tarvin and Subrinea walk out to the big barn. They walk side by side in the blustery wind. The skies are coated by frost until they cannot see the moon and stars. They hear the ewes bleating in the barn. They walk through the mist to the barn door. They open the door and walk down the rows of lambing pens. They look around at the ewes. The ewes look up at them with soft innocent eyes.

"Here's one," says Subrinea. "Look, Tarvin! Aint he a purty little thing!"

"Dead, aint he?" Tarvin asks.

"Nope, he's not dead," says Subrinea, bending over the

lambing pen and lifting the lifeless lamb in her arms. "It aint dead. I feel its heart beatin. It's only cold—the poor little baby is—"

Subrinea takes a pencil from her pocket. She marks a figure 5 on a post in the lambing pen that is near the entry. "Hold this lamb," she says. Tarvin takes the lamb in one arm, holds the lantern with his other hand. Subrinea takes a twine string from her pocket and a piece of paper. She writes "5" on the tag of paper and ties it around the lamb's neck. They walk down the rows of lambing pens on the right side of the entry where they first entered the barn. They do not find another lamb. "Can't tell," says Subrinea; "might be ten lambs born on this side of the barn before mornin."

Tarvin carries the lamb as they walk over the straw-covered barn floor to the other side of the barn. They walk down one row of lambing pens and up another. "Look," says Subrinea, "look, Tarvin! Here's two, look!"

"Yep," says Tarvin. "One is sucklin his mammie. We'll leave 'im. Other little fellar is all pooped out."

Subrinea bends her tall thin body over the lambing pen. She picks up the lamb in her arms and holds it as if it were a young baby.

"Can you hold it, Tarvin," Subrinea asks, "while I mark the post on this pen?"

"Yes, I can hold two in my arms."

Subrinea marks "7" on the post.

"Why did you mark '7'?"

"Because '5' is in your arms and '6' is there with his mammie."

Subrinea takes a tag and puts it around his neck. She takes the lamb from Tarvin's arms. She carries one lamb. Tarvin carries the other lamb and the lantern. They walk toward the sheep shanty. Subrinea caresses the lamb, calling it "a little doll—a poor little baby about to die in the cold—" while the shrill wind sweeping over the ridge top blows her golden hair about her shoulders and down over the collar of a heavy well-worn frizzled coat.

Tarvin lights their way with the lantern through the frosty mists to the shanty. He sets the lantern down. He opens the door. Subrinea dashes into the shanty in a hurry so as to avoid a puff of winter wind that will chill the warm room. She lays the lamb down on the floor. Tarvin hurries into the shanty. He puts his lantern on the floor and lays his lamb down beside the lamb Subrinea just laid down.

"Now let's warm 'em," says Subrinea. She gets the pan of warm water from the stove. She puts her hand into the water to see if it is too warm. "The water is a little warm but it's about right fer these lambs," Subrinea says. "They air very cold. We must hurry." She puts her lamb into the pan of water. She keeps its nose above the water and rubs its legs and back with warm snow-water. The legs begin to move. The lamb begins to show life. "See, it aint dead," says Subrinea. She is greatly pleased at what the warm water will do. "It aint goin to die if I have anything to do with it. I've been where babies were born and I know what to do. I've had to shake breath into a few of these lambs."

Subrinea feels sure of herself with lambs because she has helped with the births of babies among the women of her people. She has learned from her experiences going with her mother. Her mother taught her all she knew and all that was handed down from her grandmother. When it comes to working with the lambs, it is easy for Subrinea. She loves to work with them.

"You can do most anything," Tarvin says. "You'd be a good wife fer a farmer."

"Yes, if I loved 'im."

"A woman must have a strong backbone, nerves solid as a rock cliff, and muscles strong as wild grapevines to go through with all my mother has gone through," Tarvin says, as he watches Subrinea bathe the lambs in the pan of hot water. "There aint many wimmen that could do it. I jest look at Ma goin around in shoes without stockins on her legs. I see the big clumps of blood showin under the skin in the broken veins. I see the strain of toil on her face. I jest wonder if life is worth livin when a woman hast to work like Ma has had to work. Ma is still workin and Pa is still workin. They have had to pay the price to git a little ahead."

The little lamb baa-baas in the pan. He kicks the warm water from the pan trying to get on his feet. "Ah, comin to life, aint you, Honey—ah, comin to life!" She lifts the lamb from the pan of water. "Take 'im, Tarvin," she says, "and put 'im under the blanket until he dries. Take 'im away while I bring life back to this 'n."

Tarvin takes the lamb while Subrinea works with the one in the pan, saturating him with warm water, rubbing his feet, legs, and his body. Subrinea's long shapely fingers work over the lamb's body. Tarvin turns back the heavy blanket and puts this lamb with his tag around his neck beside the other lambs. "That's funny, Subrinea, this puttin lambs to bed," Tarvin laughs. He pulls his pipe from his pocket and loads it with bright burley leaf. He walks over to the stove, takes a stick of kindling and lights his pipe from the blaze in the stove.

"I'm beginnin, Honey, to like to work with sheep fer the first time in my life," Tarvin laughs. "I can't hep it about the weather. Sunshine is bound to come back again. The grass will grow. The trees will leaf. The birds will sing. We'll see lambs on the pasture then and we'll think about this night."

"Yes, Tarvin," says Subrinea. "He's kickin and baain! Come and git 'im. Put 'im under the blanket." Subrinea stands up with the lamb in her hands. The water drips from his body to the floor. Subrinea shakes the water from his body and hands the lamb to Tarvin. Tarvin carries him over and puts him across the cot.

"I'm beginnin," Tarvin continues, "to love you more and more. It seems that you air gittin as close to me as a pair of birds I skeered from the bull grass on yan side of the hill tonight. They flew into the winter storm together. I know they will freeze to death in this storm. They flew away in the mists chirrupin to one another. I feel that way toward you, Subrinea. The kinfolks of yourn that offered you that money, I could kill 'em free as I ever et a bite of grub. When I think about that, my blood biles."

"But nothin happened," says Subrinea. "You can forgit that. Nothin won't happen with them. I've found you, Tarvin. I love to work with you. I love to hep you saw wood. I love to work with lambs. I like to hep you do anything on a farm. It is a lot of fun fer me. I git away from home. I slip away. I've got eyes like a possum. I know the paths. You can't lose me, Tarvin, in any of these woods. I've hunted over all of 'em with a rifle. Like a rock, Tarvin, I will stand by you. I know your people don't like squatters. I've heerd 'em talk. Not anybody around here likes squatters. Squatters don't like themselves. They hate to be squatters. They would rather be somebody else. But I can't forsake my people and run away. I've often prayed that my name wasn't Tussie. That don't do no good, fer my name *is* Tussie. Tarvin, I don't keer what happens so I'm with you."

"Why don't you keer, Subrinea?" Tarvin asks. "You ought to keer."

"If I'd have a baby by you it would be a Bushman," says Subrinea, "and not a Tussie. I'd be havin my babies by somebody out'n the family. That aint happened among the Tussie wimmen. I know they have had their babies by Tussie men 'r Beaver men. We air all a-kin! That is what's the matter with us! We have married one another. Look what has happened. We aint nothin! That's the way people look on us. They look right! We aint nothin and if I ever have a baby it won't be a Tussie! I hope it's a Bushman!"

"I aint thought about that," says Tarvin, "but I'm thinkin now."

"Well, I have," says Subrinea. "I've thought a lot about it when I look at my people."

Tarvin lifts one of the dry lambs from the bed. The lamb kicks Tarvin with his long strong legs. He looks at Tarvin with his big innocent eyes. If it had not been for Subrinea he would have been dead. His eyes would have been cold and glaring now and his little body would have been carried out and buried under the snow for the foxes, or it would have lain there until the snow melted and the crows would have stripped his carcass clean. "It's a purty lamb," Tarvin says. He fingers over its dry fluffy body. "You couldn't freeze this lamb to death now."

"Let's take them to their mothers," says Subrinea. "You can carry two lambs and a lantern and I can carry two lambs. Let's take them to their mothers before the milk cakes in their sacks."

"Yes, we'd better."

They carry the lambs to the barn, they walk down the entries to the lambing pens with numbers marked on the posts corresponding to the numbers on the tags around the lambs' necks. They put each lamb with its right mother. The ewe knows her lamb by the smell.

"That's funny," Tarvin says, "that in a pasture where there air three hundred yowes and over three hundred lambs, each lamb can find his mother. He smells of a lot of the yowes sometimes before he gits the right one, but he allus gits the right one."

"Look at that mother," says Subrinea, "she won't let number four suckle."

"Yes, she will," says Tarvin. "I'll hold her and you milk a little milk into the lamb's mouth."

Subrinea and Tarvin climb over the rails on the lambing pen. Tarvin catches the ewe by the flanks and holds her. Subrinea milks a few drops from the ewe. She puts the lamb in the right place and in position. She milks tiny streams into his mouth. The lamb starts to suckle his mother. Tarvin holds the ewe and makes her own the lamb. "About one yowe out'n every forty," he says, "won't own her lamb. It's a lot of trouble when a yowe won't own her twins."

Tarvin and Subrinea walk up and down the rows of lambing pens in the darkness of the night amid the sour scent of sheep smell. They carry lambs to the shanty when they chill. They put them in a pan of heated snow-water and warm their bodies back to life. They put them under the warm blanket and dry them. They carry them back to their mothers. They work side by side in the cold blustery night, a night that freezes birds, chickens, pheasants and rabbits to death. Tarvin and Subrinea, with heavy garments clothing their young strong bodies, do not mind the cold. They are happy at their work and happy to work with each other. They are working with living things—something they can see, feel, love, and have sympathy for.

"Honey, I'm all pooped out," says Tarvin. "It would do me a lot o' good jest to stretch out on the bed."

"Wait a minute," says Subrinea. "I don't want you to mash one of our baby lambs."

Subrinea places the lambs on one side of the bed while Tarvin unlaces his boots. She puts the lambs, in a row crosswise at the foot of the bed.

"Now, you big long thing," Subrinea laughs, "when you git in bed don't put the weight of your big feet on the lambs. You jest put your feet down against their wool. They'll keep your feet warm."

"Thank you, Honey," says Tarvin. "You know how to fix me a place to rest."

Tarvin removes his heavy coat, his sweater and his heavy wool shirt and lays them across the stool chair in front of the stove. "It's like skinnin a possum," says Tarvin, "to pull off all this wool." Tarvin pulls off his pants in the dim yellowish glow of lantern light. Subrinea turns down the quilts on the bed. Tarvin climbs in the bed and Subrinea pulls the quilts over him. She starts to tuck the quilts down close to his long body.

"What air you doin, Honey?" Tarvin asks.

"I don't want you to git cold," says Subrinea.

Subrinea stands beside the bed and looks down at Tarvin's brown face half buried in the white fluffy pillow. Tarvin looks up at her face with wide blue eyes. They look silently at each other. Subrinea sits on the side of the bed and removes her shoes. She removes her coat and sweater and lays them with Tarvin's clothes on the stool chair. She lifts the quilts and slides her long slender body under the quilts beside Tarvin. Not a word is spoken. Silence fills the room. Piece by piece Subrinea flings the rest of her clothing from under the quilts onto the floor. Tarvin removes the rest of his clothes and throws them from under the quilts on the other side of the bed.

Tarvin puts his strong brown arms around her shoulders

and pulls Subrinea against him. Subrinea reluctantly lies against him—her long beautiful warm body completely relaxes. Her lips meet his lips and her ripe cornsilk-colored hair falls across his face. "Subrinea, do you know what we air doin?" Tarvin asks. "Air you afeard?"

"I do know what we air doin, Tarvin," says Subrinea, "and I aint afeard."

"I've allus wanted to love you like this, Subrinea," Tarvin says.

"I've kept myself fer you, Tarvin," Subrinea whispers. "Be easy with me, Tarvin. You won't hurt me?"

"No, Honey."

They lie limb to limb, lip to lip, and breath to breath; the twitch of each body muscle is dear to one another. Sweat breaks from Tarvin's face and runs in little streams onto her face and into her eyes. It runs across her face to the pillow and dampens her cornsilk hair. The lambs with a new breath of life revived in their bodies wriggle at the foot of the bed. Subrinea and Tarvin lie embraced in their first fulfillment of joy, beauty and quickened powers of their strong youthful bodies. Seconds are minutes and minutes are hours while this God-given beauty and ecstasy of youthful love is first consummated.

"I'll make you a biler of coffee," says Subrinea, "before I go home. You need coffee to keep you awake until your Pappie comes. I'll haf to slip home and crawl through my winder to bed."

"What if Boliver finds you've been here with me all night?" Tarvin asks.

"I don't keer," says Subrinea, "a big lot if he does find it out. He won't like it—but what can he say atter his own people and my own people have acted like they have? He can't say anything. I can take keer of myself—I'll tell 'im that, too. He don't take keer of me. He knows it."

Subrinea fills the coffeepot with black grains of coffee and with clean snow-water. She sets it on the stove. "And I'd better make a pan of flapjacks fer you to eat with butter and sorghum molasses while you take these lambs back to their mothers and look over the lambin pens again. You can't tell when a lamb is comin. Think of twenty-five lambs tonight and all of 'em livin!"

"No one could beat that record," says Tarvin. "Pa was right when he said lambs air like babies and a woman is needed around a sheep barn on a night like this. Honey, atter you leave me I'll do my best to save every lamb. I'll do my best to keep our record."

Subrinea washes her hands in the melted snow-water. She pours flour from the sack into a crock, mixes it with milk and stirs the batter thoroughly with her spoon. She places the big skillet on the stove, takes a yellow hunk of butter from the crock—watches the butter melt and run over the skillet. Subrinea pours her batter into the skillet. She sees it cover the bottom of the skillet. It runs over the bottom of the skillet with a sizzle. She lets it remain and cook while she pours sorghum molasses from the jug for Tarvin's breakfast. A golden strip of molasses streams from the can to Tarvin's plate. She places the butter dish beside his plate. Subrinea turns the flapjacks over on the other side to let them brown. They sizzle for a minute. She lifts four flapjacks onto Tarvin's plate. She pours him a cup of hot black coffee. "You have your breakfast now," she says. "I must be goin."

Tarvin sees on the small table the breakfast that Subrinea has cooked for him. He has never seen flapjacks that smelled so good. Maybe it is because he is hungry. "You must eat with me," says Tarvin. "You cannot leave me now."

Tarvin sits down at the table and begins to eat. He does not hear an answer. "Have you gone?" thinks Tarvin, as he turns to look. Subrinea is not there. Tarvin jumps up from the table. He runs to the door. He looks at a tall dark figure moving through the morning mists. "Subrinea, Subrinea," he cries to her, but she goes like a ghost through the night over the drifts of snow gritting beneath her boots. She goes over the hill and down Cat's Fork toward her slab-built shanty, a tiny dark speck upon a land of desolation. It is a place where the winter snow-birds chirrup plaintively day-long in the waves of dark rag-weeds, a place where the loud angry winds sweep up the Cat's Fork valley like wind roaring up a chimney flue.

Tarvin looks from the open door of the sheep shanty until the room gets cold. He has the door wide open.

"Subrinea comes unbeknowins and she leaves unbeknowins," thinks Tarvin as he closes the shanty door and walks over to his once-steaming hot breakfast. "She comes like a tall ghost and she leaves like a tall ghost. I can see how she can slip away from a dark room when they air asleep at home. She can slip away from a lighted room here while I am watchin her. I never heerd the door close behind her."

Tarvin pours sorghum molasses over the flapjacks on his plate. He cuts frozen clumps of yellow butter and mixes it with the sorghum molasses. Tarvin eats the flapjacks covered with sorghum molasses mixed with butter and he drinks the hot black coffee. "That's good coffee and it revives me in these gray winter mornin hours. It keeps me from wantin to go to sleep. This is good grub. Subrinea knows jest what I like to eat."

Tarvin eats his breakfast by lantern light. As soon as he has eaten he gets up, fills his pipe with bright burley crumbs of tobacco, lights his pipe with a stick of kindling, takes a lamb from the cot in one arm, gets his lantern and moves toward the barn.

Tarvin hears a big hoot owl whooing in the tall frozen timber near the barn. He hears another owl answer this one. He hears them hooting and laughing to each other as he walks up and down the entries in the sheep barn inspecting three hundred lambing pens. He does not hear the roar of the frost-laden wind as he has heard it the night long. "Mornin must not be long away," thinks Tarvin. "When the winds lay and the hoot owls start hollerin, it's not long until daylight."

When the winds subside and the loneliness of the mocking hoot owls among the tall barren silent oaks begins, there is a loneliness that fills Tarvin's heart. He has suddenly found himself alone. He has found himself without sturdy Subrinea by his side. Now he must depend upon himself to lubricate the bodies of the lambs in warm water. He must gather more snow in the pan and melt the snow and heat the snow-water. It is work for him. He never knew how Subrinea could do all these little things. Subrinea knows how to do everything. He misses her when she goes away. His heart becomes lonely as the January wind sweeping over the white oaks' clinging brown leaves on a desolate wind-swept point. The desolation looms before his eyes in satiny-colored ghosts. "I will save all the lambs I find in the pens," thinks Tarvin. "I'll do jest what I told Subrinea I'd do."

As the gray daylight creeps over the big rough slats of a high ridge-top covered with snow and the clean clear air feels too dense to breathe, Tarvin walks out to the barn and forks down hay to the mangers for three hundred sheep. He takes sacks of cracked corn and pours it in their feed boxes. The sheep stand in their pens and eat the cracked corn and nibble the hay. Tiny streaks of white air come from their nostrils and the ewes seem to talk to their little lambs in the pen as the lambs suckle their mothers.

"It seems like a dream that Subrinea come last night," thinks Tarvin. "I jest can't believe she hepped saved my life last night. I can't believe she saved the lambs until I got here. She hepped me save 'em atter I come. She even got my breakfast. She made me a biler of snow-water coffee that makes me feel like a new man. What will Pa think when he comes?" Tarvin hears the owls still hooting in the silent dark trees. He can hear the morning wind that has just risen, sighing among the treetops around the barn.

Tarvin finds another lamb lying lifeless in a pen. He picks it up, carries it under his arm to the shanty. He heats water, lubricates the lamb while the ewes eat in their pens and the lambs suckle. He brings life to the lamb and he smiles. "I'm might' nigh as good as Subrinea bringin life back to lambs," he thinks, as he carries the lamb over to the cot to put it under the blanket. He looks at its little black nose and its spotted feet as he puts it to bed under the blankets. "That cot will shore smell of sheep," he laughs. Tarvin puts wood in the stove from the dry wood-stack in the shanty. He waits for the sheep to eat so he can turn them from the lambing pens to get water from the spring below the barn. As he sits before the fire and listens to the owls, he hears the caw-cawing of crows. There must be thousands by the racket they make out in the shanty yard. He walks to the window and looks at the sky darkened with swarms of crows. They fly above a rounded heap of snow. "That's where Pa buried the lambs yesterday," thinks Tarvin. "How do they know the lambs air there under the snow? Lambs jest died, and the crows here the next day to git 'em."

The crows alight in the tall pine trees near the shanty. They alight in the tops of the oak trees around the barn. They fly down on the heap of snow. They do not dig into the snow. It is too deep for them to get to the dead lambs. They fly back up into the tops of the pines and the oaks. The frozen tops of the oaks and the pines are sagging with the weight of the crows. There are thousands of them cawing. Tarvin has never heard them caw this way before. As Tarvin walks to the barn to open the lambing pens, the crows do not fly away. They sit up in the trees and caw-caw. "They air hungry," thinks Tarvin. "The cornshocks and all the loose corn grains scattered over the fields air snowed under. There air thousands of them to git their breakfast and there's nothin to git."

Tarvin opens the lambing pens and the ewes with their lambs trail down the path to the spring, where the big sluices of warm water spout from under a rock on the hill slope. The gray sheep trail over the white path of crusted snow. Before Tarvin opens the last lambing pen he hears the crows cawing louder than ever. He hears the sheep bleating and the lambs baaing to their mothers. He runs to the barn door and looks. The crows are flying down in great numbers attacking the sheep and trying to pluck their eyes out. He hollers at the crows but they do not mind. He runs to the shanty and gets his automatic, loaded and ready to use. He runs back to the barn, down the path a few steps from the barn. He opens fire into the mass of dark wings. Dozens of crows drop to the earth. He reloads and fires into them again. The ground is black with crows. They start to rise into the air in a black mass of wings, hiding the winter-gray sky from his vision. He reloads his automatic and pumps six more loads of number-three shot into their hungry bony carcasses. They fall like ripe apples shaken from a tree. The snow is black with crows and there are blotches of blood over the snow. "I'll let 'em eat their own kind," says Tarvin, reloading and firing again. There are more than two hundred crows dead and dying over the snow-covered earth. "In all the days of my life I've never seen that before. Crows fly down and try to pluck the eyes out'n the lambs and the yowes." The crows rise in a black cloud of fanning wings, screaming as they fly—over the ridge-top and across the valley below. Wounded crows are flapping and bleeding and cawing on the snow.

Tarvin puts his automatic down as the scared sheep start for the barn. They run headlong toward the barn entry, baaing as they go, each lamb following his mother. Tarvin walks out, picks up the dead crows and stacks them in heaps. He wrings the necks of the wounded crows and throws them on the stack. There is a stack of crows piled near the shanty as high as a small doodle of hay. "Now when the crows come back, they can see this stack of their own dead. They'll never make another attack on my sheep. When it aint dogs, it's foxes. When it aint foxes, it's crows. Everything tries to eat the sheep. The copperheads even try to kill 'em."

Where Tarvin puts his automatic down on the snow, the hot barrel melts the snow. Tarvin picks up his automatic and takes it into the shanty, rubs a meat rind over the barrel, and a rag with a wire fastened to it, through the barrel. "Must keep my gun in condition." After Tarvin cleans the gun barrel, he goes to the barn and fastens the lambing pens. "If Subrinea could only have been here to see this fight," thinks Tarvin, "she would have seen somethin. She would have seen crows fallin from the air like big black drops of heavy rain."

6.

ANSE WALKS over the crisp snow. His big boots crunch-crunch the snow as he walks over the path. He breathes deep into his lungs the clear clean January air. He smokes his cigar and looks over the white earth and the big black silent trees. He hears the wind rustle the white-oak leaves that cling to the boughs of the tough-butted white oaks. He finds a dead bird in his path. He picks it up in his big mittened hand. "Froze to death 'r starved to death," he says, blowing smoke from his cigar. "Stiff as a board." He finds a rabbit sitting in a clump of briars. Anse slips toward it. Its eyes look at him. The big scared eyes stare at the red-bearded man. Anse jumps and flings his body on the rabbit. "I'll have me a rabbit to eat," he says, his thick body sprawling in the snow. "Ah—a rabbit froze stiff as a board. Don't know how long it could've been dead." Anse gets up. He brushes the snow from his mackinaw coat, his mittens and his corduroy pants. He leaves the rabbit on the snow. "Suppose Tarvin is all right," thinks Anse. "Don't guess he froze to death. Guess he lost a lot of lambs last night in that storm." Anse walks toward the sheep barn worrying about the lambs that Tarvin has lost during the night.

Anse can see the ground spattered red with blood before he gets to the barn. "How can that be?" thinks Anse. "Has somethin been in the sheep? Has dogs come and got the sheep from the barn? Has foxes carried out the little lambs and et them on the snow? I'll soon find out." Anse sees a black doodle of something piled high. It is a dark heap on the snow. He walks up to the stack of crows. "Gentlemen," he says, "the biggest doodle of crows I ever saw in one doodle."

"Good mornin," says Tarvin. Tarvin walks from the shanty when he sees Anse looking at the pile of crows. "What do you think of that many crows in a pile!"

"Who kilt 'em?" Anse asks.

"I did," says Tarvin. "They come down this mornin when I started to water the sheep. They flew down from the trees and tried to pluck their eyeballs out. I don't think they blinded nary lamb ner yowe but they would have if I hadn't jest happened to have that automatic out here."

"Gee Christ," says Anse. He puffs his cigar and looks at the pile of crows.

"There's between two and three hundred in that stack,"

says Tarvin. "I put twenty-four loads of number-three shot into that bunch of crows. 'Peared like two dozen crows fell at a shot."

"How did you git along with the lambs, Son?" Anse asks.

"Yowes drapped thirty-one lambs," says Tarvin, "and I've saved thirty-one!"

"I—I—" Tarvin repeats, stammering and looking at the pile of crows.

"Saved 'em all!" says Anse.

"Yes," says Tarvin," "saved 'em all!"

"Seein is believin with me," says Anse. "I didn't think you'd live through a night like last night. Gentlemen, we don't usually have a night in this country like last night. It's the worst night I've ever seen in this country."

"If you don't believe me," says Tarvin, "go out there in the barn and look in the lambin pens."

"How did you do it?"

"Took the lambs when they didn't have no life in 'em and put 'em in hot water. Worked with 'em until they come to. Then I put 'em under the blankets and dried 'em."

"Did you think of that?"

"Well, yes, I did."

"How did you ever think to do that? I never heerd of it."

"I heerd a woman say if you'd do that you'd save the lambs."

"I'll do that from this on."

"It will pay you. It will save the lambs."

Tarvin and Anse walk into the shanty together.

"I see you've had your breakfast."

"Yes, I got hungry about three o'clock this mornin. Worked hard last night. I got me some breakfast."

"You've done well to kill the crows, cook your breakfast and save the lambs. I couldn't do all that."

"You aint young as you ust to be, Pa."

"I aint begun to show my age, have I?"

"Nope, but a man at seventy can't do what he did at eighteen."

"But I'm still as good a man as you'll find in these parts. I can work the tails off'n all the young men I know."

Anse smokes his cigar and looks at the pan of water on the floor.

"Is that the pan you het water in to soak the lambs?"

"Yes, that's the pan I used."

"Looks like you've used the old shanty last night."

"Shore did, but I saved the lambs."

"I'll take over now and you can go home and git some rest."

"All right, Pa, I need it."

7.

THE JANUARY snow lies on the ground. The yellowish winter sun comes into the clear sky on the short winter days. It is too weak to melt the snow. Anse goes to the sheep barn during the day; Tarvin goes at night. The first days of January the ewes drop more lambs. As January passes, fewer yewes drop lambs. There are more lambs to care for in the barn. Many ewes will not give suck to their lambs. These lambs must be put on bottles. They must have milk from a certain cow and the milk must be warmed before it is put into the bottle. As the days pass, work accumulates around the barn. There is more work than there has ever been before. Tarvin does not lose a single lamb at lambing time, nor one that he feeds from the bottle.

"It's a fine thing," Anse tells Fronnie, "jest to see how well that boy gits along with the sheep. Honest, he knows more about 'em than I do. He has better luck than I've ever had. If Tarvin keeps on he's goin to make a real shepherd among the sheep. I'll have plenty of land fer 'im, too, if everything turns out the way I hope it does." When Anse speaks of the future he always turns his face toward the tract of land that he anticipates buying.

On extremely cold nights, Subrinea slips to the barn to work with Tarvin. Before the January morning dawns, Subrinea, like a tall ghost bounding over the frozen snow, under the sound of the winter winds in the barren oak limbs and under the dry rattle of the tough-butted white-oak leaves, slips back to the slab shack down deep in the hollow of desolation. She cares for a sick lamb. She brings a helpless lamb back to life. She smiles when she sees him open his big innocent eyes and kick with his strong legs. It is fun for Subrinea and she loves to work with the sheep. "I love to work with growin plants," says Subrinea. "I love to see corn in the field. I love to see the growth of corn and plants and I like to work with livin things."

As the month of January draws near a close, the heavy lambing season is nearly over. There are a few late ewes left to drop their lambs. The snow begins to melt from the earth. The ravines are choked with blue water running over the rocks with a purring sound. Snow leaves the south hill slopes but the snow is heavy on the ridge-tops and on the north hill slopes. Anse walks out where he buried the lambs in the snow. "Looks like somebody's been gougin around here in the snow," Anse says to himself as he kicks with his boot heel. "Aint no lambs here. I put eight here on the most miserable day I ever spent at this barn. I'll never fergit the money I lost on that day. Since that day, I've put two more lambs here. That aint bad, so hep me God, to lose only ten lambs. I've lost ten lambs out'n three hundred and eight lambs and I've got forty yowes to lamb yit."

Anse kicks the loose snow about, digs into the snow with mittened hands. "Ah well, I guess the foxes had a bait of dead lambs. If the foxes didn't git 'em, guess the hound dogs did. Crows didn't git 'em. They aint been back since they lost a lot of their carcasses here." Anse puffs on his cigar and leaves the snow pile. "Jist thought I'd bury 'em if they's still under the snow. Won't have the trouble buryin 'em now."

Anse spends the day at the barn, feeding the ewes, caring for the lambs and inspecting the lambing pens. When he isn't working with the sheep he is out digging into the earth, lifting handfuls of dirt up and examining them carefully, rubbing dirt between his bare hands, smelling of it, and fondling it as Subrinea fondles the lambs.

Anse walks over the winter earth, wanting spring to come. Somehow he can feel the touch of spring coming into his blood. "Soon it will be plowin time again," thinks Anse. "How glad I'll be to git away from these lambs. Foolin with lambs is like settin in the house with a dress on and a baby in your lap. Aint no place fer Anse. I want to be behind my mules turnin the sod over. I'll have a lot more newground to plow this year, I hope."

Anse walks down the point today toward Cat's Fork after Tarvin comes to stay at the barn for the night. Anse surveys the dark loamy earth on Cat's Fork. He picks up a handful of the loam and sifts it through his fingers. He smells at the handful of loam as a hound dog smells a possum track. "Now if I jest owned this land," thinks Anse, "God Almighty, what corn it would fetch! I'd corn this land three years, then I'd sow it in wheat and orchard grass. I'd sprinkle a little Korean clover seed with my orchard grass. My dream would come true. I'd be the biggest landowner in these parts."

Anse walks down the hollow, smelling the sweet rich soil where the snow has melted in spots. There are white spots on the dark and desolate land where there is the big graveyard of stumps. It is a land that looks like a black hound dog's side with white spots. Anse can see the desolate land as it now stands. Anse can see this land when it belongs to him. He can see great fields of grass knee-deep, with white-faced cattle and hundreds of gray sheep rolling in fat, with little lambs tagging at their sides. Anse can see gray sheep instead of gray rocks on the stubborn slopes and he can see the white faces of cattle instead of the seasoned light brown tops of the oak stumps and the white tops of the beech, ash and maple stumps.

Anse hears the sound of an ax and the laughter and cries of children. He approaches a clearing on his right; upon a high flat he sees a shack made of slabs. He sees his old friend Boliver Tussie chopping stove-wood poles over a block. He sees a half-dressed child carrying wood from the pile through the winter wind into the kitchen. Anse stands and looks at the slab house. He pulls at his red beard that stands out from his chin like a heavy ear of corn stands out from its stalk. "If I'd rent to that man," thinks Anse, "I'd move 'im in the house on my fur place. I wouldn't let 'im live in that polecat's den. I couldn't stand fer a renter of mine to live in a shack that bad. I'd take 'im to that three-room shack I've got."

Anse looks at the clearing around the house. He sees a path leading over the hill to a spring. He observes the hollow. He calculates the fields he will have cleared for corn the first year. He walks down the hollow below the house. Anse remains unseen as he walks down the hollow to the timber road and then down Cat's Fork toward Ragweed Hollow. He digs up a handful of dirt, fondles the soil, smells of it and lets it slip between his fingers back to the earth that he has always loved.

"Is that a voice I hear?" thinks Anse as he cups his big mittened hand over his ear and listens the way the sound comes. "Wish I had a ear like a mule. I could twitch it around anyway and catch a sound. Man's ears air too small. They aint no good. No wonder the mule can hear more than we can. The Lord didn't do a good job on a man's ear like he did on the mule's ear."

It is a woman's voice. Anse walks down the hollow, walks easily with his heavy boots on the partly snow-covered ground. He walks over the slush, rocks and the sand. Anse walks slowly as he gets nearer the voice. Anse can hear singing and praying and he can see tall slender trees—leafless in the winds of winter with their naked tops pointed against the sky.

"It's that gal that Tarvin sparks around," Anse says, observing a tall girl under the trees of Heaven. "Wonder what she's singin and prayin about away down here by herself." Anse stands half hidden behind a cluster of fallen treetops that are wedged against the side of a ravine. He watches Subrinea take a dead lamb, say a few words of prayer over its body, sing a stanza of a hymn, then lay the lamb in a grave. Subrinea then takes a shovel and throws dirt over the lamb, sticks a stick at the head and one at the foot of the grave. He stands and watches her bury the lambs. Anse does not want to be seen watching her. He does not want Subrinea to see him. He crawls back under the treetops to hide as she passes him going back up the hollow to the desolate slab shack that he has just seen. She is carrying a mattock and a shovel on her back as she passes him, singing an old hymn that Anse loves to hear.

"A funny gal," thinks Anse as he crawls from under the treetops that still hold the leaves on their boughs that were green when the trees were cut. "I jest wonder if she's a little off in the head. Them's the lambs that I had buried under the snow in the barn lot. Wonder how she found them? Wonder how she knowed the lambs was there?"

Anse walks down the hollow wondering at what he has seen. Anse wonders if it was a dream or a reality that he saw this girl burying dead lambs, singing hymns and preaching their funerals. It is hard for Anse to believe. "Squatters air funny people," Anse thinks. "Durned if I can understand 'em."

"Fronnie," says Anse, "a funny thing happened today. If I tell you I know you won't believe me. You might think I'm losin my mind." Anse laughs with a big hee-haw. He bends over, slaps his stubby short legs with his big fire-shovel hands. He looks at the blazing fire and he laughs again.

"What's so funny about it, Anse?" Fronnie asks. "You tell me and I'll laugh with you."

"I was comin down Cat's Fork today and I saw a funny thing," says Anse. "I saw Subrinea Tussie down there under the trees of Heaven buryin my lambs. You know the ten lambs I lost and buried under the snow? I missed 'em today when I looked fer 'em to bury 'em. I jest happened to be out galli-vantin around lookin over that Sexton timber tract. I come down the hollow a-past Tussie's and heerd a voice. I could tell it was a woman's voice. I slipped up close and then closer until I could see Subrinea Tussie. She buried my lambs jest like you bury people. She sung a song and preached a funeral."

"Air you right shore you didn't dream it, Anse?" asks Fronnie, as she blows smoke from her pipe into the fireplace.

"Right shore," says Anse, "I should say I am. I was in thirty feet of the gal. I hid under a treetop. It sorty plagued me. Jest somehow I couldn't rush right down past her. It would a-plagued me somehow. I jest stayed fer the funerals. I wonder if she's right in the head."

"I don't see any reason why she wouldn't be," says Fronnie. "She 'pears to be smart and good to work. She's jest been to a lot of funerals this winter, fer that's about all the places there's been around here this winter fer a body to go. How did she know you had dead lambs buried under the snow?"

"I don't know, Fronnie," says Anse. "I know I aint told her. Tarvin is the only one that knows where the dead lambs air. Guess he's seen 'er and told 'er about 'em."

"Guess he hast," says Fronnie. "I think Tarvin is sorty sweet on that gal."

"Aint many gals in this country fer a boy to spark right now," says Anse. " 'Pears like they git married anymore before they air knee-high to a grasshopper. 'Cept the squatter gals. They don't git married. They jest live with their kinfolks."

"Now don't talk like that, Anse," says Fronnie. "You married me when I was fifteen. If Tarvin wants to marry a squatter's gal, that's his business. He's a man now. Tarvin is eighteen. He ought to know what he's doin. If he wants to git burnt he'll haf to sit on the blister."

"If he makes hisself a bed of fire he'll haf to sleep on it," Anse says, pulling a cigar from his pocket and lighting it. "Jest as I have said before, Fronnie—the squatter wimmen have legs, arms, eyes, hair like all other wimmen—but their skins air tough. I know what I'm talkin about. I say, their skins air tough. They air thick and tough."

"We air all tough wimmen through these parts," says Fronnie, blowing smoke from her clay pipe in big circles. Fronnie spits in the fire. "We haf to have our babies on the run. In three days atter we have a baby we air out'n bed and in eight days we air in the field again hoein corn and terbacker. That's why Tarvin ust to be sick so much when he's a baby. I know it was because I worked in the field and got hot and he nursed my milk. That's all that was the matter with 'im. I've thought a lot about it."

"Yep, come to think about it," says Anse, "I guess we air all tough. I can stand more than a young mule and I'm seventy. I've jest had a little stummick trouble. I think I know what's wrong with my stummick."

"What is it?" Fronnie asks Anse, as she turns toward him. She looks at Anse sitting reared back in his chair, like the patriarch of his fellow hillsmen. His face is surrounded by his massive red beard. His blue eyes are as bright as a young man's eyes. His big hands are resting on his legs as he talks.

"What makes me think I know," says Anse, patting his leg with his hand and smoking with ease, "I et some honey out at the shanty. I felt a little sick at my stummick atter I et. I got sicker. I vomited up a couple of worms. That's what's the matter with me. I'm wormy, Fronnie. I'm jest glad it's only worms."

"Aint you too old to be wormy, Anse?" Fronnie asks.

"Nope," says Anse, "you can't git too old fer the devilish things."

Anse sits and blows smoke into the fire. Fronnie sits and blows smoke into the fire. The two sit alone looking at the fire, dreaming, maybe, of the days gone by. Anse is dreaming, too, of the future years as a young man dreams. He is dreaming of the big farm that he will have, with hundreds of sheep and cattle in the velvety knee-deep grass. Anse dreams of loamy earth, the smell of the earth, and the feel of the earth in his hands. Anse dreams more than a young man dreams and he plans at the age of seventy to go on living forever and forever.

8.

FEBRUARY SUCCEEDS January and inherits her barren desolate earth and her flying snow. Water pours over the cliffs mumbling words and laughter. Trees stand barren and lifeless on the slopes. The ground remains too hard to plow. Anse cannot do any spring turning. All he can do is look after the sheep and cattle, reset posts in his fences, spread barnyard manure over the garden and the potato patches. He cuts firewood from the dead undergrowth, hauls it to the house and stacks it in a rick.

"That timber has all been cut, so I hear," Anse tells Fronnie. "Now all I can do is wait until the land is sold. I'm all worked up about it. I want to hear the Master Commissioner git upon the courthouse steps and hit the courthouse door with a gavel. I can't wait. I jest haf to wait, 's all."

"It won't be long," Tarvin tells Fronnie, "until we'll go right back to hard work agin. December and February have been the only months I've not had to work like the devil. When Pa gits all that land, then we'll haf to work. January was the hardest month I've had among the last twelve months but I liked to stay out there at the sheep barn and work. I enjoyed it more than any work I've done in a long time."

"Oh, tell me, Tarvin," says Fronnie, "while I think of it. Did you ever tell Subrinea Tussie about the dead lambs your Pa hid in the snow?"

"Yes, I did, Ma," says Tarvin. "I passed there one mornin on my way home."

"I jest wondered," says Fronnie. "I knowed she found it out some way. Your Pa come down the holler one evenin and Subrinea was buryin the lambs under the trees of Heaven. She was preachin their funerals and singin songs over 'em jest like they's dead people."

"I didn't know she'd done that," says Tarvin. "I know she loves sheep. She loves lambs."

"Your Pa thought she might be a little off in the head," says Fronnie. "He laughed about it."

"She aint off in the head," says Tarvin, jumping from his chair to his feet. "She's got plenty of sense. She's got a heart that feels. Subrinea aint hard-hearted. I know Subrinea better than to think she's off in the head. Pa aint got no business talkin like that nohow."

"He jest laughed about it," says Fronnie. "He didn't say no harm of Subrinea. She plagued your Pa a right smart. He got under a treetop and listened to the singin and preachin. He didn't say anything to 'er. He watched 'er take 'er mattock and shovel and go back up the holler home."

Tarvin stands and smokes his pipe. He looks out the window toward the barn. He sees the fine snow sifting through the trees. He sees the birds alighting on the barren sassafras twigs by the hogpen. He sees a dull barren world, a world that will quickly change, the last of March. This cold ugly earth that he sees now will quickly burst into a green liquid beauty—a strange beauty that seems to rise out of the ugly earth. He will see trees leafed in green tender clouds beneath a high sky that will be the color of robin's-egg blue. He will see grass grow on the slopes and the sheep will walk over the carpet of velvety green. And February will pass strangely as the months of the seasons pass. It will pass unknown and unmarked into oblivion—this strange passing of time, marked only by the washing of new gulleys, the decaying of leaves and the slithering of frozen rocks.

Part III

1.

"Ma, do i have any clean clothes this mornin?" Tarvin asks. "I'm goin with Pa to town this mornin. Pa's ast me to go along with 'im."

Tarvin stands before the looking glass in the kitchen. He has a pan of hot water that he has just dipped from the teakettle. The pan is set on a split-bottom chair beneath him. He has a shaving mug in the middle of the pan of water. Tarvin takes the shaving brush and makes up big gobs of white foamy lather. He smears the lather in white fluffy streaks across the thin dark red beard on his face. He takes a long black-handled razor and cuts swathes down his lean cheeks as Anse takes a wheat cradle and cuts swathes of wheat on the mountain slopes. The beard nick-nicks as the big black-handled razor cuts it clean—so clean you cannot see a stubble.

"Your blue serge pants air hangin on the clothes line upstairs," says Fronnie. "You will find a clean shirt in the dresser drawer upstairs. You'll find socks in the bottom dresser drawer. Your shirts air in the top dresser drawer."

Fronnie strains the morning's milk as she talks to Tarvin. She pours the milk from the big three-gallon bucket into the separator.

"I'll tell you," says Fronnie, "your Pa is buyin more land

137

and he's too stingy to buy milk buckets, slop buckets and dishes. I aint got enough good dishes, knives, forks and spoons to set the table when company comes. I haf to use my milk buckets fer slop buckets. I take a bucket half-full of clear water and atter I pour out slop to the pigs, I rinse the slop buckets out with the clear water. It don't git them exactly clean but I guess it'll do. Your Pa wants big farms, full barns, and plenty of everything to eat and to spare but he don't want anything in the house. I'm afraid to ast 'im fer the money to buy house plunder. When I do he takes the top of the house off with vile oaths. He stomps his big boots on the floor hard enough to break the planks."

"Yes, Ma," says Tarvin. He gives his face the last-over with the razor. "Pa likes the out-of-doors. He says a man that will wash dishes aint no good. Pa allus told me to watch that sort of men. Said they warn't good providers fer their families. Pa got mad when he talked about men that would wash dishes and wouldn't git out and do a day of hard work."

"Ouch," says Fronnie, raising her arm up and working her shoulder backward and forward. "It's a ketch in my shoulder. My arm gits so I can't raise it above my shoulder half of the time. It's too much hard work, Tarvin. I'm gittin old before my time and your Pa is buyin more land fer us to conquer. You don't know how we've worked to put this big farm in shape. You air my youngest child and you don't know about it."

"Don't work so hard, Ma," says Tarvin. He washes the soap from his clean-shaven face in a pan of cold water. The water has a thin layer of ice frozen across the top of the pan.

"I work because I haf to work," says Fronnie. "I've larned a lot of it from Anse. Jest the same as you washin your face in that ice water. Anse ust to make the boys wash in ice water in the winter. He said it made 'em tough. I've seen Anse come in and wash in a pan filled with mush ice. I've seen 'im wash his face, throw the pan of water into the air and it would be ice before it hit the ground. Anse would dry his face on a meal-sack hand-towel. He would rub his face with the meal-sack hand-towel until it was red as a sliced beet. Then Anse would sit down at the supper table and eat like a hoss. His face would look like the blood would bust from it any minute. Anse had the strength then of a hoss. He didn't know his strength. He was a hard man fer a woman to live with. You don't know, Son, what I've had to go through with in my life-time, bearin children fer Anse, cookin grub to feed a family of gluttons and doin all the housework and heppin with the work outside when Anse was crowded in the crop seasons."

"Yes, I do know, Ma," says Tarvin. "I've taken all the work off'n you I could. You know that, Ma."

"Yes, you have, Tarvin," says Fronnie. "You've been a good boy to hep me. I hope and pray if you ever marry as purty a woman as the one you danced with the other night that you won't have her lookin old before her time. I hope you won't be as land crazy as your Pa. He dreams about land. He's wakes up in the night talkin about cattle and crops. He's wakes up milkin cows and breedin white-faced bulls to Jersey cows. Your Pa don't know nothin but to take care of land and breed livestock, save money, raise big crops and buy more land. He takes better keer of his land and his livestock than he ever did his children. He made it so hard on his children that they left home soon as they got big enough to git away. Anse is more in love with his farm than he is with me 'r any of his children. I've gone out to work with 'im on Sunday and I've seen 'im dig a handful of dirt up and fondle it in his hand like I would a baby. He'd tell me what kind of dirt it was and what kind of crops it would be good to grow. I've seen 'im find a stalk of clover growin from a cow pile in the woods someplace. He'd git down and dig dirt up around it, pull the weeds from around it and put stakes down beside it so the cattle couldn't git it before it seeded. We'd go back past this place two years atter and find a clover patch. That is Anse. I could tell you things about 'im you don't know. When he was a young man he'd lift the ends of saw logs in the clearin and put them on the fire. Anse aint afeared of anybody that wears pants. I aint talkin about my husband, but if everybody would take keer of his farm like Anse has, this would be a purty country. This would be a wealthy country. I believe Anse could make a livin on a rock. He's sich a thrifty man. He's jest a hard man on his wife and his family. He's a honest man when it comes to payin debts. Anse don't owe any man one penny."

"Yep," says Tarvin, "I never had anybody to tell me that Pa wasn't a good man to pay his debts."

Tarvin walks up the stairs to get his pants, socks and shirt. Fronnie washes the milk buckets, dries them with a big rag, hangs the buckets in the pantry. She pours the dishwater into a big slop bucket that sits beside the kitchen stove. She saves every drop of dishwater and every crumb of bread for the hogs. There is not a crumb of bread left for a rat or a mouse in Anse Bushman's house. Anse will see that everything is saved. "I've seen wimmen wasteful enough that a family could live on what they throwed in the slop bucket," says Anse. "They could carry out grub faster than their men packed it in."

Tarvin puts on his blue serge pants, his white shirt and his striped necktie. He puts on clean soap-smelling socks and his shined black low-cut slippers. He pulls his coat from the clothesline and squeezes his broad shoulders into it. "I'm about to outgrow this coat. I aint had this suit but three years either."

Tarvin walks down the stairs. His tall muscular body creaks the steps as he walks. He bends to go under the door-facing. He walks back in the kitchen where Fronnie is. "Has Pa come?" he asks.

"No," says Fronnie. "He went to see about the sheep this mornin. Must be they've got out'n the pasture and air over in the rock cliffs on the Artner place. Yowes air still drappin a lamb now and then. It's dangerous about foxes and dogs."

"Yes," says Tarvin, looking out at the window. "I see Pa comin. I can see 'im comin through the flyin frost."

Anse opens the door. He is blowing his warm breath on his knuckles. Icicles are hanging from his beard. His cap is pulled over his ears and there are clumps of ice hanging from his bootlaps. "It's a bad mornin," says Anse. "It's a cold mornin. Two yowes got out'n the barn and lambed in a rock cliff on Artner's farm. I carried the yowes and the lambs to the barn and made the yowes let the lambs suckle 'r they'd a-died. I saved both lambs."

Anse holds his fingers over the bright blazes that leap up the big-throated chimney. He looks pleased since he found the yowes and saved the lambs. He pulls his fingers from over the fire. He puts his fingers in his mouth. "Bring me a pan o' cold water, Tarvin," Anse says. "My fingers might be bit with frost."

Tarvin brings a pan of ice water. Anse souses his hands in the water and holds them there. He grits his broken teeth. His face is lined with pain.

"Take off my boots, Tarvin," he says. "Put my feet in another pan of water. My feet air numb. It's a cold time out and we haf to be in town today by one o'clock."

Tarvin unlatches his father's boots. He jerks them from his feet. He strips the socks from his feet. Fronnie brings another pan of ice-cold water. Anse puts his feet into the water. He sits with his feet in a pan of cold water and another pan in his lap with his hands in it. "This will take out all the frost," Anse says. "Sheep air a lot of trouble through January, February and March. The yowes never know when to quit drappin lambs. A body hast to do a lot of watchin now. These lambs won't be much. They'll go to the late market. But a body hast to save 'em same as he does the early lambs."

Outside the window, Tarvin and Fronnie can see the white waves of flying frost among the leafless trees. The world is a white mist. The trees are covered with frost and the dirt is covered with frost. The blustering March winds go singing over the earth. They howl around the eaves of the big house. They howl songs without words among the leafless creeper vines where the English sparrows roost and chirrup lonely throughout the long dark and gloomy nights.

"I'm all right now," says Anse. He takes his hands from the pan of water and wipes them dry on his heavy mackinaw coat. "I got so cold I got sick. I thought my ticker was goin to stop tickin. 'Pears like it's so much colder than it ust to be, 'r I can't stand the cold like I ust to."

Anse lifts his feet from the pan of water and holds them before the blazing log fire to dry. The water on Anse's feet evaporates into steam and the draft from the chimney pulls it upward through the swallow-throated chimney with the smoke and heat.

"Fronnie, look around and see if you can't dig up some money," says Anse, "and while you git it I'll be gittin ready to go to town. I've got business in town at one o'clock."

"All right, Anse," says Fronnie. She obeys Anse's orders. "You give me a little time and I'll have the money."

Fronnie puts a wool shawl around her shoulders. She fills her pipe, dips it into the bed of hot ripe-persimmon-colored charcoals. She beds the bright burley crumbs with living firebrands. She puffs big streams of smoke that thin on the hot air in the room. Fronnie walks to the door. She opens it, darts out like a cat after a mouse to keep a gust of March wind from filling the warm living room. Tarvin watches his mother go to the smokehouse. He sees her lifting down the old buckets where the wrens build their nests. He sees her taking down old coffee-pots. He has often wondered why she would never let children play around the smokehouse. Now he knows. He sees her walk into the cellar. He thought he'd seen loose rocks in the cellar wall; now he understands. He sees her walk out the frozen hard path to the barn—a path that is crumpled with frozen cow tracks. The cows walked over this path when the ground was thawed and left tracks. They have frozen in the earth and the walking is rough. Fronnie's hair is blown loose on her head by the powerful gusts of March wind. Her gray-streaked hair is white now. It is white with frost. Crows fly low over the barn. The crows' black wings fight the tyrannous wind. Their wings are as black as Fronnie's hair was once black. Now time is against her and she is getting the savings of a lifetime to buy more frozen land, wastelands, with mountains of wrecked treetops with brown leaves still clinging to the dead sapless boughs.

"Pa's boughs will soon be sapless," Tarvin thinks, as he looks out of the window watching his mother going after money, he never knew how much, and kept he never knew where. "Ma's boughs will soon be sapless like the fallen giant trees. She has been a giant tree in the forest of human trees. Pa has been a giant tree in the forest of human trees. Neither of them will stand forever; yet they want to grow forever in their forest of human trees. They want to stand against the heavens forever. They cannot stand forever. They air givin the strength that they have gathered from the land back to the land. They will soon sleep in the Plum Grove earth and the land they own will fall into my hands. My hands and maybe Subrinea's long purty shapely hands. Her golden hair, too, will turn to the color of flyin frost someday. The land will do Subrinea like it has done Ma. It will break Subrinea. Wonder if Subrinea will ever have money in coffeepots, rusted buckets and behind rocks in the cellar walls and hollow logs in the smokehouse like Ma has had. Wonder if Subrinea will save like Ma. Ma will lay back a few pennies from every dozen of eggs she sells. She will lay back money when she sells cream and butter and sorghum molasses or when she sells a pig, cow or bull, or veals a calf. Ma has looked ahead fer the dry seasons, the cropless years, the hard days to come. Pa has looked ahead. Pa and Ma have worked shoulder to shoulder to turn the hard wheel of life. They have been strong and sturdy through the hard years and the plentiful years."

Anse walks upstairs, puts on his peg-legged blue suit that he has had since his wedding day. He wears a big striped tie with a big gold-headed tie-pin pinned to the tie beneath the knot. Anse has a pencil and fountain pen in his coat pocket, a big black umbrella hat on his head. He pulls his Sunday shoes from beneath the bed. They are shined and the hooks and eyes look shiny and bright beneath his short pants legs. Maybe Anse has grown taller since he bought the suit the week before he was married.

"I'm ready," says Anse. He puts his .32 Smith and Wesson in his hip pocket. The ends of brass cartridges show from the chamber of the pistol. "I'll have money on me and I'll take pertection. If a man tries to rob me he'll rob my dead body. I've made all I have, and by God, so hep me, I'll fight to beat hell fer to hold it."

"Must I take my pistol too, Pa?" Tarvin asks.

"What pistol?"

"The one I took off'n Bollie Beaver at the cane-mill last October."

"Yes," says Anse. "We'd better both be armed. You know when it comes to auctioneerin off land at the courthouse block there's goin to be trouble and plenty of trouble."

"Here, Anse," says Fronnie. She walks into the front room. She closes the door quickly behind her. "Here's the money. Here's $4100. Somebody might try to bid it from under your nose. If you haf to have more, send Tarvin back atter it."

"All right, Fronnie," says Anse. He pulls from his pocket a big black leather purse that has a drawstring at the top. Fronnie's lips are blue with cold and her frizzled hair is filled with frost. The air from the warm room melts it and the steam rises from her head like mist from a mountain top. With her long shriveled hands she lays out one hundred ten-dollar bills. Anse puts them in the big pocketbook.

"That's enough to put in the pocketbook," says Fronnie. "Now put five hundred dollars in each vest pocket and a thousand dollars in each shoe. Let Tarvin carry the other hundred."

Fronnie counts out five hundred-dollar bills for each vest pocket and Anse places them securely in the bottom of the vest pockets. He pins the top of his pockets with safety pins.

"Now the big bills, Anse," she says. "Remember when you sold your work oxen that time. Twenty yoke of 'em."

"Yes," says Anse, "I remember. I had to shed a few tears when I sold them cattle. They broke the roots in the ground and tore up the stumps where we got grass today. They hepped me to conquer this land."

Fronnie takes four five-hundred-dollar bills from her apron pocket. Anse pulls off his shoes. He puts a thousand dollars under each foot. He slips his shoes back on his feet, runs the strings through the eyes and around the hooks, ties the strings in bowknots at the tops of his Sunday shoes. "I'm walkin on the money today," Anse laughs.

"Here, Tarvin," says Fronnie, "you'll haf to larn to carry money and to handle it. Remember money is precious. Here's a twenty-dollar bill fer each front pocket and six ten-dollar bills to put in your slippers."

"All right, Ma," says Tarvin.

He puts a twenty-dollar bill in each pocket. He pulls off his low-cut slippers and puts three ten-dollar bills in the toe of each slipper. "I'm walkin on money too," says Tarvin. "It's the most money I ever saw at one time in my life. This is the most I've ever carried."

"You see what a savin wife means, Son," says Anse. "If it hadn't been fer Fronnie I couldn't a-done it, Son. It takes a savin wife to hep a man along among these hills."

"You've made it, Anse," says Fronnie. "I've hepped, but I aint done much."

"I've made and you've saved," says Anse. He strokes his

beard that is warm and dry now. It is bright red like the flames that leap from the forestick up the chimney. "Fronnie, we've made it together. Now we need more land and new houses, renters and bigger fields of grass. We're jest gittin to the place where we can live."

"You wait a minute," says Fronnie, "and I'll bake you some bread in a skillet here on the coals. I'll pour you some buttermilk. It's nearly time you's goin. It's nearly eleven now."

"We won't have time to wait, Fronnie," Anse mutters. "We've got to be in town by one o'clock. Atter the biddin on land is over we'll git a bowl of hot soup at a restaurant. Have us a big supper fixed tonight. We'll be tolerably hungry."

Anse walks out the door. Tarvin follows Anse. They walk into the flying frost. Tarvin wears a long sweeping overcoat, a checkered hawk-billed cap that he pulls down over his ears. Anse wears his big mackinaw coat. They walk across the pasture, follow a barren streak of earth, frozen hard as a rock. It is a cow path that leads to the top of the ridge. Fronnie can see two white bulks of men moving toward the top of the hill. She watches them from the kitchen window. She sees them stop on top of the hill. She can see Anse pointing over the valley. She can see them standing by a big oak stump in the pasture. They stand there and talk a few minutes and then move on.

The ridge road they walk on is whipped by a volleying wind that thunders across the knolls with a tremendous gusto. It is hard for them to draw enough of this wind to breathe. Often they turn their backs on the frost-coated wind long enough to get their breaths. When they get a good breath of wind into their lungs, they turn and face the charges of the wind that is sweeping across the high hill tops and cleaning the knolls of every dead leaf. It breaks the limbs from the frozen trees, carries them over the frozen valleys and drops them.

The earth now looks desolate and doomed. It looks as if the vegetation will never spring from its barren frozen sides.

The rocks, frost-covered and gray, snarl their ugly teeth at them like scaly monsters. They are looking at the two men from every bluff. Snowbirds chirrup languidly from the fodder shocks standing on the Maddens' farm. "A no-count farmer," says Anse, "that would have corn in the shock this time o' year. I'll bet he shucks his corn as he feeds it."

They walk under the pine grove to the midpart of the Chester hill. They find the county road that comes up to Chester's house. They walk down the hill to Hungry Hollow. They walk down Hungry Hollow to Greenwood. Tarvin can hear people say when they pass them on the road, "Old Anse Bushman all dressed up and goin to town. Must be a sale of some sort in town. That's what brings old Anse out in his ground-hog whiskers this time of year. Ground hogs air out, you know. They didn't see their shadders last month."

Anse and Tarvin come to the street where people are passing. Anse walks straight as a solid hickory trunk stands. His big muscular legs fill his boots and his tight pants legs. If Anse were to bend the muscles in his legs too much, he could split his pants legs. His dress coat is tight around his shoulders. His mackinaw is filled with immense shoulders. His whiskers are filled with frost and it looks as if Anse is carrying a snowdrift fastened to his chin into Greenwood. Children look from cozy windows at the funny-looking old Santa Claus with the long frost-filled beard. They look at him and laugh. Mothers hold their small children to the windows so they can see the funny-looking old man and the tall boy walking down the street.

"Thought Christmas was over and Santa Claus had gone home," says a very pretty girl slamming the door quickly.

"What did that gal say, Tarvin?" Anse asks.

"I didn't ketch it, Pa," says Tarvin. "Think she was hollerin at me."

Tarvin hears what she says. He doesn't want to tell Anse. There would be trouble.

"Shoo of these town gals," says Anse. "They aint wimmen fer a livin. They have life too easy."

"I'll bet that old buzzard's headin for the poorhouse," says a well-dressed man. He is putting his car in the garage. He stands and looks at Anse and Tarvin. Anse turns to Tarvin and asks, "What did he say?"

"Said he bet we's headin fer the poorhouse."

"Ast 'im what he wants fer that trap of a house and that fine car," says Anse. "Tel 'im if he aint got enough to eat to come out in Ragweed Hollow and git a square meal."

The man hears what Anse says. He walks slowly into the house. He does not engage in conversation with Anse. He does not want to argue with Anse. Anse and Tarvin walk down the street. It is a path that their feet are not accustomed to walking over. It would be much better if it were a hill path. Anse would not feel lost. "I don't like to be called a buzzard," says Anse. He walks along and wipes the frost from his beard. He wipes the frost away and his beard looks shiny and wet as an apple tree after a March rain.

Anse walks in front. Tarvin walks behind. The two men walk with long strides down the wet street, across a bridge and to the main square of Greenwood. The courthouse stands in the middle of town. It is a bluish brick building with a sagging roof. It was built in the days of Daniel Boone and Simon Kenton. It is crippled with age.

"I don't like a damned town," says Anse. "It aint no place fer me. My heart could never be here. I wouldn't have no place fer my livestock and no place fer my chickens. I wouldn't give my farm fer this whole damned town. 'Pears like the folks will haf to lower their heads here when it rains. It might rain in their noses. A man can come to this town well-dressed and have everybody makin fun of 'im right to his face. Thank God, I don't make my livin kissin dirty babies' mouths and people's tails to git their votes. That's the way they live here.

They live from us. We feed 'em. There aint many people in this town that knows how to work. No wonder they air all the time hollerin about hard times."

2.

THERE IS A big crowd gathered on the courthouse block. Men with their wives are standing shivering in the March frost storm. They are standing all over the courthouse square. There is a tall man standing on the courthouse steps looking down over the crowd of men and women. His hair is as white as the flying frost. The white locks fall beneath his gray soft felt hat. He has a pleasant smile as he looks at the people. His eyes are keen and strong and his handsomeness makes the women from the hills, dressed in tattered dresses, bundlesome coats, and fascinators wrapped around their heads, look admiringly at him. He stands upon the high stone steps as the crowd draws nearer to him. He holds a bundle of papers in his trembling hands.

"That's the Master Commissioner," says Anse. "He's the man that sells the land. He don't look like a man that's done a lot of hard work, does he?"

"No, he don't, Pa," says Tarvin. "He looks like he's had a purty easy life. His nerves aint settled, though. Guess that's the way that a pencil job works on a man. It works on his nerves and brains and makes his belly stick out and his hands grow soft. See, that man's got a paunch that fills his clothes almost to the place where they'll split."

"Master Commissioner Sebastian Litteral," says Anse. Anse looks at the Master Commissioner standing on the high stone perch looking down on the broken faces beneath him. "He aint a bad-lookin man, but I don't see anything about him to make the wimmen cast sheep eyes at 'im."

A small short man walks out and hits the courthouse door with a mallet. He hits the courthouse door with a bang, bang, bang. The crowd comes to attention to see whose farm will be the first sold for debts or taxes. They are anxious to see who will bid it in. They whisper to each other. There are a few well-dressed men in the swirling mass of people. Anse is one of the better-dressed men. He stands among the milling crowd, caressing his beard and looking at the Master Commissioner.

"Hear ye, hear ye, hear ye," shouts Sebastian Litteral to the milling crowd of dark broken faces below him on the court-house square, "by virtue of the orders of the Greenwood Circuit Court, Commonwealth of Kentucky in the case of Blunder Keaton versus Buck Coonse, case number 2813, in favor of the plaintiff at the July 1931 term of court for the sum of six hundred and forty dollars ($640) with interest from November 10th, 1930, I will, to make said sum and $100 probable court costs, sell at public outcry, to the highest and best bidder at the front door of the Court House in Greenwood, Kentucky, at about one o'clock P. M. March 4th, 1932, upon a credit of six months, the following described real estate, to-wit:

"Beginning at a stake within one or two feet of the S. E. side of a large broken-off high chestnut stump, called by said Commissioners to be in A. Womack's line and in the line of Herndon's survey (but the parties of the first part do not recognize Womack's title to that portion of the land, and do

not know that it is the true line of Herndon but only refer
to it as it is mentioned thus by said Commissioners) thence
running S. 54 deg. E. 10 poles to a stake on the west side of a
very small drain where a beech tree once stood and near the
house now occupied by Lewis Large (from which stake a mark
on a large poplar stump bears N. 53 W. 4½ poles); thence
S. 40 deg. W. 8 poles to a stake close to a very small hickory
bush, marked at the foot of the hill; said to be corner of Lot in
Logwood's Division, now claimed by Charles Callihan; thence,
with the marked line of said Lot S. 10 deg. E. 24 poles 8 links
to two hickory bushes near a large rock; thence, S. 37½ E. 26
poles to a large white oak by the road on the ridge; thence,
crossing said road S. 42 deg. E. 10 poles to two white oaks
and a chestnut oak (the last three courses being the marked
lines of said Callihan's Lot but which differ from the course
of said Commissioners' plot) thence, leaving said Callihan's
line and re-crossing said road N. 51 deg. E. 31 poles to old
down black oak by three dogwoods growing from one root;
thence, N. 11 deg. 33 poles 3 links to a chestnut oak stump,
near the bluff and opposite and in full view of the house now
occupied by Emore G. Smith; thence, S. 88½ E. 45 poles
descending the spur of the ridge along, parallel with said bluff
to a stake bearing S. 15 deg. E. 11 links to a large white oak
stump; thence, S. 1½ E. 1½ poles to a stake bearing N. 12½
E. 21 links to a large white oak stump; thence, N. 1½ E. 1½
poles to a stake bearing N. 12 ½ E. 21 links from the same
stump; thence, S. 88½ E. 8 poles to a stake by a down beech;
thence N. 18½ E. 22 poles to a stake in the bottom bearing
S. 18½ deg. W. 2 poles 14 links from a very large white
oak stump; thence, up a branch of Ragweed Hollow N. 16
W. 18 poles to a stake 3 feet on the N. E. of a white oak
stump; thence, N. 88½ W. 44 poles to a ravine in the rear
of the said Smith heirs and continuing the same course 51 poles
further, making 95 poles in all to a sourwood and dogwood
claimed by said Commissioners as being in the Herndon line;

thence, with their line S. 35 deg. 45 min. W. 36 poles 17 links to the beginning. This is the true course of the Herndon survey but along the Commissioners' marked line, which if not the true line, is not binding on the parties of the first part as to the Herndon survey.

"The said property will be sold subject to the payment of unpaid County and State taxes, if any. For the purchase price, the purchaser will be required to execute a sale bond with good security to be approved by the Commissioner and bearing interest from date and as additional security, a lien will be retained on said property to secure the payment of the purchase price. Purchasers should be prepared to execute bond on the day of the sale.

"Now ladies and gentlemen," says Master Commissioner Sebastian Litteral, "you have heard the fine description of this land. I've been informed there's twenty level acres of good terbacker land on this farm. I've been informed there is a good apple orchard—that there is a pine grove that is worth untold money if cut into saw-timber. It is a land rich in resources. It has a good house, barn, cellar, and springs of flowing water the year around. Drouth cannot faze the good water supply. Gentlemen and ladies, it is a farm well worth the money you put into it. Now, do I hear a bid? Come on, gentlemen and ladies! Do not pass up the chance to buy this land flowing with milk and honey and—"

"Master Commissioner," says a small man dressed in overalls, blue shirt and lumber jacket, "don't say any more about my farm. I owe debts that I'm goin to try to pay. I want to hold that land. I know every foot of that land. Pap growed up on it. He married on it and lived all his life. Grandpa married on that land and lived all his life. I married on that land and I'm livin on it today and by God, I aim to keep livin on it. If I haf to fight, I aint goin to have it sold from under my nose."

Master Commissioner Sebastian Litteral shifts his feet on

the cold stone steps. He fumbles the bundle of papers nervously and begins to ask for bidders.

"I said you warn't goin to sell it," says the small man. His
face is covered with scattered black beard. His small black eyes
dance like puddles of fire. "I'll take a sledge hammer and I'll
maul the goddamn brains out'n the first son-of-a-bitch that
comes in to take it. By God, I will. I aint standin to have my
land sold from under my nose."

"He's a riled man," says Anse. "He loves that farm. I can
understand why he don't want it sold. Maybe somethin has
happened—sickness and death!"

"You're right, Uncle," says the small man. " I bought good
coffins fer Ma and Pap. I laid them away nice as I could.
They'd worked so hard fer me that I paid too much fer a poor
man to pay fer their coffins. I mortgaged my farm. My terbacker crop was good and I didn't get anything out'n it. But
by God, I'll die when my land goes. I aim to stay on that land.
I'll fight the son-of-a-bitch that bids it from under my nose."

"Don't interrupt me again," says the Master Commissioner.
"It's not me sellin your land. It is the Commonwealth of
Kentucky."

"To hell with the Commonwealth of Kentucky and God
damn you," he says. "I've hepped make Kentucky. By God,
I have. My people have worked before me. They have fit in
wars fer America. They fit the Indians and then by God, you
sell all I have. You sell the grove of pines I love. You sell my
rock cliffs and you sell my shack. God damned if I don't fight
till I die before you take my land."

"Oscar, call the Sheriff," says Sebastian, "so I can do my
duty. I'm not goin to stand up here and be humiliated by a
whipper-snapper like that. I am here to do my duty. I'm a
Kentuckian too. I'll do it fer this Commonwealth of Kentucky."

Oscar leaves his wooden mallet by the door. He waddles
down the frost-covered stone steps. He goes through the

milling crowd after the Sheriff. While he is gone Master Commissioner Sebastian asks for bidders. When he asks for bidders he is interrupted by vile oaths from the small man. He tries to make his way to the Master Commissioner, but two men catch him and hold him until Sheriff Bradley comes. Sheriff Bradley comes waddling like a goose in his fat. He is almost out of breath by the time he walks to the courthouse yard. He has two big pistols buckled in holsters on his hips. The butts of the big pistols stick out of his holsters.

"What's the matter with you, Buck?" red-cheeked Sheriff Bradley asks him.

"Tryin to sell my farm, Sheriff," he says. "I lost my head. I can't bid it in. I don't have the money and I can't git it. I guess I lost my head, Sheriff."

"It's my duty to arrest you," says Sheriff Bradley. "I'm sworn on my oath to do my duty."

He pulls a pair of handcuffs from his pocket and locks them around Buck Coonse's wrists. He takes him through the milling crowd, the hisses, curses and jeers, toward the old brick jail. Men and women in the crowd feel sorry for Buck. Sorrow and sympathy are written on their silent dark faces. They whisper to each other. "Remember," Buck hollers back to the crowd as the Sheriff takes him off to jail, "I'll kill the son-of-a-bitch that bids in my farm as soon as I git out'n the buggy jail I'm headin fer. I'll bust his goddamn brains out with a sledge hammer."

"That man means what he says," says Anse. "I can see it in his eyes. He has fightin fire in them eyes."

"Yes, he means that," says a big man, sanctioning what Anse says. "He hates to lose his farm."

"Do I hear a bidder, gentlemen, among you," says Master Commissioner Litteral. He waits awhile, shifting the papers restlessly in his hands. There is not a voice from the crowd. Sebastian shifts his feet and stomps them on the cold stone steps to keep them warm. There is still no one bidding on Buck Coonse's farm.

"Don't I hear a single bid?" Sebastian asks.

"If my ears air tellin me the truth," says John Porter, "you don't hear a single bid, Master Commissioner."

"Then the Commonwealth will bid it in," says Sebastian, "and we'll proceed with another farm. I've got a long list of farms here to sell."

"You won't sell many," says a voice from the milling crowd. "We aint got the money to buy the farms with. If we had the money we wouldn't lose our farms."

"You say you haf to do your duty, Master Commissioner," says Hoggie Morton. "You git a divvy when you sell our farms. That is your duty. Your duty is the pay you git."

Sebastian does not pay any attention to the comments of the crowd. He proceeds to pull another sheet from the stack and read. It is the Dan Hensley farm, mortgaged first and second mortgage. Taxes for two years are due. There is more money against the farm than it will bring. Sebastian begins to read that the Commonwealth and the county courts have made it possible for him to sell Dan Hensley's farm. He reads the names of the men whose farms join Dan Hensley's farm. He reads the trees, rocks, stumps and corner stones in the line fence. When he speaks of trees, corner stones and stumps it is

music to Anse Bushman's ear. He cups his hand over his ear so as not to miss a word. He gets closer to the stone steps by pushing his way through the crowd.

"Howdy, Mr. Bushman," says Boliver Tussie. "You remember me, don't you?"

"Oh yes," says Anse, "you live on Cat's Fork of Ragweed Hollow, don't you?"

"Yes," says Boliver, "I live there. I was down to the cane-mill frolic on your farm last October."

"Oh yes," says Anse, "you're the man that larnt me how to make amber-colored sorghum molasses."

"I'm the man that can make purty sorghum," says Boliver. "You remember my gal, don't you, that called at the dance that night—Subrinea?"

"Yes," says Anse, extending his big hairy hand to shake hands with Subrinea. "I remember a purty woman wherever I see 'er."

Anse laughs as he shakes hands with Subrinea. Tarvin walks from behind.

"What air you doin out on a cold day like this, Subrinea?" he asks. "Where have you been in the crowd that I aint seen you?"

"I've been smothered in this crowd," says Subrinea. She avoids answering why she has come to Greenwood with her father. Tarvin could make a good guess, but he remains silent.

"Jest to tell you the truth, Mr. Bushman," says Boliver, "we come to see who bid in the Sexton Land Tract. We want to know. We don't own it, but it is dear to us as our home. We've lived on it all our lives, hunted over every foot of it, and we hate to leave it."

"Silence down there," cries Oscar, beating his mallet on the courthouse door and looking down at Anse, Boliver, Tarvin and Subrinea. "Quiet, please, so we can bid on this farm."

"Quiet, please," says a man, staggering through the crowd. "Quiet so we can sell farms today—quiet, I said, quiet. God

damn this sellin a man's land nohow. God damn sicha work
to hell nohow."

Sheriff Bradley walks alongside the man. He locks his handcuffs on his wrists. He takes him through the crowd to jail.
"Handcuff me, you son-of-a-bitch," he says. "You aint gittin
no virgin. I've been in your goddamn jail before. Jest so you
feed me corn bread and beans." The Sheriff takes the drunk
off toward the brick jail.

"Another good man gone West," says Alf Perkins.

"Do I hear a bid on the Dan Hensley tract?" asks Commissioner Sebastian.

There is silence in the crowd. There isn't anybody bidding.

"Give me time," says Dan Hensley, "and give me work and
I'll clear up my debts. I don't want my house sold from under
my nose and I won't use a ax on the man's head that buys it.
I'll kill 'im a easier way. I'll plug his heart with a rifle ball.
My farm is a sheep farm. It's high among the hills and I don't
know who'd want it. I'm layin on my belly with a rifle. I'll
lay on frozen ground, muddy ground, or in the snow. He'll
never take possession of my farm while there is breath in my
body. I'll fight fer the land my father, grandfather and great-
grandfather has owned before me. I won't have it sold at the
block. God damned if I will."

"This looks like war," says Subrinea. "Everybody is goin to
fight over his land."

"It looks bad to me," says Tarvin, "to take their land away
from them. If they love their land well enough to fight fer it
they ought to be allowed to keep it some way."

"What's the Commonwealth goin to do with all these
farms?" an old woman asks. "That's what I'm here fer. I'm a
widder woman. I've lost my farm. I'm goin to fight, too. I
won't be moved out. I'll burn my house before I'll let somebody else have it. Damned if I don't burn it. When they try
to take my land, the old Devil gits in me. I can feel the old
Scratch start down at my navel and work up to my throat.

When he does that, somethin is bound to pop. Wish my man was above the ground. This wouldn't happen. Fred would see to that." She turns from Subrinea and spits a bright sluice of ambeer spittle from her toothless mouth onto the sloppy sour-smelling ground where hundreds of broganed feet have trampled the frost and earth into a loblolly. She pulls the gray wrinkled shawl around her shoulders a little tighter.

"If no bids," says Sebastian, "on the Dan Hensley tract, the Commonwealth will bid it in."

"The Commonwealth will haf to just bid in," says Dan Hensley. "God damned if I don't give the Commonwealth some trouble. I'll fight like a son-of-a-bitch fer my land."

"Another man, Sheriff," says Sebastian. "There's too much disorder here. I can't perform my duty."

"Don't handcuff me, Sheriff," says Dan. "I'll go to jail with ye. All I want is a good warm bed and three meals a day no-how."

Sheriff Bradley walks away to jail with Dan Hensley in front of him.

"Master Commissioner," Anse hollers from below, "aint you got a Sexton Land Tract to sell? If you have I'd like fer you to bid it off now. I've got a fur piece to walk and a lot of work to do when I go home."

"Yes, I have," says Sebastian, fumbling with jerky hands down among the sheaf of papers. "At your pleasure, my friend, if you are interested in bidding it in."

Sebastian pulls a paper from the stack. He looks down at Anse. He looks at the paper again.

"It's a big land tract," Sebastian says.

"Yes, I know it is," says Anse.

Sebastian fumbles among the armload of papers. He finds the right paper. He begins to read.

"Hear ye, hear ye, hear ye," shouts Sebastian, looking down at Anse.

"Yes, I hear ye," says Anse—

"By virtue of a judgment and order of sale, of the Greenwood Circuit Court, Commonwealth of Kentucky, in favor of the plaintiff at its January 1931 Circuit Court term, for the sum of three thousand three hundred dollars ($3300) with interest from March 6th, 1929, in the equity action of the First National Bank, Greenwood, Kentucky, versus Jad Sexton, et al., I will, to make said sum and one hundred dollars ($100) probable court costs, sell at public outcry to the highest and best bidder, at the front door of the courthouse in Greenwood, Kentucky, at about 1:00 P.M. March 4th, 1932, upon a credit of six months, the following described property, to-wit":

Sebastian reads the names of the men whose farms it joins. He reads about the Anse Bushman farm, the white oaks, black oaks, blade oaks, chestnut oaks, beeches, stumps, rocks and creeks it follows. He reads three pages of landmarks, rods and feet. This is music to Anse Bushman's ears. It is sweeter music than the lowing of white-faced cattle. Anse gets up closer so he can hear every word. Tarvin and Subrinea talk, unmindful of the land. Boliver listens to the boundaries read. He watches Anse and Sebastian.

Sebastian finishes reading the boundaries of this large tract of land. He wipes his mouth with his handkerchief. He looks over the crowd.

"Do I hear a bid?" he asks.

"Two thousand dollars," says a well-dressed chubby-cheeked man smoking a big cigar.

"Twenty-one hundred," says Anse, looking toward his competitor.

"Twenty-five hundred," says the chubby-cheeked man, peering through his nose-glasses at Anse and chewing the end of his cigar.

"Twenty-six hundred," says Anse.

There is silence as Anse's competitor eyes him more closely. There are whispering and muttering of voices from the shivering crowd on the courthouse square.

"Has that old buzzard with the red beard got that much money?" someone mutters. "He don't look like it. Looks like he might be from the poorhouse."

"You can't tell who's got money and who aint when the men come from the hills. He's from Ragweed Hollow. Owns a big farm out there."

"He looks like Santa Claus."

"Twenty-eight hundred dollars," says Anse's competitor. He seems to wonder if Anse will bid any higher.

"Twenty-nine hundred," says Anse.

"Three thousand," he yells.

"Thirty-one hundred," says Anse.

"You have it," says the man.

"Do I hear any higher bid?" says Commissioner Sebastian Litteral. "It's a big farm, well watered. The soil is virgin soil. It's not had a plow stuck in it. It is a land flowin with milk and honey."

Anse's heart is in his mouth. He wants the land. He feels that he has to have the land. He can look into the distance and see before his eyes in a future vision, houses everywhere on the slopes near his home; he can see the smoke from the ugly chimneys; he can see their cattle, hogs and chickens. Again he can see before him steep slopes with knee-high grass, herds of sheep, herds of white-faced cattle rolling in fat standing knee-deep in a June stream of blue gurgling water. This belongs to Anse Bushman.

"If I do not hear a higher bidder," says Master Commissioner Sebastian, "it is sold to the man with the red beard. What is your name, please?"

"Anse Bushman."

"Are you prepared to give sufficient bond?"

"I am."

"Who's the bondsman?"

"I've got the bond in my boots."

"What do you mean?"

"I'll pay you cash right now."

The crowd laughs.

"All right," says Master Commissioner Sebastian. "Oscar, take him to the clerk's office. Get a lawyer and proceed."

"You aint goin to take that land either," says a man walking up to Anse. He is tall, with discolored front teeth, and a scattered black beard over his face. "I say you aint goin to buy that land."

"Who the hell said so?" says Anse. "I've already bought it."

"I said so."

"Who air you?"

"Lonsey Beaver."

"A squatter, huh!"

"You're goddamn right," he says. "Do you want to make somethin out'n it?" He looks at Anse with mean eyes. His lips quiver.

"I'll take that land," says Anse, "if I haf to fight everybody in this goddamn town. When it comes to runnin me off'n that land somebody is goin to git shot. I aint afraid of hell and high water and all the goddamn squatters in this county pitched in fer good measure."

Anse squares himself. Stubborn as an oak he stands. He puts his hand on the butt of his pistol. The crowd becomes silent. Women start running back from the two men. Men have been shot down on this courthouse square.

"A rich man," he snarls at Anse. "Buy land poor people live on."

"I aint a rich man," says Anse. "I've worked fer what I've got. By God, I'm buyin that land if money will pay fer it. I'll keep it, too. What ornery son-of-a-bitch is goin to tell me what I can buy and what I can't buy? When it comes to sich a thing as this, this county aint a safe place to live any more."

"I'll see you don't git it," says Lonsey. "I'll fill your behind with buckshot the minute you put a plow in it."

"Pay 'im no minds," says Boliver Tussie.

"Sheriff," says High Commissioner Sebastian, "more trouble on the ground."

"Don't call the Sheriff," says Anse. "I can fight my own battles. I'll let you call the undertaker if he keeps on."

Anse pulls his gun in the open. The crowd pushes back farther. The two men stand face to face. Men whisper in the crowd.

"Look behind Lonsey Beaver," says Tarvin. "You can see why all the trouble. It's my old friend Bollie Beaver."

Tarvin walks in with the pistol in his hand he took from Bollie Beaver at the cane mill.

"Bollie, if you want to start anything," says Tarvin, "I'll give you a longer sleep than the one I gave you at the cane mill. You remember that night, don't you? I know you and your kind. Guess this fellar is your brother. He looks like you."

"Stay back, Sheriff," says Anse. "I'm a law-abidin man. I pay my taxes. I'm not a charge on the state. I'm a good citizen. If he molests me I'll kill 'im dead as four o'clock and save the county taxpayers the expense of feedin 'im in jail."

Lonsey Beaver slips through the crowd. Bollie follows him.

"That old man means business," says a young man standing near the cold stone courthouse steps.

"You goddamn right," another sanctions, "he means business. He's a Bushman and the Bushmans all mean business. They'd fight at the drap of a hat and drap the hat theirselves."

"I haf to go with Pa," Tarvin says to Subrinea. "I'll see you soon as I can, Honey. There might be trouble."

"I'm glad you're gittin that land, Mr. Bushman," says Boliver. "I prayed all the time you'd bid it in. I's afeared you didn't have the money and somebody else would git it."

"Thank you," says Anse, hurrying across the courthouse square among the milling crowd toward the clerk's office. Anse gets a lawyer. He has the old deeds inspected and a new deed made. Anse pays in cash for the farm. Tad Sexton signs the deed. He was the man that was bidding against Anse on the courthouse square. He leaves the deed in the clerk's office to have it recorded.

Anse walks up the street. He smokes his cigar. He is the proud owner of five hundred acres more land. He passes the courthouse square. He can hear vile cursing as the farms are put on the block for sale. He can see the Sheriff arresting men and taking them to jail. He can hear threats: "We ought to combine and fight. We ought to rebel. Let's don't let them sell our land. God damn the Commonwealth of Kentucky. By God, we'll fight fer our rights. We'll fight fer our farms."

"We must hurry home," says Anse. "We've got to look about the yowes. If more yowes drapped lambs today they'll freeze to death. One of us ought to be there now."

"Yes, Pa," says Tarvin, "we'll haf to hurry."

Anse's short legs take long strides. The muscles of his legs bulge in his tight-fitting pants legs. The blue trails of cigar smoke stream back across his shoulder. Anse walks like a proud man. He is going home with a thousand dollars of money he started with. He has one of the biggest farms in the county.

Frost ceases to fly through the air. The sky becomes clear. Stars come into the sky. Anse and Tarvin walk up the Chester hill to the pine grove. They walk under the pines that the starlight shines down through. Their feet crunch-crunch on the hard frozen earth.

"I'm a happy man," says Anse. "I'm so happy I fergot somethin."

"What's that, Pa?"

"The bowls of hot soup."

Tarvin laughs.

"I never thought about soup when them Beavers tried to start somethin with us," Tarvin says.

"I'll put their hind-ends off'n that farm," says Anse. "I want 'em to git off'n there right now."

They walk out the ridge path toward the house. They walk across the sheep pasture. They come to a little clump of black-oak trees. Anse sniffs like a dog.

"March here," says Anse. "It's come in like a lion. It'll go out like a lamb. I can smell the spring in these woods. I can smell the land awaitin to be plowed. I can smell the livin roots workin under the moldering leaves.

3.

"SON, THEY like their grub, don't they?" Anse says as he bends over the fence laughing. The shoats root each other from the trough. They lie down in the trough and bite each other on the necks. "They shore like their grub."

"Yes, Pa," says Tarvin, "a hog's the hoggishest thing I've ever seen. A hog is worse than a dog to fight over grub."

"Yep," says Anse, "but I like to listen to 'em chomp their grub and eat. 'Pears like they enjoy their grub more than any livin thing. God Almighty, but I like to see fat hogs on a floored pen. I like to see shoats on the ground. I like to see pigs drinkin troughs of milk. It looks like livin when a body sees hogs on a farm."

"Spring will soon be here," says Tarvin. He changes the subject from hogs to the seasons. "We'll soon be turnin the sod over agin."

"I can feel spring in my blood," says Anse. "I'm goin to have Fronnie to make me a good spring tonic out'n herbs and bark—bile them together to a bitter gall—drink 'er down and give my system a spring cleanin. I don't need it, but I'll feel a lot better."

"You'll haf to be thinkin about a renter fer next year," says Tarvin. "Do you have anybody in mind?"

"I've been thinkin," says Anse. "I'm not shore yit. I've been thinkin about tryin Boliver Tussie. I know he can make good sorghum molasses. I know he's a plum good hand when it comes to butcherin. I jest don't know about his farmin, only what you said. I know if I rent to him 'r any other man, I'm goin to bind 'im with a good ar-tickle. I'm goin to know where we stand. I want 'im to know where we stand before we start the season together."

"I think he'll make you a good renter," says Tarvin.

"Yep, you would think so, Son," says Anse. "You're sorty sweet on that gal o' his'n, aint you?"

"Jest tolerable sweet," says Tarvin. He looks at Anse with a smile on his face. "Jest tolerable sweet, Pa—"

Fronnie is sitting on a stool milking a cow. Anse and Tarvin have been watching the hogs eat. When they see Fronnie milking a cow, they walk toward the barn. Anse dips cracked corn from the barrel into a feed box. He carries the box out in the barn lot. A cow follows him. Anse finds a suitable place, places the box on the ground and pulls up a milking stool made from a block of wood that has four stout legs set in auger holes. Anse puts the milk bucket under the cow. He throws down his cigar butt. He begins to milk with both hands. Tarvin milks a cow near Anse. They talk about hogs, sheep, cattle and spring crops as they milk. Fronnie smokes her pipe and milks her cow.

Don runs down the road barking. "Here, Don!" Anse shouts. "Come back here, you rascal!"

"What's he barkin at?" Fronnie asks.

"Jest me, Mrs. Bushman," says Boliver Tussie. "Leave 'im alone. There's a sayin that all dogs know one another. A dog won't bite me. I've never had a dog to bite me in my life."

"Dogs don't like me, it 'pears like," says Anse. "I've got four big scars on each thigh where dogs have nailed their teeth to me. But I got the dogs. I jest let a bulldog hold to me once when I's peddlin green beans and went into a home. I pulled my knife from my pocket. I opened the big blade and slit his throat. The other dog bit me and tried to run. Jest as it happened, I had my gat on me. I pulled it and fed 'im a load of hot lead. It was too much fer 'im to carry."

"I never kilt a dog," says Boliver. " 'Pears like I could never have the heart."

"You've never owned sheep," says Anse. "If you ever owned sheep, durned if that soft heart of yourn wouldn't harden a little when you saw a bunch of dogs come to your sheep pasture and start tearin flakes of flesh from your livin sheep. Your soft heart would change when you'd see the dogs tear entrails from your pet yowes and stringin 'em on the ground and the yowes keep runnin."

" 'Speck that would rile me," says Boliver. "I never thought about that. I've allus had huntin dogs. I've done a powerful lot of huntin. Guess them days air over now. Timber all gone and the land sold."

"Yep," says Anse, "fer as I'm concerned it's all over. I'll have sheep on that farm one of these days and I don't want huntin among my sheep. Give me a little time and all that huntin ground will be conquered. It will grow big fields of

terbacker, corn and cane. Atter growin these it will be sowed
down in Korean clover and orchard grass."

"That's jest what I come to see you about, Mr. Bushman,"
says Boliver. He rubs his big rough hand over his stubble of
red beard. "I've come to see you about rentin from you next
year. I was there to see if you got the land and you got it. I
don't want to leave that land."

"Yep," says Anse, "I'll talk to you about rentin, but dad-
durn me if you aint got some onery kin that's goin to git
their tails off'n that place soon as Sheriff Bradley can serve
notices on 'em. If he can't git 'em off, then I can. I'll take a
.30-.30 rifle and pick 'em off as they come out'n their dens if
they don't go. And when they air gone, I aim to fire them little
log-pole shacks they lived in. I don't want one left standin. I
aim to burn that slab shack you live in if we come to an agreement, and put you in a better shack."

"That will suit me," says Boliver. "It don't make no difference to me nohow fer I could live in a pole shack with a dirt
floor. I've lived in shacks like that all my life. I'm livin in the
best shack now that I ever lived in. It has a plank floor. I
don't like it durin the summer. I've wanted to take the floor
out so my bare feet could git back on the ground, but Crissie
wouldn't let me."

"I don't blame her nary bit," says Anse. He gets up from
the milking stool with a three-gallon bucket filled with milk.
"I don't see how a body can go barefooted and plow new
ground."

"Well, I can," says Boliver. "The bottoms of my feet air
tough as shoe leather. I can show you right now that I can pull
my shoes off and walk through the biggest briar thicket and
under the thickest locust patches on this place. A locust thorn
—don't care how hard it is seasoned—won't go through the
bottom of my foot. I walk over briars jest like they wasn't
there. I could stand to go barefooted winter and summer. I
ust to go barefooted the coldest winter that come."

"If your feet air that tough," says Anse carrying the bucket of milk to the corncrib and setting it inside the door, "you won't haf to buy any shoes. You'll save a little money there."

"I never thought about that," says Boliver. "I jest know my feet air tough."

Anse walks back with a feed box filled with cracked corn. He gives it to another cow. He moves his stool over to the cow. He sits down and starts milking with both hands. He keeps talking to Boliver. Tarvin is milking a cow near Fronnie. Fronnie and Tarvin are talking to each other as they milk the cows.

"Now if you think you can tend a good crop," says Anse, "about sixty acres, I'll be willin to rent to you if you will come to my terms. I believe you air a tough man. You can stand a lot. How much of a force do you have to put in the field?"

"There's my old woman Crissie," says Boliver, "she can hoe more corn than any man I ever saw. Subrinea is a good worker. I have two boys and two more gals I can work in the field. That makes a half a dozen to hoe and one to stay behind the plow."

"That's a good workin force," says Anse. "You ought to devilish nigh tend God's creation with a force like that. You can take six rows at a swarp around a newground slope. It'll shore look purty to see where you slice down six rows of weeds."

"It will that," says Boliver. "I can raise a mighty big crop."

"That's what we both want," says Anse.

"I'll haf to be goin," says Boliver. "I'm glad you feel the way you do about rentin to me. I'll try to make you a good man on your place."

Boliver gets up and starts through the gate. His overalls are patched and ragged. His face is red with stubbled beard. It looks as if Boliver has just kept his beard clipped off with scissors during the winter. His long dark poking-stick teeth hold his thin red lips far apart.

"Funny how a man that ugly could pappie a gal purty as Subrinea," thinks Tarvin, as he looks at Boliver standing by the gate and talking back to Anse.

"Jest a minute, Boliver," says Anse. "I'll walk a piece of the way with you and talk about this year's crops. It aint long, you know—jest a few more days until we'll haf to start work."

Boliver waits at the gate until Anse finishes milking the cow. He takes the bucket of milk to the corncrib, sets it inside the crib and walks away with Boliver. Tarvin and Fronnie finish milking the cows. They can see Anse and Boliver as they walk down the road together. They can see Anse talking with his hands. They can see Anse pick up a handful of dirt, stop long enough to smell the dirt and sift it between his fingers.

Anse and Boliver soon disappear into the dark deep desolate hollow, while Tarvin and Fronnie carry two buckets of milk to the house at a time. They carry the milk buckets onto the path, under the pine trees to the house. The March wind is cool on their faces. A redbird comes to the oak grove above the house. It alights on a dark barren limb of an oak tree and sings a song of spring. Tarvin stands with a bucket of milk in each hand and listens to the redbird sing.

"Spring can't be fer away," says Tarvin, "when the redbirds come to these dark hills in the spring. It riles my blood to hear a redbird sing in the spring. It brings back happy days. I can see the big mules steppin along with the plow. I can smell the earth agin."

4.

"Come in, Boliver, and git you a chear," says Anse.

"I aint got much time, Mr. Bushman," says Boliver. "I've jest come over to see if you'd made up your mind to let me rent from you. It's been botherin me a lot, you know. I don't want to leave the old place where we've lived all our lives and where my people have lived ever since they've been in this country. It's awful hard fer us to tear up stakes and leave now. We don't know where we could go. We don't want to go. Every tree and every crick, rock cliff and patch of ferns means something to us on your farm. It is your farm now. It ust to be a wild tract of land where the squatters lived."

"Yes," says Anse, "I've got a ar-tickle I had drawed up by Lawyer John Oscar Simmons. I thought I'd put my terms in the word and on big white sheets of paper. That is the only way to do business, Boliver, like men do at the People's Bank. They have everything down in ciphers and in the word in big books with horsehide leather backs and big white sheets of ruled paper. I don't have much education but I larnt to cipher well, and to read and write the word, and it has been a lot of hep to me in this world."

"I never larnt my ABC's," Boliver says. He follows Anse into the house swinging his hat in his hand over the seam of blue drilling pants. Boliver's shoulders are slightly rounded by heavy lifting. Deep lines have started grooving his face. It has happened too soon for his years. His teeth are discolored. They stand like two rows of uneven stumps on a red clay hill. His red beard, stubbled on his long lean lantern jaws, looks like saw-briar stubble after Anse has cut the saw briars with a briar scythe.

"I've often thought about the larnin I got," says Anse, "and how much more I'd a got if it hadn't been fer the devilish mean boys burnin the schoolhouse. They's bad'ns around here in my day and your day, Boliver. The boys were tougher than they air today. That's why so many men our age air ignorant as hosses. Jest like the word in the Bible—people grow weaker and wiser all the time. When I went to school we jest had readin, ritin and rithmetic. We all called 'em the three R's. The teacher called his classes by the name of a boy in the class. My class was called the Anse Bushman class. I was the biggest boy in the class. Mister Armstrong named it atter me. Atter we recited from our books, he let us go out and run over the hills until time to recite agin. We'd git out and fight yaller-jackets' nests. We'd dig 'em out'n the ground. What did we care fer fifteen or twenty yaller-jacket stings. We'd dig bumblebee nests from the ground and burn hornets' nests from the trees. We'd take long poles with fire on the end of 'em and fire the hornets' nests. Sometimes we kilt ground squirrels with rocks. We hunted rabbits and tracked down possums, coons, polecats and minks in the winter when the snows come if we's still in school. Our schools was only three months long in them days."

"I don't know about the schools," says Boliver, "only what I've heerd. I went one day and the place was too tame fer me. I took my dinner bucket and slipped back through the woods home. I couldn't stand to sit in a schoolhouse on a split log and look at a book. I kept my eye on the hole sawed in the house fer a winder, that day I was in school. When I laid my Primer in the door to show I went to the bushes, I picked up my dinner bucket and hauled my carcass through the woods fer home. I knowed I'd never need my Primer again, and I would need my dinner."

"It was the Anse Bushman class that burned the schoolhouse," says Anse. "I allus hated it. I allus watched over the boys fer Mister Armstrong when we left the schoolhouse. He had about one hundred scholars in the school. He had a lot of trouble with the big scholars. He had to bring his gun. A snow fell early that year. I remember it like it was yesterday. The one-room log schoolhouse was built high off'n the ground and Mr. Young's sheep laid under the schoolhouse when the weather was cold. We walked around back of the schoolhouse. We saw what a good warm bed they had on the leaves. We run the sheep out and went under the floor. We's all sprawled out on the good warm places the sheep left—one of the boys lit his pipe and throwed the match down and ketched the leaves on fire. We fit the fire with our caps but it got back under the floor where it was too low fer us to fight it. I never seen sich a blaze in my life. We run from under the floor in time to see the boys and girls runnin out the door and jumpin from the winders. It was a skeery sight to see them jumpin with their books and dinner buckets—screamin as they jumped. We left our books and dinner buckets and took to the brush like rabbits. I never went back. I couldn't go back atter that. It ended my education. If it hadn't been fer the Anse Bushman class burnin the schoolhouse, I'd know a lot more than I know today."

"Children don't know what they've got today," says Boliver. "They've even got one-room painted schoolhouses with a lot of big winders in 'em. They aint jest holes cut in the walls either. The winders have big sashes of glass in 'em. They've got wagon roads to the schoolhouses too. We jest had a little dog-path to the school I went to that day. It aint no trouble fer a boy to git his larnin now. He don't haf to walk six 'r seven miles either. There's a lot more schoolhouses than there ust to be."

"Children air growin weaker and wiser," says Anse, "jest like the word in the Scriptures. I don't believe it's a good thing. You take my boy, Tarvin. He's a fast larner in school. He can't do nigh as much work as I could do when I's his age. He jest thinks he hast to work. He don't haf to work like I did."

Anse and Boliver sit down in the front room. They sit before the log fire in hickory split-bottomed chairs and watch the fire burn the dry seasoned wood. Fronnie walks from the kitchen to the front room. Fronnie has been washing the dinner dishes. She lights her pipe to sit before the fire and rest as long as her pipe of tobacco burns. That is the way Fronnie rests after each meal.

"Howdy do, Mr. Tussie," says Fronnie.

"Howdy do, Mrs. Bushman," Boliver greets Fronnie.

"Fronnie," says Anse, "before you sit down and make yourself comfortable will you git that ar-tickle and bring it in here. Bring Tarvin with you. We haf to have two witnesses to sign this ar-tickle if Mr. Tussie wants to rent part of my farm fer next year."

"All right," says Fronnie.

Fronnie walks back through the door to the kitchen. She is not gone very long before she comes back holding a sheaf of paper in her hand. Tarvin walks by her side. The contract was written by a lawyer. It is on the kind of paper Anse wanted, long sheets of clean white paper with red printed margins down the side. Anse takes the paper in his hand. He pulls his glasses from his vest pocket. He puts them on, fondles the paper in his hand and begins to look over the typed contract.

"Now, Boliver," says Anse, "I think I'd better read this and explain it as I go. We don't want any misunderstandin. I've never rented to a man in my life. I've looked about me at the men who've rented their farms. I'v seen killins and the like over ground rentin and crop sharin. I thought to myself if my crop-lands got too big fer me to handle and I had to rent part of my place, I would have the contract down in black and white. Now I've done that very thing. I went to Lawyer John Oscar Simmons and had 'im to fix the ar-tickle. I'm a law-abidin man and I don't want trouble. That's why I've had this contract made. I don't want to kill anybody or git kilt."

"I don't want no trouble either," says Boliver. "I don't want the stain of death chalked up against me on the Lamb's Book of Life in Heaven. I want to do what is right. I've allus been like that. I never thought about the land where I've lived all of my days bein sold from under me; but it was sold and the timber has been cut. I feel like the farm is mine, though I don't own a foot of the land. I still want to stay on this land. Jest somehow I hate to leave it. My people come here from God knows where durin the days when they had the iron furnaces in this country. They hepped cut all the timber off'n that land. They cut big trees down fer cordwood. Jest stripped these hills bare of a sprout. The company helt the land—God knows how many companies helt it—I don't know—a lot of 'Big Men' helt it—passed it on from father to son and the big timber growed back. Now they've cut the timber agin and sawed it at the mill this time and that wasn't enough. They've sold the land to 'clear off debts,' they said. It leaves me without a home—and all our dead has been planted on that land fer the past hundred years. We've lived there jest like the land belonged to us."

"You didn't haf to pay no rent, did you?" Anse asks. He peeps over his big black-rimmed glasses at Boliver.

"No, we didn't," says Boliver. "We jest sorty looked over the land like it was our own. We hunted over the land, picked up the chestnuts and hulled the walnuts in the fall. We gathered all the beechnuts that our hogs didn't git. We let our hogs run out and fatten on the mast. We let our cows run out the year long. They lived on wild pea-vine durin the summer. We raised a patch or two of corn to feed 'em durin the winter. Then they found a lot of dead grass when the snow didn't kiver the land. Our cows allus stayed fat enough fer beef. Durin the summer we dug ginseng roots, May-apple roots and yaller roots and sold them; we picked the wild blackberries, wild strawberries and wild dewberries. We canned all we wanted and sold the rest. Them years was good years. The last years have been hard years. I've been cuttin timber fer the past three years. We've had seven big sawmill sets before we could git all that timber cut and sawed. The wild pea-vines in the coves is all snowed under with dead treetops. The chestnut trees, hickory-nut trees and beech trees have all been cut. The mast is all gone. We can't let our hogs run out any longer. What would our cows have to eat among the dead treetops? Where could we find ginseng, yaller root and May-apple root now to dig? We can't go under that mass of treetops and find 'em. The berry vines air all smothered under the wreckage of trees. We don't have nothin now only what we raised on the clearin patches back of the shack. All that we have left on that big timber tract is a place to hold our dead. Our dead air buried in that land—that land we love."

"You've had a easy life and a good time," says Anse, "all

your days. That was a easy life. While you hunted in the woods,
kicked up your heels and danced at the square dances at plat-
forms built under the trees—while you squatters played your
fiddles, picked your banjers and guitars and lived a easy keer-
free life, I was over on this side of the valley workin like a
brute—clearin land, farmin land and sowin grass. I was savin
my pennies. I knowed the time would come when the last of
the charcoal timberland would disappear. That was the last
tract of it in this county—and I had money waitin to git it
when it was sold under the hammer. It was too close to me.
I had to buy it. Now it must be put into shape like the rest of
my land. I hate to tell you, Boliver, but your good days air
over and you must come under the yoke—jest like a colt hast
to be shod and go to work atter the good days of kickin up his
heels air over—jest like young bull calves in the pasture when
their big hoofs air trimmed down and iron shoes nailed on
their feet. Heavy yokes must go on their necks and when the
drivers git through loggin with 'em—and atter they git old—
they sell 'em fer beef. I aint goin to beef nobody atter he gits
old—but he must come under my yoke if he stays on my land."

"Yes," says Boliver. He looks at the fire dancing above the
dry sticks of wood. He rubs his big hairy hand down his red
briar-stubbled beard.

"All the squatters has come under the yoke," says Boliver.
"They've been run out'n the county but the Beavers and the
Tussies. We're all that's left."

"Jest the Tussies left," says Anse, "fer I give Sheriff Bradley notice to give the Beavers ten days' notice and if they aint
off'n my premises to set 'em off at the boundary line. I'm lettin the Tussies stay over until they can find some place to go.
I'm goin to let your family rent from me if you will agree to
the ar-tickle of agreement. I aint takin no chances on the
Beavers. They aim to try to kill me. It is either I'll kill a few
Beavers 'r they'll git a few Bushmans. It will be the Bushmans
git the Beavers if I can hep it."

"Where did the Beavers go?" Boliver asks.

"I don't know where they went," says Anse. He pulls a cigar from his pocket. "I don't keer where they went. Mort Hargis told me he seed a whole swarm of 'em on the county road with a mule cart loaded with plunder—men and wimmen and children walkin behind—livin on the country as they went—goin some place. They will go anywhere they can find a place to light. You know they didn't have nothin, never had nothin and never wanted nothin. They was a triflin lot and mean as striped-tailed snakes."

"They didn't make much atter they started cuttin timber," says Boliver. "They was ust to the old life. They was ust to the freedom of the hills. They didn't make but a dollar a day cuttin timber. They couldn't keep their cows and hogs like they ust to. They missed their milk and meat. It cost too much when they started buyin it."

"They didn't know how to spend their money," says Anse. "They didn't know the value of a dollar. They'll larn the value now. They'll larn that money has value. They'll larn to treat people right when they git a home. They'll haf to git away from here to git a home. People all over this county knows that name and they don't like it. You know why they don't like it."

"Not exactly," says Boliver.

"Well, they stole so much of this land atter the cordwood was cut off," says Anse. "They had deeds made fer it and they got it. They tried to whop the old settlers out. Plenty of people in this county got their land that way. Don't think the old people don't remember. Don't you believe they will ever fergit either."

"The Tussies didn't git no land," says Boliver. "It would have been better if we had got some land. We would have a place now. I don't want to move from place to place."

"No, the Tussies didn't take any land," says Anse, "I know that to be a fact. That is one reason why I'm givin you a chance to farm on my land this year. Now the Tussies have no home. I'm givin you all a home. I aint afeared anybody will git my land. I had Lawyer John Oscar Simmons to go back over the old deeds. I have a clear deed fer all the land I have. I looked into that before I put my money into the land."

Tarvin and Fronnie sit before the fire and smoke their pipes. They listen to Anse and Boliver talking. They do not talk. It would not do Fronnie and Tarvin any good to say anything, for Anse is the head of the house. Anse is running his farm. He will run everything on the farm long as he can get about. Anse will be master of his acres long as there is breath in his body. Anse was born to rule. Anse was not born to be ruled. Tarvin and Fronnie know this.

"Now this is our ar-tickle," says Anse. He smoothes the paper across his lap in front of him. He bends over and begins to read. Boliver turns his head toward Anse, his chin resting in his hand and his elbow on his leg. He bends over and listens to every word. Tarvin and Fronnie look toward Anse.

5.

"THIS CONTRACT made and entered into this 15th day of March, 1931, by and between Anse Bushman, party of the first part, and Boliver Tussie, party of the second part. Wherein it is agreed that Anse Bushman, party of the first part, does let and rent to Boliver Tussie, party of the second part, a portion of one farm, located on the west side of Ragweed Hollow in Greenwood County, Kentucky, containing approximately five hundred acres; that the said Anse Bushman, party of the first part, shall furnish Boliver Tussie, party of the second part, a three-room house, a garden, potato patch, free of all charges except for the consideration hereafter named; further, and for the same consideration, the said Anse Bushman, party of the first part, shall furnish Boliver Tussie, party of the second part, pasture for two cows.

"The said Boliver Tussie, party of the second part, agrees to farm and cultivate in a diligent manner, fifty acres of corn; the said corn is to be planted and well cultivated, cut and shucked by the said Boliver Tussie, party of the second part; and then, said corn is to be divided by the barrel in the cornfield in the presence of both parties or their agents. Anse Bushman, party of the first part, is to have one-half of said corn and one-half of fodder; and Boliver Tussie, party of the second part, is to have the other half of said corn and the other half of said fodder. The said Boliver Tussie, party of the second part, is to haul said Anse Bushman's half of the corn and fodder to said Anse Bushman's barn, sort the said corn and throw the big ears in one crib and the nubbin-corn in another crib and house the fodder in the barnloft.

"That means," says Anse removing his glasses slowly and wiping his eyes with his hands after the laborious task of reading the contract, "that you air to put my corn and fodder in either one of the three barns that I want it in. I'll tell you when we gather the corn this fall, where I want you to put it."

"That's a lot of corn to farm in newground," says Boliver. "It will take a lot of work to dig out fifty acres of corn among these big stumps and rocks on these steep hills."

"You air right," says Anse, gesturing with his hand as he talks, "but if you and your family works, you can do it all right. This aint all I want you to do. This just takes keer of the house, garden, tater patch, cow pasture and corn."

Anse puts his glasses back over his eyes. He picks up the contract and reads again.

"The said Boliver Tussie, party of the second part, agrees to raise and diligently cultivate, and prepare for market, five acres of tobacco on said farm; and said tobacco is to be marketed at an equal expense to both parties, sold in their names as partners at the tobacco warehouses in Maysville, Kentucky; and the returns are to be divided, one-half going to said Anse

Bushman, party of the first part, and the other half going to Boliver Tussie, party of the second part."

"The reason I put in the contract that we sell our terbacker at the Maysville warehouses," says Anse, looking over his glasses at Boliver, "is that I'm afeared that you might want to sell the terbacker crop to some pin-hooker that talks you into sellin your crop fer nothin. I've been stung by 'em before. I've been over the road in this terbacker game. I know what can happen, fer it has happened to me."

"That's all right," says Boliver. "You know more about it than I do. All the terbacker I've ever raised has been fer our own use. I know how to raise it. I never raised that big a crop before. It's a big field of terbacker to raise when a body has a big corn crop."

"That aint much," says Anse. "I've raised forty acres of terbacker and a big corn crop. If you make any money you got to work. You just remember what I tell you. Boliver Tussie wants to make money, don't he?"

"Yes," says Boliver.

"Then he's got to work," says Anse. "He can't set in the shade of the oak trees and dream money into his pockets. I want 'im to make money fer hisself and money fer me."

Anse begins to read the contract again.

"The said Boliver Tussie, party of the second part, further agrees to raise and diligently cultivate, and prepare for market, five acres of cane at an equal expense to both parties; and sorghum molasses made from said cane, is to be divided at the mill, one-half going to said Anse Bushman, party of the first part, and the other half going to Boliver Tussie, party of the second part; the cane blades and cane tops are to be equally divided between Anse Bushman, party of the first part, and Boliver Tussie, party of the second part.

"The said Anse Bushman, party of the first part, is to furnish Boliver Tussie, party of the second part, a span of mules to use for plowing and hauling, seeds and working tools. Said Boliver Tussie, party of the second part, is to be responsible for said span of mules, if he hurts or maims in any way said mules, unless by act of God, such as thunder, lightning, storm, said Boliver Tussie, party of the second part, will pay for said mules from contents of the crop. Said Boliver Tussie, party of the second part, is responsible for all tools that are broken, lost and stolen. Said Boliver Tussie, party of the second part, must pay for said tools at a fair and reasonable price, by money, or labor (at one dollar per day) or from contents of crop.

"Said Anse Bushman, party of the first part, is to furnish Boliver Tussie, party of the second part, with orders to Grubb's General Merchandise Store, in Greenwood, Kentucky, until the crop is made if said Boliver Tussie needs credit; said Anse Bushman, party of the first part, will assume said credit for Boliver Tussie at said store; Boliver Tussie, party of the second part, paying account to said Anse Bushman, party of the first part from his crop at harvest time."

"I like that part of the ar-tickle," says Boliver. "I've jist been wonderin how I's goin to git grub fer the family and tend all that crop. I aint got nothin to go on but a few taters and canned berries."

"That will all be taken care of," says Anse. He removes his glasses and wipes his eyes with his hand. He looks straight at Boliver. "I've allus said it took grub under the belt—grub that would stick to the ribs and plenty of it fer a hard-workin family in crop time. When you dig and plow among roots and rocks it takes a powerful lot of grub. I eat like a hoss when I work. I eat sow-belly, soup beans, turnip greens, corn dodger bread—grub that will stick to the ribs. The reason I said Grubb's General Merchandise Store in the contract is, I trade with Grubbs. I've traded with 'em forty years. Old John Grubb's word is good as gold. He buys from me, too, and I buy from 'im."

"It makes no difference where I git grub," says Boliver, "jest so I git grub."

"Now this takes keer of the crops," says Anse, "the house garden, tater patch, the mules, seeds, workin tools—I've got a few more things in this contract that I want to read you. They may not set well on your stummick and you may not mind. I don't know. I do know that I want an understandin between us."

"I want that too," says Boliver. "I want to know what to do and what not to do."

Anse puts his glasses over his nose. He puts the black celluloid frames behind his ears and he continues to read.

"Said Boliver Tussie, party of the second part, will not be allowed to have any dances, any sort of frolicking in said Anse Bushman's house until the crops are laid by and until the crops are harvested. Said Anse Bushman, party of the first part, will not tolerate this because Boliver Tussie, party of the second part, will not be in any condition to work after long nights of frolicking in crop time.

"Said Boliver Tussie, party of the second part, will not be allowed to fish from beginning of crop season until the end of crop season. Said Anse Bushman, party of the first part, regards fishing during the summer as a waste of time and costly to crops.

"Said Boliver Tussie, party of the second part, will not be allowed to make moonshine whiskey on the property of Anse Bushman at any time. Said Anse Bushman, party of the first part, will not tolerate moonshine making on his premises at any time or under any consideration. If said Boliver Tussie, party of the second part, or any member of his family is caught directly or indirectly operating a moonshine still and making illegal whiskey, his entire crop and all the work he has done is to fall into the hands of Anse Bushman without any cost and he is to vacate Anse Bushman's premises within ten days.

"That's one thing I won't stand," says Anse looking at Boliver. "I know there's plenty of moonshine goin on over on the farm I bought. When the wind blowed this way all last summer, I could smell moonshine whiskey poured from the still. The Government can take a body's property when the Revenuers find a still on it. The Lord aint kind to moonshiners nohow. Look what happens to 'em. Git in jail, in the pen—and lose all the money they make makin moonshine. Lots of 'em lose their eyesights. Here fer a while I never saw so many blind men. I never saw so many men walkin on canes with the jake-leg. Moonshinin don't pay."

Boliver does not say anything. He turns and looks toward the fire. Anse resumes reading the contract to Boliver.

"Said Boliver Tussie, party of the second part, will not be permitted, nor members of his family be permitted, to attend church revivals more than two nights out of each week. Said Anse Bushman, party of the first part, knows it is extremely dangerous to crops by past experiences; and said Anse Bushman, party of the first part, furthermore believes if his renters want to pray and worship God, they can do it at home and their prayers will be answered at home same as they will be at church.

"Said Boliver Tussie, party of the second part, will not be allowed to bring a baby into his home each year. Said Anse Bushman, party of the first part, will not tolerate this since he knows by past experience it is extremely dangerous when the crops needs attention; when the season is here it is time to work and every available hand is needed in the field."

"Why is that?" Boliver asks looking strangely at Anse. "Some things a body can't hep."

"If you have a baby at your house," says Anse, "I know who'll haf to foot the Doctor's bill. It will be old Anse Bushman, party of the first part."

"I aint so shore about that," says Boliver. "We aint had no Doctors yit."

"Maybe not," says Anse, "but it takes a hand out'n the field and with the crop you'll have in, you'll need every hand you've got."

"Guess you're right," says Boliver. "Go ahead with the contract."

"Said Boliver Tussie, party of the second part, will not be permitted to engage in, nor allow among members of his family, any immoral conduct; he will not be allowed to harbor on his premises person or persons of immoral conduct; said Anse Bushman, party of the first part, will not allow nor tolerate people living on his premises to engage in any kind of immoral conduct.

"If either party fails to do as herein described and mentioned, this contract becomes void and the party breaking contract is to turn entire crop to other party without any trouble and vacate premises within ten days, and if not broken and it is said Anse Bushman's wish, said Boliver Tussie agrees to vacate said Anse Bushman's premises on or before the 15th day of March, 1932."

"Now air you willin to sign?" Anse asks. He drops the contract on his lap and removes his glasses. He wipes his eyes as if a hard task is done.

"I don't like what it says about babies," says Boliver. "I can't hep it if one comes sooner than we expect it."

Boliver looks at the fire. Tarvin looks at Fronnie and Fronnie looks at Anse. There is silence in the firelit room.

"But I don't want to leave," says Boliver. "I ain't got no place to go unless I leave the country. I can't write my name, Mr. Bushman. I'll haf to make my cross and you sign fer me."

"All right," says Anse. "Make your cross right here."

Anse holds his big stubby index finger on the spot for Boliver to make his cross. Boliver takes Anse's pencil and scrawls two uneven lines crossing midway. Anse writes Boliver's name on the paper.

"Now," says Anse, "our ar-tickle is signed. It is an under-

standin down in word and ciphers. It is down in black and
white. Fronnie you be first witness to our signatures."

Fronnie takes the pencil. She scribbles her name down as
first witness. Tarvin takes the pencil from his mother. He
writes his name down as the last signature.

"I have two copies of this ar-tickle," says Anse, "one fer
you to keep and one fer me to keep. Now let's git our signatures on the other copy. You can take either copy you want to
take."

Anse sits before the fire. He fondles his beard and smokes a
cigar. He blows the blue clouds of smoke toward the ceiling.
Tarvin sits before the fire and blows out small clouds of smoke
from his pipe. Fronnie sits between Anse and Tarvin and
smokes her long-stemmed clay pipe. There is silence in the
room. Anse holds the contract. It is the first time Anse has
ever had a renter on his farm. Anse has always done his own
work. He has lived his own life and he has helped other members of his family to live their lives. Anse feels that he is the
head of his family and he is ordered by God to run his own
home according to the dictates of his own conscience, and to

help direct the lives of all connected directly or indirectly with him and his premises.

Boliver walks down the hollow. The folded contract sticks from his hip pocket. Night is coming on; the March sun is going down beyond the ridge. Boliver can feel the sharpness in the March air that is close akin to the clear cool nights of October. Boliver's brogan shoes grit on the hard crust of frozen earth. There is the silence of death on the earth about him, silence among the dark naked trees that stand listlessly on the stubborn slopes waiting for green leaves to burst from their boughs, and blooms to burst suddenly from their buds.

PART IV

1.

ANSE, TARVIN and Fronnie finish milking the cows. Anse lights his cigar. Fronnie smokes her pipe. The shoats bite each other and squeal over the scraps of bread left in the trough. The pigs have eaten until their sides looked puffed out like the sides of a toad-frog. They lie down by the side of the trough and grunt. They get their breath hard. Anse swings a big bucket of milk at each side as he walks out the path toward the house. Fronnie follows Anse with two big buckets of milk.

Tarvin puts the harness on Jack and Barney. He fastens red tassels to their bridles. He polishes the leather straps on the harness with an oily rag. He takes a currycomb and combs the mules' backs, flanks, shoulders and bellies. He sleeks down their hides with a brush. "They must look good," Tarvin thinks. Tarvin works like a Kentucky redbird building her nest in the spring. "Mules must look purty this mornin."

Tarvin drives the mules out past the house. Anse and Fronnie walk out from the cellar as Tarvin drives up to the pine trees in the front yard and stops. Tarvin is singing:

> "The last time I saw Darlin Cora,
> She was sittin on the bank by the sea;
> With a big forty-four around her waist
> And a banjer on her knee—
> With a big forty-four around her waist,
> And a banjer on her knee."

187

"You're shore happy this mornin," says Anse. "Son, you act pliam-blank like a spring redbird buildin a nest." Anse laughs and blows smoke from his cigar. He twists his long red beard with his big rough hand. Fronnie stands by the pine tree and smokes her pipe. She looks at Tarvin standing in the wagon bed. Tarvin is wearing clean overalls, a clean blue shirt, his checkered hawk-billed cap and a sweater. Tarvin has his low-cut slippers shined.

"What air you all dressed up fer, Son?" Fronnie asks. "Looks like you might be goin to a protracted meetin, a funeral 'r a dance."

"You air dressin up to do some hard work, Son," says Anse. "I allus hated the job of movin people."

"I like to move people," says Tarvin. "I jest love to do it. Jest to think you air takin people to a new place. I'll be movin Subrinea to a better house."

"I'd never looked at it like that, Tarvin," says Anse. "I've never seen the mules all dressed up like that to git down and haf to pull on a muddy road. Won't look like that by the time you git Tussies moved over on the hill. You've even got the jolt-wagon brushed up."

"Yep, I brushed the old buggy up a little yesterday," says Tarvin. "Atter you told me to move Tussies, I went to work to git the mules and wagon lookin good."

"Be careful, Son," says Anse. "Don't have any bad luck. I 'spect you'll be able to haul all their house plunder at one load. Them mules could pull that slab shack they live in, house plunder and the family if you could git it all on the wagon."

Tarvin stands in the wagon bed. His head is up among the lower limbs on the pine tree. Tarvin looks good in his clean clothes in the warm March sunshine. Tarvin looks happier than he has ever looked. He fondles the leather check lines in his hands. He looks at the sleek-combed mules. "Git up, Jack and Barney," he says. He shakes the leather check lines and lets the wagon brake off. The mules step briskly down the road.

The heavy wagon wheels make heavy sounding rattles as the wagon rolls along. It leaves the prints of the heavy wheels in the yellow clay bank below the house as it rolls over the hill. Tarvin puts the brakes on as the wagon shoves against the mules' breastyoke.

"Mules air powerful things," says Anse to Fronnie. "If it wasn't fer mules and cattle God knows how we'd conquer these hills. Mules air tough as hickory sprouts. When it comes to plowin these hills, it takes mules to stand these steep hills and these roots."

"And that is a powerful fine boy in the wagon drivin the mules away," says Fronnie. "I can't hep it if I do haf to brag on my own boy. He's good to work and he's got good judgement about things."

"I aint so shore about his judge-ment about wimmen," says Anse. "Honey, when I's a young man you wouldn't see me runnin around with a squatter gal. You never heerd of it, did you?"

"No, Anse, I never heerd of it if you did," says Fronnie. She blows a wisp of smoke from her pipe that circles in a tiny cloud up among the green branches of the yard pine tree. "Times have changed, Anse, and people don't look down on the squatters like they did when we was young. Aint many squatters left now. Ust to be so many of 'em. People jest look on 'em and think of 'em as folks like the rest of us now. They've got to have a place to live like other people. They air people like we air, Anse."

"I've changed a lot too, Fronnie," says Anse. "You know, I wouldn't a-let a squatter set his foot on my land if I'd a-knowed it ten years ago. Now, I'm lettin one move on my place. I'm wonderin what old Ed Justice, Tom Rankins, Jad Jenkins and a few of the old boys will think of me."

"It won't matter what they think, Anse," says Fronnie.

"Tarvin's caused me to do it," says Anse. "Out of all eleven children we've had, Tarvin's the only one that's stood by us.

We owe a lot to Tarvin. I'd do purt nigh anything fer that boy. He's got to take over here one of these days, Fronnie. It aint goin to be long as it has been nohow. You know we aint young as we ust to be. I've jest been thinkin that I've lived my span of years. The Word says threescore and ten is a good long life fer a man. I'm goin beyond that. Life, then, becomes uncertain."

Anse looks down the hollow to watch Tarvin make the last turn in the Ragweed Hollow road. Fronnie watches Tarvin as he rolls out of sight around the curve. Tarvin stands in the wagon straight as a cove-poplar sapling. The check lines are in one hand, the brake beam is in the other hand. The heavy wagon rolls down the hollow behind the giant span of mules.

2.

TARVIN SEES a redbird on the bank above him. It sings in the leafless brush. It is a pretty redbird. It is the rooster redbird. Its feathers are red as beef blood. It sings to its mate. The mate answers the rooster redbird. Tarvin sees the hen redbird. She is up on the hill picking up straws. She plucks a brown straw of bull grass from the slope. She flies through the brush up the hill. Her feathers are not as red as the rooster's feathers. "That looks good to me," thinks Tarvin, as he whistles and drives the mules along. "That is a shore sign that spring is jest around on yan side of the hill. These old winter-scarred hills will soon be clothed in green. Lord, but I do love the redbirds. It jest looks so good and makes a body so happy to see 'em back among the hills in the early spring."

Tarvin drives down Ragweed Hollow. He turns to his right at Cat's Fork. He drives up the timber road. He looks at the brown slopes on each side of the road. He whistles and sings as his mules step briskly along. He drives up Cat's Fork until he comes to the tall trees of Heaven. As he gets closer he can see the white March clouds rolling across the blue March skies that are far above the trees of Heaven. Tarvin stops his mules beneath the trees of Heaven.

"The little mounds over there," thinks Tarvin, "is where Subrinea buried the lambs. Subrinea hast to have a good heart in her. She has a heart that feels fer life that can't hep itself. Subrinea is a good girl to work. She is a purty girl. She aint like a lot of her people. I am in love with Subrinea. She jest seems like she belongs to me now."

Tarvin looks at the little mounds beneath the trees of Heaven. They are not the mounds where the lambs are buried. They are the little mounds where the squatters have been buried for the past hundred years. Tarvin can see the ugly field stones at the head and foot of her people's graves. He can see the green bunches of wild ferns planted on their graves. There are rows of graves under the trees of Heaven. Tarvin does not whistle and sing now. He sits silently on the wagon seat. He looks over the barren earth that holds her dead. There are sprouts grown up beside the graves. There are clumps of briars growing there. There are wild iris, trillium and percoon springing from their leaf-covered mounds.

"People of the past," thinks Tarvin. "They didn't waste their lives away buyin land and more land and workin like brutes to pay fer land like Pa has. They didn't work their wives like Pa has worked Ma. They took life easier and I don't know but what it was better. They lived from the land until they's crowded off'n the land and squeezed up on too little a boundary of land. They lived sorty wild and free and thought life would go on forever like this fer their people. They didn't look fer the future. They lived while they lived. They come at last from these hills to this plot of ground beneath these trees of Heaven. It is a good place to be buried, too. It's the purtiest place among these hills. It's the only timber in this big boundary they hunted over that is left. It marks the last remains of a bygone people. This makes me love Subrinea more. I'll marry Subrinea. I don't care what my people

think. I don't care what her people think. I know her mother
wants me to marry her. She is the only one. By God, I'll marry
her. I don't care what anybody thinks. I haf to live my life.
They can't live my life fer me. I know who I want to live with.
I'm the one that's doin the marryin."

Tarvin shakes the check lines. He lets the brake loose on
the wagon. The lively mules step up the hollow toward the
slab shack on the hill. Tarvin looks back from the wagon at
the trees of Heaven. He remembers the days and the nights he
has met Subrinea here. He remembers the trees of Heaven in
summer when he could smell them and when their tops waved
with pretty blossoms against the heavens. He remembers the
words Subrinea has said to him here. He remembers the moonlit nights when he has held her tall ghostlike body close against
his own—when he has looked into her green eyes and has
seen the colors of green leaves in her eyes. He remembers the
nights when he has seen the petals of the bloodroot in her
teeth. He remembers the nights when he has felt the torrents
of snow-melted waters rushing in her veins. Subrinea is the
forest, earth, flowers, water, and everything on the land.
Subrinea is made of the earth. She is more beautiful than the
earth. Tarvin cannot forget her. She is with Tarvin all the time.
She has become an unforgettable part of him.

As Tarvin reins the mules around the curve in the road by
the ash log, he sees the slab shack in the morning sunlight. He
sees Boliver Tussie, Crissie, Subrinea and the children in the
yard waiting. The house plunder has been carried outside of
the shack. It is waiting to be loaded on the wagon and hauled
away. Tarvin rises from the wagon seat and stands with the
leather check lines in both hands now. He does not need to
handle the brake, for the mules pull the wagon up the bank.
He reins the mules in a circle, and he drives beside the furniture. He has the mules heading down the hollow. He is ready
for the furniture to be loaded.

"Good mornin, young man," says Boliver.

"Good mornin," says Crissie. "I'm glad you've come."

"Good mornin," says Subrinea.

"Good mornin," says Tarvin. "I'm glad to be here. I've seen two redbirds on my way. They have made me happy. Spring is here."

"You air right," says Boliver. "Spring is right on us. I want to git to my new home. I want to start my new work."

"We'll soon be there," says Tarvin. "Jest this one load. I can take all there is here but I don't believe I can haul the family."

"Oh, we'll walk," says Boliver. "Shucks, it aint no fur piece around up the creek past the Coon Den Holler over to that house. We can walk it in 'n hour."

Tarvin ties the check lines to the jolt-wagon brake beam. He climbs down from the wagon. "These aint runaway mules," says Tarvin, "but I jest aim to be shore they don't run away. Now I'll need some hep here loadin this house plunder."

"You've got plenty of it," says Boliver. "Big Aaron, you and Snail git in here and hep us now. Snail is a hoss on a lift."

Crissie, Subrinea and the little girls stand by and watch Tarvin, Boliver, Big Aaron and Snail load the furniture on the wagon. " 'Spect I'll haf to dump the corn-shucks from the bed-ticks," Boliver says, "before we can git all the plunder on the wagon."

"Nope, jest throw 'em upon the wagon," says Tarvin. "We'll rope 'em down. I can take all that's here and the house, too, if we could load it on."

"We don't want the house," says Subrinea. "We'll leave it where it is. I'm glad to git to a better house."

"It's the first time I've ever moved from this land," says Boliver. "I've lived here all my life. My people lived here before me. I'll still be farmin on this land."

They load the beds, stove, safe, chairs, bedticks—all their furniture on the wagon. Tarvin ties ropes to the front beam of the wagon bed and throws them back over the load of furniture. Boliver and Big Aaron pull the ropes over the wagonload of furniture, and tie them to the beam on the rear part of the wagon. They tie ropes to the side of the wagon bed and throw them across the load of furniture. They pull the ropes tightly and tie them. The furniture is tied until it can't move.

"I'll ride with you, Tarvin," says Subrinea. She climbs upon the wagonload of furniture with Tarvin. She sits where she can handle the brake. Tarvin climbs up beside her.

"Do you suppose I'll haf to rough-lock the wheels goin over this bank?" Tarvin asks Subrinea.

"Not if the brakes air good," says Subrinea. "I can stand with my weight on the brake beam and rough-lock both hind wheels."

"Good fer you," says Tarvin. "The brakes air good. They will hold."

"Farewell, old shack," says Subrinea.

"Good-by to everything here," says Boliver—"great huntin days, dances, hard work and good times."

"Good-by to the place where all you youngins was born," says Crissie. "I'm glad to git away. But this is one spot in this big wide world that I can't fergit."

Tarvin sees Crissie walking down the hill with a baby in her arms. He sees Boliver walking along leading two hound dogs. The children follow. Each is carrying a load in his arms—a picture, a pitcher—something that might be broken if hauled on the wagon. Tarvin and Subrinea see them walk down the path toward the spring. They will walk up the little creek and over past the big chestnut tree coon den where Tarvin and Subrinea sawed the wood last winter. They will walk into Ragweed Hollow here. They will walk up the hollow to the shack on the hill. Tarvin and Subrinea must follow the timber road down Cat's Fork and turn to their left up Ragweed Hollow. They must follow a road that is wide enough for a wagon.

"Set on the brakes, Subrinea," says Tarvin. "I'm ready to start the mules."

Subrinea stands on the brake beam. She holds to the furniture. Both hind wheels are rough-locked until they slide over

the dirt. Tarvin reins the mules carefully over the bank. He chooses the best parts of the road. He dodges the big stumps, trees and rocks. He avoids the ditches. The big wagon behind the span of powerful mules rolls slowly and clumsily over the yellow clay bank to the oxen road. Tarvin stops the mules. Subrinea releases the brake. The mules step briskly now down the hollow with the load of furniture.

"Aint this the purtiest day you might' nigh ever seen?" Tarvin asks Subrinea.

"Yep, it is," says Subrinea. "I'm jest as happy as a spring redbird, too."

"I am too," says Tarvin. "Don't know why unless it's you movin closter to my home. Jest seems like you ort to be there."

Subrinea smiles. She sits beside Tarvin on a bedtick. They can look down on the backs of the mules. The wagon rolls down the hollow, past the ash log beside the road. It rolls around the turn in the road.

"Look, Tarvin," says Subrinea. She points to the trees of Heaven. "This is a place I can't fergit."

"I can't either," says Tarvin.

"Whoa, boys. Whoa-ho."

The mules come to a stop. Tarvin and Subrinea sit silently on the wagonload of furniture. They look at the tall trees above them. The trees' slender bodies seem to reach the sky. They look at the graves below them. They can see the ugly field stones dotting the earth under the trees of Heaven. Subrinea turns her eyes from the graves. She looks at Tarvin. She pulls him close to her. She kisses his lips.

"Let's move on," says Subrinea.

"Git up, Jack and Barney," says Tarvin. He shakes the leather check lines. He lets them go slack. The mules start quickly, lifting their front feet high in the wind as if they are pawing the wind. The wagon rolls down Cat's Fork to Ragweed Hollow. The air is filled with sunlight. There is a layer of mud on top of the earth now. The sun has melted the top layer of the half-frozen earth. Mud cakes on the wheel rims and gathers among the heavy wagon-wheel spokes as the big wheels roll over and over.

"This load will be hard pullin up this holler," says Tarvin. "We air goin up grade all the way. But these mules will pull this load. A little mud won't matter to them. Take the lines a few minutes, Subrinea."

Subrinea takes the lines and drives the mules. Tarvin fills his pipe with the ripe burley tobacco crumbs. He tamps them down securely in his pipe. He strikes a match on his shoe. He lights his pipe. He blows swirls of smoke out to the morning wind. He takes the lines from Subrinea and drives the mules. The wagon rolls over the thin layer of mud up Ragweed Hollow. They drive slowly along until they reach the cliffs where Anse has a grove of chestnut oaks.

"Stop the mules, Tarvin," says Subrinea. "Look over yander on that bank. It is white as cotton. Look at the bloodroot."

Tarvin stops the mules. The mules' sides go in and out like a bee-smoker.

"Mules need windin anyway," says Tarvin. "I'll bet I can guess what you want."

"Bet you can't."

"All right, you want me to go over there on the bank and pick you a bouquet of percoon. Now aint that what you want? Tell the truth!"

"Yes, it is," says Subrinea. She smiles and looks at Tarvin. "How could you guess it, Smarty?"

"I know you too well, Subrinea," says Tarvin. "I know how you air about wild flowers. But it is spring now. We air all wantin to see the wild flowers bloom."

"They look so purty over there," says Subrinea. "I jest want a few of 'em."

"All right," says Tarvin. "Hold the lines. I know the mules air glad you air on this wagon."

Subrinea holds the lines. Tarvin climbs off the wagon. He walks lickety-split through the sloppy mud. He crosses the creek and climbs the bluff on the other side. He pulls up the bluff by holding to the chestnut-oak trees. He climbs up among the cliffs. He picks a bouquet of sweet-smelling snow-white tender blossoms of spring bloodroot for Subrinea. He scoots back down the hill to the hollow—crosses the creek and walks back to the wagon.

"Here, Honey," he says. He reaches the wisp of bloodroot blossoms up on the wagon to Subrinea.

"Thank you," Subrinea says. Tarvin climbs back upon the wagon.

"Here's another thank you," Subrinea says. She kisses Tarvin. "That kiss is for your labor. Honey, when you scooted down the bluff you got the seat of your pants muddy."

"Yes, I can feel the dampness too," says Tarvin. "That cold wet mud soaks right through a body's pants."

"Another thank you," says Subrinea. She kisses Tarvin again.

"Give me the lines now," says Tarvin. "The mules have rested long enough."

Subrinea hands Tarvin the check lines.

"Git-up, Jack and Barney. Let's be goin, boys!"

Tarvin slackens the lines. The mules brace their rear legs, twist their bodies and start the heavy wagon rolling up the hollow. The green ferns look over the rocky bluffs at the blue creek water below them. May-apple patches are springing here and there. Mouse's-ear has started to grow from the earth. Green briars are showing tiny tendrils of green. Alders are sprouting tiny tender leaves. The brilliant sunshine of March is playing over the dark desolate hills of early spring. Birds chirrup brightly. They sing spring songs of love and work. Life is beginning to spring from the loamy earth.

"Talk about a change in these hills," says Tarvin. "You jest wait until atter the first thunder showers. We'll have plenty of wild flowers, green swellin buds, terrapins, turtles, lizards, frogs and snakes. That's the trumpet that wakes the livin spring from its long winter sleep."

"Yes, Honey," says Subrinea, "but you jest look over yander on that bluff."

"More flowers," says Tarvin. "I'll tell you that before I look."

"Honey, you air so smart," says Subrinea. "Yes, it's more flowers."

"Trillium?" Tarvin asks.

"Yes, how did you know?" Subrinea asks.

"I've already been to that patch."

"Git me some of the blooms to go with this bloodroot."

"If the mules could talk, they would thank you."

"Poor mules air tired. They need rest."

"Whoa-ho, boys. Whoa-ho."

"See how quick they stop."

"Here, you hold the lines."

Tarvin scoots down off the wagon. He walks across the hollow to the rocky bluff. The steep slope is blue with wild trillium. Tarvin jumps over the broad creek. He plucks the tender stems of trillium for Subrinea until his big hand is filled with the flowers. "This is shore purty," says Tarvin, "and it smells plenty good."

Subrinea watches Tarvin leap the broad creek with his long legs. He does it with ease. She looks at his tanned face, his big muscular arms, and his big hand around the bunch of tender flowers. Tarvin walks up to the wagon. Subrinea bends over and takes the flowers as Tarvin reaches them up to her. "Here, Honey, is my thank you," she says. She bends down, holding with one hand to the rope that holds the furniture. She kisses Tarvin.

"I'm jest goin to start carryin you wild flowers all the time now that they have come," says Tarvin. "I like the thanks you give me."

Tarvin laughs. Subrinea takes the wild trillium and puts it with her wisp of bloodroot blossoms. Tarvin climbs back on the wagon. He takes out his tobacco pouch and pours the light burley crumbs in his pipe. He tamps them down in his pipe with his index finger. He strikes a match on his shoe and lights his pipe. Subrinea hands him the check lines.

"Git along, boys. Git-up, Jack and Barney!"

The mules slowly press against their collars, zigzagging their powerful bodies against the heavy load. Tarvin blows out wisps of smoke as the wagon rattles slowly up the twisted snake-curved road behind the straining mules. Tarvin guides them so the big wheels will not hit a chug-hole, ditch, stump or big rock in the road.

"Hope we don't find any more flowers," says Tarvin. "Your folks might wonder if we aint got lost with the furniture. It's time we's rollin in there now."

"Honey, we can tell 'em the mules needed to rest along,"

says Subrinea, "and you know they have needed to rest. They air pullin a heavy load."

The road before them is a rough road. There are little banks to climb and little banks to go down. Tarvin guides the mules up past the old charcoal pits where the earth is black and deep with ashes. He crosses the creek and bends to his left under the giant beech grove on his father's farm. He crosses the creek again and turns to his right. He drives across a little bottom, under a grove of tall poplar trees. He goes down a little bank and crosses the creek again where the sawmill used to stand.

"We'll let the mules wind a minute," says Tarvin, "before we tackle that hill. Honey, we'll haf to git off'n the wagon here. You'll haf to follow behind and chock the wheel. Jest haf to let 'em pull a little at a time up that steep bluff."

Tarvin and Subrinea climb off the wagon. Subrinea takes the lines while Tarvin looks around to find a rock. Tarvin turns over several rocks. They are flat rocks. He finds a big thick rock. It is partly round.

"Here's the rock," says Tarvin. "It will hold the wheel."

Tarvin and Subrinea stand beside the wagon. They watch the mules pant. Subrinea holds her bunch of flowers. She puts them to her nose and smells. She looks at them. She looks at Tarvin and the sweaty mules. There are blotches of mud over their sleek bodies now. Their hind legs are muddy to their hocks. Their front legs are muddy to their knees.

"Honey, you will haf to lay your flowers down," says Tarvin. "This is a hard hill to pull and you'll haf to use both hands. Now let's git ready."

"All right, boys," says Tarvin gently to the mules. He rubs Barney's back. He pats his shoulder. The big mules brace their hind feet against the earth—digging out tiny holes in the earth as they strain against the ioad. The wagon moves slowly. Tarvin drives and climbs the spokes in the rear wagon wheel—giving all the weight in his body to help turn the wheel.

Subrinea follows with the round rock. The mules climb half-way up the bluff. They get slower and they breathe harder.

"Chock the wheel," Tarvin shouts.

Subrinea puts the big rock under the wagon wheel. The wheel drops back against the rock. Tarvin pulls the brakes down to rough-lock the wheels. The mules rest their bodies. They let their muscles relax. They stand on the bluff and get their breath hard.

"All set," says Tarvin, "let's go again."

"All right, boys," says Tarvin, "let's go to the top this time."

The mules know what Tarvin says. As they strain against the load, Tarvin lets the brake beam up. The mules pull the wagon snail-slow until they go over the steepest part of the bluff. Subrinea follows the wagon carrying the rock. If the mules fail to pull the wagon to the top of the bluff, she will have the rock to chock the wheels.

"Good boys!" says Tarvin as they reach the top of the bluff. "See, you never haf to whop these mules to make 'em pull. All you haf to do is speak to 'em. They do the rest."

The mules stand at the top of the bluff. They lean their bodies forward against their load. They get their breath hard and fast. Subrinea goes back down the bluff to get her wisp of flowers. Tarvin holds the check lines in one hand. He rubs Jack's shoulders with the other. He speaks kind words to the mules. Subrinea comes up the bluff carrying her flowers.

"It don't tire you to run up and down the hills," says Tarvin.

"No, fer I'm ust to it," says Subrinea. "I am lean and tall. My breath comes easy fer me. My legs never git tired. I can run all day and never git tired."

Subrinea's cheeks are flushed red. Drops of sweat cling to her forehead. They shine like white soup beans in the March sunlight. Sweat runs in tiny streams and drips from Tarvin's forehead. Sweat drips from the flanks and the bellies of the mules.

"Git-up, boys," says Tarvin. "Come along. This is your last pull."

The mules strain for their last time against the heavy load. They roll it along over the newground road to the little shack. Boliver and Crissie are waiting for the furniture at the house.

"We's about to give you out a-comin," says Boliver. "Thought you might a-got stuck sommers."

"Didn't git stuck," says Subrinea, "but it's been a hard load fer the mules to pull up this holler. You ought to jest go out there and look how that bluff is skived up where the mules dug in with their hoofs to pull this load."

"Thank God it's here," says Crissie. "We want to git the stove set up first so we can git a bite of dinner."

"We'll jest set the plunder off on the ground," says Boliver, "so Tarvin can git home with the mules. The mules air gittin hungry too."

Tarvin, Boliver, Big Aaron and Snail untie the ropes and set the load of furniture off in the yard. Tarvin and Boliver lift the stove from the wagon. Tarvin helps Boliver carry it into the house. Subrinea and Crissie carry loads of clothes and dishes into the house.

"Thank God," says Boliver, "we air in our new home at last. It's the first time in my life that I've lived off'n Cat's Fork of Ragweed Hollow."

"It's sicha purty place," says Crissie. "The house is so much better here. We have glass in our winders. We can make this sicha purty place in the summertime. I've jest been lookin around here at the place where I can plant flowers."

"We can see your house from here," says Subrinea. "But it's a fur piece over there to it."

"Jest across Ragweed Holler," says Tarvin, "and up on yan bank a piece. It aint fur. Jest a pipe of terbacker fer me."

"I'll be gittin a snack for dinner," says Crissie, "while you all carry in the old contraptions."

"All right, Ma," says Subrinea.

"Ma, I'm awful hungry," says Snail.

"I'd better be gittin over the hill," says Tarvin. "Pa's been expectin me back fer some time now. The road was muddier than I'd expected it'd be."

Tarvin climbs into the wagon bed. He takes the reins. He lifts the brake beam. "Git up, Jack and Barney."

Tarvin slackens the check lines. Jack and Barney move the empty wagon with ease. They step mildly over the road the way they came. Tarvin lets them trot over the bluff, across the creek, under the beech grove, down over the charcoal hearth and down alongside the rocky bluffs. Tarvin turns to his left and goes up the left fork of Ragweed Hollow where his house stands.

Tarvin sings as he drives the mules up the bank below the house. He whistles as he drives by the pine tree in the front yard. He takes the mules to the barn. He unhitches them from the wagon. He takes the harness from the mules and hangs it in their stalls. He takes the mules to water. He forks down hay into their mangers. He puts ten ears of yellow corn into each mule's feed box.

"The trip is over, boys," says Tarvin. "You jest done fine."

He pats each mule's nose as he rolls the ears of corn over into his box.

3.

"Now Boliver," says Anse, "I've jest come over to tell you that I can see the smoke from your chimney. It don't look good. Looks like we've got neighbors near us fer the first time in our lives. I jest want to tell you now is the time to fire this big hill on this side the Ragweed Hollow road. The fire will jest about clean your crop land fer you."

Boliver stands at the wood-block hacking off sticks of woods from dry locust poles. He stands with his ax handle in one hand. He has one hand on his hip. Anse stands on the other side of the wood-block and points to the hill across the hollow from Boliver's house.

"That is the hill I aim fer you to take," says Anse. "God Almighty, it will be a sight to see the corn that hill will fetch. Damned if a man don't might' near sink up in them big black loamy coves. I've jest come around that hill. I'd like fer you to fire that and burn that hill before the sun brings out all the lizards and the black snakes. If you fire the hill atter they git out, the fire will git about all of 'em. Lizards air sicha good flyketchers and the black snakes git the moles and the mice."

"It's gittin about time," says Boliver, "that a body wants to git his ground ready to plant. A body ought to have the ground stuck full of seed next month. It's the time to burn now while the March leaves air dry. It's hard to burn woods atter the big spring thunder showers come and wet the ground and bring the green back to the hills."

"You git a ring raked up this holler back to the ridge road," says Anse. "We can fire from this holler and let the fire burn up the hill. We can fire from my pasture from yan side. We can fire from the ridge road all the way around the hilltop and let the fires meet each other."

"That will jest about clean the land," says Boliver.

"Won't be much left," says Anse. "Jest a few black brands to pick up and a few old rotten logs to pile and a bent-down saplin here and there to cut. Fire is man's friend and fire is man's enemy. In this work, it will be our friend. It would take a body two years' steady work to clear that hill with axes and hoes."

Beyond them lies the hill slope covered with wreckage of trees. Dead dry leaves are still clinging to sapless boughs. There are masses of dead tufted bull grass. There is a layer of leaves on the ground almost knee-deep on Tarvin's long legs. There are patches of dead briars. There are piles of dead logs in the deep ravines. It is almost impossible for man or varmit to get through this mass of dead and living vegetation. Anse crawls through it like a polecat. He digs up dirt here and there and feels it. He smells the dirt. He tells himself that it will make good corn. Anse gets his long beard tangled in the briars. He shakes it loose when it pulls his chin. Anse climbs over the dead logs like a lizard. He goes under the treetops like a mink. He climbs up among the treetops like a gray squirrel.

Boliver takes a rake, hoe and ax. He goes up the hollow. He rakes a broad ring over the earth. He cuts through briar patches with the hoe. If there is a fallen log, he cuts it in two and rakes the ring. He rakes it to the top of the hill and connects the Ragweed Hollow road with the ridge road. Now there is a ring all the way around the field. To clear this mass of vegetation, all Boliver needs is a little match. It is unbelievable the work it will do on a sunshiny March afternoon when the wind is still.

4.

ANSE, TARVIN and Fronnie walk down the path from the house. They walk toward the great brown mass of dead treetops, logs, leaves and briar thickets. The sun is high in the March sky. The vegetation on the earth is dry as powder. It is the time to burn since the wind has dropped. Anse walks in front with an armload of rich pine kindling. Anse smokes his cigar and looks toward the big slope that is sleeping beneath the comforting rays of March's sun. Tarvin walks behind Anse and smokes his pipe. Fronnie walks behind Tarvin and smokes her pipe.

"Boliver and Crissie and all their youngins air goin to meet us down here at the beech grove," says Anse. "He aims to take his youngins and fire up the holler. We air to fire along our pasture to the ridge road. We'll meet sommers back yander on the ridge. We air goin to see somethin we've never seen before."

"It will remind one of hell and torment," says Fronnie. "Jest imagine, this hill will look like hell."

Anse does not speak to Fronnie when she speaks about hell. He walks down the path and Tarvin and Fronnie follow. They walk up to the beech grove. Boliver and Crissie and the children are waiting for them.

"You have come, Mister Bushman," says Boliver as he pulls the brown cured burley tobacco crumbs from his hip pocket and crams a handful into his mouth. Tiny tobacco crumbs hang in his red briar-stubble beard.

"Yep, we air here," says Anse. "Now we want to git this hill on fire while the wind is still. Then there won't be any danger of the wind blowin the fire across the ring."

"If you don't mind, Pa," Tarvin says, "Subrinea will hep me. We'll fire the side of the woods next to the sheep pasture. You and Ma can hep Boliver and Crissie fire up Ragweed Holler to the ridge road."

"Suits us, don't it, Fronnie?" Anse asks.

"Yep, it suits me," says Fronnie.

Anse distributes a stick of pine kindling to each person. Anse strikes a match to a stick of kindling. The oily resin begins to ooze and the black smoke rolls from the tiny blaze. Fronnie, Tarvin, Subrinea, Snail, Big Aaron and Crissie stick the ends of their kindling sticks over the blaze. They catch fire. The fire burns the oily kindling sticks like an oil wick from a lamp. Tarvin and Subrinea start setting fire along the sheep pasture's edge to the massive waste piles of trees and worthless vegetation. Anse leads the way up Ragweed Hollow. Crissie, Fronnie, Boliver, Snail and Big Aaron follow Anse. They hold the pine torches to the dead leaves long enough to get the fire started; then they move on. There is a long line of fire along the Ragweed Hollow road. There is a long line of fire along the sheep pasture's edge. Tarvin and Subrinea walk rapidly up the hill, daubing fire to this leaf pile and that wisp of dead bull grass. The fire leaps into the air as if it is flashing from a powder keg. Tarvin and Subrinea have to run to keep away from the fire. They move further along the timber line and start setting fire again until they get to the hilltop.

"We'll haf to hurry, Tarvin," Subrinea says, "and git the fire set out on this ridge road so it can burn back and meet the fire comin up the hill. The fire is goin fast up the hill."

Great clouds of smoke rise up Ragweed Hollow. There is a yellowish flame leaping up with the smoke. Tarvin and Subrinea walk rapidly out the ridge road, setting fire to the leaves and grass. They can hear the fire popping in the brush below them. They can see the flames leaping to the saplings' tops. They can see the saplings falling before the flames. They can see rabbits running across the ridge road to the hollow below. A red fox darts across the road. He is leaving the fire. A polecat slowly runs over the hill with his black shaggy tail high in the air.

"Let's slow down a little with the fire," says Tarvin. "Don't meet Pa and his fire-setters yit. We'll have all the wild game surrounded if we do. Let's give every livin thing a chance to git out'n there."

Subrinea and Tarvin stand and watch the fire. Amid the sounds of snapping brush and clouds of smoke ascending to the sky, they can hear Anse shouting to his fire-setters. They can hear him telling them where to set the fire. They can hear him rushing them along. They can see squirrels running from the fire. They can see rabbits, weasels, possums, foxes. They are making a dash to save their lives. A gray fox passes with the hairs on the end of his bushy tail on fire.

"We'd better meet the rest of the fire-setters," says Tarvin, "and close the gap. If we don't close the gap, a rabbit 'r fox is goin to run through here with fire on his tail and set the woods on fire over here. We'll have hell if fire ever gits below us."

"Aint it awful to destroy the last place the wild game has to run over," says Subrinea. "Jest to think Pa has hunted over these woods all his life. I'll bet he hates to set fire to 'em and burn up the dens of the wild game. I'll bet it breaks Pa's heart."

"It pleases my Pa," says Tarvin. "He can see big fields of corn here. He can see fields of grass and sheep and cattle. It is his dream to see all this land in cultivation."

Tarvin and Subrinea walk out the ridge, setting fire. They meet Anse and his fire-setters. The gap is closed. The wild game fleeing from the fire now will have to run through a ring of fire. The ring has broadened until it is so wide that it is impossible for any living creature to run the gauntlet of fire. The only way it can save its life is to find a hole back in the earth and crawl into it—dig under the earth and lie there until the fire passes over. Flocks of birds soar over the flames to escape the fire.

"Fire's goin up that hill faster than a hoss can run," says Anse. He wipes the sweat from his forehead with his big hand. He wipes the sweat from his long red beard. His beard is filled with particles of burnt leaves, sticks and stems of grass. Fronnie's face is wet with sweat. Big Aaron and Snail are wet with sweat and gray with wood ashes. Sweat drops hang all over Crissie's leather-tanned face. Boliver's face is sweaty and dirty. It is flushed red from the heat.

They stand with burning pine torches in their hands and watch the fire burn.

"It's shore poppin things," says Anse. "Listen down in them woods, won't you? It's great to see fire clean land like that. Won't be anything to do behind that fire."

"It's killin a lot of wild game," says Boliver. "I hate to see that."

"We can't hep that," says Anse. "This land hast to be cleaned. It's the wild game's bad luck. It is our good luck."

Subrinea and Tarvin do not speak. They watch the fire sweeping the tops of the saplings. It looks as if the flames are leaping to the clouds. The whole mountain slope is a blazing inferno. Bright flames leap high among the treetops that cover this rugged earth. Fire twists around the saplings and burns them to the ground.

"I didn't think the green saplings would burn too," says Anse. "That's so much the better. Let the fire sweep all before it. Let it burn the land clean. You'll have some of the awfulest terbacker in them ash banks and that loam that ever growed in this holler."

"Anse, that burnin hill reminds me of what I think hell is goin to be like," says Fronnie. "Anse, you air a weaked man. You aint a 'saved' man."

"Don't tell me about it here," says Anse. "Don't be talkin about hell all the time, Fronnie! You vex me here among people."

"Vex you!" Fronnie repeats. "Vex you! You will be vexed someday with hell, damnation and torment. You will be glad that I reminded you here on this earth."

"Gee Christ, Fronnie," says Anse. He turns and walks out the ridge road.

"Fronnie didn't ust to act like this," thinks Anse. "What on earth is the matter with Fronnie? I've been hearin her talkin to the cows and chickens like they's real people but I didn't

think anything about it. She can't be losin her mind. I've allus
kept Fronnie plenty to eat and a good home. Fronnie aint
never wanted fer nothin."

Fronnie looks at the fire and talks to Boliver and Crissie
about hell, damnation and torment. Crissie and Boliver do not
talk with Fronnie. She talks about Anse. Anse stands off by
himself and watches the fire burn. He breathes a wind that is
pleasant for him to breathe. It is a breath that reminds him of
spring. It reminds him of plowing and growing crops of
grain. Anse breathes the smell of woodsmoke into his lungs.
Anse loves the smell of woodsmoke. There is but one smell
that is more pleasant to Anse. That is the smell of polecat.
Anse loves the smell of new-mown hay too. He loves the ripe
rich smells of harvest.

As fast as the flames ascend to the tops of the saplings,
they descend as rapidly. They sink to the earth. Patches of
smoke rise here and there where the giant clusters of treetops
were interwoven into mountains of brush piles. These have
fallen into gray ash heaps. Just the bones of giant tree-bodies
remain. These are burning rapidly. The earth that was brown
three hours ago is a black and gray earth. The fire has cleaned
it. One can see each ravine now. One can see a rock here and
there. One can see stumps dotted all over the slope. One can
see the banks, the steeps, the sinks all over the land.

"We'll git in there, old woman," says Boliver to Crissie,
"and chunk the log heaps, pick up the brands and cut a few
saplins that didn't burn down. We'll soon have the ground
ready fer the plow."

"It won't take us long, Boliver," says Crissie. "It will be
awful dirty work."

Anse walks back toward the house. He does not get close
to Fronnie. He is afraid she will start talking to him about hell.

"I'd better git home," says Fronnie, "and put a fire in the
stove. Anse will be hungry. I'll haf to git 'im some supper.
Crissie, you all come over sometime and see us."

"We will; you come and see us," says Crissie.

"It sounds awful good to hear that," says Fronnie. "It reminds me of the days before I married Anse. That was in the days when we had neighbors close fer a body to talk to."

Fronnie walks along the ridge road smoking her pipe.

"I 'spect we'd better be gittin along too," says Anse to Tarvin. "We've got all our work to do up yit. Aint no danger in the fire now. It's burnt down low."

"If the wind raises I'll be over here to look about it tonight," says Boliver.

Anse and Tarvin walk along the ridge road behind Fronnie. Anse looks at the hill below him. He looks at the big coves that spread away from the deep ravines. He looks at the smoking snags, log heaps and stumps. Anse walks slowly around the ridge road and surveys the mountain slope beneath him. "That's the way to clean land," Anse thinks. "That land will be easy to farm. Weeds air slow to ketch holt in new ground atter the fire has burnt over it."

Subrinea, Crissie, Boliver, Snail and Big Aaron walk down the hill toward Ragweed Hollow. They walk over the land where the fire has burned. Crissie and Boliver can feel the hot earth through their brogan shoes. Subrinea, Big Aaron and Snail watch where they step with their bare feet. They walk over the burned earth where ashes are shoe-mouth deep. They can see white wisps of ashes here and there. It is where snakes have burned to death. They have been thawed from winter sleep by the warm March sun. They did not sleep until the spring thunder resurrected them and the spring showers washed off their ragged skins and the spring sunlight gave them new ones.

"God Almighty," says Boliver, "this is land. If we don't raise a crop here it will be our own fault."

"If we don't raise a crop," says Crissie, "it will be because you start puttin rot-gut licker down your old rusty bull neck agin. You know Mister Bushman won't stand fer it nohow.

If he'd a-knowed you liked that stuff better than a cat likes cream he'd a-never rented you this place."

"I jest said this land would raise good corn," says Boliver. "I didn't say anything fer to argue with you, Crissie. You air ferever on my bones. Jest seems like I git tired of work and haf to have a drink now and then. If I didn't git it, Crissie, life wouldn't be worth livin. I wouldn't say a word to you if you'd git drunk with me."

"What would our youngins do if I'd start drinkin with you?" Crissie asks Boliver, with a snarl on her lips. "Jest what would become of our youngins if I acted like you? I'll tell you right now I aint a-gittin drunk with you."

"Watch, Snail," Boliver says, "don't git too fur out in one of them deep ash heaps. You'll step on livin coals and burn your feet. This whole hill slope is a bed of livin coals."

Crissie, Boliver, Snail, Big Aaron and Subrinea walk across the newground to the hollow. They walk up the bank to the little three-room shack on the hill.

"I'll tell you this is a better home than we've ever been ust to," says Crissie. "I'm proud of our new home."

"I like it too," says Subrinea. "We can have a lot of flowers around this house. It has good floors in it and glass in the winders too. We won't be ashamed fer people to visit us here."

5.

"Crissie, you can take Big Aaron and Subrinea and go to Grubb's General Store and git our provisions," says Boliver. "Big Aaron is a stout boy to pack a load from town. I'll take Snail with me to the newground. We'll start chunkin this mornin."

"All right," says Crissie. "We'll bring in the grub. We need it. We aint got another bite in the house."

Snail and Boliver go to the newground. They take an ax, saw, sprouting hoe and a mattock. They walk down the hill in front of the shack, cross the hollow and climb the hill to the newground. They walk into the beds of cold ashes. There is a stream of smoke here and there over the vast dark fields blotched with gray heaps of ashes. The smoke streams upward from the giant stumps, old log heaps and beds of half-decayed loam. The fire has gone down into the dry earth, burning out holes into the loam.

Boliver and Snail pick up the brands scattered here and there over the land. They throw them into heaps. They set fire to the heaps. If a big log has not burned, they saw the log in two and twist one half around and pile small brands between. They set fire to the log heaps and leave them to burn. They work in heaps of gray ashes and black charcoal. They pick up all loose poles, pieces of stumps and chunks and throw them on the burning heaps. They leave the land clean for the plow.

"We want to hurry and git this land fixed fer the plow," says Boliver. "We want to git this done before April. It's along toward the last of March and the first of April when the heavy rains come. The brands and logs will git soaked with water and we'll never git the stuff burnt. We want to do our burnin while the dry days air here."

Big Aaron carries home 35 pounds of soup beans. Crissie carries a sack of flour and a basket filled with soda, salt, pepper and sugar. Subrinea carries a sack of meal and a slab of sowbelly. They walk five miles to Greenwood on a snake-curved path across a range of big hills. They walk back over this path and carry the loads of provisions. They have to sit down along the way and rest as they climb over the big hills home.

"Soup beans and corn bread fer dinner and supper," says Boliver, "and sow-belly, gravy and biscuit bread fer breakfast. It takes grub if a body is to stand liftin them logs. We air chunkin the brands and clearin up the newground atter the fire. Jest like Mister Anse Bushman said, when a body works it takes grub to stick to the ribs."

"Sallet greens will soon be back to the hills," says Crissie.

"When sallet greens comes back to the hills, I can pick greens to cook with the meat. We can have big pots of greens and we all like greens so well."

"Greens will be a change," says Boliver. "God Almighty, but I like to eat from a big pot of greens that has been biled with a piece of fat meat. I like to jest set down and fork 'em up like you fork up hay and put it on a sled. Lord, but I jest love to eat greens biled with fat meat. 'Pears like fat meat seasons the greens. It makes my mouth water to think about it."

Boliver, Crissie, Big Aaron, Subrinea and Snail work clearing the newground. They carry pieces of logs and put them on the log piles. They pick up the last brands and pile them in heaps. They cut down the sharp stumps where the fire burned down the saplings. "A mule is liable to fall on a sharp snag," says Boliver. "If he'd step on a rock and fall he'd rip out his guts on a sharp snag. I'd haf to pay fer the mule. It would take my crop. When Mister Bushman said in the ar-tickle that I'd haf to pay a fair and reasonable price fer the tools I destroyed 'r if I hurt a mule, he meant that he'd set his own price. He'd set the price of the mule sky-high. I aint wantin to pay fer no mule."

The March days pass. The sunshine plays brilliantly over the earth. The wind blows over where the woods have once been. Swirls of ashes rise toward the skies. Subrinea gets ashes in her yellow hair. Subrinea gets her face soot-black. She gets her body soot-black. It does not matter to Subrinea. She works like a man in the newground beside her father, mother and brothers. It takes all hands and cooks to get the newground ready before the spring rains.

While Tarvin and Anse walk behind their plows and turn the cold March dirt over in the slick layers from the mould boards of their turning plows, Boliver, Crissie, Subrinea, Big Aaron and Snail get the newground clean of brands, sharp stumps, snags and logs. They get it in shape for the plow.

"I'll tell you, Tarvin," says Anse, "Tussies air goin to make good renters. They air workin people. They've got their new-ground in shape fer the plow. They'll have their land ready to plant by the time we air ready to plant our land. We don't want them to show us up. We air the best farmers in this holler. I can't stand to let a squatter beat me doin anything."

"Squatters air good as anybody else, Pa," says Tarvin. "You jest can't git over Tussies bein squatters. It don't matter to me what they air. I like Tussies. I think they air good people to work and good people to git along with. They air good neighbors."

"I guess we need neighbors too," says Anse. "Look at your Ma, Tarvin. I hate to think about Fronnie. I jest haf to git away from her. She talks to herself all the time. She talks to the chickens and the cows. Your Ma has allus been a silent woman until here lately. She's jest started talkin like she has never been allowed to talk in her life. Ah, poor Fronnie—she's right on my bones all the time about hell and damnation. I hate to think it, Tarvin, but I believe your Ma is losin her mind. God knows, I hate to think about it."

6.

THE NIGHT is dark. The dark skies quiver in the distance. There is the slow rumble of thunder. "It is the spring thunder showers comin," says Anse. "It is the trumpet of the spring. Now you will hear the frogs. Now you will see the snakes crawlin over the earth. You will see snakes with new coats of skin goin here and yan. You will see turtles along the creek banks. You will see them sunnin on logs out'n the water. They'll fall off in the water as you pass along the creeks. And you will see terrapins crawlin on the sandbanks. You will see the green git back to the hills and you will see the flowers spring from the earth and bloom as they have never bloomed before. I can tell that thunder is the trumpet to awake the spring. Boliver has his newground ready in time. We've got our spring plowin done jest in time."

The heavy thunders shake the earth. The lightnings cut across the vast fields of velvety thick darkness. When the lightning flashes across the earth, it shows thin clouds racing across the sky. They are a yellowish-gray color. They race above an earth yet barren of green vegetation save for a few wild flowers, willow leaves, alder leaves and green-briar leaves. They race above the earth that is still dark and desolate—an earth that is ready to wake from its long winter's sleep.

The thunders roar. The lightnings flash. The rain falls in heavy torrents. "Jest 'pears like the sky has opened wide," says Anse, "and the water jest falls from the sky. It's a powerful rain. This rain will wash the earth clean. It will clean the trees and wake them from sleepin. It will bring new leaves to their limbs and new blossoms to their buds."

"This storm reminds me of the end of time," says Fronnie. Fronnie looks at the window when the lightning flashes. She can see a yellowish glimmer of light. She can see the torrents of water sliding down the windowpanes. "There will be a time like this. The rain will pour from the heavens and the thunder will roar. The lightning will light up the whole earth." Fronnie smokes her pipe and watches the storm. "I'd be afeared to go to bed now," says Fronnie. " 'Pears to me like the whole earth is tearin apart."

"Ah, Fronnie," says Anse, "it aint the end of time. The world will be destroyed by fire the next time. It won't be destroyed by water like it was before. It will be fire. God Almighty knows I'd ruther it would be destroyed by water. I'm skeered of fire. Drownin's a easier death than bein fried by fire."

Anse stands before the window. He puts his face against a windowpane and looks out at the pouring sheets of water. Anse doddles his head as the lightning flashes.

"Lord, but this will be more like the resurrection," says Anse, "than it is the end of time. It is the resurrection of spring. Tomorrow there will be life among these hills where today life was asleep. Tomorrow you will see new life. Tomorrow you will see the buds swellin on the trees and you will see flowers springin over the slopes. I've seen these spring thunder showers too many years not to know about them. Spring is the awakenin of new life and the resurrection of old life among these hills."

All night long the thunder roars. All night long the lightning flashes. The rain pours from the skies in great torrents. Fronnie sits up and smokes her pipe. She will not go to bed. Fronnie is afraid of a storm. She is afraid to go to bed. Anse sits up and watches the storm. Anse loves a storm. His eyes twinkle as he watches the lightning flash.

"I can't see enough of this storm and sit in here," says Anse. "I aim to go out in the storm and git a good soakin. If I git a soakin now, I can git wet any time this year and it won't hurt me. I love a storm. I jest got to git out in this resurrection of spring and see how I like a night of resurrection."

"Pa, you aint goin out in that storm, air you?" Tarvin asks.

"I am," says Anse. "I love a resurrection."

Anse opens the door. He walks out into the storm.

"Is Anse losin his mind, Tarvin?" Fronnie asks.

"I don't know, Ma," says Tarvin.

"He must be, the way he acts," says Fronnie. "He wakes me every night drivin the mules in his sleep. Honest, he just cusses and hollers 'gee-haw' all night long. He's allus fightin old Barney. 'Pears like he has more trouble drivin 'im of a night when he plows in his sleep. He shoos the sheep over the pasture too. It's all night long I hear Anse drivin mules in his sleep. I hear 'im shooin the sheep to the barn. I git so tired of hearin Anse I can't stand it. Am I sleepin now? Did Anse go into the storm? I might be dreamin. I can't be in bed with Anse though, fer I'm smokin my pipe and talkin to you."

Tarvin looks at his mother. He glares at her as she sits in the rocking chair smoking her pipe. Tarvin looks back over the years. He has seen his mother, strong as a man, go to the fields and work like a man. He has seen her come to the house and do the work of a woman around the house. He has seen her work all day and part of the night. "It is hard work that makes Ma like that," thinks Tarvin. "She has come to this long before her time. Poor old Ma! I feel so sorry fer her I could cry. If I cry, Ma will see me. She will wonder what is the matter with me. I'll pretend that I don't know Ma is the way she is. She aint never had company like the other wimmen in the neighborhood. She has lived here fer weeks at a time and never had a neighbor woman to speak to her."

"No, Tarvin," says Fronnie, "I wouldn't live with a man that wore a long red beard like Anse wears if it weren't fer you. I tell you there is something the matter with Anse. We jest won't talk about what is the matter with Anse. Look at 'im tonight. He is out in this storm. He loves a storm. He thinks it is a resurrection. I'm afeared when resurrection mornin comes, the trumpet won't wake Anse. He will sleep right on. Anse aint nigh right with the Lord. He can't say that I didn't warn 'im when we burnt the newground. I'll tell you, Anse loves his farm more than he loves me. Anse loves his mules more than he loves me. If it wasn't fer my cows, pigs and chickens, Tarvin, I wouldn't stay here nary minute with Anse. That's the only reason I stay here and put up with 'im. If I's to leave, what would you do? You would git along all right. You would marry Subrinea. She is all right, Tarvin. She is a good gal. She will make you a good wife. Anse don't know it, but she will. She will make you bilers of black coffee at midnight if you want 'em. She will darn the heels of your socks. She will sew buttons on your clothes. She will wash your clothes and patch the holes fer you. Subrinea is a purty gal. Pay no mind to her bein a squatter's gal. That makes no difference, Tarvin. She has a heart in her bosom."

Tarvin looks at his mother. He sees her once crow-black hair streaked with gray. He sees the wrinkles in her face getting broader each year. The skin on her face is wrinkled like the peeling on a roasted sweet potato. "Ma shouldn't be like that," thinks Tarvin. "Ma is gittin old before her time. Ma aint but threescore years and four. Ma's gittin to look like she is a hundred years old. I like to remember the days when Ma was strong. I like to remember the days when Ma danced with Pa like I dance with Subrinea. I like to remember Ma when she could set down and eat a whole pot of green beans and a big piece of fat meat that she cooked in the beans to give 'em flavor. Ma was a powerful woman then. Time hast been unkind to Ma. Time and hard work hast changed Ma. I never want time, hard work and childbearin to change Subrinea like they've changed Ma."

7.

ANSE STANDS out in the torrents of pouring rain. He looks toward the heavens and the rain hits his open eyes. It washes his face and his red beard clean. The lightning flashes around Anse. He reaches out his hand as if he is trying to grab the lightning. Anse listens to the roar of thunder. It is sweet music to Anse Bushman's ears. Anse walks across the pasture back of the house. He stops as the lightning flashes. "A night like this one will only come once," thinks Anse. "This is the resurrection of spring. I must be out. I must go over my farm. Dull stupid people air sleepin behind thick walls and under roofs that don't leak. They don't know how much they air missin. Tomorrow we will have a new earth. We will have a purty earth. The air will be sweet to breathe and the woods will be clean to smell. This is the best night in all the year."

Anse walks up the pasture path to the ridge road. He walks out past the big newground where Tussies have been working. Anse remembers the dry afternoon when the fire nearly cleaned the land. When the lightning flashes, he can see a strip of black earth. He cannot see very far for the rain. He can see water running over the clearing. Anse looks into the valley on his right when the lightning flashes. He can see a dim outline of the hills. He can see the great white sheets of rain descending on the valley. "The snakes air wakin down in that valley," thinks Anse. "The turtles have started crawlin from their beds. The terrapins air stirrin from the sand piles. It is a great night. If Fronnie could jest appreciate a night like this. She talks funny. She's allus on my bones about the hereatter. I want to live while I live. My farm is heaven to me as long as I keep my farm and long as I am alive."

The water streams from Anse's beard in tiny streams. His clothes are rain-soaked. They cling closely to his skin. They outline the shape of his strong thick body. It is knotty with muscles, as an ancient tree is gnarled by time. The water squashes in Anse's brogan shoes. The water feels good to Anse's feet. The water feels good to his body. This is a night that Anse Bushman loves. He walks over the loamy newground. Now the loam is soaked with water. Anse walks in the newground mud across the field. He goes down Ragweed Hollow. He walks by the cliffs beneath the chestnut oaks. He walks over the farm while the storm roars over the earth. The lightning flashes. The thunder roars. The rain pours. Anse drinks in the resurrection of a Kentucky mountain spring.

8.

WHEN MORNING dawns, Anse walks out to feed the hogs. A few stars are in the clear sky. He breathes deeply of the new clean air. It is sweet for Anse to breathe. As the morning fades into day, the sun rises and the wisps of mist ascend toward the heavens. The earth looks fresh and clean. The oak trees are beginning to bud. The willows have leafed out. Their tiny tendrils tremble in the wind. The apple trees are putting forth little mouse-ear leaves. The frogs croak in the swamps. Anse walks out to pour slop in the chute for the hogs. A snake crawls down the hill toward the hog pen. "He's the old mouser black snake that ust to stay in this hog pen to ketch the mice and rats," says Anse. "He looks so much better than he did when I saw him last. He has a new coat of skin. He's slept up there under the oak leaves the winter long." Anse does not bother the black snake. He lets him crawl under the hog pen. That is the place he stayed last year until dog days set in. Then he went blind and he worked his way under the bed of leaves and went to sleep until the resurrection of spring.

"It's sich a purty mornin," says Fronnie. "Spring is here agin. But I worry about you, Anse. I've spent many a spring with you. What makes you go out at night when there is a storm and run over the hills? You air a old man. You air seventy-one years old. You act like a child. Anse, somethin is happpenin to you."

Anse does not speak to Fronnie. He goes ahead with his work around the barn. Tarvin and Fronnie milk the cows. Fronnie talks to the cows as she would talk to a child. "Purty Thing, you won't fersake me. Purty Thing, Fronnie loves you. Purty Thing, if it wasn't fer you and the chickens, Fronnie wouldn't stay here with old Anse Bushman nary minute. Anse is a man lost deep in sin and out in the storm at night with the Devil. Purty Thing, Anse has fersook me. It is fer you that I stay in this God-fersaken hole."

When the work is done at the barn, Anse walks over to see Boliver. He walks briskly. Anse is a new man in a new world. He crosses the sheep pasture and the newground. He walks around the hollow to Boliver's shack. Boliver is out in the yard looking across the hollow at his newground. Boliver is chewing the brown burley leaf. It looks as if he has a goose egg in his jaw.

"Good mornin, Boliver," says Anse.

"Good morning, Mister Bushman," says Boliver. "It's a fine mornin this mornin."

"Jest like God has made the world over new," says Anse. "I feel that way about it. I feel like a new man this mornin."

"I'm jest takin a look at my newground," says Boliver. "I don't believe I'll haf to plow that land. All I'll haf to do is go in there and double furrow the land and plant it. There aint a weed on that newground, there won't be fer a long time yit. It's as soft as if it had been plowed. What do you think about it?"

"My Pap raised all his newground corn like that," says

Anse. "I think it will save you a lot of work. It is the very thing to do. Jest go in there and lay the land off with two furrows in a row and plant it. The mules, seed corn and plow air ready any time that you air ready. Spring is right here on us now. It will be a busy time. It is the season to plant. This is the time to work."

Anse and Boliver walk over the newground hill. They look at the ravines. They walk among the ash banks. "Now, Boliver, all you will haf to do," says Anse, "is to sow your terbacker seeds in one of these ash banks. Sow plenty of them. You will need a lot of plants fer five acres of terbacker. You won't haf to burn a terbacker bed. It is already burnt fer you."

"I'll have my crop in one piece of newground," says Boliver. "That will make things handy. I'll have enough land here fer my terbacker, corn and cane. There'll be a few acres over what the ar-tickle calls fer. Do you want me to farm them too?"

"I do," says Anse. "I want you to farm this newground. It will make you a big crop. You will raise plenty fer me, fer yourself and plenty to sell. You won't be buyin soup beans and sow-belly next year. You'll have your own grub. You can come over to my house and git one of my cows. You need milk fer your family. You can pasture her in the pasture back of your house."

"Thank you, Mister Bushman," says Boliver. "We do need a cow. We got in a hard place last winter and had to sell our two cows. Now we need 'em. We've missed 'em too!"

Anse leaves Boliver and walks toward his house. He breathes the wind of spring into his lungs. He looks at the grass starting in little green blotches over the pasture slopes. He sees his sheep with their young lambs playing on the green swards of tender grass. Anse stands and watches the lambs hunting their mothers. It pleases Anse to watch a lamb smell at a half-dozen ewes before he finds his mother. It pleases Anse to watch a lamb fall on his foreknees and suckle his mammie. Life is back among the hills for Anse Bushman. Anse is proud as a black snake that has his new spring skin. Anse, too, like the snake, turtle, terrapin and the frog, has been resurrected into a new spring of life.

9.

BOLIVER TAKES Barney and a cutter plow to the newground. He lays off the newground for planting. He drives a furrow through the field. Subrinea follows him, dropping three grains of seed corn after a long right step and a short left one. She drops the corn at the tip of her big toe on her left foot. Big Aaron follows with a hoe and covers the corn. Big Aaron plants pumpkin seeds around the rotted half-charred stumps.

"This is the land fer corn, punkins and beans," says Boliver. "You'll see a crop grow out'n this earth. It is a good earth. This is the kind of land to farm. It will be work to plow this corn since we didn't plow the land. We air jest layin it off and plantin it. We haf to work to git our crop planted."

Anse and Tarvin take their span of young mules, harrow

their land and furrow it for planting. Anse can see the long rows on Boliver Tussie's newground slope from his house. He can see the fresh dirt furrows—the red clay furrows among the dark burned-over earth. The big field, with furrows running in contours with the lay of the hill, is pleasing to Anse Bushman's eyes. He works fast to keep his work ahead of Boliver. "I like to raise more than other farmers," says Anse. "I jest can't hep it. Like to have more than other people. It is jest in my blood to be like that. Tarvin, you take atter your Ma and her people. You aint like your old Pa when it comes to gittin ahead."

"I wouldn't turn my hand over to git ahead of the other fellar," says Tarvin. "I jest can't git interested. I jest want to do what I've got to do and let the other fellar do the same. I want to see Tussies git along. I want to see them raise plenty to use and to spare."

"Jest because you love that gal," says Anse.

"That's one reason," says Tarvin; "and another reason, all the old settlers air down on the squatters. I hope they raise the best crop in the holler."

Green clouds of tender leaves come to the trees. Weeds grow in the coves. Wild flowers spring up on the banks, coves and under the cliffs. The air is a water-over-gravel color. The sky is high and blue. The birds sing songs of cheer. They sing songs of love as they carry straws to build their nests. The redbirds sing in the coves. The larks rise from the meadow with songs pouring from their hearts. Spring is here. It is the greatest season of the year—that great prolific sudden burst of spring among the dark Kentucky hills where there is loam in the coves and where there is clicking of gooseneck hoes on the newground slopes.

Life has come back to the hills after a long sleep and the thunder showers of resurrection. Life has come back to the birds, turtles, terrapins, frogs, snakes, scorpions and ground hogs. Life has come back to the trees and the flowers. "If I could jest go on forever and forever like the snakes," says Anse. "Jest sleep the winter long and be resurrected every spring like the snake with a new skin on my body, I would be a proud man. But I'm not cold-blooded like the snake and the frog. Maybe I will be resurrected like the snake. Jest so I git back to my farm, that's all I keer about. I want to keep on raisin big crops of cane, corn and terbacker. I jest want to keep my feet on the dirt, to plow the dirt, to feel the dirt with my hands and feet and to smell the dirt. I love to work in the dirt. I love to smell the spring. I love to smell the woodsmoke and the new-plowed land. I feel like a stronger man."

Anse walks behind the young mules. He plows Dick and Murt on the old ground slopes. "The old mules know how to plow in newground," says Anse. "The young mules air too fiery. They'll haf to live a while longer before they know how to plow in newgrounds. It takes Jack and Barney fer the newground."

As the earth blooms into flowers and song, Anse and Boliver plow the earth and plant. They work as the days of April pass. The earth is fragrant with flowers now—the wild flowers by the cliffs—and the green clouds of tender leaves on the trees. The pulse of the earth is beating. It is beating high. It is an eternal beating pulse that will beat high in the spring and beat during the prolific growth of summer—it will ebb during the death of autumn. It will die in the sleep of winter and be resurrected by the warm suns of spring when the blood flows freely in the veins of the trees, in the stems of the flowers and the blades of grass.

"By April twentieth," says Boliver, "I'll have my corn planted. I will have my cane planted. All I'll haf to do is git my terbacker ground plowed and ready to set. I'll haf to wait fer a rain in May before I can set it in the loamy newground rows."

"Boliver won't beat us none, plantin," says Anse. "We'll be done by April fifteenth. By May tenth, if there comes a good rain and by God's grace, we'll have our terbacker set."

Twisted green stems of corn, the color of May-apple stems unfolding from the coves in early spring, peep from the furrows. Tiny tendrils of corn, stubby and dark green, line the long newground rows. Three stalks spring from each hill. Two pumpkin leaves on a tiny stem spring beside the half-rotted fire-charred stumps. There is not a weed in the field. "Must a-been fire that kilt the weed roots in the ground," says Boliver. "Mister Bushman said the fire would do that. He hast lived a long time and Mister Bushman knows. Mister Bushman knows what he is doin when it comes to farmin these hills."

Tiny cane stalks peep like tiny stems of timothy grass along the cane rows. Tiny cane stalks that look so weak and frail. "Strange about cane," says Boliver. "It is so weak when it first peeps from the earth. A body jest hast to throw a little dirt over it so it can git up through the earth. If you kiver it with too much dirt, it won't come up. August is when cane begins to grow. I've seen cane stalks big as my wrists. Sorghum molasses made from newground cane is the sweetest sorghum molasses in the world."

10.

"TARVIN, WILL you go with me Sunday?" Subrinea asks. "There's somethin I want you to hep me do."

"I'll go with you, Subrinea," says Tarvin. "I'll go with you and hep you do anything that I can."

"I want you to hep me decorate some graves," says Subrinea.

"I will," says Tarvin.

"I'll show you where we can find plenty of flowers," says Subrinea. "I've never seen so many wild flowers in bloom. They will all be gone if I wait until Decoration Day."

The sun is coming up over the green clouded hills. The air is fresh and fine to breathe. Subrinea and Tarvin walk down

Ragweed Hollow. Tarvin carries a gooseneck hoe. Subrinea carries a basket and a case knife. Subrinea does not look as she did when she planted corn in the newground. Subrinea does not have the charcoal black on her face. She does not have the gray wood ashes clinging to her sweaty legs. Subrinea looks clean and fresh as a mountain flower. Her love-vine-colored hair falls loosely over her shoulders. It is fluffy as a dried wisp of timothy hay. Her strong muscular legs are stockingless in the April wind. She walks beside Tarvin down the Ragweed Hollow road. They breathe the pungent odor from the pennyroyal on the slopes.

"I know where we air goin," says Tarvin.

"Where?" Subrinea asks.

"To the cliffs."

"You air right. You know where every patch of wild flowers is. I can't hide one from you."

Tarvin laughs at Subrinea. He carries the hoe across his shoulder. His strong bronzed face looks down at her tall body and her pretty face that looks up at him. Subrinea is swinging her basket along as she walks. She looks at Tarvin. She does not look where she steps. They walk down the hill from Subrinea's shack. They cross the creek under the poplar grove. They cross a little bottom. They walk under the thin-leafed beech trees and cross the creek again. They walk over the dark earth where the charcoal kilns used to be. They walk down to the cliffs.

"Look," says Subrinea. She points to the bluff filled with wild flowers. She has the case knife in her hand. "Look at the wild iris, won't you! Look at the blue ageratum and the dusty miller!"

"We'd better jump the crick together and git 'em this time," says Tarvin.

"All right," says Subrinea.

Tarvin takes Subrinea by the hand. The two strong young people leap across the broad spring-filled creek together. Their long legs split the blue April wind. They laugh as their feet find a place on the flower-covered bank below the steeps where the cliffs hang over.

"Flowers a-plenty here," says Tarvin. "There's enough flowers here to decorate all the graves among these hills. God knows, there air plenty of them that is flat now. They air forgotten because their people have moved away and because their people air dead."

Tarvin plucks the blue ageratum from the cliffs. He plucks it with his long hard fingers. Subrinea cuts the stems with her case knife. They gather bouquets of ageratum and wild trillium. They gather pinks from beneath the tall chestnut-oaks. They gather wild phlox from the creek banks. They fill their basket with bouquets of wild flowers.

"We need some wild roses," says Subrinea.

"We'll git 'em," says Tarvin. "You follow me."

Tarvin and Subrinea walk up the pasture hill by an old fence row. The wild-rose stems are thick as wild trillium on the bluffs. "Here they air," says Tarvin. "We'll gather all you want."

"You know where all the wild flowers grow," says Subrinea.

"I ought to," says Tarvin. "I'm over this ground enough. I've been goin over this pasture to hunt the cows since I've been able to walk."

Tarvin and Subrinea gather bouquets of wild roses. They cut the wild roses from their briary stems. Tarvin cuts them with the case knife and Subrinea bundles them. She lays the bunches of wild roses in the basket with the rest of their wild flowers.

"There is only one layer of petals around the wild-rose blooms," says Subrinea. "I've allus wondered why it was. The tame rose has many layers of petals."

"I don't know that," says Tarvin. "I've jest noticed it, that's all. I don't know why you air purtier than other gals. I jest know you air. That's the way I feel about wild roses."

Tarvin carries the hoe across his shoulder. Subrinea carries the basket of flowers on her arm. She holds to Tarvin's arm as they walk down the pasture hill to the Ragweed Hollow road. Tarvin carries the case knife in his hand. The young lovers walk down the road arm in arm. They walk down to Cat's Fork. They turn to their right and walk up the oxen road toward the trees of Heaven. They see the slender tops leaned against the heavens. They see their dark green tender leaves trembling in the April wind. They walk under the grove of trees of Heaven. They walk out among the graves.

"I'll haf to cut the briars," says Tarvin, "before you can decorate the graves."

"I cut the briars last year," says Subrinea. "It is the dark loamy earth. The briars grow up over night here."

Tarvin cuts the briars with his hoe. He whacks them down. He rakes them from the graves with his hoe. He picks up armloads of briars and carries them from this ancient graveyard. He cuts the sprouts from the graves. He carries armloads of poplar, sassafras and hickory sprouts and piles them with the briars. Subrinea gets down on her knees and places bits of torn sod back in place. She pulls weeds from the graves. She lays bunches of wild roses, dusty miller, wild trillium, blue ageratum, bloodroot and eggplant on the graves. She pushes the dead leaves away from the headstones.

Tarvin looks at the undecipherable names on the crude field-rock headstones. He looks for the names, dates of birth and dates of death. "Subrinea," Tarvin calls, "here is Clarista Tussie's grave. What kin was she to you?"

"My great-grandmother."

"Put an extra bunch of wild roses on her grave."

"Why?"

"I jest like that name."

"She was Pa's grandmother. She lived on the Sexton Land Tract. She never lived anywhere in her life but Cat's Fork."

"She's walked under these very trees then."

"Yes, she has."

Tarvin cuts loads of sprouts and briars until he has cleaned this ancient graveyard under the ailanthus trees. It has not been blotted out by time and the elements. There is mound after mound under these trees of Heaven. The mounds look like sweet-potato ridges. Very few mounds are marked. They remain under the trees of Heaven, unmarked and unknown except to a few of the squatters Anse didn't run away from the Sexton Land Tract. Soon they will be forgotten by dust, eternal time and the elements. Timber and briars will hide this place where graves used to be. Dead leaves will rot to loam and enrich their mounds. They will be forgotten by all human beings except the squatters.

"I feel like I haf to decorate my people's graves," says Subrinea. "Who on this earth that aint a squatter by blood would stoop to decorate one of our graves? People hate us. God knows why we air all that bad."

"I would decorate your graves," says Tarvin. "I would feel good to put flowers on squatters' graves."

"Oh, Honey," says Subrinea. She walks over and puts her arms around Tarvin's neck. She pulls his face down to her face. She kisses his lips.

"You do love me," she says.

"You know I do."

"Tarvin, I love you. I'll allus love you."

Tarvin holds Subrinea in close embrace. Her limbs are close to his limbs. Her face is covered with his face. His arms are about her shoulders. He is pressing her close to him. He is holding her tightly. They stand above the graves of Subrinea's dead. They stand beneath the trees of Heaven. The wind of April blows Subrinea's hair about Tarvin's arms. It rustles the green tender leaves on the trees of Heaven above them. Around them are more than a hundred graves cleaned of briars and sprouts and decorated with wild flowers.

"I've never loved any gal but you, Subrinea," says Tarvin

as he releases Subrinea from his strong embrace. He looks into her cat-colored eyes and speaks these words. "I've never kissed any gal but you, I've never known any gal but you."

"And I've never loved any boy but you," she says.

"We'll be buried beneath these trees of Heaven someday," says Tarvin. "We'll be buried side by side. I'll be buried among the squatters. I loved a squatter gal. Her name was Subrinea. I liked the way the squatters lived. They had a good time while they lived. They didn't work themselves to death. They didn't try to hog all the land; yet they lived. They were a happy lot."

"I'm glad somebody likes us," says Subrinea. She pulls Tarvin's face down close to her face. She kisses his cheeks. She kisses his lips. "Honey, I would do anything fer you," she says. "You don't know what a good wife I could make fer you. I could love you to death."

"I could return that love," says Tarvin. "I could love you to death."

"We don't want to do that," Subrinea laughs.

"We'd better be goin," says Tarvin. "It's about dinner time."

"Jest a minute," says Subrinea. "I got a few bunches of wild roses left."

Subrinea takes a bunch of wild roses for each lamb's grave. She drops the bunches on the lambs' graves. "We air ready to go now," she says.

Subrinea carries the empty basket on her arm. Tarvin carries the gooseneck hoe. They walk down Cat's Fork toward Ragweed Hollow. The April world about them is filled with wild bird cries. It is filled with blossom and song. The earth is alive. It is breathing. It holds Subrinea's dead. It holds their dreams beneath the trees of Heaven. It will hold them eternally here. Many springs will be resurrected; many crops will be planted and reaped; many generations will be born and many will die away; but Subrinea's people are a part of the earth; Subrinea is a part of the earth and she and her people will lie forever enfolded in the rich cover of the earth under the trees of Heaven on Cat's Fork.

11.

BOLIVER GOES to the tobacco bed. He carries a big two-bushel basket. Big Aaron carries a basket. They pull the rank tobacco plants from the bed. They leave the tiny tobacco plants for another setting. They carry the big baskets filled with fresh plants across the muddy field. They carry them beyond the field of young sturdy growing corn.

Clarista and Winnie Tussie drop the plants along the deep furrowed rows. Subrinea, Crissie, Boliver, Big Aaron and Snail follow along the rows and set the plants. They work fast to set the tobacco before another rain. "It's a good terbacker-settin season right now," says Boliver. "We want to git our terbacker set, fer next week our corn will do to hoe. Our cane will be ready to plow. Our work is comin on us right at once."

"And I want to git out long enough," says Crissie, "from this terbacker settin to pick us a lard can full of sallet greens and cook 'em with a big piece of meat. My mouth jest waters fer the taste of 'em. I'm gittin tired of that old grub we've been eatin. I want somethin fresh."

"God Almighty, I do too," says Boliver. "Don't talk about them good sallet greens here. I might start eatin these green terbacker plants."

"You jest about eat 'em atter they git ripe," says Snail. "If I's to chaw terbacker like you do, I'd git sick as a hoss. 'Pears to me like you eat terbacker, the way you cram big chaws back in your jaw."

"Son, you aint old enough," says Boliver, "to chaw your terbacker like a man. Wait until you git older, then you can talk about chawin your terbacker. You will take a bigger cud in your mouth then. You won't be talkin about your Pa."

Clarista and Winnie walk along the deep furrows in the newground and drop tobacco plants. They walk fast. Their slender bare legs are spotted with clumps of mud. Their feet are muddy. The mud has caked to their feet until it is hard for them to lift their feet and carry the baskets of plants. They walk through the mud and drop the plants as fast as Boliver, Crissie, Subrinea, Snail and Big Aaron can set them.

"God Almighty, but this is a back-breakin job," says Boliver. "It takes a weak mind and a strong backbone to walk through the newground all day and set out terbacker. I feel like all my blood has gone to my face I've stooped over so much today."

" 'Pears like my eyeballs air goin to pop out any minute," says Crissie, "I've stooped over so much today."

Crissie stands up in the tobacco row. She throws her shoulders back and puts her hands on her hips. "Whew!" she says; "it's my eyes."

"It don't bother me a bit," says Subrinea.

Subrinea does not stand up straight. She bends over and keeps setting tobacco. Her strong brown legs are spotted with mud. Her knees are covered with mud where she has often bent on her knees when she set a tobacco plant. One cannot tell what Subrinea's feet are made of. It looks as if Subrinea is walking on feet and legs made of newground dirt that is mixed with water and shaped into a pulpy loblolly. Subrinea takes the bottom row and is far ahead of the tobacco setters. Her long slender body moves along with ease. She laughs as she takes the green smelly plant and puts its silk-hair roots into a little hole she has made with her hand in the muddy furrow. She pulls the water-soaked dirt over the tobacco roots and presses it down with her hand. Then she drags over a handful of loose dirt and levels it around the plant. She moves on to another tobacco plant.

"I don't mind settin terbacker plants," says Subrinea. "I think terbacker is sicha purty weed. I like to see it when it really starts growin along the middle of July when the sun starts beamin down to make the damp earth hot. That's when terbacker grows. It has a purty blossom too. I love to see a terbacker patch in bloom about the middle of August."

"You air right, Subrinea," says Boliver; "terbacker does its growin right in the hot days. I think terbacker starts gittin purty about the time when the suckers start poppin from behind the leaves. I love to feel a summer wind stir then. I like to hear the flap-flappin of the terbacker leaves in the wind. God Almighty, but I like the smell of green terbacker plants on hot days. I guess I'm jest a little a-kin to the terbacker worm. I can smoke it, snuff it and chaw it. I jest love the taste of this fragrant weed."

Below them are long rows of set tobacco plants. They twist around the newground slope. They follow the curves of the ravines, the flats and banks. They dodge the big stumps. They stop for the cliffs and the big rocks. The ground is loamy and black. It looks like a winter-colored earth where no weeds grow nor flowers bloom. It is a black-loam land, a gray-ash land. It is a land filled with roots, stumps, rocks. It is a land that was hard for the mules to plow. It is a new land that is hard to conquer. There is a wildness in the dirt that is hard to kill. It will take years to kill this wildness and tame the land as Anse Bushman has tamed his land. But from the black bosom of this newground earth will spring a heavy crop. Prolific roots will sink into the bosom of this rich earth. Giant stalks of tobacco will grow.

"I'm about all pooped out," says Big Aaron. He straightens his tall body and stands in the tobacco row. His hands are covered with mud. Thin mud works up and down between his toes. Thin mud works up and down between Crissie's toes. Thin mud works up and down between Boliver's toes. "Whew," says Big Aaron, "I feel a swimmin in my head. Bent over all day, and it 'pears like the blood has rushed to my fard. Terbacker settin in newground is enough to poop a body out. It's all right to set terbacker in old ground where the ground is all worked up and a body can rake plenty of dirt around the terbacker roots with his hands. It's jest hard to set terbacker in newground, where there's so many roots, rocks and stumps."

"But it takes newground," says Snail, "to raise good terbacker. We'll raise the terbacker here in these coves."

"Enough to fill two big barns," says Boliver. "You jest wait and see if we have a good growin season. If we don't have another drouth to fire the terbacker we'll have an awful crop."

"Lord, I'm so hungry that I feel like my belly has growed to my backbone," says Snail.

"We jest have two more rows," says Subrinea. "Let's finish the terbacker settin and have it over with. We can't leave the field with jest two rows to set."

"You air right," says Boliver. "The skies might git clear tonight and the wind start blowin. The ground will dry out and we'll haf to wait fer another rain to fall before we can set the rest. Then we'll have the field in early terbacker and two rows of it in late terbacker. Let's stick with it until we git done. I know you youngins air about all pooped out, but look at me and your Ma—you air young and on your first legs and we aint no more on our first legs."

"You air right, Boliver," says Crissie. She stands in the

furrow and wipes the mud from her hands on a stump. Then she wipes her hands again on her apron. She puts her hands into her apron pocket and gets her pipe. She holds her long-stemmed stone pipe in her left hand. She reaches into her apron pocket with her right hand. She pulls out a wisp of bright tobacco crumbs. She puts them in the bowl of her pipe. She tamps them with her index finger and thumb. She reaches back into her apron pocket with her left hand. She fingers for a match and finds it. She strikes the match on Boliver's pants leg. She lights her pipe.

"Terbacker smoke allus stops my hunger," says Crissie. "All I haf to do is taste smoke, then my hunger is gone."

"Terbacker heps my hunger too," says Boliver, "that's the reason I'm chawin so much terbacker today. We want to stick to this terbacker field until we git done."

Boliver, Crissie, Subrinea, Snail, Big Aaron, Winnie and little Clarista struggle through the long deep furrowed rows. The day is done. It is time for darkness to fall. They walk through the mud barefooted until all the tobacco plants have been set. They slick the heavy mud from their hands. They kick it from their feet as they walk from the field.

"Now Subrinea," says Crissie, "we'll haf to git home and git a bite of supper. I'm might' nigh too tired to eat."

"I never was so hungry in my life," says Subrinea.

"That's why I say you ought to chaw 'r smoke terbacker," says Snail. "You won't git hungry then."

"When I want to use terbacker," says Subrinea, "I'll use it. I won't ast you fer your advice."

"I guess Tarvin Bushman told you not to use it," says Snail. "I guess he thinks it looks bad to see wimmen chaw and smoke."

"Turnin agin the things his poor old Ma likes if he feels like that," says Boliver. "That's heathen-like. I like to see everybody use the fragrant weed that likes it. Nearly all of 'em like it. God Almighty put terbacker here fer a purpose. That

purpose was to use it. Preachers preach against it. When I hear
'em start that kind o' preachin I git up and git my hat and
walk out'n the house."

Boliver walks in front. He walks down the bank from the
newground tobacco field. Crissie follows Boliver, and the
children follow Crissie. Their bare feet walk silently over the
dark muddy earth. They swing their arms as they walk down
the path and across Ragweed Hollow. They walk up the bank
to their shack under the oak trees. The stars have come into the
sky. The wind is getting cool. A bull-bat flies over them and
screams. A whippoorwill calls to its mate.

Part V

1.

"I AINT kickin Boliver," says Anse, "but he don't know how to handle mules. Jack and Barney have lost a hundred pounds apiece since Boliver hast been plowin 'em in that newground. One mornin I says to Boliver: 'Boliver, what is the matter with my mules? Air you givin 'em all the water they'll drink three times a day?' 'Yes,' he says, 'I'm givin 'em all the water they'll drink three times a day. I'm waterin 'em in that big hole o' clear cool water under the beech grove above the charcoal bottom. It's Ragweed Crick water. It's runnin in a fast stream.' Then I ast 'im: 'Air you feedin 'em plenty? You know the feed is in the barn fer 'em.' 'I'm givin 'em ten years of yaller corn at a feed,' he says, 'and I'm fillin their mangers plum full of clover hay. I'm givin 'em all they'll eat.' 'Then there must be somethin wrong,' I says, 'fer when you work Jack and Barney, that's when they start lookin good. If you let 'em run out and kick up their heels they git poor as snakes. They git so poor you can count their ribs. I know somethin is happenin to my mules. My mules may kick the hat off'n your head but to me they air like children. I haf to watch over 'em.'

"Boliver didn't say anythin more. I didn't say anythin more. But I thought a lot jest the same. I thought I'd slip over there some day and see what they's doin to my mules."

"Won't you have some more coffee, Anse?" Fronnie asks. Fronnie takes the coffeepot from the flat-topped stove in the corner of the kitchen. She carries the coffeepot with a dishrag around the handle to keep from burning her hand. She pours

239

Anse's coffee cup full of hot foaming coffee. Anse does not speak while the coffee is pouring from the pot. He watches the black stream of coffee leaping from the spout. He whiffs the fragrant scent of coffee into his nostrils. Fronnie fills her empty coffee cup.

"You can pour me another cup too," says Tarvin.

Fronnie fills Tarvin's empty coffee cup.

"Aint nothin better than strong coffee fer a body when they git up at three o'clock in the mornin," says Anse. "I jest love the taste of coffee. I like it without sugar and cream."

"So do I, Pa," says Tarvin.

Fronnie does not speak. She walks back to the stove and sets the coffeepot on the stove. She lays the dishrag on the kitchen table. She walks over to the table. She sits down at the table across from Anse.

"Did you find out what was the matter with the mules, Pa?" Tarvin asks.

"Yep, I did," says Anse. "I slipped back across this end of the newground where they've got their terbacker set. God Almighty, I've never seen sicha purty terbacker. It's a long ways ahead of ourn. I slipped up to the knoll and I looked over that ledge of rocks. I'll tell you what I saw. I saw that damned lazy Snail Tussie ridin the plow and Boliver drivin the mules. I didn't stay in my hidin place long. I took out through the terbacker patch. I went over where they were.

" 'Boliver,' I says, 'that's what's the matter with my mules. Have that goddamn lazy Snail to git his tail off'n that plow. You know that my mules can't pull that big cutter plow through this newground and break these balks that have never been plowed before with a load on the plow. I jest don't want this to happen ever again. My mules air worth more to me than all this newground corn and this terbacker. I've plowed these mules since they's colts. I know they was broke to plow and they know how to plow. They air the best plow mules fer newground in this country. They ought to be. They've plowed enough newground.'

"Boliver looked plagued. You ought to a-seen Snail crawlin off'n the plow. I took the mules and plowed a couple of rounds. I says: 'Jest one man to these mules. Snail, you can git you a hoe and git with the rest of 'em and do a little work. Boliver ought to stand all these mules can stand in this rough plowin. They haf to pull the plow and break this bed of roots beneath the ground. All you haf to do is guide the plow.' "

"Did Snail git his hoe and go to work with the rest of 'em?" Tarvin asks.

"You're damned right he did," says Anse. Anse pushes back his red beard and takes another sip of coffee from the mustache coffee cup that Fronnie got him five years ago for a birthday present. Part of the coffee cup is covered to keep his beard and mustache from getting into his coffee. There is just a hole in the top of the cup to pour the coffee in from the pot. "If he hadn't a-got off'n that plow," Anse continues, "I'd picked me up a root from the corn balk and I'd a larruped that young man until he'd a-been glad to a-got off. I'd a done it if I'd a-had to fit all the Tussie family."

"What did Boliver say when you told him to git off'n the plow?" Tarvin asks. Tarvin takes another sup of coffee and looks across the table at Anse.

"He didn't say a damned word either," says Anse. "He jest looked at me. I says to him: 'Remember, Boliver Tussie, you air under a contract to pertect my mules and take care of all the tools you use. Remember these mules air worth your whole crop.' Boliver jest looked plagued. He didn't say a word. I think Boliver is a man that don't want trouble. He's jest got a family that don't know how to do nothin. I thought I'd better larn them how to plow before I left the mules. You ought to a-seen the mules step along when I got a-holt of 'em. I showed 'em how to plow newground. They air a people that aint never been under the yoke. They've been ust to a good time. Now their feet air shod like a colt's feet and their work is jest beginnin. They've jest run around and danced and cavorted and had a good time all their lives. They've lived like wild people. It's time they's larnin to work and by God, if they live on my land they haf to work. They aint no better than we air."

"How did the corn look over there in their newground?" Tarvin asks. "I aint seen it in a long time."

"I'd a-thought you'd a-seen it, Son," says Anse. "God Almighty never let purtier corn grow out'n the earth. Tarvin, it is a sight to see. Great rank stalks of corn air poppin from them coves over there jest like pokeberry stalks grow from a rotted stump. Crushaw vines and punkin vines air runnin all over the corn balks. Bean vines air climbin the corn stalks at the bottom of the newground like mornin glories. It's a sight to see. And the smell of that newground cornfield is better than the smell of a good coffee early in the mornin."

"How many were workin in the cornfield when you's over there?" Tarvin asks.

"Boliver and Snail were workin at the plow," says Anse. "Crissie, Subrinea, Big Aaron, Winnie and Clarista were down below 'em with hoes. Crissie was takin the bottom row. Subrinea was at her heels with her row. That Big Aaron was a way behind 'em. He needs a brush took to him too. He needs a club around his rump—any big stout young man like he is lettin his poor old Ma and his sister take rows of corn and lead 'im halfway through the field. The little girls were a fur piece behind."

"Whop—hop—" yells Tarvin as his chair reels beneath him. There is a splintering of wood and Tarvin up-ends heels over head on the floor. The chair breaks beneath his weight. "I jest moved to git up," says Tarvin. "Thought I'd been hearin somethin poppin beneath me. It was that chear."

Tarvin gets up from the floor. He brushes his pants legs. He rubs his hips.

"Air you hurt, Son?" Anse asks.

"Nope," says Tarvin. "Jest a chear broke down in the floor with me. I'm glad it was me instead of you 'r Ma. It's liable to a-hurt one of you. It would a-broke down with you, Pa. You know that. You air a lot heavier than I am. It is a good thing you've never set down in this chear."

"My furniture aint no good," says Fronnie. "It is rotten. My dishes air all broke up. I've lost nearly all the knives, forks and spoons I've got. I guess the rats hast carried 'em under the floor. Aint got enough dishes to set the table when company comes; yit Anse buys more land. Anse wants more land and more land."

"No I don't, Mother," says Anse softly to Fronnie. "I've got all the land I want. I've got all the land I need. I'll never buy another foot of land. You have hepped me to buy the land I have, now I will hep you buy all the furniture you want. I'll go to town with you this mornin and git it. We'll jest go buy all the furniture you want."

Fronnie looks at Anse. She sips coffee from the cup. Anse sips coffee from his cup. He pulls it through the hole in the mustache cup with a snort. It is not pleasing for Fronnie and Tarvin to hear Anse drink coffee. After Anse takes a sup of coffee he sets the cup on the table and presses his beard down against his chin. It looks satiny soft in the yellow glow of the morning lamplight. It has a sparkling red luster about it that Fronnie and Tarvin cannot help but notice.

2.

AFTER ANSE, Tarvin and Fronnie milk the cows, Anse feeds the hogs and the chickens. Fronnie strains the milk and puts it in the cellar. Tarvin harnesses Murt and Dick. He hitches the young mules to the jolt-wagon. He drives the team out from the barn to the house. He ties the leather check lines around the yard pine tree that stands by the front-yard gate. Anse and Fronnie get ready to go to Greenwood. Tarvin takes the bright-worn gooseneck hoe from where it hangs on the garden palings. He walks around the hillside path toward the tobacco field.

Anse and Fronnie drive down the Ragweed Hollow road. Anse sits on the front seat with the strong leather check lines in one hand. He holds the brake beam with his other hand. Anse is dressed in his blue serge suit. He wears his big umbrella hat. Fronnie wears a new gingham black-checkered dress. She wears her new bonnet with the long slats. The bonnet strings are tied under her chin. She wears an apron and in the pocket on the left side of her apron is her pipe, tobacco and matches. Fronnie sits beside Anse on the jolt-wagon seat that is softened by coffee sacks wrapped around the seat-board.

They ride away together down the hollow. Anse is smoking a cigar and there is a stream of smoke following the wagon. Soon the wagon disappears into the deep hollow and the stream of smoke thins and dies on the wind.

When Anse and Fronnie return at noon, they have twelve new chairs. They have two new sets of dishes. They have two sets of knives, two sets of forks, two sets of spoons. They have glassware, pitchers, glasses, crocks, churns, bread pans, pots, tin cups, water buckets and two new beds. "When I git furniture," says Anse, "I believe in gittin it. I don't believe in gittin two or three dishes and two or three chears. I've heerd 'furniture' at this house until I'm sick of hearin about it. When I buy land I want acres. When I buy furniture I want pieces of furniture and plenty of 'em. I jest let your Ma pick the furniture and I stood back and told her to buy plenty of all she wanted. She jest kept wantin furniture and I jest kept buyin. We brought back all the mules could pull on the jolt-wagon. It was a big load fer the young mules comin up Ragweed Holler. We'll never need all the plunder we've got. We can't make use of it."

"That will do Ma good," says Tarvin. "She's been wantin new house plunder fer a long time."

"I jest hope it will," says Anse. Anse pulls the harness from the young mules. He hangs it on the forked limbs that are used as harness hangers above the mangers. He carries corn from the crib and puts it in the mules' boxes. He forks hay down from the loft into the mules' mangers. "I'll tell you, Tarvin, I've had to stand a whole lot. I aint grumbled about what your Ma hast said to me. Your Ma hast been actin funny here lately. She aint been talkin nigh right. She's been talkin to the cows, hogs and chickens. She talks all night long in her sleep. She talks about me in her sleep. She's getting me worried. She talks about seein me in a lake of fire. She talks about hell, damnation and the hereatter. She's allus sayin I'm lost. Jest goes on continually."

Anse brushes the dust from his blue serge suit. He takes off his big black hat and knocks the hayseed from the brim. He walks from the barn toward the house where there is a stream of gray smoke rising from the kitchen flue. Tarvin walks beside Anse. They can smell bread and sizzling bacon. They can smell the appetizing scents of cooking food. They pass the wagonload of furniture under the pine tree by the front-yard gate. There is a big rock under the hind wagon wheel to chock the wagon. The brake beam is pulled down.

"Thought we'd wait until atter dinner," says Anse, "and unload the furniture. We haf to be mighty careful."

After Fronnie, Anse and Tarvin have eaten their dinners, they unload the furniture from the jolt-wagon. Fronnie smiles and smokes her pipe as she helps carry dishes, spoons, knives, forks, glassware and crocks into the house. Fronnie is a happy woman. She does not talk to Anse about hell's fire. She does not remind Anse that his soul is lost. "We'll lose this day in the terbacker patch," says Anse to Tarvin when Fronnie goes into the kitchen with a load of dishes. "I'd ruther lose this day than to hear what I've heerd the last month. I hate to lose a day's work, but it's the best."

Just as Anse, Tarvin and Fronnie are carrying the last load of dishes into the kitchen, Crissie walks up to the kitchen door and knocks on the door. Fronnie walks over to the door.

"Howdy do, Mrs. Bushman," says Crissie politely.

"Howdy do, Crissie," says Fronnie. "Won't you come in?"

"Nope," says Crissie, "I jest don't have the time to spare. I've jest come from the terbacker patch. I come over to git your old furniture."

"My old furniture!" says Fronnie. "I didn't send fer you to come over and git it, did I? If I did I don't remember it."

"Yep," says Crissie, "a little bird flew over and told me you's gittin a lot of new furniture. It told me that I might git your old furniture since you's gittin brand-fired new furniture."

Fronnie stands in the kitchen door and looks at Crissie.

"That same little bird," says Fronnie, "that flew over your terbacker patch and told you I's gettin new furniture fer my house, can fly back over your terbacker patch and tell you that you can't have my furniture. Jest to tell you the truth, I've never heerd of sicha work in my life. I want to keep my old furniture. I want to keep my old chears. I love my old furniture fer what it has been and I want to keep it."

"There aint nothin in the ar-tickle of the ciphers and the word," says Anse, "where it said we's to give you our old furniture, is there? If there is we'll give it to you. Young woman, you'd better git back to the terbacker patch where you come from. If we want you to have our old furniture we'll let you know."

Crissie opens her mouth and shows her catlike teeth. Tarvin does not speak. Anse stands beside Fronnie and looks at Crissie as she turns and walks down the path from the house toward Ragweed Hollow.

"That beats anything I ever heerd of," says Anse. "How did she know we'd gone to town this mornin to git new furniture? What right did she have to come over here and ast Fronnie fer her old furniture?"

Anse lights a cigar. He walks madly through the house. "Can't expect nothin more from squatters," he says. "You give them a good house atter they've lived in hog pens and they start wantin more. They never know when they git their wants. I'll fly loose here one of these days and I'll clean house. It aint like it ust to be. I've done everything fer them that was in the ar-tickle fer me to do. I've done my part. Yet they aint satisfied. I've furnished 'em a cow and opened a store account fer 'em. Jest let 'em go and git what they want. They couldn't a-made bread this summer if it wasn't fer me."

"I DON'T like it," says Anse to Fronnie. "I tell you I am a decent man. That is what I told 'em."

Anse squares himself beneath the yard pine tree. He holds his smoking cigar in his left hand. With his right hand he strokes his beard. Fronnie stands beside Anse—a tall mountain tree, Fronnie is, with winter in her hair. Time finds it hard to bend her tall strong body with hard work, childbirth and the weight of the years upon her shoulders.

"What air you talkin about?" Fronnie asks.

"Wimmen," says Anse. "Don't guess I should tell you but it plagues me. It plagues a man of my years. I aint a huntin wimmen. I got a good wife. Fronnie, you have been a good woman. You have been a good wife. You have been a wife good to me as any man could have."

"What air you drivin at, Anse?" Fronnie asks. "Tell me about these wimmen."

"Bad wimmen," says Anse, "and I think they were Tussie wimmen. They had red hair and freckled faces like the Tussies. They were tall and thin like the Tussies. Looked like razor-back hogs to me. That's the Tussies."

"Bad Tussie wimmen," Fronnie says. She puffs her pipe. "Bad Tussie wimmen atter you, Anse. Bad wimmen. The old low-down strollops! When did you see 'em, Anse? Where did you see 'em?"

"I was out lookin over the sheep pasture a little bit ago," says Anse. "I was lookin fer sheep drippins over the pasture field to see if any of my sheep has stummick worms. I was down there by the chestnut-oak grove on the bluff. I saw two wimmen comin up the holler. They's doin a lot of talkin and laughin. They 'peared to be happy as two medder larks. I jest stood there and watched 'em. They saw me. 'Yander's a purty bearded man,' says one of the wimmen. Then she laughed and laughed. She bent over laughin. She slapped the other woman on the back as she laughed. 'He is my man,' says the other woman. Then the other one says, 'No, you can't have 'im. He's my man. I want a old man with long beard. I'll take 'im out in the terbacker patch with me!' 'No you won't,' says the other woman. They argued and argued like they's goin to fight over me. They both laughed like they thought it was funny. I was so dumbfounded that I couldn't talk fer a minute 'r two. Then I started becomin Anse Bushman again. My heart quit flutterin and my mind got clear. I'll tell you right now, Fronnie—you have been a good wife to me. You have been the woman I wanted and I got you. I thought about all of this and I says: 'I'll tell you strollops somethin right now. You air talkin to Anse Bushman and you air on his land. I aint wantin to go into the terbacker patch with you and I aint goin with either one of you. I want you to hike your tails off'n my farm. I want you to git off in a hurry. I'll have you to understand that I've got a wife and a good wife.' They went up the holler. They didn't talk back to me. When they saw how mad I got they didn't laugh any more. I'll tell you, Fronnie, it don't pay to fool with people like Tussies. I never did like squatters. I've told you they was low-down. Jest because Tarvin wanted Boliver on his place and you uphelt fer 'im, that's why we've got 'em on the farm now. These wimmen went up the holler toward Boliver Tussie's."

"I could cut their hearts out with a butcher knife," says Fronnie. "I could kill 'em, Anse, free as I ever et a bit o' grub. I could take a garden hoe from the palins and chop their damned necks in two."

Fronnie quivers like a winter leaf in the wind. She looks at Anse. Anse looks at Fronnie.

"Mommie," says Anse, "you know if I'd been out with 'em I wouldn't be tellin you about seein 'em. I couldn't hep it because they found me in the woods and talked like they did to me. It riled me, Fronnie."

"I could cut their necks off with a briar scythe," says Fronnie "I didn't know I loved you so. I hate the old gallivantin low-down strollops. Out tryin to take another woman's man."

Fronnie looks wild out of her eyes as she talks to Anse. She puffs harder on her long pipestem. The pipestem jimmeys in

Fronnie's mouth because several of her front teeth are out and
it is hard for her to hold the pipestem between her lips with
the weight of a pipeload of tobacco out on the end of a long
stem.

"I feel like goin atter them wimmen," says Fronnie.

"Now Mommie," says Anse with his rough tone of voice
softened as he speaks to Fronnie, "aint no use to do that. Jest
let that pass. We'll haf to git shet of that bunch over there
some way. I slipped out in the cornfield and hid behind a
stump this mornin and watched 'em work. I know what's goin
on. I know I love terbacker much as any man. I love to smoke
cigars and I can chaw terbacker. But I've never seen sicha family of terbacker worms as the Tussies. They have terbacker hid
in all the stumps over there in their cornfield. Boliver found a
package of Red Horse scrap terbacker that Snail had in a
holler stump. I saw 'im take it out'n the stump this mornin.
Then I saw Snail go over the hill to look fer his terbacker.
When he didn't find it he says: 'Who in the hell stole my sweet
terbacker?' He looked all around. Not a person opened his
mouth. Boliver had it in his hip pocket. Old Boliver workin
barefooted in there among the copperheads and fightin sweat-
bees and wipin sweat, diggin with a long gooseneck hoe."

"Did Snail git his terbacker?" Fronnie asks.

"Nope," says Anse, "you know he didn't. Boliver found it.
I saw 'im mixin Snail's Red Horse sweet scrap terbacker with
his home-growed burley that I give 'im. I saw him takin a
chaw that looked big as a goose egg behind his red-bearded jaw.
I heard Big Aaron down in the cornfield cussin. He said somebody had stole his poke of Honest Scrap terbacker. I heerd
Boliver cussin when he went down to his big black-oak stump
and said somebody had stole his plug of Brown Mule terbacker.
Said somebody had got his sweet terbacker. Crissie went down
to a holler beech stump in a bean-vine cove and said somebody
had stole her Shoe Peg twist terbacker. 'If I find out the
youngin that got my terbacker,' says Crissie, 'I'll stand 'im on

his head and pour a bucket of water in his touch-hole.' Crissie
was mad as a hornet. Boliver give her a chaw of the Red Horse
scrap terbacker that he stole from Snail. I never heard sicha
fussin over terbacker in my life. 'Peared like every youngin
over there but Subrinea's got terbacker hid in a stump to keep
the others from stealin it. All jest a-workin to beat the band
and smokin terbacker 'r chawin it. I'd ruther see 'em smokin
and chawin as to see 'em out there standin in the dust under
the brilin sun with their mouths open like they's tryin to beat
the lizards catchin flies.''

"Have they got a good crop?" Fronnie asks.

"The best I ever saw" says Anse. "They've got better corn
and terbacker than we've got. They've got the best land.
They've got land that aint had the wildness taken out'n it yit.
And they air good workers. They jest git right down with a
hoe and dig. They dig up too many roots from the ground and
carry 'em off to the fur edge of the field and burn 'em. It's goin
to make my ground wash when the heavy rains come this fall.
I've warned Boliver about it. I can't kick on their work. It's
jest funny the way they like terbacker. It's strange how each
person tries to hide his terbacker from the other. They jest cuss
and dig and chaw terbacker.

"I'll tell you somethin else, Fronnie," says Anse. "I've been
over to the wild raspberry patch. Somebody has got 'em all.
Somebody has picked the berries fer us and tromped the vines
into the ground. Somebody has picked all the wild strawberries. Somebody has made a road through the woods to my
turnip patch. The road goes toward Boliver's shack. It goes
to the fur edge of their corn patch and atter I got there I lost
the path. There wasn't any more path to follow. It petered out
in the corn rows. Somebody has stripped my cutter plow of all
the plow pints, bolts, washers, beam-rods, and the cutter. Somebody has even stole the teeth out'n my harrow. Who's doin all
this stealin here, nohow?"

"I don't know, Anse," says Fronnie. "It ust to wasn't like

this. We never had to lock our corncrib and our smokehouse."

"I haf to lock 'em now," says Anse. "I padlock 'em. I aint takin no chances. Anybody that will steal harrow teeth will steal anything."

"You air right," says Fronnie. "There air a lot of thieves here in Ragweed Holler now. There is even bad wimmen here now."

"Jest come to think about that terbacker," says Anse, "they air buyin it at the Grubb's General Store. I'll haf to go down there and see how the account is runnin. They might be runnin me in debt bigger than all their crop is worth. I'll haf to see about it."

Anse looks toward the Boliver Tussie shack. He can see the tall green stalwart stalks of corn waving in the wind. He can see the knoll densely covered with green burley tobacco stalks. He can see the tobacco leaves moving in the wind. He can see the dark green top sides of the leaves when the wind is still and when the wind rustles the leaves he can see their light green under sides. It looks pretty to Anse Bushman. Anse can see the tall stalks of cane growing from the newground ravine. They look good to Anse—cane stalks shooting skyward in the golden summer sun. Cane shooting from the dark loamy earth, green and pretty in the summer wind! When Anse sees these crops, his beardy lips curve in smile. He holds the cigar in his hand and a tiny stream of smoke curls from the gray-ashed end.

"Where is Tarvin?" Anse asks Fronnie.

"He took the gun when you's out this mornin runnin over the pasture," says Fronnie. "Said he was goin atter you a mess of squirrels."

"Jest because we've sorty ketched up with the hardest part of our work," says Anse, "aint no reason fer 'im to go on a holi-day. It's too early in the season to squirrel hunt nohow. The old she-squirrels 's got youngins now. He oughtn't to be out shootin among 'em."

4.

"Anse," says Fronnie, "I want you to do somethin fer me."

"All right, Mommie," says Anse, "I'll do it if I can."

"You can, Anse," says Fronnie. "You air big and strong. You can do anything. I want you to go over to Boliver Tussie's and see if them wimmen air over there. If they air over there, I want you to run 'em off'n this place. I can't stand the thoughts about 'em comin here. I jest can't stand it. I can't stand old bad wimmen on the place. Remember Tarvin is a young man. And you air a man, Anse. And you air near 'em. I'd jest feel safer if you'd go and run 'em off."

"I'll do it, Mommie," says Anse. "Jest as you say. I've been thinkin about doin it nohow. I'll go over there now."

Anse puffs his cigar. His thick short body moves as quickly as a cat. He takes short strides across the potato patch toward the sheep fence. Fronnie stands under the yard pine and watches Anse step over the potato ridges. She watches Anse's body slowly disappear from sight as he walks over the bank into the sheep hollow—down toward Ragweed Hollow. Fronnie stands under the pine tree and waits. If there is loud talk Fronnie can hear it. It is too far for her hawk-gray dimming eyes to watch the Tussies moving around the house. Fronnie can see the house. On the days when the wind is blowing toward her house as it is today, Fronnie can hear them talking. She can hear what they say. Fronnie waits beneath the yard pine. She smokes her pipe while she waits.

Fronnie can hear vile swearing. She can hear Anse. She can hear children screaming. She can hear women cursing. She can hear women running to the bushes screaming. She can hear women calling Anse all sorts of bad names. Fronnie puffs her long-stemmed clay pipe harder and harder until small clouds of smoke ascend into the limbs of the yard pine and grow colorless on the blue summer wind. Fronnie can hear Anse hollering. She can hear the walloping of a club.

"I aint afeared of Anse gittin hurt," Fronnie thinks. "I've seen Anse in too many fights. Look at the election days when I have had to pull 'im out'n a fight. Anse will fight anything. Anse is a good fighter. He can lick three men his size. Anse is a much of a man. I can't hep it if Anse is seventy-one years old. Anse can whip the Tussies all right. Anse will clean 'em up. Jest to think I'm havin this done, too."

Fronnie smiles as she hears the racket over at Boliver Tussie's shack. She remembers when Crissie came to her house and asked her for her old chairs. She thinks about her wild raspberries stolen from the patch where Fronnie has picked each year and canned. This year Fronnie's jars must lie in the cellar empty and the spiders spin their webs in these jars. Fronnie's strawberries have been picked. And the things those women said to Anse, Fronnie cannot forget. Fronnie sits under the yard pine and waits for Anse to return. She looks over the potato patch toward the sheep-pasture gate.

She sees Anse's head bobbing up from the hollow. Anse is walking quickly up the bank. She watches Anse open the gate. She watches him fasten the gate behind him. Anse walks across the potato patch toward Fronnie. He is walking fast. His short legs carry him quickly toward his wife. His giant arms swing

like pistons at his side. His fire-shovel hands pull through the
evening air like boat paddles on a swift mountain river.

"I jest had to do it, Fronnie," says Anse.

"Do what?"

"Clean house over there."

"What did you do, Anse?"

Anse gets his breath a little hard. His words come in short
hard sentences.

"Boliver was over there on the porch drunk with his feet
hangin over. He was hollerin that he was fallin. All the children, Crissie and the two strange wimmen I saw this mornin
was there. I didn't see Subrinea—come to think about it. I was
so mad I couldn't remember—I jest got me a bresh and I
whopped Boliver until he got up and staggered in the house. I
followed 'im in the house and I whopped 'im until he rolled
under the bed and I whopped him clean back to the fur side of
the bed—over fernenst the wall. I made 'im think he was
fallin. I cut me a four-year-old club before I got to the house."

"Did anybody try to fight you back?" Fronnie asks.

"Big Aaron and Snail did when I's layin it to their Pap,"
says Anse, "and I give them a larrupin apiece and they took
to the bushes screamin. I made fer the strange wimmen and
they run to the woods screamin. I told them never to set foot
on my land agin. They ast me where the boundaries of my land
was. I told them that was fer them to find out and not fer me
to show 'em. Crissie didn't keer nary bit. She was glad of it. I
jest about skeered her little children to death when I went to
cleanin the house with a club. They run like wild turkeys and
screamed. All over their drinkin that old hooch and chawin
terbacker and spittin all over the floor! Old Boliver has right
now went agin the ar-tickle. If I want to go to law about
it, I can take every blasted stalk of corn, cane and terbacker
that he's got. 'I'll give 'im another chance,' I told Crissie."

"We air right now into it," says Fronnie. "We air goin to
have a lot of trouble. I've been worried a long time now. I've

been thinkin that this was goin to come. This world is too sinful. You know that, Anse. While you air a good husband to me anymore, you air a sinful man. You will be in court before this thing is over."

"That is all right," says Anse. "You know how I stand with Judge Whittlecomb. We stand united. Boliver won't have a chance."

"I don't care," says Fronnie. "Anse, I'm proud of you fer straightenin that place up. It jest had to be done. It makes me love you more, Anse. It makes me feel that you air a better man."

"I aint a bad man at heart, Mommie," says Anse. "When I see things aint goin right, I want to do somethin about it. We aint had anything on our place since we've been man and wife as vile as squatters. We've allus got along. We've raised our family. Now our trouble is beginnin in our old age."

5.

"I DIDN'T git you a squirrel Pa," says Tarvin, "but you see what I brought you!"

"Yep, I see," says Anse—"a ground hog! Where did you git 'im, Son?"

"Back yander in that fur cornfield," says Tarvin.

Tarvin lays the ground hog down on the kitchen porch. Its body is covered with dark gray hair. Its short tail is almost black. Its head is covered with light gray hair. There are blotches of blood on its nose.

"Its a fat'n," says Fronnie. "I'll git a lot of grease out'n that'n to bathe my jints for these rheumaties. Can't git my arms above my shoulders half the time. My knees air stiff. My neck hurts. Ground hogs' grease is good medicine fer rheumaties."

"I'll tan his hide fer shoe-strings," says Anse. "I'm needin shoe-strings."

"Pa, I went up the holler," says Tarvin. "I saw a lot of corn down. I jest wondered if the crows air atter our corn. Then I looked around a ear of corn. I saw tracks in the loam. I didn't know whether they were coon tracks 'r ground hog tracks. I jest set down and waited. I knowed if it was a ground hog he'd be out to git his dinner. I waited a few minutes. Here he come. Big fat ground hog waddled up the corn balk. I plugged 'im in the head so I wouldn't hurt his body."

Anse picks up the ground hog. He feels the weight of it. He feels the flesh over its ribs.

"It's shore a fat'n," says Anse. "You can't feel nary rib. It'll be good eatin. We'll pick his bones. I've jest been a-cravin a ground hog fat on newground corn. I'll take 'im out and skin 'im, Tarvin, while you eat your supper."

"Aint you goin to eat your supper now?" Tarvin asks.

"We've et our supper," says Fronnie. "We've waited supper on you until it nearly got cold. We jest went ahead and et our suppers."

Tarvin takes the washpan from the table on the kitchen porch. He walks over to the water bucket. He pours the washpan half full of cold water. Tarvin reaches to a mussy cracked dish over on the side of the table and gouges up a handful of lye soap that Fronnie has made from wood ashes. He smears the soap on his hands and then on his face. He slaps cold water on his face and on his hands. The lye soap lathers on his face. He rubs his face. With closed eyes he feels his way across the porch to the hand-towel that is placed on a roller. Tarvin rolls the towel down to get a dry part to wipe his face. After he rubs the coarse-thread meal-sack towel over and over his face, the skin is reddish-brown.

Fronnie lifts the table spread from over the supper that has been left for Tarvin. She takes a fly swat and shoos away the fat flies. Tarvin sits down at the table with a clean face and clean hands. Anse walks out behind the smokehouse and takes the dead ground hog. He takes his pocketknife and slits the ground hog's tough hide on its hind legs below the leaders. He makes little holes behind the leaders and hangs them over two nails that he has driven into a smokehouse log to hold rabbits when he skins them. Anse hangs the ground hog on the nails. He begins to remove the ground hog's pelt.

"God Almighty," says Anse, "but this ground hog is fat. He's been livin on pokeberries and my corn. Fat enough to render lard from. Fronnie will git lots of grease fer her rheumaties from this ground hog. I'm glad Tarvin likes to hunt the way he does. We'd miss old Tarvin about bringin home wild game if he's gone from this place."

While Tarvin is eating his supper and Fronnie is carrying him an extra pitcher of buttermilk and an extra plate of brown corn bread, Anse finishes skinning the ground hog behind the smokehouse. He lays the pelt upon the top of the wood-ash barrel that Fronnie uses for making lye soap. He covers the pelt with wood ashes to make the hair slip. Don eats the entrails and the paws. Anse wipes his pocketknife on his pants legs. He shuts the long sharp blade and puts the knife in his pocket. He carries the ground hog's carcass folded double in a two-gallon crock into the kitchen.

"Here he is, Fronnie, fat as a butterball," says Anse. "Put a little water and salt over 'im and let 'im soak until mornin."

"I'm sorry, Pa," says Tarvin, "that I didn't git home in time to hep you and Ma milk the cows and feed the hogs."

"It's all right, Son," says Anse, "long as you bring home the bacon. Aint nobody around here goin to kick about it. It's all right when you bring home a ground hog purty and fat as this'n."

Fronnie puts a layer of coarse salt over the ground hog. Fronnie pours the crock half full of water from the water bucket. She carries the crock to the cellar. Anse takes a cigar from his pocket. He picks up a stick from the kindling pile underneath the kitchen stove. He holds the stick of rich pine kindling over the smoked globe of the kerosene lamp. Drops of resin run from the pine kindling stick. A yellow blaze leaps

up the throat of the dingy smoked globe and catches hold of
the kindling. Anse lifts the stick from over the lamp globe and
holds it to the end of his cigar.

"This allus saves a match, Son," says Anse. "You remember that."

"All right, Pa," says Tarvin, as he puts away more corn
bread and buttermilk into his long hollow stomach. "I know it
don't pay to be wasteful."

Anse puffs clouds of smoke into the room. He stands and
watches Tarvin eat. Tarvin's brown sun-tanned lips cover the
brown-crusted bread as he takes big bites from the square of
corn-bread pone that he holds in one hand. He hold his buttermilk glass in the other hand. He takes a bite of corn bread and
then a sup of buttermilk. Tarvin drinks a glass of buttermilk
at three sups.

"Son," says Anse, "I love to watch you eat. You can shore
put the grub away. Jest like I ust to be. I can't do it now.
'Pears like my stummick won't let me. I'd love to be able to eat
like I ust to eat. Lord, but I like to watch you eat. No wonder
you air powerful as a bull to break my pitchfork handles when
we air loadin hay onto the wagon. No wonder you can lift a
doodle of cane hay at one lift onto the hayrack if the pitchfork handle will stand you."

"Pa, I never git enough to eat," says Tarvin. "After the
skin on my stummick gits tighter than the ground-hog skin
over a banjer head, I jest crave to eat more and more. I have
the blamedest appetite. And I sleep like a log every night. I'm
full to my ears now but I jest want to keep on eatin. I want to
eat and eat."

Tarvin looks over the table. The corn-bread plate is cleaned.
The buttermilk pitcher is empty. Tarvin gets up, pats his
stomach with his hands. He stretches his arms above his head
and lays his hands flat on the kitchen loft. He bends his
stomach in and out. "Ahhmm," he says, "I feel better." He
takes his pipe from his pocket. He fills the big pipe bowl with

dry burley tobacco crumbs. He takes the stick of kindling Anse used. He holds it over the lamp globe until it catches fire. He lights his pipe. He whips the stick of kindling in the wind until the fire goes out. He throws the stick back down on the kindling pile beneath the stove. He puffs tiny clouds of light blue smoke from his pipe.

"Think I'll git out and walk around in the yard a little before I turn in," says Tarvin. "Moonlight's so purty in the yard tonight. I like to see the moon shinin down on the yard pines."

"I ust to feel that way when I's a young man," says Anse, "but now I'd soon see the moon shinin down on any other tree as a pine tree."

Tarvin walks out of the kitchen door onto the porch. Fronnie walks back from the smokehouse.

"Where air you goin, Tarvin?" Fronnie asks.

"Ah, jest lumberin about, Ma," says Tarvin. "Et a good supper and I'm afraid if I go to bed on it jest now I'll have a lot of wild fightin dreams. Think I'll walk around in the moonlight under the pine trees and smoke my pipe."

6.

ANSE AND FRONNIE go to bed. Anse puts the kerosene lamp in a split-bottom chair by the head of his bed just as he has always done since he has been married to Fronnie. He lays two matches down beside the lamp. At three o'clock in the morning he will awaken just as accurately as if he were an alarm clock. He will wake one hour before the rooster crows. He will light the lamp, carry it into the kitchen and put a fire in the cook-stove. He will put water in the teakettle. Anse will wake Fronnie and she will start getting breakfast. Anse will go to the corncrib and throw corn over the fence to the hogs so they can eat before the chickens get off the roost to help the hogs eat their corn. Anse will carry big yellow ears of corn and put them into the feed boxes for the mules. He will have all the

work done but milking the cows by the time Fronnie has breakfast ready. Tarvin will sleep until breakfast is ready.

"I'll let 'im sleep now," thinks Anse, "but when he gits a
wife he'll find it different. But I don't worry. Tarvin will come
sound. He won't allus be a sleepy head. He'll wake up when
he starts runnin this farm. He'll haf to hustle. He'll haf to
move. He's got the blood in 'im. Jest like a good fox hound—
old Tarvin will know the right track to follow. It's bred in his
blood, in his flesh, bones and brain."

Anse crawls in bed beside Fronnie in his shirttail. He does
not wear underwear during the hot summer months. He has
always slept in his shirttail. He blows out the lamp. Anse lies
with his eyes wide open peering into the darkness of the room.
He can see the window with a broad strip of moonlight falling
across the floor. Anse cannot sleep. He squirms and twists in
bed. Thoughts flash through his brain as lightning flashes on
a sultry summer night when the earth is starved for water—
when the intense heat makes streams of sweat run down his
body and drip to an earth that has parched lips and that is
thirsting and crying for water.

"I aint heerd Tarvin come back to this house," thinks Anse.
"If he was quiet as a mouse, I would hear him. I wonder if he
has smoked his pipe of terbacker. I wonder where Tarvin is
and what he is doin. I am a man. Tarvin looks sad-eyed.
Tarvin looks strange. Somethin is goin on around the place.
Somethin is wrong—I jest feel it."

While Fronnie snores, Anse rolls under the one thin quilt
that covers their bed. Anse cannot sleep. He gets up from bed.
Quietly he slips on his pants so he will not wake Fronnie. He
walks across the dark room. He does not walk over the strip
of moonlight on the floor. Anse does not want Fronnie to see
him. Quietly he walks to the front-room door. Anse lifts the
latch—quietly he opens the door—slowly—slowly—he slips
out of the house and closes the door behind him. Anse walks
out into a hill world flooded with moonlight. The night is

around him with a million insect sounds. The whippoorwills sing love songs to each other from the hilltops. Anse loves the night around him. He is a free man out in the big out-of-doors. Not even Fronnie is beside him now. That is fine. He is free as the summer night wind is free. He can look over his farm. He can can see the growing crops. He can see the quiet stir of night life on a Kentucky summer night when all life stirs.

"I'll slip over through the cane patch in Boliver Tussie's newground," thinks Anse. "I'll see how the cane looks at night. It ought to be awful purty now. It's time the cane started headin. I'd like to see his terbacker patch at night when the night winds stir the terbacker leaves in the moonlight. That's when I think a terbacker patch is purty. And I'd like to see that mighty newground corn of his'n in the moonlight. Jest somethin tells me to go to the newground tonight."

Anse walks down the path barefooted toward the sheep gate. His feet are wet with dew where he walks through the wet grass. When he walks in the path the dust gathers on his dew-wet feet. There is a little layer of mud gathered on Anse's feet. "Copperheads won't be likely to bite me when my feet air muddy," thinks Anse.

Anse opens the gate and walks into the sheep pasture. He closes the gate and looks over his potato patch in the moonlight. The long rows of dark potato vines between the sheep pasture and the house look good to Anse Bushman. He walks down the little grassy bluff to the hollow. He hears the little streams of cool mountain water trickle over the rocks. Anse sees the big square shadow of a man in the moonlit pool of water when he looks down at the water. He sees the shadow of a basket beard on the man's face. Anse walks up the hill to the cane patch. He walks up the ravine where the cane is planted. "Taller than fence rails," thinks Anse, "with the purtiest heads startin on the stalks." Anse stands under the tall stalks of cane. He looks toward their tops. He can see the moon above the tall cane stalks in the water-over-gravel-colored sky. He can see the big round moon, the color of an autumn beech leaf—big and round as a wagon wheel. It is flooding his fields with light.

Quietly Anse walks under the tall cane. He walks in the furrowed balk. The loose mulched loamy earth is soft to Anse Bushman's feet. Anse feels the strength of youth as he walks over the furrowed earth. Anse can feel strength in his bare feet as he puts them back to earth and walks slowly—looking at the tall dark stalwart stalks of cane on the earth and the moon and stars in the sky above him. Anse feels delighted to hear the music of insects about him. His heart leaps up when he hears the songs of the whippoorwills on the hilltops. He crouches with fear when he hears the terrifying screams of the bull-bat. "Reminds me of the days when I ust to bring the cows up to the milk gap fer Ma," Anse thinks. "Days that air gone by like dead leaves in the wind in years past."

Anse walks into the tobacco patch at the far end of the cane patch. He can see a green cloud of leaves moving slowly in the moonlight. He can smell the green tobacco wet with dew. It is a pleasant odor for Anse. Anse whiffs of the night air as he stands in the tobacco patch. "God Almighty," thinks Anse, "I could throw my hat out in that terbacker patch any place and it couldn't fall to the ground fer the broad terbacker leaves. I've never seen sicha terbacker grow." Anse parts the leaves in the balk as he slowly walks along, touching the plants, smelling the plants and fondling them with his hands. "I jest love the touch of green growin terbacker," thinks Anse. "No wonder man likes to use that purty fragrant weed. It is purty to see; it is good to smell; and it is sweet to chaw and good to smoke."

Anse walks slowly, lifting his big bare feet high and setting them down carefully—feeling with them as he places them on the shadowy ground so that he will not feel a coil of soft flesh bigger than the stem of a wild grapevine, for that is the way the copperhead lies when he hears footsteps. Anse's footsteps cannot be heard though. His bare feet tramp on the damp shadowy earth under the leaves of broad tobacco. "Somethin white," thinks Anse. "It's at the fur end of the terbacker patch. Looks like a ghost to me. I'll see what it is. I'll go toward it."

Anse walks toward the white object. "If it's a ghost, I'll see," thinks Anse. "I've heerd of ghosts but I aint seen one in my life." Anse moves closer and closer to the object. He can see another object beside the white one. It is a tall dark object. Anse can hear them speaking softly to each other. Their words are soft as the mumble of night wind along the tobacco stalks.

"Hi there!" Anse hollers as he nears the two objects. He is close enough that he can see two human beings. "What air you doin?"

The two tall ghosts leap the tobacco rows. They break the broad leaves as they run—faster than the wind—faster than Anse Bushman can run. Anse takes after them. He forgets about the tobacco leaves in the balks. Anse runs to the edge of the newground cornfield. He stops and he can hear his breath coming hard. But he listens for the rustle of the corn blades the way the two went.

"Man and woman," says Anse. "Ah, I have it now. I see why Tarvin went out'n the house to smoke his pipe. I can see through it all now. I'll jest go to Boliver Tussie's shack. I'll see that little lady when she gits home with straw and leaves on her back and in her hair. Out in the terbacker patch at night. I'm a ruint man. I'm goin to lose my only boy. Out at night like two varmints when all life stirs on a warm night."

Anse breathes hard as he walks. He walks under the tall stalks of corn where floods of moonlight pour upon the new-ground earth. Anse walks under stalks of corn that are six feet above his head. He is lost under the tall corn. He cannot sense his direction. He just walks and walks. When he reaches the edge of the cornfield, he is up the hollow above Boliver Tussie's shack. Anse climbs over the fence to the sheep pasture. He walks quickly toward Boliver Tussie's shack. The hound dogs bark as Anse walks in the yard.

"Boliver!" Anse hollers. "Oh, Boliver!"

"Who air you?" asks a voice from within the shack. "What do you want comin around a man's house at this time of night?"

"I'm Anse Bushman," says Anse gruffly, "and I want to know a God's plenty. Git out'n that bed before I come in and pull you out. Come to the door!"

"All right, Mr. Bushman," says Boliver. "I jest didn't know it was you."

Boliver gets out of bed and comes to the door in his shirt-tail. He stands with the door half open, yawns, rubs his bald head with his hands, looks at the stars and moon in the summer sky and talks to Anse.

"Jest what do you want, Mr. Bushman?" Boliver asks. His bald head shines in the moonlight as he stands on the doorstep in his shirt-tail shivering in the night wind.

"I jest want to know if your gal is in bed," says Anse.

"I reckon so," says Boliver. "I'll go and look. Somebody been in your chickens? Am I dreamin 'r what's this all about?"

"Ast no questions," says Anse. "Go look and see if she's in the bed."

Boliver goes back in the house. Anse waits for him to return. Boliver is gone two minutes. He comes to the door.

"She's in there in bed, Mr. Bushman."

"Was she sound asleep?" Anse asks.

"Yes, she was snorin, Mr. Bushman."

"Air you shore she was in bed?"

"Yes. If you want to see you air perfectly welcome to come in."

"Nope, I'll not come in. I must be gittin back over home."

"What's this all about, Mr. Bushman? I'd like to know."

"Never mind," says Anse. "Good night to you."

Anse walks over the bluff toward Ragweed Hollow. Boliver stands in the door in his shirttail and watches Anse walk over the bluff.

"Little innocence," says Anse. "She jest beat me to the house is all. If I hadn't lost my way in that tall corn I would a-ketched 'em. I ought to a-slipped upon 'em in the terbacker patch, and nailed holt of 'em instead of hollerin. Jest like varmits. I'll be out over this place from now on. If I catch 'em I'll use a two-year-old club on 'em. I'll whop 'em worse than I did Boliver fer gittin drunk."

Anse walks down Ragweed Hollow to the little creek that leads up to his sheep gate below his potato patch. He turns to his left—walks up the creek and through his potato patch home. As Anse walks along the potato vines, the dew cleans the dirt from his feet. He will not have to get a washpan of water and wash his feet before he goes to bed. Anse walks over the yard grass into the house. He slips upstairs to Tarvin's room. Anse lights the lamp. Tarvin is in bed. The sweat is streaming from his face. He is snoring. He does not wake when Anse lights the lamp. Anse blows out the lamp, walks down the stairs. "Little innocence," Anse mutters, as he goes down the stairs. He mutters these words loud enough for Tarvin to hear.

7.

ANSE, TARVIN and Fronnie sit at the breakfast table. It is long before daylight. The rooster has just crowed for four o'clock in the morning. The moon is down. Light streaks are breaking in the east.

"More coffee, Ma," says Tarvin.

Fronnie pours Tarvin another cup of strong coffee.

"I'll take more coffee too," says Anse.

"You're both drinkin more coffee than usual," says Fronnie.

Anse does not speak. Tarvin does not speak. They sit silently and sip their coffee from the saucers. Anse does not talk to Tarvin. They get up from the breakfast table and walk toward the barn. Tarvin walks into the barn. He starts putting the harness on Murt and Dick.

"You can take the mules to the field this mornin, Tarvin," says Anse, "I got some business I got to tend to soon as I hep Fronnie milk the cows."

"All right, Pa," says Tarvin.

Tarvin drives the mules toward the tobacco patch in the twilight of morning. The harness jingles as Tarvin walks behind them and guides the span of big mules out the wagon road from the barn. There is a stream of smoke coming from Tarvin's pipe that smells good to Anse. He stands and watches Tarvin's long body out of sight around the bend beyond the pine trees.

"It's a shame," thinks Anse. "I'll git 'em off'n the place before it's too late. I know he is guilty. I'll not tell Fronnie. It will worry her. There will be plenty of trouble among the wimmen folks. I'll not trouble anybody. I'll do it myself, then I know it will be done."

Anse helps Fronnie milk the cows. He helps her carry the milk to the cellar.

"Anse," says Fronnie, "you air awful good to hep me this mornin. Why air you stayin back to hep me?"

"I've got to go around the sheep fence this mornin," says Anse. "I sent Tarvin to the field with the team."

Anse walks down the hill from the cellar toward the sheep pasture. The morning sunlight falls on the dewy grass—millions of dewdrops sparkle in the short grass on the sheep pasture. There are bunches of oak, sourwood, persimmon and black-oak sprouts here and there over the grassy hill that the sheep won't eat. Anse takes his pocketknife and cuts down a few of these clumps of sprouts as he walks toward the new-ground tobacco patch.

Anse climbs over the sheep fence and walks into Boliver Tussie's tobacco field. He can see Tussies working in the tobacco. They are pulling tobacco suckers from the tobacco stalks. They are pulling the long green worms from the plants. They take the worms from the leaves and pull them in two and throw the slimy mass of green tobacco fluid down in the tobacco balks. Anse walks slowly out toward Boliver and Crissie.

"Good mornin, Mr. Bushman," says Boliver.

"Good mornin," says Anse.

"You air out early this mornin, Mr. Bushman," says Crissie.

"Late," says Anse. "I git out four hours earlier than this every mornin."

"Did you want somethin, Mr. Bushman?" Boliver asks.

"Yep, I do," says Anse gruffly. "I jest come to tell you that you've been violatin the ar-tickle. You've done it more times than once too."

"How have I violated the ar-tickle?" Boliver asks.

"You've been drunk," says Anse. "You know that. You've had bad wimmen on these premises. Look at your wife there—she's goin to have a baby!"

"What if I am," says Crissie. "I know I'm goin to have a baby and I've been goin to have a baby ever' since I've been on this farm. And we air goin to have two babies at our house. What air you goin to do about that, Mr. Bushman?"

Anse looks at Subrinea as she stands in the tobacco balk.

She stands with her hands on her hips. "She is behind with her terbacker row," flashes through Anse Bushman's brain. "She's allus led the workers in the field. She is pregnant. Why aint I noticed this before now? She was as tall and thin as a bean pole. Now she is wearin her apron high." While Anse looks at Subrinea, she pulls a tobacco worm from a tender leaf. When she pulls the worm in two, she vomits quickly on the tobacco plant. "She's shore pregnant," thinks Anse. "That's what wormin terbacker done fer Fronnie when she was packin her youngins." Anse looks at Subrinea and madness inflames his brain.

"God Almighty," says Anse. "Jest as I expected. I aim to put you off'n my place. By God, I want to hike your tails off'n this place and do it within ten days. If you don't I'll put you off. I'm gittin goddamn tired of all this foolishness. I ought never to a-let the goddamn trash of this country moved on my land. There's where I missed it. I'll take this crop back and set you out on your tails in the big road."

"The hell you will, Anse Bushman," says Boliver. "You whopped me with a club when I was drunk. You'll never whop me agin unless I'm drunk. By God, I'll git drunk when I git damned good and ready. I'm gittin tired of all this petticoat gover-mint you got us under. Tryin to tell me how many babies my wife is to have. Tryin to tell me when to pray and where to pray; when to go to church; when to dance and when not to dance. I say, God damn you!"

"I never had a man to talk to me like this," says Anse. "I aim to bust your goddamn purty face with my fist."

"If I can't whop you with my fist," says Boliver, "I'll knock your goddamn teeth down your throat with a rock. If I can't do that, all my family will hep me fight you. You aint got a chance, Anse Bushman! This is one time you air goin to git a real whoppin if you come a step further. You'd better stay where you air."

"Let 'im come on, Pap," says Snail, "me and Big Aaron will

take care of him. We want to git our hands on him nohow. He whopped us with a club. He'll never do it agin."

"I don't have my gun," says Anse; "if I did, this terbacker patch would run red with blood. I can't fight all of you. You got me fouled. But by God, you remember that I'll win this fight. I'll put you off'n my land. This crop will be mine."

"It won't be yourn," says Boliver, "if we haf to come in here at night and cut it all down while it's still green. We've made this crop and we're goin to have our half. You've made half of it and never turned your hand over."

"Turned my hands over, hell," says Anse. "I've got all the work of my lifetime into this land. I've got my life's work tied up in this land. I've got everythin in this land. I've got my whole life in this land."

"This land don't belong to you, Anse Bushman," says Boliver. "You might have your whole life wrapped up in it, but what is one life to a hundred lives? This land belongs to the Tussies and the Beavers. It belongs to us. It belongs to me. My blood, flesh, heart and soul is wrapped up in this land. It is part of me. I am part of it. Look at the men and wimmen you put on the road! They air somewhere—God knows—I don't know where they air—but I know their hearts air here. They air here among these hills. They air buried here. The wild game you destroyed is buried here with the hearts of the squatters."

"Talk all you damned please," says Anse. "You aint goin to fight me fair. I'll let the Law decide this. I know you have violated the ar-tickle. You signed that ar-tickle. This crop will go to me."

"You aint nothin but a nosey old polecat," says Boliver. "You jest go around smellin trouble. Out at night snoopin around. Don't you ever git me out'n bed again. If you do I'll feed you a load that you can't carry!"

"I aint said nothin, Mr. Bushman," says Subrinea, "but I'll tell you I was in this terbacker patch last night. I was here with Tarvin."

"You don't haf to tell me," says Anse. "I know you was here with Tarvin. I know about the Tussie wimmen. I met two onct down the holler. I know what they said to me. They air all alike—all the damned squatter wimmen! They air huzzies! I jest want you off'n my place. You air dangerous as copperheads! I aim to have you off'n my place if the Law says so. If it says fer you to stay, then powder and lead will be the only way to decide this."

Anse walks away. Boliver watches Anse as he walks back toward the sheep pasture. Anse does not cross the sheep pasture fence toward the house. He walks up the hill to the top of the ridge. Anse walks toward town.

"I'd better see what kind of a store account Boliver Tussie hast run up at G. G. Grubb's General Store," thinks Anse, as he walks out the ridge road under the hot July sky. Anse can hear the crickets singing in the glimmering heat. He can see the crows fly over by twos to the pine grove on the hill. Anse can smell the smelly green tobacco as the hot July wind blows up the hill toward him from Boliver Tussie's newground tobacco patch. He can hear the rustle of the green corn blades in the slow summer wind. Anse Bushman walks fast strides along the ridge path. His jaws are firmly set. His thick short body moves quickly as a snowbird hunting for dead ragweed seeds in winter.

"Jest to think Tarvin's in a mess," thinks Anse. "Subrinea's got Tarvin. God damn that outfit to hell nohow. Why did I ever let them move on my place? I'm gittin old and soft. Jest to think they've got my only boy hooked up with the squatters. He'll jest about haf to marry Subrinea. If I could jest git four men to prove her character, that would make her a whore. Tarvin would not haf to marry her. That hast been done here. I could git 'em. I'd like to take that crop and set that bunch out on the road. It would be farewell to the squatters then. They'd all be gone. This is one way out and if I can git 'em out like this I'll do it."

Anse's brain flashes moods of madness like heat glimmers on a sultry evening over the summer sky. "Jest to think I had to take a insult from that family this mornin! Boliver threatened to maul my skull in with a rock. I didn't have a chance agin that whole squatter family. Jest to think they run me off'n my own premises! I'll git even with 'em! I'll fix 'em!"

8.

"Howdy-do, Mr. Bushman," says George Grubb. "Aint seen you fer some time."

"Howdy, George," says Anse. "I aint jest had the time to spare to loaf in town any this spring. I've been a busy man with my crops."

George Grubb takes Anse Bushman's big rough calloused hand into his own small tender hand. He shakes Anse's hand. He looks at Anse with dimming eyes that peer from behind big black-rimmed glasses. His clean-shaven face is close to Anse's face. Anse's face is covered with a mat of sweaty beard. Anse stands squarely and soberly before George Grubb and looks at his dimming eyes with his bright blue twinkling eyes.

"Somethin I can do fer you, Mr. Bushman?" George Grubb asks.

"Yep," says Anse. "You can let me see Boliver Tussie's account here."

"All right, Mr. Bushman," says George Grubb. "I've jest been wonderin when you's comin in to look over this account. I've been lookin fer you every day."

Anse follows George back to the office. They walk unmindful of the farmers and people of the town that have come to buy groceries and to sell products. The store is filled with busy people. It is filled with well-dressed townspeople and tall lean people from the hills with broken faces and calloused hands.

George Grubb comments about crops and the weather as he turns to a big account book on his desk. He keeps talking to Anse as he fingers the place where the letter "T" is indented on the pages of the account book. Anse does not answer the questions he asks. Anse is watching the big book. Anse is wondering what the account will be. George Grubb does not pay any attention when Anse does not answer his questions. He goes on talking to Anse just the same. He keeps piling meaningless words at Anse. He keeps turning the pages of the book and peering over the scribbled writing and the figures on the pages.

"At last, Mr. Bushman," says George. "Right here is his account."

"Let me see it," says Anse. "Let me see how much he's spent fer grub since he's been on my farm makin his crop."

"Several pages of this account," says George. "You know

you told me to let 'im have what he wanted. You have never been in to check his account, Mr. Bushman."

"That's right," says Anse. "I've been a very busy man and I aint had time to loaf in town. You know I raise jest about all I use. I barely haf to come to town. That's the reason I aint checked on Boliver Tussie's account. I didn't think he'd run me in debt much until this mornin. Now I don't put anything a-past 'im."

"He's got a big account here, Mr. Bushman."

"How big is it, George?" Anse asks.

"Over four hundred dollars."

"Jesus Christ," says Anse, "it can't be that much. He aint been buyin grub from this store four months yit. That's a hundred dollars a month."

"Well, it is over four hundred dollars, Mr. Bushman," says George Grubb. "I've jest done what you told me to do. You know we've traded together fer years. This is my business to sell. When you tell me to let a man have anything and you will stand good fer it—I know you will, Anse Bushman. I know you are good as gold. I thought the man was runnin you in debt but it wasn't my business to tell you. It was your business to check this account long before now."

"You air right," says Anse. "Jesus Christ—over four hundred dollars! My store account never run over ten dollars a month in my lifetime. What on earth has he bought, George?"

"Look fer yourself, Anse," says George Grubb. "I've got everythin down right here in black and white that the man bought."

Anse looks at the pages of accounts. Anse gets down close to the page and runs his fingers along the words and works his lips as he silently reads.

In account with

G. G. GRUBB'S GENERAL STORE

Poultry-eggs, Hides, Calves & Furs

Roots Sorghum and Feeds.

Boliver Tussie

March 22—		
6 bars Big Ben Soap		.25
3 lbs. loose soda		.25
25 lbs. navy soup beans		3.00
10 lbs. pintoes		1.35
Plug star tobacco		.25
" granger "		.25
" brown mule "		.25
Shoe peg "		.15
Sugar		.50
Corn meal		1.50
Flour		1.79
Lard		1.04
Baking powder		.25
Salt		.10
White salt bacon		1.14
2 Overall jackets		1.79
coal oil		.10
	Total	$13.96

March 29—		$13.96
White beans		.50
Star Tobacco		.35
Honest scrap		.50
Brown mule		.40
Shoe peg		.25
Meal		1.50
Flour		1.85
Lard 5 lbs.		1.04
Sugar		1.00
Jowl butts		1.00
Coffee arbuckle 3 lbs.		.60
Calico 10 yds.		1.00
Thread 2 spools		.10
10 lbs. flaked hominy		.45
Oat meal		.25
crackers		.25
	Total	$25.00

April 5—		$25.00
3 lbs. arbuckle coffee		.60
6 bars O.K. soap		.25
Side pork (sow belly)		2.50
Baking powder		.25
Sugar		1.80
Pinto beans		1.50
Navy beans		.75
Micky twist tobacco		.50
Shoe peg "		.70
Honest scrap "		.50
Loose crackers		.25
	Total	$34.60

April 12—		$34.60
Coal oil 5 gal.		1.00
Can lard		5.25
Flour		1.85
2 lbs. yeast		.50
Chop (cracked corn) 100 lbs.		2.25
Sugar 100 lbs.		5.00
White salt meat		2.25
15 lbs. barley malt		1.00
Mickey twist		.50
Granger rough cut		.50
Shoe peg		.50
	Total	$55.20

April 19—	$55.20
Coal oil 3 gal.	.60
Walker's twist	.50
Day's work	.50
Honey cut	.50
Picnic twist	.25
Cracked corn 300 lbs.	6.75
Sugar 300 lbs.	15.00
Navy beans 25 lbs.	3.00
Sow belly	3.15
40 lbs. barley malt	2.50
Corn meal	1.50
6 lbs. yeast	1.50
Potatoes	1.25
3 lbs. arbuckle coffee	.60
Total	$92.80

April 26—	$92.80
3 lbs. Arbuckle coffee	.60
O.K. soap	.25
Honest scrap	.50
Granger rough cut	.50
Shoe peg	.40
Sugar 200 lbs.	10.20
Cracked corn 200 lbs.	4.50
Can lard 50 lbs.	5.25
Potatoes	1.35
Jowl butts	2.20
Flour	1.85
2 cans lye	.25
3 bandana handkerchiefs	.25
2 doz. gallon jugs	2.40
Total	$123.30

May 3—	$123.30
Honest scrap	.25
10 lbs. cracked hominy	.45
Overalls 2 pairs	2.19
Calico 10 yards	1.00
Oilcloth 3½ yds.	.85
Broom	.35
Coal oil 5 gal.	1.00
Sugar 100 lbs.	5.25
Chop (cracked corn) 100 lbs.	2.00
Mickey twist	.75
Star	.75
2 lbs. yeast	.50
Day's Work	.50
15 lbs. barley malt	1.00
Meal	1.50
3 lbs. arbuckle coffee	.60
Total	$142.24

May 10—	$142.24
Granger rough cut	.50
Picnic twist	.50
Lugs (jug corks) 500	2.50
Chop (cracked corn)	4.50
Sugar 200 lbs.	10.50
15 lbs. barley malt	1.00
Day's Work	1.00
Apple jack tobacco	.75
4 lbs. yeast	1.00
Beans (white) 25 lbs.	3.00
Beans (pinto) 10 lbs.	1.35
Loose soda 3 lbs.	.25
O.K. soap 6 bars	.25
White salt bacon	2.50
Candy	.25
Total	$172.09

May 17—	$172.09
Potatoes 100 lbs.	1.50
Sugar 200 lbs.	10.20
Chop (Cracked corn) 200 lbs.	4.50
Salt coarse	.25
2 cans lye	.25
2 pair overalls	2.50
yeast 2 lbs.	1.00
Barley malt 40 lbs.	2.50
Flour	1.89
3 lbs. arbuckle coffee	.60
Beans 25 lbs. mixed	3.00
Total	$200.28

May 24—	$200.28
Potatoes 2 bushel	1.50
Chop (cracked corn) 200 lbs.	4.50
Sugar 200 lbs.	4.50
Sow belly (side pork)	3.50
Baking powder	.25
O.K. soap	.25
5 yards calico	.50
10 yds. unbleached muslin	1.00
8 doz. gallon jugs	9.60
Granger rough cut tobacco	.75
Day's Work	.75
Total	$227.38

May 31—		$227.38
Coal oil 5 gal.		1.00
Sugar 300 lbs.		15.00
Chop (cracked corn) 300 lbs.		6.75
Oat meal		.50
Meal		1.50
Lard can		5.50
Pinto beans 25 lbs.		3.00
Loose crackers		.25
Yeast 2 lbs.		.50
Barley malt 30 lbs.		1.00
Coffee 3 lbs. arbuckle		.60
Day's Work		.75
Picnic twist		.50
Star plug tobacco		.60
White salt meat		4.15
10 lbs. course salt		.25
Flour		1.85
	Total	$271.08

June 7—		$271.08
Picnic twist		.75
Day's Work		.75
Sugar 200 lbs.		10.20
Chop (cracked corn) 200 lbs.		4.50
Meal		1.50
Flour		1.89
Jowl butts		5.25
White beans 25 lbs.		3.00
Star soap		.50
Yeast 2 lbs.		.50
Natural leaf tobacco		.50
4 doz. gallon jugs		4.80
3 lbs. arbuckle coffee		.60
2 lbs. yeast		.50
40 lbs. barley malt		2.50
3 lbs. loose soda		.25
	Total	$309.07

June 14—		$309.07
40 lbs. barley malt		2.50
coffee arbuckles 3 lbs.		.60
Sugar 200 lbs.		10.20
Chop (cracked corn) 200 lbs.		4.50
Meal		1.50
Can lard		5.25
Natural leaf tobacco		.50
Flour		1.85
Day's Work		.50
Red horse "		.50
Pinto beans 25 lbs.		2.75
Jowl butts		4.50
	Total	$344.22

June 21—		$344.22
Walkers twist tob.		.50
10 lbs. cracked hominy		.50
5 gal. coal oil		1.00
6 lbs. yeast		3.00
Arbuckles coffee 3 lbs.		.60
Sugar 300 lbs.		15.00
Chop (cracked corn) 300 lbs.		6.75
Beans 25 lbs. white		3.00
Flour		1.85
Granger		.50
12 bars Big Ben soap		.50
60 lbs. barley malt		3.25
	Total	$380.67

June 27—		$380.67
Sugar 300 lbs.		15.00
Mickey twist		.50
Arbuckle coffee 3 lbs.		.60
Day's Work		.75
Chop (cracked corn) 300 lbs.		6.75
45 lbs. barley malt		3.00
Meal		1.50
Beans 25 lbs.		3.00
6 lbs. yeast		1.50
Baking powder		.25
Calico 5 yds.		.50
Thread 1 spool		.05
O.K. soap		.25
	Total	$414.32

July 3—		$414.32
Chop (cracked corn) 500 lbs.		10.00
Sugar 500 lbs.		25.00
Day's Work		.50
Picnic twist		.50
Arbuckle coffee 3 lbs.		.60
60 lbs. barley malt		4.00
8 lbs. yeast		2.50
Flour		1.85
Potatoes		1.25
3 lbs. loose soda		.25
Oatmeal		.25
Crackers		.25
Can lard		5.25
	Total	$466.52

"Sweet terbacker," says Anse. "God Almighty, look at the sweet terbacker they've been buyin. I'm out there smokin cigars made from home-growed terbacker. When I take a chaw of terbacker I chew home-made. I take the plant jest as it comes from the earth—aint a lot of sugar on it! Their terbacker account is more than their bread account. Jesus Christ, they love sweet terbacker better than a cat likes cream. Crissie could a-smoked my burley—got it from my barn—and saved all this money she's spent fer twist terbacker. She's a wasteful woman. When she has the right to spend money she don't know how to spend it."

"What is pintoes?" Anse asks.

"Soup beans," says George.

"It's all right," says Anse. "Soup beans air grub to fill their bellies. I aint kickin on soup beans."

Anse reads down the first page of accounts.

"I see they air gettin plenty of sugar here," says Anse. "The further I go in this account, the more sugar they air buyin. It didn't take this much sugar in berry-cannin season."

"Yes," says George Grubb, "they got more sugar and more sugar as time went on."

"My God Almighty," says Anse, "they've even been buyin cracked corn. They have bought hundreds of pounds of chop and they aint got a chicken to feed it to. Look at this account, won't you! If they had to have corn why didn't they come to me? Why didn't they git my old corn? I know why they didn't come to me. You know, George, what they wanted that corn fer."

"I felt like I knowed, Mr. Bushman," says George Grubb.

"You ought to a-told me," says Anse. "You know, George, I've traded with you fer the last fifty years. We have growed to be old men together. We've trusted one another. I know you want to make all the money you can—but let them run up a debt like this! Let 'em buy all this sugar and cracked corn! You know what they wanted with it same as I do. I've run the risk of stool pigeons comin out there and findin moonshine stills on my place. I've run the risk, George, of losin my farm. You know if a still is found on a body's land, the Gover-mint can take it."

"Yes," says George, "if a still is found, they can take your property."

"I have a ar-tickle with Boliver Tussie of agreement and it was signed in the presence of witnesses," says Anse, "that he would not be allowed to make moonshine on my place— nor be ketched with moonshine in his possessions—nor would be allowed to drink moonshine. I tied him up hard and fast and he won't stay tied. He's got loose every place I tied him in the ar-tickle."

"I couldn't understand how you ever let a Tussie on your place," says George Grubb. "You know the name the Tussies has. It aint a good name, Anse. We make 'em pay the cash when they buy anything. Their credit aint worth the paper it is writ on. I can't understand how a sound-thinkin hard-workin man like you, Anse, ever let a Tussie move on your farm. You know the Tussie wimmen, don't you, Anse? They have been in jail here. You know they aint no good. They will give you trouble if you have boys at home. They will go to the woods and stay all night with anything that wears britches."

"I believe that," says Anse. "Two wimmen come out home. I was down in the woods. They tried that on me. It nearly worried Fronnie to death when I told her. I took me a four-year-old club, George, and I went over to Boliver Tussie's and I cleaned house. I went to their newground terbacker patch this morning and I tried to clean house again. But Boliver's whole family would a-jumped on me. I didn't have a chance. I got so mad I could a bit tenpenny nails in two. They threatened me with rocks. I didn't have my gun with me. I've jest come to town to check this account and to see a lawyer. I'm puttin 'em off'n my place. Lord, but I aint goin to stand no sicha doins. My boy out there in love with Boliver's gal! Jest can't do a thing with 'im! The only boy I got at home. The only boy I got to give all my land to when I'm too old to do any more work. Jest got to resign all my farm to my boy, Tarvin."

"Tussie wimmen air good-lookin wimmen," says George. "When a Tussie woman passes you in the street, you got to turn your head if you air any kind of man at all and look at her the second time. Tussie wimmen are all tall, fair-skinned, light-headed and purty. They air the color of the autumn weather. They air good-lookin wimmen and it hurts a man to look at 'em."

"You air right," says Anse. "That gal Tarvin's been sparkin is the purtiest gal you ever laid your peepers on. She looks like an angel sent from Heaven above. And she works hard as any man. She's the only Tussie woman I know that don't chaw or smoke. You can see how that family uses terbacker that's on my farm. They don't smoke and chaw it—they jest eat it. They air terbacker worms, all of 'em—big long hard green terbacker worms. Jest low-down long hard greasy no-count terbacker worms."

Anse stops talking. He scans the pages of the store account. Anse works his lips as he reads down the pages of the big account book.

"What's lugs, George?" Anse turns to George Grubb and asks.

"Jug stoppers," says George.

"God Almighty," says Anse, "and look here. They've been buyin barley malt by the hundredweights. They've been buyin yeast. That is enough, George. I know what they've been doin. They air makin moonshine on my place. Not only air they makin moonshine—but they air sellin it. Look here— look at the jugs they've bought. No wonder I couldn't git them boogers to do a day's work fer me atter they got on my place. They trapped me. I've been buyin their supplies to make moonshine. They've used my credit to buy their sweet ter-backer too. Terbacker account is might' nigh as big as their grub account. Why did you ever let them have all this yeast and barley malt, George?"

"I jest keep books here anymore, Anse," says George. "My clerks sold it to them. I told the clerks to let this family have credit because you told me to let 'em have credit. I don't do much waitin on people anymore. I look after the credit end of things here, do the buyin, and the bookkeepin. I aint young as I ust to be, Anse. You aint young as you ust to be. We air goin to haf to step aside one of these days and let younger men wear our shoes, Anse."

"I aint givin up until the end," says Anse. "I've got a fight on my hands right now, George. And by God, I aim to win this fight. I aim to clean the Tussies off'n my farm. I got into this scrape. I listened to a younger man that was tryin to wear my shoes. And his mother put her jib in fer 'im and now she is sorry about it. She sees where Anse Bushman was right. I'm a ruint man. Them damned low-down copper-heads! Got me in debt until I won't make much off'n my crop."

"You didn't give 'em enough work to do, Anse," says George. "Why didn't you give 'em a crop to tend! They wouldn't a-had time to 've made moonshine licker and a-stayed drunk if you'd a-give 'em land a-plenty!"

"Give 'em land a-plenty in newground," Anse repeats. "I give 'em sixty acres of newground. That's enough fer two families. I didn't think they'd be able to tend it. They've farmed that, made moonshine and stole every wild berry on my farm. They've carried off my turnips, too. Jest like a bunch of crows. They pilfer, and they work, they drink and dance. I've never seen sich a family in all my born days. Jest live like wild people. Work in the hot sun with their mouths open when they aint chawin and smokin terbacker. Crissie Tussie has worked all summer and she is carryin a baby. It is ready to be born any time. When I rented the place to 'em it was last March—I didn't know then that she was goin to have a baby. She looked jest like a healthy strong woman. Jest seemed like all of a sudden like a flower that pops into blossom in the spring, she looked like she was ready to have a baby. She's right out there now in the terbacker patch workin and suckerin terbacker. She's keepin her row of terbacker right along beside of Boliver."

"My Lord!" says George, "but they must be a tough set."

"I've never seen people like 'em," says Anse. "They air a red-blooded lot. I've bred a lot of hogs, sheep, horses, chickens, dogs and cattle in my day. I've crossed different breeds. I jest wonder what a cross between a Tussie and a Bushman would be like. Think I'm goin to see——"

"You mean——"

"My boy and his gal, George—so I hear," says Anse, "and I don't doubt it. It's a mess, George. You jest hold this account until I sell Boliver's cane and terbacker and fer God's sake don't let 'em have another thing. Let 'em eat roasten ears, green beans, greens and young taters. They can live now. Let 'em chaw and smoke home-made terbacker fer a while. They aint no better than I am. Crissie aint no better than Fronnie. I'd never buy her store plug terbacker to smoke. I wouldn't buy sweet terbacker fer myself good as I like to chaw sweet terbacker. When I take a chaw, I take a chaw of the bright burley leaf that growed on my farm. I can't see any use buyin terbacker when I raise it."

"All right, Mr. Bushman," says George. "Jest as you say. I'll not let 'em have anything more at the store and I'll hold your account here until you git your part of their terbacker crop this fall."

"My part!" says Anse. "I hope to git it all. I'll pay you out'n their part. I'll keep the rest. I've got to git a writ of possession to git Sheriff Bradley to put 'im off'n the place within the next three days." Anse walks out of the store with his long arms swinging to the rhythm of his walk. The weight of his big hands makes his arms swing like pendulums moving in opposite directions.

Part VI

1.

"Sheriff, I aint goin to leave this place," says Boliver. "I went to town and got me a lawyer. He will file the answer to old Anse Bushman's notice fer me to leave this place. I got a little money now and I will fight 'im. He aint got all the money that there is in Ragweed Holler. I can git more money if I need it. I voted fer you, Sheriff. You air on my ticket. Why do you bring sicha goddamn notice as that out here?"

"Boliver, it is a part of my work," says Sheriff Bradley. He is getting his breath hard after he has walked up the hill to Boliver's shack. The two pistols' butts shine brightly above the leather holsters that are suspended from his broad leather belt. "It is my duty, Boliver, same as it is your duty to cut the weeds from your corn and worm and sucker your ter-backer. I am sworn on my oath to do my duty. You know, Boliver, what a man's oath means."

"Duty, hell," says Boliver. "You air tryin to set me out on the road like old Anse did the rest of my people. You know what it means to set a man and his family out in the road when he aint got no place to go. Aint you goin to run fer somethin else agin when you git out'n the Sheriff's office?"

"Well, you know, Boliver, a Sheriff can't succeed himself," says Sheriff Bradley, "and I can't run fer this office agin. To

285

tell you the truth, I've had so many close calls in this office that I don't want it agin. People all the time fightin here—all the time shootin—it's a hard office to hold. I'm lucky to git out'n this office alive. And I've sent my deputies out to arrest my hardest men. I keep the tax books and make an arrest now and then—you know jest sorty stay behind the curtains and run the thing, but I've had two or three close calls when the bullets come might' nigh findin me behind the curtains. I've been thinkin about runnin fer County Judge atter I learn to write."

"Sheriff, I'll vote agin you if you try to hep Anse Bushman," says Boliver. "You know I got a lot of distant kinfolks and we vote as one, you know. We haf to fight fer ourselves. Everybody is agin a squatter here until election times. We decide the vote fer our party. If we vote agin our party, our men will lose, you know that. You will lose. You can't be elected Judge unless you sorty stand by me."

"I'm jest standin here thinkin," says Sheriff Bradley, "if there can't be some sort of a compromise between you and Anse Bushman. I'll be the go-between. What do you think about that?"

"I don't know about that," says Boliver. Boliver spits a bright sluice of tobacco spittle on the dry July earth. He wipes his mouth with the back of his broad rough hand. "That man Bushman won't listen to reason. He aint never listened to reason yit. He is a mean old man. He is a man that will fight at the drap of a hat when he draps the hat hisself. You haf to kill 'im to whop 'im."

"We can try," says Sheriff Bradley. "How about us walkin over to Anse Bushman's house?"

"I'm willin to try," says Boliver. "Jest wait a few minutes. I got to go in the house."

"To git your hat?" Sheriff Bradley asks, " 'r your shoes?"

"Nope," says Boliver, "I aint got no hat. My old bald head can stand the July sun. I can stand more sunshine on my head that a lizard can stand. Sun can't bake out my brains, and thorns can't git in my feet. I never wear shoes unless I go to town. They make fun of a man goin barefooted in town anymore. People there air stuck-up. My feet air too big. People laugh at my feet. Lord, but I love to go barefooted."

Boliver and Sheriff Bradley walk down the path to the hollow. They talk as they walk along the sheep path. Boliver chews his quid of tobacco behind his red-bearded jaw. He chews his tobacco as a cow chews her cud. He spits ambeer about every twenty steps as he walks in front of Sheriff Bradley and shows him the path to Anse Bushman's big house on the hill. Sheriff Bradley follows Boliver and smokes his pipe. He wipes streams of sweat from his pinkish forehead and his round chubby cheeks. He gets his breath hard and his words come slowly when he talks to Boliver Tussie. Boliver is not short of breath. Sheriff Bradley walks too slowly to suit Boliver Tussie. Boliver has to wait along on Sheriff Bradley.

"I don't think I'd vote fer 'im fer Judge," thinks Boliver, "even if he stands by me through all my trouble. He is too soft. He needs to work in newground corn and terbacker. That will give 'im wind. That will harden his flesh. That will give his face color. It would do him good. He can't even go bare headed in the sun. Wears a hat big as an umbrella. He wouldn't make a good Judge. Let 'im work a little bit and sweat like the rest of us."

Boliver and Sheriff Bradley reach the sheep-pasture fence. Sheriff Bradley cannot roll under, for the wires are too close. He cannot climb over the fence. Boliver takes his hand and helps him over the fence. They walk down the hollow across Anse Bushman's hog pasture and climb the rocky bluff up to Anse Bushman's woodyard.

"Ah, Anse," Sheriff Bradley hollers.

Don runs toward the woodyard barking. Boliver stands beside Sheriff Bradley with his hand on his hip pocket. The

July sun creeps over the hickory trees behind Anse Bushman's smokehouse.

"What d' you want?" comes a rough voice from inside the house.

"Want to see you on business," Sheriff Bradley answers with a bullfrog coarse voice that seems to come from a deep hollow within his mountain body of flesh.

"Come in and eat some dinner," Anse hollers.

"Have been to dinner," Sheriff Bradley answers.

"Come have some more," Anse requests.

"Nope, thank you," says the Sheriff.

"Will be out in three shakes of a dead sheep's tail," Anse answers.

"Here, doggie," says Sheriff Bradley, "we ain't goin to hurt you. Come here, boy, to me."

Don walks up to Sheriff Bradley. He whines and looks wistfully at Sheriff Bradley. He walks over to Boliver Tussie and smells of his pants leg. Don begins to growl.

"Funny about a dog," says Boliver, "they like or don't like a man by his smell. Aint many dogs likes me atter they smell me. Call 'im over to you. The longer he smells me the madder he gets. He seems to be takin up his master's troubles. He don't like me either."

Sheriff Bradley calls Don over to him. He pats Don's head. Don turns again to Boliver and looks with mean eyes and growls. He shows his long tushes with clean white powerful teeth between them.

"Don't you try to bite me, you son-of-a-bitch," says Boliver. "I know you don't like my smell. I don't like yours either. I'll shoot your goddamn heart out if you ever try to sink them long tushes in my leg."

Don keeps showing his teeth and growling when he looks at Boliver. Sheriff Bradley rubs Don's nose. He looks pleased at Sheriff Bradley and licks his hands.

"Howdy, fellars," says Anse as he walks off the kitchen porch smoking a cigar and patting his full stomach.

"Howdy, Anse," says Sheriff Bradley.

Boliver does not speak. He stands and looks at Anse with mean hard eyes.

"What in the hell air you doin over here, Boliver?" Anse asks. "Three days ago you were goin to beat my head in with a rock over in the terbacker patch. Now here you air over on my premises. Ah, the Law will larn you somethin yit."

"Glad to see you, Anse," says Sheriff Bradley. He shakes Anse Bushman's big rough hand with his small soft pudgy-backed hand.

Anse does not shake hands with Boliver. He looks at Boliver with his hardened blue eyes. He blows out big wisps of smoke when he looks at Boliver. Boliver looks at Anse with hard eyes. His bald domed head glistens in the sunlight. The sweat glistens like sunlight on a small round pool of water when the autumn vegetation has thinned and all that is left has turned to reddish brown.

"What brings you here, Boliver?" Anse asks.

"Jest come over to tell you I aint goin to move," says Boliver. "Jest come over to let you know that I've got me a lawyer and I aim to law you until hell aint bigger than a gnat."

"I'll fight you, Boliver," says Anse, "until hell freezes over. You've goddamn nigh broke me up and ruint my reputation now. I've jest been to George Grubb's General Store and checked your account. You've been makin moonshine on my premises. You've run me in debt over four hundred dollars. You've been stealin everything loose on my farm. You and your family pilfer like a bunch of thievin crows. This is the first time I've told you. I jest want you to know that I know it. You aint got sense enough to know how much mules can stand. You've hurt my mules by lettin your goddamn big lazy boys ride the plow in that tough newground."

"Jest a minute, boys," says Sheriff Bradley. "I've come over here with Boliver to see if we can't work out some kind of compromise."

"Compromise, hell!" shouts Anse. "God damn a compromise! I want this goddamn hellion and his whole works off'n my place. Sheriff Bradley, why don't you set 'im out!"

"I can't set 'im out and you can't either," says Sheriff Bradley. "His lawyer has filed the answer to your writ of possession notice. The court is goin to make you show why you have the right to put him off'n your place. I didn't know it until this mornin atter I come to Boliver Tussie's house. I come to put 'im off but I can't put 'im off."

"You can't put me off'n that land," Boliver laughs with a sarcastic snarl. His lips quiver as Don's lips quiver when he growls at Boliver. "You can't put me off. I am with you to stay. I've got the money and I aim to fight you. You'd jest better be nice to me and give me my way a little bit now, old Anse Bushman. It will never be *Mister Bushman* again either. From now on you air old Anse Bushman to me—a rough old beardy skeleton that tries to tell everybody what to do! Anse Bushman, you aint tellin me what to do no longer."

"You was awfully nice until you got on my place," says Anse. "I felt sorry fer you and your family. Never again will sympathy enter the bargain when I'm gittin a man on my place. Don't think I'll ever let another man move on my premises. I'll let the land grow up first. I'll let it grow up in a wilderness jest like it was."

"Now you air talkin, Anse Bushman," says Boliver. "Let it grow up wild like it was. Let the wild game come back. I'll move off'n your place right now if you will sign a ar-tickle that you will do this."

"I own this land," says Anse, "and I aint runnin it the way you want it to be. I want to see growin crops and flocks of sheep and herds of cattle on this land. If Anse Bushman's hands hold out and the Good Lord will let 'im live long enough you'll see 'em. Jest because I've passed the threescore-year-and-ten mark, don't mean that I'm not still a man. I'm as good a man as ever et cornbread."

"I aint leavin this place," says Boliver. "I'll show you that."

"I'll show you that you will," says Anse. "Powder and lead will put you off if nothin else. I'll git my kinfolks and we'll carry the war to your shack. We'll shoot it out across that holler."

"I've got powder and lead right here," says Boliver, "any time you want to start that." Boliver puts his hand on his hip pocket. "Old boy, I'm layin fer you."

"Now, boys," says Sheriff Bradley, "let's git our heads togither here and come to some settle-ment."

"Settle-ment, hell!" shouts Anse. "Sheriff Bradley, you can side in with Boliver Tussie and be damned. Remember you air goin to run fer Judge! I'll spend money agin you and do everything in my power to beat you. I don't care if you do belong to my party. What air you doin with your nose stuck in my business? That's why your nose is so goddamn long and sharp. You've got it stuck in everybody's business. You'll git it whacked off clean agin your face. You air takin Boliver Tussie's side. The only thing I have in common with 'im is that we belong to the same party."

"That's jest it," says Sheriff Bradley, "this thing is goin to split the party in this county and let that den of thieves in and take the offices. You can swing the election with your money."

"And we can swing it with our votes," Boliver breaks in.

"Swing, hell," says Anse; "your bunch is all sell-outs. My money will buy 'em. You know that, Boliver. A jug of moonshine will buy your vote. Moonshine and sweet terbacker will buy all the Tussies."

"It will take more than that if Sheriff Bradley runs fer Judge," says Boliver. "We air fer 'im. We'll elect 'im too. Damned if we don't."

"I'll beat 'im too," says Anse.

"Boys," says Sheriff Bradley, "I'm in a spot. I'm tryin to git you fellers to stand togither like brothers. You fight like dogs."

"You try to git us to stand fer your own good," says Anse.

"Not that," says Sheriff Bradley. "It's jest a bad thing to have trouble like this. Somebody might git kilt. You fellers air both riled. It's the best to do things in a peaceful way."

"Let a man make moonshine on your place," says Anse. "That's the way to do it! Let the stool pigeons come and find a still on your place and let the Gover-mint take your farm. That's the way to do it! Let a man steal from you. Let his children carry off his turnips! Let his kinfolks come in and invite a old man like me to the bushes. Let sicha old strollops worry my wife! God damn the low-lifers!"

"What's the matter, Anse?" Fronnie asks from the kitchen porch. She stands on the kitchen porch and smokes her pipe.

"Nothin's the matter, Mother," says Anse. "Jest a little business here to take care of. You go back in the house and wait until I'm through here."

Anse speaks with soft words to Fronnie.

"Thought you's all riled up, Anse," says Fronnie. " 'Peared like I could hear vile oaths comin from out here."

Fronnie walks back into the kitchen. She smokes her pipe as she walks. A blue trail of smoke follows Fronnie as she walks back into the kitchen.

"I know why you air fightin me," says Anse. He turns and looks at Boliver as he speaks. "I know where you air gittin your money to fight me. I know who is payin your lawyer fee. You aint foolin me. It is the Moonshiners' Association in this county. Old Flem Spry is your president. He was kicked out'n the Forty-Gallon Baptist Church. He had to do somethin. Now he's your President. You've got their hep and you've got money that you've been paid fer moonshine. I've bought your cracked corn, your yeast, and your malt.

Yit you come right back fightin the hand that hast fed you!
You air a old reprobate! That is all you air. You can take
your Moonshiners' Association and go to hell with it."

"Old Flem is one of our party too," says Sheriff Bradley.

"Can't hep that," says Anse. "You know what he is. I've
seen 'im take a horse-quart of moonshine when his hand
shook so he couldn't hardly git the horse-quart to his mouth.
His mouth would water and his eyes would twinkle as he
watched that old one-ply hooch bead in the horse-quart. He
would finally git it up to his mouth and he would drink it
like a hog starved for slop. Then he would start talkin about
the Scriptures. He would go to the church house and preach
one of the awfulest God-fearin hell's-fire and brimstone
sermons that ever fell from the lips of a man! That's old
Flem. Now he's fightin fer the moonshiners fer all the three-
ply hooch he can git to drink and the fees they pay each
month to the Association."

"I'll git the money," says Boliver. "The moonshiners air
backin me. Did you ever hear of any barns burnin with
cattle and terbacker in 'em because people didn't keep their
mouths shet? People can do too much talkin."

"All right," says Anse, "jest go on about your business.
We won't compromise. We'll fight this thing out in court.
I can't stand fer all that's goin on around this place. I'll fight
it to the end—jest as I said—until hell freezes over."

"And remember," says Boliver, "you got somethin else
to remember. You've helt your damn nose so fer above my
family. You must remember that Subrinea is goin to have a
baby soon. Your son Tarvin is the daddy of it. Jest keep that
in mind. There will be another baby fer you to keep and you
will haf to foot the doctor bill. You will haf to keep the
baby. What air you goin to do with a baby that has red blood
in it, Anse Bushman? A child that hast squatter blood in its
veins? A child that is half Tussie?

"Ha ha ha ha!" Boliver laughs as he turns and walks away.

Sheriff Bradley turns and walks away with Boliver.

"Sorry, Anse, that you fellars couldn't git your heads to-gither," says Sheriff Bradley, as he follows Boliver over the hill through the hog pasture toward the sheep pasture. "If you ever make up your minds, let me know."

"Let you know, hell," says Anse. "I think jest about as much of you as I do Boliver Tussie. Birds of a feather flock togither. You and Boliver Tussie air both buzzards out lookin fer somethin to die. I jest don't want to see neither one of you buzzards back on my premises."

"Jest as you say, Anse," says Sheriff Bradley. "We've allus been on the same side. We've been good friends but you have come to the place you won't listen to reason. If you don't want me fer a friend any longer—then there's not anything more I can do about it."

Anse watches Sheriff Bradley walking in a slow dog trot to catch Boliver Tussie. Boliver is walking along the path whittling a stick as he walks.

2.

"TARVIN, COME here," says Anse. "I've jest had a row with Boliver Tussie."

"Soon as I put the mule up, Pa," says Tarvin.

Tarvin leads the mule in the stall. He walks back out and fastens the stall door.

"What happened, Pa?" Tarvin asks.

Tarvin leans on the barn-lot fence and listens to Anse. Tarvin picks up a corncob and whittles with his pocketknife as Anse talks.

"Sheriff Bradley was with 'im," says Anse, "when he come over here. They come fer a compromise. That was Sheriff Bradley's idear. Thought he might win the Tussie votes, I guess."

"What did you do, Pa?"

"I told both of 'em to stay away from here," says Anse. "Old Sheriff Bradley was sidin in with Boliver. Big lot of votes there now. You know the Moonshiners' Organization of this county is backin Boliver in his fight agin me."

"What fight, Pa?" Tarvin asks.

"I give Boliver a three days' notice to git off'n my property," says Anse. "He got him a lawyer and filed an answer to my writ of possession."

"The hell he did!"

"Yes, he did," says Anse. "He's damned nigh ruint me, Tarvin. His store account is over four hundred dollars jest fer four months. He's bought barley malt, lugs, jugs, malt, sugar and cracked corn. You know what he got all these fer. I've been payin fer the moonshine he's made to drink and sell. He's holdin the money he got fer his moonshine to fight me with. I'll tell you the Tussies air a dirty bunch."

"What else did he buy, Pa?" Tarvin asks.

"Bought all sorts of sweet and plug terbacker," says Anse. "You ought to go down to the Grubb General Store and have George Grubb to let you look at the account. Where I ought to have my end kicked is fer lettin 'em git in debt the way I did and never checkin up on his account. I didn't think about this."

"Is he really goin to law you, Pa?" Tarvin asks.

"Yes he's goin to law me," says Anse. "If he can't git me

one way, he is goin to git me another. Boliver said jest before he left the house that Subrinea was goin to have a baby by you and that I would pay fer it. Ast me what I was goin to do about it. Said a lot of smart things jest like he had the bull by the horns."

"What did you tell 'im?"

"I didn't tell 'im anything," says Anse. "There aint anything I can say to 'im before I talk with you, Tarvin. I jest want you to tell me the truth about all of this talk. Is it the truth? Is Subrinea Tussie goin to have your baby?"

"I 'spect she is, Pa," says Tarvin. "I don't see anything to keep her from it."

"God Almighty," says Anse. "We air into it all the way around. I aint goin to fight your battle jest now but I'm goin to fight my own battle. I'm goin to put Boliver Tussie and that family off'n my place."

"That is your fight, Pa," says Tarvin. "You jest leave my fight alone. There aint goin to be no fight to it."

"I can git you out'n it, Tarvin," says Anse. "I can git four men to swear they monkeyed with her. That will make her a whore. The Law won't do nothin to you."

"You aint doin that, Pa," says Tarvin. "She aint that kind of a gal."

"Why?" Anse asks. "Do you aim to marry that Tussie gal?"

"I am already married," says Tarvin. "We've been married a long time. We've got to have a weddin ceremony yit. That's all."

"God Almighty," says Anse. "That will finish me and your Ma. What will we do with her in our house? I jest won't have her, that's all."

"You air right," says Tarvin, "you won't have her. Two families air one too many under the same roof. I don't keer how big the house is."

"What do you aim to do, Tarvin?" Anse asks.

"I aim to build me a little log shack like the Tussies ust to live in, and I aim to live on this farm."

"You will haf to be married by a preacher," says Anse, "before the baby comes so it won't be called a wood's colt."

"We'll haf to marry and keep people from talkin," says Tarvin. "Goin to a preacher and havin 'im to say somethin aint goin to marry us any more than we've been married fer the past year. I've allus knowed Subrinea was my wife. I've been seein her most every day fer the past year."

"You have!"

"Yes, I have."

"Don't you mean to be married under the holy bonds of matrimony by God's laws and man's laws?" Anse asks.

"It don't matter to me," says Tarvin, as he whittles away on the corncob.

"God Almighty, Tarvin," says Anse, "have you lost all your raisin?"

"The Tussies aint married, have they?" Tarvin asks. "They've got along, aint they? They've been married by God's laws. Man's laws aint mattered none to 'em."

"Do you aim to live like the Tussies have lived?" Anse asks.

"I like the way the Tussies have lived," says Tarvin. "They aint tried to git every loose dollar in the world. They have lived on the land and they have loved livin on the land. They love the land much as you love the land, Pa. You took their land when you bought the Sexton Timber Tract. You know you did. They hated to see you buy it. They had lived here in peace all their days. They had hunted over this land. They had farmed little patches of it. They had made their moonshine. They had their dances. They laughed and cried and loved and enjoyed the comin and goin of the seasons. Look what you did. You stopped all of this. You run 'em all away but Boliver Tussie and his family. You put 'em under the yoke. You can't do a Tussie that way, Pa. They have the same wildness in their blood and flesh as you have found in new-ground. You've got to work easy with the Tussies. They air a red-blooded people and I don't care what you say."

"I don't look at it like this," says Anse. "Old Boliver Tussie is a-carryin a pistol fer me right now."

"You've thought about carryin a pistol fer 'im and shootin 'im," says Tarvin. "He is goin to fight you back, Pa. You can't tramp 'im under your feet any longer. You can't boss 'em like you have bossed Ma and me. You can't whop 'em with clubs like you do mules. You can't herd 'em like you herd sheep."

"I can't tramp 'em under my feet, Son," says Anse, "but it will be a strange Court that will uphold the things they've done since they've lived on my place atter Boliver signed the ar-tickle. I know Judge Whittlecomb. We stand jest like two peas in a pod. We stand together, Son. I jest hate to see you live with Subrinea. I hate to see you git in that mess. I hate to see Bushman blood mix with Tussie blood."

"It's already mixed," says Tarvin. "I'm glad to have Subrinea Tussie fer my wife. I'm glad to mix my blood with her blood. I expect to live on this farm. I expect to have more sheep. I expect to raise the crops that you have raised, Pa. I couldn't git a better wife than Subrinea. I know that I can't. I'll be tickled to death when she has my baby."

"Lord hep the pitiful," shouts Anse. "Have you lost your mind? That baby will be callin you a son-of-a-bitch by the time it can talk."

"Nope, Pa," says Tarvin. "I aint worryin about what it calls me and I aint losin my mind. I know what I'm doin."

"Then you air goin to marry her?"

"Yep, I'm goin to marry her," says Tarvin. "Guess it would be better than to go on havin youngins and not be married by the laws of man."

"She is a low-down woman, Tarvin," says Anse, "and you know it."

"Pa, I don't like to hear you talk like that," says Tarvin. "You aint got no room to talk."

"What do you mean, Son," Anse asks, "by talkin to me like that?"

"I mean," says Tarvin, "that there's a lot of good people today that would like to fergit their yesterdays. They talk about the bad young people of today. Pa, I know about you and Ma. You aint got no right to talk."

"Good Lord!" says Anse. "What air you drivin at, Son?"

"Do you want me to tell you?"

"I do," says Anse. "I want to know what you air talkin about."

"You had to marry Ma," says Tarvin. "Why is it any worse when I haf to marry Subrinea? I want to marry Subrinea. You didn't want to marry Ma."

"How do you know so goddamn much?"

"You'd better burned all the old letters that your Pap wrote to Ma's Pap," says Tarvin. "If I's you I'd git 'em out'n the bottom of Ma's old trunk and burn 'em."

"My God," says Anse, "is she still holdin them old letters?"

"Somebody is holdin 'em," says Tarvin. "Pa, to tell you the truth it don't bother me. I aint never told it. I jest happened to know about it. You talk like now that you have been a angel. I jest know you haven't. That's the reason I'm sayin this to you. I aint been a angel either. I love Subrinea Tussie. I am goin to spend my days with her. She will live in the same house with me. We'll raise sheep together. We will live on this farm. I don't care what you do with Subrinea's Pa; I'd ruther you'd let 'im stay. He loves this land more than you do."

"Let 'im stay, hell!" Anse storms. "I aim to hike his tail off'n that place. I aim to put the skids under 'im soon as the third Monday in this month. That's when court begins."

"Do as you want to do," says Tarvin, "but I'm tellin you what I aim to do."

"Son," says Anse, "you know too much about your Pa."

"It makes me like you, Pa," says Tarvin. "I've knowed this fer a long time. I jest let you go on and talk about other people. I jest let you talk about the squatters. I know about you and Ma goin out and stayin in that rock cliff on the hill. I know about how you slept on the leaves like the foxes slept. I know about Ma's Pa and your Pa. They had to go atter you and Ma and fetch you down from the cliffs. I know about what a time there was atterwards. I know how the 'good' people talked about my mother. I don't care what you and Ma have done. I love both of you fer all that you have done. You jest don't have any right to say anything about Subrinea. We've been to the sheep barns and stayed nights together. Subrinea saved all them lambs last winter. I didn't do it. She saved my life too. I was lost in that snowstorm on that cold winter night and she found me. We've cut wood in the woods together. We have run over the fields and terbacker patches in the moonlight together. We have been in rock cliffs together. I jest thought about you and Ma when I was sleepin with Subrinea under the rock cliffs on the leaves like the foxes."

"Good Lord," says Anse. "Son, you skeer me the way you talk."

"You'd better burn them old letters, Pa," says Tarvin.

"To tell you the truth, Son," says Anse, "I didn't know that your Ma kept 'em."

"She had to keep somethin, Pa," says Tarvin, "fer you didn't buy Ma no weddin ring, you was so stingy with your money. She allus wanted a weddin ring. You bought all the land you could buy with the money. You can't blame Ma fer keepin the old letters. They air bundled and tied with a ribbon and put away among some old deeds and things in the bottom of the trunk."

"Marry her, Tarvin," says Anse, "if you aim fer her to be your wife. Stop all this talk goin over the country. But wait until atter the third Monday in this month. If you marry her now it will hurt me when we have our trial. We'll be akin to the Tussies atter you marry her. That means a lot in a court here. It will damn near ruin me in the trial."

"All right, Pa," says Tarvin, "I'll wait until atter the trial providin you won't raise hell fer me livin on this place. You'll haf to let me build a shack somewhere on this place and settle here."

"Son," says Anse, "I expect you to settle on this place. I don't want you to move away. I don't care who you marry. I jest want you to stay near me and your Ma. We aint as young now as we have been. We need you near us. We need you to take this farm over. You air all we got now. We'll let you build you a house and live any place on this farm."

"Jest don't ever tell Ma," says Tarvin, "that I know about them letters."

"I wouldn't fer the world," says Anse. "I don't want her to know that you know about 'em."

Tarvin throws down the whittled corncob. The sun drags down a patch of fire behind it over the ridge's rim. The whippoorwills start calling from the hilltops. The insects start singing from the dewy grass. Fronnie walks toward the barn with milk buckets in her hands. Tarvin starts after the cows. He calls Don to help him drive the cows up to the milk gap. Anse walks toward the house to get slop for the hogs.

"It don't look like a body can do anything," thinks Anse, "even if it is fifty years ago, but it will be found out. Maybe that is what is the matter with Fronnie. Maybe she is right when she tells me I am a sinful man. Fronnie is right. I am a sinful man. I am a weaked man. I cuss; I fight; I work my renters to death."

Fronnie walks out to the barn. She looks at Anse as he

passes her walking toward the house to get the slop. Anse looks at Fronnie.

"I've been worried," says Fronnie. "I told you, Anse, that you would have trouble with the Tussies. I told you that you'd haf to go to Law to git 'em out'n that house. I tell you, Anse, you got to git right in your own heart. I've been thinkin more all the time about the hereatter. Anse, I want you to go with me wherever I go atter I leave this world. I'll be lost without you."

Fronnie stops in the path. She holds the milk buckets in her hands and talks to Anse. Anse walks slowly past her. He listens to the words that Fronnie is saying.

"Anse, you will not be in this world as long as you have been," says Fronnie. "You know that you won't be runnin a farm in the land where smoke oozes from the dirt; where the lake of fire is hot enough to melt the dirt. You will pray fer the rocks to fall on your face. You won't be out cussin and whoppin the workers. You won't be out whoppin Boliver Tussie with a four-year-old club fer gittin drunk. Boliver will be right there with you. You will be friends in hell. I've jest set out at the house and thought all atternoon about you, Anse. What is the worth of this big farm when a man has lost his soul? You ought to belong to the Lord, Anse."

3.

"Look at the crowd gathered in fer the trial, Pa," says Tarvin. "Looks like all the people in Greenwood County has left their crops to hear this trial."

"You air right, Son," says Anse. "Every sharecropper in this county and everybody that hast any sympathy fer the squatters will be here. They will see somethin they aint seen before. This trial ought to stop the trials among the share-croppers. It will larn 'em that they aint runnin this county."

The courthouse square is filled with people. Women stand among the men. Women with lean sun-tanned bony faces, dressed in percale and gingham dresses—women wearing aprons with pockets on the corners to hold their pipes and tobacco crumbs—women carrying babies in their arms and letting the babies nurse their long broken breasts. Men stand with quids of tobacco behind their lean beardy lantern jaws and talk to their wives. Men stand with pipes, cigars or cigarettes in their mouths and talk to each other. Men stand like trees. They speak words to each other and they swear oaths. They speak about the Lord, crops and the fights over line fences. They talk about the North Fork boys meeting the Allcorn Creek boys at the Raccoon Church and fighting it out to a finish in church.

"They even pulled the seats up from the church-house floor," says Kim Grace, "and throwed 'em at each other. I got my wife and little youngins and got out'n there. Wimmen was faintin all over the church-house. Jest one boy got knifed. Boys didn't use powder and lead. That is one thing that can be said fer the boys. They's nice about that. They jest used the butts of their pistols, and knocked each other cold as cucumbers. I guess there's forty boys in that fracas. Got so anymore you can't go to the Lord's house on Sunday night and be safe."

Anse hears them talking as he walks in front of Tarvin and

Fronnie. Anse pushes his way through the milling crowd.
Tarvin and Fronnie follow Anse. Tarvin helps Fronnie through
the crowd. Anse smokes his cigar and the blue smoke swirls
in puffs bigger than the puffs from any cigar on the courthouse square. Tarvin smokes his pipe. Fronnie does not smoke
her pipe. The stem is too long for Fronnie to get through
the crowd without jabbing her pipe against a spectator and
running the stem down her own throat. She will wait until
she can get a seat in the court-house so she can sit and listen
to the trial and smoke in peace.

"There's an awful big crowd here," Fronnie says to Tarvin.
"Can't understand why so many people have come to the
trial."

"Yes, Ma," says Tarvin, "I can understand. It's the first
trial on the new court docket. People aint got no place to go.
They come to court. It is a good place to go. People love to
hear a trial. Lovers meet each other here. Men come to
talk about their crops. They come to swap hosses. They come
to trade and to drink together. They come to have a good
time. Before this trial is over, they'll be having a good time."

"There goes Anse Bushman," Tarvin hears a man say.
Tarvin sees him pointing to Anse. "Anse Bushman is tryin
to put a man off'n his place. You've heard of Anse Bushman!
He's got a barrel of money. He knows how to keep it. Don't
think the trial will be much good. A lot of people will be
disapp'inted."

Anse is pushing his way toward the court-house door. He
wears his blue serge suit. Anse wears a high celluloid collar
with a broad striped necktie twisted around the collar. He
wears a watch chain and fob over his vest. He wears a rose in
his coat lapel. Anse Bushman is a man to be respected in the
community. Men look at Anse from all sides as his strong body
pushes a path for his wife and son among the milling
crowd.

"Make way fer the Judge, boys," says a voice from the

crowd. "Judge Whittlecomb is now enterin the courthouse."

Judge Whittlecomb walks down the broken concrete street toward the courthouse door. Men, women and children step aside as the Judge speaks to this one and that one—tipping his gray felt hat as he walks down the street. The Judge nods "Good mornin" and smiles and the people smile as the Judge speaks and nods. The Judge calls them by their first names. "Judge Whittlecomb has one of the finest pair of legs of any man in Kentucky," says a woman. She looks at the Judge and smiles.

"He lifts his feet up and sets them down—pawin in the air as he walks like a thoroughbred Kentucky race-hoss."

The Judge wears broad-rimmed glasses. He wears a pin-striped suit that fits tightly and shows the shape of the lower extremities of his body and his long race-horse legs. The Judge wears a white rose in his coat lapel. His big bright blue eyes roll in their red-rimmed sockets behind the black-rimmed spectacles and he bats them as a bull-frog bats his eyes.

"He's a fine Judge," says a man from the crowd. "He's a man, Steve, like we air. The Judge is a common man. He aint a stuck-up man. He knows everybody. He is a deep man the way he can turn to them big law books and repeat the law. He never went off to school like a lot of fellars. He's got his education at home by a pine torch while the other young men in this county was out with their bottles and pistils a-kickin up their heels and shootin up the place. Now the other fellars' heels air in the Judge's hands."

"He's a fine-lookin man," says a young woman in the crowd. "Wish he wasn't a married man. Any woman would be proud to be the wife of Judge Whittlecomb. He could make any woman happy. My heart melts when I see 'im. He's the finest-lookin man in Kentucky. Smokes big cigars. Wears good clothes. Look at the Judge, won't you!"

"I'm tired of hearin all the wimmen rave about the Judge," says the tall bean-pole man with a beardy face standing beside her. "I can't see why he's so damned good-lookin. He's even got a paunch the size of a bushel basket under that purty gold watch chain and fob he wears."

The path is opened down the street for the Judge. He walks briskly—pawing the wind with his race-horse legs—setting down his big slick-shined shoes on the broken pavement. The Judge carries a satchel in one hand and a law book in the other hand. He follows Anse, Fronnie and Tarvin into the courthouse. He walks down the broad middle aisle of the courthouse. On each side of him are long plank seats. People are sitting crowded together on these homemade seats. Lovers sit by each other with their arms entwined. Families are sitting together awaiting the coming trial. Over the heads of the lean faces and the broken bodies—the lovers, wives, husbands, grandpas, and grandmas—the drunks—is the low dark rain-stained courthouse ceiling. There are many spiderwebs spun around the dark paintless posts that support the roof over this room. This room holds the big fate of the little justice meted out to Greenwood County's citizens. Spiders spin away on their web of destiny of their fellow citizens. The whispering, restless, sun-tanned, broken-bodied, beardy-faced men, breast-nursing women and young lovers sit below and watch and listen to the making and shaping of these webs of destiny in the Greenwood County Court. They see the well-groomed, handsome Judge with the satchel and the big law book and the "finest pair of legs in Kentucky" take his seat on the bench. They see him pull off his coat and hang it on the back of his chair. They see him roll his sleeves to his elbows. They see him unfasten his collar and loosen the knot in his tie. They see him pick up the morning paper that has been placed at the bench for him. They see him sit down in his swivel chair—light his cigar—put his feet on the top of the desk with the soles of his big shoes facing the people. They see him smoke his cigar and read the morning paper while the jurymen come to the long front seats just down below the bench where the Judge sits. Twelve men and women come to the jury box. The Judge glances slowly down on them with his light blue eyes turning slowly in their sockets. It is just a glance for the Judge continues reading his morning paper.

4.

BEHIND THE *Judge are the pictures of George Washington, Abraham Lincoln, Theodore Roosevelt and Woodrow Wilson. If these venerable men could only arise from their graves and attend this court! If they could only see hill justice in the land they helped to shape, make breathe as a nation—the most powerful under the sun—if they could only sit among their people as bystanders—if they could only listen! Better they cannot!*

5.

SHERIFF BRADLEY walks into the courtroom through a side door behind the Judge's bench. Slowly he walks across the courtroom toward the Judge's bench. Many eyes are focused upon the short fat Sheriff. They look at the two pistol butts gleaming above the leather holsters.

"Sheriff, call the court to order," says Judge Whittlecomb. The Judge looks up from his paper when he sees Sheriff Bradley. As soon as he speaks these words to him, the Judge looks back at his paper. He continues to read while Sheriff Bradley pounds on his desk with a gavel. The whispering, laughing, talking crowd becomes solemn. The faces look grave and sober when the Sheriff pounds on the Judge's table for order. The eyes of hill people are focused on the jurymen and women in the jury box.

Anse sits on the left side of the courthouse facing the Judge's bench. Anse sits in a chair with his elbows on the table in front of him. Waddell Burton, Anse's lawyer, sits beside him with a scroll of paper lying on the table. Tarvin and Fronnie sit in chairs beside Anse. They look across the open space in front of the Judge's bench to the other side of the courtroom. Boliver Tussie sits there. Subrinea and Crissie sit beside him. Flem Spry sits with them. Boliver's lawyer,

Charlie Baskwell, sits beside them behind the table. Beyond them sit the Beavers, Tussies and the members of the Moonshiners' Association. Anse looks at the mass of fighting, face-dilapidated, mean-eyed human beings. Anse knows he has a fight on his hands—even if he wins this lawsuit. Anse and Tarvin know the second step in a Greenwood County lawsuit for the losing side is powder and lead. But Anse is not afraid. He is not afraid of any human being that walks the earth. Anse will fight to a finish.

Tarvin looks at the woman he loves. She has been drawn into an inevitable conflict. She knows the background of this conflict. Tarvin and Subrinea look at each other across the courtroom. They see their own blood fighting each other. "Marriage by man's law," thinks Tarvin, "might tie our families together." Tarvin remembers the days he has had with Subrinea, as he sits and stares across the courtroom at the woman he loves who is heavy with his child. Her cat-green eyes look at Tarvin's sun-tanned face. Tarvin remembers the sheep shanty, zero weather, the lambs, the trees of Heaven, the wild flowers on the slopes and the newground tobacco field in the moonlight. He remembers the tall newground corn and the moonlight on the green stalwart stalks, the seedy crab grass in the balks and the light rustle of the summer wind among the talking corn blades. Tarvin remembers life with Subrinea. He cannot forget. Subrinea is a part of him just as the earth is a part of him; the earth that he has known and never lost. He is part of Subrinea. He has become part of the wild flower that Subrinea is. He has learned to laugh, to work and play from Subrinea—that volcanic outburst of Nature that she is.

"What says the Plaintiff in the Anse Bushman case versus Boliver Tussie?" Judge Whittlecomb asks. He looks up from his paper and puffs his cigar.

The eager spectators strain their long skinny necks and their big bull necks. They look toward the Judge. They look at

Subrinea and Crissie. They look at Boliver and Flem Spry whispering to each other. They hear the coarse whispers of the mean-looking men that sit on the rows of seats behind the Tussie family. They look at Fronnie, Anse and Tarvin. Young girls in the courtroom look at Tarvin with eager eyes. Subrinea watches the girls looking at Tarvin. Subrinea does not like it.

"Pal, you don't know me and I don't know you," says a small man with mean eyes looking in at the courthouse window, "but I jest want to show you a pitiful sight."

"Okay, friend," says a tall freckled-faced man with a quid of tobacco behind his lean horse jaw. "I'll be right over to look."

The tall man walks over from a crowd of men to the courthouse window. Men follow him toward the window. They want to look at the pitiful sight.

"See that purty gal over yander," says the small man with the mean eyes and a mouth filled with broken discolored teeth. He points with his index finger toward Subrinea Tussie.

"Yes, I see 'er," says the tall freckled-faced man. He spits a bright sluice of ambeer on the sour-smelling foot-trampled courthouse yard. "I believe that purty gal's in the family way, ain't she?"

"That's jest it," says the small man. "She is my cousin. I'm Bollie Beaver. You see that low-down polecat right over yander by that old red-bearded Santa Claus?"

"Yep," says the tall man.

"That's the fellar that got 'er in trouble," says Bollie. "That's Anse Bushman's boy. Anse got my Uncle Boliver on his farm jest so that ornery boy of his'n could have a decent gal to ruin. You fellars can see that he's ruint 'er."

"It won't be long," says a tall bearded man, "before she'll be havin a baby."

"I'm a bad man," says Bollie. "I'm a dangerous man. I'm gittin away from here before I lose my temper. I come to town today to riddle that young Bushman with my knife until his hide won't hold shucks. I'm a man that don't want trouble and I don't want the stain of his dirty blood on my hands. Fellars, I jest hate to see a rich man's son take advantage of a poor girl like Subrinea Tussie."

Bollie Beaver walks away from the crowd at the courthouse window. He disappears among the milling crowd. He leaves a group of men standing at the window looking at Subrinea. They are making comments on the unfair advantage that a landowner's son has taken of a poor sharecropper's girl.

"The Plaintiff is ready, Your Honor," says Lawyer Waddell Burton. He stands on his feet behind the table and answers. He fingers nervously at his coat lapel when he speaks.

"What says the Defendant?" Judge Whittlecomb asks. He peers through his big-rimmed spectacles at Lawyer Charlie Baskwell.

"We are not ready," says Charlie Baskwell. "Your Honor, we move to continue this case in court until we can git all of our witnesses. We don't have near all of 'em here."

"Motion overruled," snaps the Judge.

"The Sheriff didn't summons all of them," says Charlie Baskwell.

"You can't expect Sheriff Bradley to do it all," says Judge Whittlecomb. "You should have done this. We can't go on usin the taxpayers' money and continuin cases in court. We've got too many now. It will take years to clean this docket. Come on now! Let's git busy."

Judge Whittlecomb puts his newspaper aside. He shifts his feet upon the table top. He puts one of his feet upon the other. He puffs the short stub of his cigar. Judge Whittlecomb looks at the jury.

"Air you or any of you related by blood or marriage to the Plaintiff, Anse Bushman, or the Defendant, Boliver Tussie?"

There is silence.

"All qualified," says the Judge.

"What says the Plaintiff to this jury?" Judge Whittlecomb asks.

"We accept them, Your Honor," says Waddell Burton.

"What says the Defendant to this jury?" Judge Whittlecomb asks. He picks up a copy of the Racing Records and begins to scan the pages.

"Hobart Hornbuckle," says Charlie Baskwell.

Hobart stands.

"Are you related to the Plaintiff by marriage?"

"Yes," says Hobart.

"Sit down."

Lawyer Charlie Baskwell questions the jury. He and Boliver Tussie retire to the anteroom. They take a list of names. The people in the courthouse laugh and talk while Boliver and his lawyer are outside in the anteroom. When Boliver and Lawyer Baskwell come back, Baskwell reaches the list of names to the Judge.

"Hobart Hornbuckle, Eif Bridgewater, Tim Hawthorne, stand aside," says Judge Whittlecomb.

"Sheriff, fill up the jury box."

"Mort Watkins, Zac Smith, Murtie Preston, fill up the jury box," says Sheriff Bradley.

"Hold up your right hands," says Judge Whittlecomb.

The three new jurors hold up their right hands.

"You do solemnly swear or affirm that you will to the best of your ability truly answer such questions that may be propounded to you, so help you God."

They fill the vacant seats left in the jury box.

Judge Whittlecomb questions the jurors. He qualifies them.

"What says the Plaintiff to this jury?"

"Plaintiff accepts jury."

"What says the Defendant to this jury?"

"Defendant accepts jury."

"You do solemnly swear that you will truly try and render a just verdict accordin to the Law and evidence, in the case of Anse Bushman versus Boliver Tussie, so help you God."

"Plaintiff, call your first witness," says Judge Whittlecomb. He pulls a new cigar from his coat pocket. He lights his cigar. He spits on the floor. He looks at the pages of his racing record. He blows his nose on the floor. He wipes his nose with his hand.

Lawyer Waddell Burton reads his petition to the jury. As he reads the petition Boliver Tussie shakes his head that statements in the petition are not true.

"Take the stand, Anse Bushman," says Lawyer Waddell Burton.

Anse gets up from his chair by the table. He walks over to the witness stand. It is a chair before the jury box.

"Is your name Anse Bushman?"

"Yes, sir."

"Do you own a farm in Ragweed Hollow?"

"Yes, sir."

"Is Boliver Tussie a sharecropper on your farm?"

"Yes, he is a thief on my farm. He is a hellion of the first degree!"

"You're a goddamn liar," shouts Boliver Tussie.

Anse leaves the witness stand and makes toward Boliver. Lawyer Waddell Burton grabs Anse by the coatsleeve. Men gather around Anse to hold him. Men gather around Boliver to hold him. They keep the two men apart.

"I don't have a chance in this goddam court nohow," says Boliver. "Look at that jury. I could have all the names called in the jury wheel and it would be the same. They'd all be agin a squatter—all for the landowner, Anse Bushman. They'd be agin a sharecropper. How in the hell did they git in the jury wheel like that! Take your court and go to hell with it. I'm through because I'll never git a fair trial. Abe Lincoln,"

Boliver points to Lincoln's picture on the wall, "there's a hell of a lot of white slaves in this country. Wake up from your sleep."

There is talking and laughing—cursing and whispering among the milling crowd. People take sides. Anse Bushman has his crowd. Boliver Tussie has his crowd. There is vile swearing on both sides. Women stand between the men as they pull their pistols from their pockets. The men will not shoot among the women.

"It's a mistrial," says the Judge. "Sheriff Bradley deputize men and preserve the peace."

Peace cannot be preserved. There is fighting all over the courthouse square. Crowds of men gather around Anse. Crowds of men gather around Boliver. They will not let the men go to each other.

"Anse, you don't live right," says Fronnie. "I have told you that you aint livin right. Your heart aint right. Boliver Tussie's heart aint right. When you all git right with the Lord, you won't need to have a lawsuit. The Lord will hep you. There won't be any trouble to settle."

Fronnie smokes her pipe as she talks to Anse. She has been waiting a long time to smoke. Just somehow Fronnie couldn't sit at a table before the jury and smoke her long-stemmed pipe. There were too many strange eyes staring at her—mean eyes—not the friendly eyes of her cows. Tarvin walks over and takes Subrinea by the arm. He leads her through the milling crowd toward home. People look at Tarvin and Subrinea and wonder how a Bushman could love a Tussie. Men stand aside as the young woman, heavy with child, walks slowly toward home. Tarvin looks back at the mingling crowd—men milling like bees in a swarm. Tarvin can hear their curses and their maddened cries. He knows his father and his mother are there. It does not matter. Tarvin has Subrinea.

6.

"JEST LUCKY," says Anse, "that I got that polecat off'n my farm on the second trial. I listened to Lawyer Waddell Burton. I didn't lose my head. I bit my lips to endure the trial. It was a sight the lies they swore on me."

"It's all over now, Pa," says Tarvin. "I was over there when Sheriff Bradley put Boliver off'n the place. I never felt so sorry fer a man in my life. Boliver was out there drunk as a biled owl. 'I won't go,' he says. 'I won't go nary step. I won't leave this land.' There was a washpan layin there. Boliver grabbed it and seized it with his teeth. The galvanize flew off in tiny white flakes. He put his teeth nearly through the pan. Then he jumped and grabbed a barb wire in the barn-lot fence with his teeth. We couldn't git 'im loose without jerkin a lot of teeth out'n his mouth. We had to take a file and pry his mouth open and throw 'im on the wagon like a barrel of salt. That's the way we got 'im off."

"Thank the Lord," says Anse, "I've got 'im off. I'll never have another Tussie on my place as long as I live to gander me around. I don't think I'll ever have another renter."

"Jest to think," says Tarvin, "Boliver was hauled to Greenwood with his family and put out in the middle of the street. Think he finally found a house jest because of the condition of his wife and his daughter. Pa, that is awful. They air human beins same as we air."

"Human beins, Son," says Anse, "but the skin on a Tussie's body is jest a little thicker than it is on other people's bodies."

"I don't feel right by takin their crops," says Tarvin. "You know atter we pay George Grubb that store account of Boliver's, we'll have a thousand dollars left out'n his half of the crop. He's raised a mighty good crop this year. Pa, I hate to say it, but he has done better than we have. You know that."

"Yes," says Anse, "Boliver is a good farmer. If he'd set his head to do the right thing, he could make a rich man in a few years. He hast a good family to work. But I'd ruther have the seven-year eetch as to be bothered with that family. Allus a-pilferin like a flock of hungry crows. Jest a bunch of hard-workjn pilferin terbacker-worms, hooch-drinkin thieves. I'll haf to be made over into a new man before I'll ever let 'em even step their feet back on my land."

Tarvin does not speak. He looks from Anse Bushman's yard toward Boliver Tussie's empty shack. He looks at the immense field of tobacco and the stalwart newground corn. Tarvin looks at the stubborn hills that belong to Anse Bushman—land as far as the eye can see for a family of three people. Tarvin looks into space.

Part VII

1.

"SON, SINCE we have that den of thieves off'n our place," Anse reminds Tarvin, "we'll have both terbacker crops to handle. We'd better go around yander to that patch of dead chestnuts in the woods pasture and start cuttin tier poles fer the ter-backer barn this mornin."

"Jest as you say, Pa," says Tarvin. Tarvin follows Anse to-ward the barn. Anse is smoking a cigar. Tarvin is smoking his pipe. Two blue streams of smoke swirl above them and mingle along the path toward the barn. There is a trail of smoke left behind them from the house to the barn. Anse puts the harness on Jack. Tarvin puts the harness on Barney. They hitch the mules to the sled. Anse takes the leather check lines in his hands.

"Tarvin, fetch the tools from the tool house and lay 'em on the sled," Anse commands.

"Okay, Pa," says Tarvin.

Tarvin gets the crosscut saw, wedge, sledge hammer and two double-bitted axes. He carries them from the tool house to the sled. He throws them down on the sled. "All set, Pa," Tarvin says.

"Git-up, boys," Anse shouts.

He slaps the mules on the rump with the leather check lines. Anse rides on the sled. He does not hold to a sled standard as the sled slides over the dead leaves, stumps, rocks and pieces of broken trees. He stands flat-footed in the middle of the sled, with a cigar in his mouth. The mules move swiftly over the rough pasture road. The tools rattle on the sled bed as Anse drives the mules over the rough road. Tarvin walks behind the sled and smokes his pipe.

"These mules will go over any kind of a rough place fer me," Anse says. "They know old Anse. There was never a better span of mules hitched to a sled than Jack and Barney. They air like their master; they air gittin old."

Tarvin walks behind the sled. He does not answer Anse.

Anse drives around the hillside road from the barn. He crosses the hollow by the pine grove. He turns to his left and drives up a narrow road that is choked by stumps, trees, rocks, brush and briars. He drives into a grove of chestnut trees the blight has killed. They stand barkless like shadowy ghosts among the living trees. When Anse reaches the top of the hill, the mules are getting their breath hard. Their sides cave in and out like bee-smokers and the noise of their breathing is noise like a swarm of bees leaving the hive.

"Whoa ho, boys," Anse commands. He does not have to tighten the reins. The mules stop still in their tracks. They are glad to get a rest. Anse gets off the sled and wraps the check lines around an oak. He ties the check lines around the oak tree.

"Aint bad mules to run away," says Anse, "but I jest want to be shore they don't run off when we start cuttin these tier poles. Mules air powerful bad to skeer at fallin trees."

Tarvin knocks the ashes from his pipe on his pants leg. He puts his pipe in his hip pocket. He begins to gather the tools from the sled bed.

"Come right over here, Tarvin," says Anse. "Here's a nice dead chestnut."

Tarvin walks over to the tree. He carries the tools. He drops them at the roots of the tree. He turns his face upward toward the tree's top. He squints his blue eyes as he looks toward the sun.

"It's a nice tree fer tier poles, but we'll never git it down," says Tarvin. "This tree leans too much toward that beech top."

"I'll notch it to fall on the right of that beech," says Anse, "and we'll use the wedge and make it fall the way we want it to fall."

"Dead chestnut wood is too brittle, Pa," Tarvin explains. "You can't fall that tree the way you want it. When you start drivin the wedge the splinters aint tough enough to hold. That tree's liable to go any way."

"I'll put that goddamn tree where I want it," says Anse.

Anse takes the double-bitted ax. He cuts a notch in the tree near the ground. He cuts the notch the way he wants the tree to fall.

"Now fetch the crosscut saw," says Anse, "and let's lay this tree on the ground."

Tarvin stands on the upper side of the tree. Anse stands below. They bend over and race the saw through the dead butt of the chestnut tree just a few inches above the notch. They do not saw halfway into the tree before it starts popping and cracking. The saw is bound tight in the tree.

"Reach me the hammer and wedge, Tarvin," Anse commands.

Anse sets the wedge in the narrow groove the saw has made. He drives the wedge with the sledge hammer with all the power of his fence-post arms and his massive shoulders. The wedge follows the groove the saw has made. The tree has to fall some way. It snaps and reels; then it rolls from the stump and twists down, raining a shower of leaves and broken tree branches as it comes.

"Watch out, Pa," Tarvin shouts. "Git out'n the way! Top's a-breakin out'n the chestnut! Out'n the way—out'n the way!" His voice rises to a scream.

But Anse cannot get out of the way. He is hemmed in by a

red-oak tree. The splintered top of the chestnut tree crashes down the open space between the mass of timber and hits Anse on the forehead above the left eye. The splintered end of the chestnut top lays Anse's forehead open to the skull. The blood spurts in a red stream. Anse wilts like a tender sassafras sprout before a newground fire. His cigar is clinched between his teeth. He holds the sledge-hammer handle tight in his hands. He lies bleeding on a bed of briars and half-decayed leaves.

"My God!" Tarvin screams. "Pa, air you kilt?"

Anse does not answer. Tarvin takes the cigar from Anse's mouth. He throws it on the ground and tramps out the fire with his foot. He tries to take the sledge-hammer handle from Anse's hands. He cannot move the hammer. He cannot pull Anse's hands from the clinched death grip. Tarvin grabs Anse around the body. He tries to lift him. He cannot lift him. He puts his hand over Anse's heart. "His heart's still beatin, and he's alive, thank God!" Tarvin shouts. "Pa's jest knocked out fer the first time in his life." Tarvin glances quickly at the splintered end of the chestnut top and wonders how his father can still be alive after a treetop has fallen sixty feet or more and hit him on the forehead. Tarvin can see flesh from Anse's forehead among the splinters.

"Can't git the mules and sled to Pa," Tarvin thinks quickly. "I'll take Pa to the sled." He gets between Anse's legs and lifts a leg up under each arm. He pulls Anse like an ox drags a saw-log. He digs his heels deep into the newground dirt and pulls Anse four to five feet at a time over the dead leaves, briars, sprouts and rocks. Anse still holds the sledge hammer in his hand. There is a red stripe of Anse's blood over the dark new-ground earth where Tarvin has dragged him. Tarvin loads Anse's feet on the sled first. Then he gets down and hauls on Anse's shoulders. The blood rushes to his pale face under the strain of the heavy lift. He loads Anse on the sled as he would load a saw-log. He ties Anse on the sled so that his big round body cannot roll off as Tarvin races the mules over the rough road toward the barn. Tarvin lopes them to the yard pine in front of the house. Fronnie looks through the window and sees Tarvin coming fast as the mules can run with Anse tied on the sled.

"Oh, my Lord!" Fronnie screams. "I knowed it would come to Anse sooner 'r later fer his weakedness. He is dead, aint he, Tarvin?"

"No, Ma," says Tarvin, as he unties the binding rope that holds Anse on the sled. "Pa aint dead. He's jest knocked cuckoo. A treetop fell sixty feet and hit Pa on the fard. If it hadn't hit 'im a glancin lick it would 've kilt 'im dead as a beef."

"Thank God," says Fronnie. "There's still a chance fer Anse to git right."

Tarvin twists Anse's body crosswise on the sled bed. His heavy legs hang over. Fronnie gets between Anse's legs and holds a foot in each hand. Tarvin gets Anse by the arms. They start up the path toward the house. Anse's head hangs down, his glassy eyes stare upward at the sky and blood drips from his matted beard. His blood-soaked beard is filled with pieces of dead leaves, broken twigs and particles of dust. His death-clutched fingers will not release their grip on the sledge-hammer handle.

There Anse lies loglike on the bed in the darkened bedroom. Doc Morris comes and goes; goes and comes again. He pulls splinters two inches long and bits of bark and leaves from the bloody pulp on Anse's forehead with his surgeon's forceps. He bathes the wound with clean-smelling antiseptics over and over again—till all the flesh is clean. Then with the surgeon's needle threaded with thin clear gut he pulls the edges of part of the gaping wound together—salves and bandages it. All the while Anse lies there making no motion, no sound except his hard breathing and an occasional groan—an inert, uninterested mass, his life, his humanness, his masterfulness taken from him and hidden somewhere while Doc Morris and Fronnie and Tarvin go in and out about him.

A day—two days—three days. Fronnie tiptoes back and forth from the kitchen to look at Anse. He seems to be in a deep sleep now. His eyes are closed, his body is relaxed, his breathing easier. Doc Morris says that he must be allowed to sleep this sleep out, however long it takes. Fronnie is getting breakfast for Tarvin and herself in the kitchen. Her stringy, gray-streaked hair falls across her forehead as she bends over the stove.

Suddenly she stops and stands rigid and upright—listening. She has heard creaks and rustlings from the bedroom, and now a croaking voice. Anse is speaking!

She runs in to him with the skillet of sizzling bacon in her hand, her tousled hair hanging down on each side of her face. Anse is sitting up in bed, supporting himself on his hands. He is talking to himself. The words are pouring out all jumbled up. His blue eyes are wide open, staring, his red beard is bristling.

"Anse!" screams Fronnie. "Anse!"

Anse stops his babble of words. He is silent. He looks at her, far off, troubled and doubtful. Then his eyes come into focus. He recognizes her. She can see the knowledge of her growing in his face. Suddenly she goes weak all over. She feels like falling. Anse has come back. That is Anse Bushman on the bed now—not the insensible lump she has been tending these three days.

"Oh, Anse!" she mutters almost in a whisper, "the Lord hast saved you—the Lord—"

But Anse breaks in on her. "Fronnie, Fronnie," shouts Anse, "you can't guess what 's happened to me! You can't guess in a thousand years!"

"Now, Anse, you mustn't get all het up. Lay down and I'll bring you a cup of coffee."

"No, Mother, no!" shouts Anse. "I've had a token. I've been in the Spirit, and the Lord has showed me things. Jest set the bacon back on the stove and come in till I tell you."

"It will burn, Anse," says Fronnie.

"Let it burn," says Anse. "Let the bacon burn. There will be more bacon when we air dead and gone. There will be bacon when we kill our hogs this fall."

"Well then, tell me about your token," says Fronnie. "I want to hear about it, Anse!"

"The token come fast," says Anse. "Seemed as I was carryin corn to the hog pen to feed the hogs before the chickens got off'n the roost, just as I might be any mornin. I saw the church house at Plum Grove. I saw the church house there in the moonlight. I saw the graveyard behind the church house. I could see the tombstones plain as I ever saw them in my life. The stars looked down on the church house and the graveyard. I could see the peckerwoods' holes bored in the church-house walls. That's how plain I saw the church house when I got the token. I'll tell you things happened fast.

"I saw the inside of Plum Grove church house," says Anse. "I saw the crowd gathered and the lamps lit. I saw that little preacher. I don't know what his name was. He called hisself 'that little preacher.' He was a little man but when it come to preachin the Word he wasn't no little man. People in the church house was hollerin 'Amen' from every corner. I saw people shoutin. I saw young men buttin their heads agin the wall. I heard 'em shoutin fer the Lord to come down through the ceilin as 'that little preacher' preached. I saw men and wimmen marchin jest up one aisle and down the other—goin around and around singin the Word and lovin one another. It wasn't the vile kind of love. It was the Love of the Lord in their hearts. I tell you the people was happy and that little preacher was preachin the Word all the time they was goin up one aisle and down the other—

" 'Brothers and Sisters,' says that little preacher, 'don't walk upon the mountainside with the Devil and his angels and feast from the Devil's table. He's here somewhere lurkin around tonight! Brother and Sister, the Lord is here too. This is a fight. You see the Angels of the Lord out there—look how happy they air! Listen to 'em shout and sing! Look at Brother shake Sister's hand! Listen to 'em gittin rid of all that meanness the old Devil has put in their minds. They air cleansin their minds of the filth the Devil has put in 'em a spoonful at a time. Hep us here tonight to whop the Devil—hep us tonight!'

"And that little preacher walked across the pulpit and beat the Bible desk with his fist hard as you hit a fence post with a maul. Looked like he would break every bone in his hand. But the Lord wouldn't let him break nary bone.

"I stood there and I could hear the Death Bells ringin in my ears. I dropped my armload of corn right in my tracks. I closed my eyes to the token. I could see it all plain as day. And I could hear: 'Listen to this, Anse Bushman! Listen to the call of the Lord! Your kinfolks have died before you—and they air buried in the hills of Kentucky—your Pappie and your Mammie have long gone back to dust. The dust that put you here, Anse Bushman—a man in this world to work and to work hard —to cuss to fight and to save your little dollars. You air feastin at the Devil's table. You air eatin the persimmon sprouts upon the mountainside—the saw briars, the green briars, the crab grass, the bull grass—why don't you come down and feast at the table in the valley that the Lord has set—you'll be in clover, wheat, barley and corn up to your eyes—not terbacker and moonshine barley either. You will feast with them that made you. You remember your prayin mother, Anse Bushman? You remember your shoutin Pappie? You remember how he ust to cuss and fight and how your poor old Mammie nagged at him until she got him down at the Lord's table in the Valley? You remember how he whopped his neighbors and stole from them? You remember how he ust to shoot at the squatters and run 'em over the hills sprinklin 'em with chilled buckshot? You remember it all—and how he repented in the end? He told God's people how sorry he was—and how sorry he was that he built a fire in the church door with timothy hay, and the prayin mothers and fathers had to climb out the winders 'r be burnt to death in the church house at Six Hickories. The Devil had 'im when he burnt that church house but the Lord forgive 'im when he come home to the Lord. The Lord forgive 'im and the Lord will forgive any sinner. The Lord will make a new man out'n you. Come and dine—come and feast—oh, come! Oh, won't you come and feast at Jesus' table all the time!'

"I thought in my mind," says Anse, "I won't come, I won't feast at Jesus' table.' I knew I was layin here in the bed yet I knew at the same time I was at the hog pen with a load of corn, lookin across into the Plum Grove church house.

" 'This aint the old Methodist Church I allus went to,' I thought. 'This can't be the old Methodist Church—it never stirred me like this—this can't be Plum Grove—' And I looked agin. It *was* the Methodist Church. I could see the little spire —and the tombstones stood all over the hill like ghosts in the moonlight—I know it is as true as I know that you air my good wife, Fronnie, and Tarvin is my son. I know what I'm sayin is true—"

"Tell the rest of it, Anse," says Fronnie; "don't stop now!"

"I am goin to tell the whole story," says Anse. "I want you to know that I am not dodgin any of it. I want you all to know what I saw. I want you to know that Anse Bushman is a changed man—

"And that little preacher," Anse continues as the spittle flies from his mouth and his fast-workin big rough hands clasp and unclasp in his eagerness as he speaks, "said a man could git all the gold he wanted and gold to spare—he could buy all the land that he wanted and land to spare—and he could have renters on his land that shared their crops with 'im—and he could live from milk and honey—the best there was on the land—and yit he wasn't happy because he had lost his own soul. He didn't walk the narrer pathway with the Lord. He was walkin the broad pathway with the Devil and his angels to a hell of fire, brimstone and eternal destruction.

"I'll tell you," says Anse, "when he said that I felt like I was stabbed with a knife—a long hawk-billed knife right through my heart. I felt the warm blood gush. I felt like the rocks from the mountains were fallin down upon me. I felt like I wanted to holler out fer the Lord. I remembered what had happened in my lifetime—I remembered my children and how hard I had worked 'em—how I had treated 'em—how I had treated Fronnie—I remembered how I had done Boliver Tussie and his family—I knowed I'd been a vile sinner. That little preacher at Plum Grove preached the Word right to me. He made the Word hit me square between the eyes like a bullet from a hog rifle. It seemed to fell me right in my tracks."

Fronnie smokes her pipe and watches Anse. She listens to every word Anse is saying. The bacon is burning on the stove. A dingy twirling smoke is ascending from the skillet toward the rain-circled newspapered ceiling. The biscuit bread is burning in the oven and the smoke is coming from the stove doors. The coffeepot is boiling over and the coffee-stained water is sizzling on the red-hot stove-top. Fronnie does not care. She listens to Anse.

"My heart was still a stone," says Anse in a slower and deeper voice. Anse's blue eyes begin to stare out of his face. They look strangely blue and alive. His big fire-shovel hands wave as he talks. Words fly from his mouth and specks of dry foamy spittle fly like December snowflakes. "I was still the old Anse Bushman. I was still the old sinnin Anse Bushman. I was still the miser hoardin his gold. I was still the brute. I was still the headstrong bull-faced know-it-all. I still hated Boliver Tussie in my heart. I jest wouldn't soften. Boliver Tussie had done too much to me. I still couldn't git over the way he broke that ar-tickle. The way he run up that big store account. The way he said he'd knock my teeth down my throat with a rock in the newground terbacker patch. I couldn't git over the way he come on my premises and boasted about not gettin off'n my place the day the Sheriff Bradley was with 'im. I couldn't git over what I saw in the terbacker patch in the moonlight one night. I couldn't git over what two Tussie wimmen said to me one day in Ragweed Holler. It all come back to me big as mountains.

"Then I looked at the other side. I'd run the Tussies from their home. I'd run 'em away from that patch of trees of Heaven where their dust is buried—dust of many generations —maybe some of that dust was feastin at the Lord's table with my Mammie and Pappie—I didn't know. It was jest a big dream that can be true. That little preacher at Plum Grove, the way he preached the Scriptures, made me wonder. I'd run Boliver away and took his crop. He's over in Greenwood now. I'd put him off'n my farm and took all he had and I didn't need it. That was my soul. I was losin my own life. I was losin my soul. I was jest as much to blame as Boliver Tussie—and I begin to shake.

"This is what shook me," says Anse. "This is what made

my blood run cold. I saw the little preacher goin away. There was light all around him. The crowd with light on their faces follered him. I saw some of the Tussie faces in the crowd and a lot of the Beavers, and I ust to didn't think squatters had souls like other people. Now I believe everybody hast a soul. I saw old Dan Perkins with his head of white hair and it was wavin in the wind. I saw old men and old wimmen—and boys and girls. I saw people I'll tell you about soon as I can recollect 'em all. I saw people left in the church house—people that we thought was servin the Lord. I saw them left there and the light got dim and dimmer and soon the church house was dark and the Devil had his own. I saw the darkness about the church house and the starlight and the moonlight fallin on the church house as it has allus done. I saw the white gleam of the tombstones in the graveyard that looked like ghosts. It was all over, I thought—

"And, Fronnie, your words of warnin come to me when I saw another sight," says Anse. "You remember what you told me about three weeks ago when I was comin to the house to git slop fer the hogs. You warned me about the Lake of Fire. I saw the Lake of Fire. I saw more than that. I hate to tell you all I saw. It was enough to make the strongest man alive on this earth tremble."

Anse's voice faltered, broke, and went on again.

"I saw old Judge Whittlecomb in that pin-striped suit he wears walkin on the Lake of Fire. The sweat was rollin from his pink soft cheeks. He had that old hoss-racin record in his hand that he reads when the lawyers air arguin a case in court. I saw 'im jest as plain as I saw 'im the other day when I had my trial with Boliver Tussie. I jest wondered what Kentucky thoroughbreds he was bettin on now? He was sweatin and walkin fast like he was in a hurry to git some place. But he wasn't gittin no place. He was jest walkin and walkin and stayin in the same place with smoke all aroun 'im. Smoke was poppin from the seat of his britches jest like he was on fire.

"I saw a scorpion beside the path. It was a striped-tailed scorpion and it had Flem Spry's head on its body. It was layin beside the Lake of Fire. I saw its forked tongue tryin to drink hooch from a horse quart. I jest thought about how old Flem had preached half his life away, and how he raved and ranted as the President of the Moonshiners' Association the other half of his life—gittin a little money now and then and layin in the fence corner drunk on hooch. He was a scorpion on earth and a scorpion in hell.

"And the smoke oozed from the earth, Fronnie. The ground was dry and parched. I could see big cracks in the land and I could see people down in the cracks and hear them weepin and wailin and I could hear the gnashin of teeth. I could see a valley filled with dry bones. I could smell the brimstone and it was awful to smell—jest like that little preacher at Plum Grove preached—jest exactly what he said hell would be like. I could see the men and wimmen tryin to hide their faces when the big rocks rolled from the mountains and crushed em. They jest rolled over 'em and mashed 'em and the people got up agin in their affliction. Bones stuck out all over their bodies and eyeballs fell down on their cheeks. They couldn't die. The Devil wouldn't let 'em die."

"Did you see Boliver?" Fronnie asks.

"Yes," says Anse, "I did. I was jest comin to that. I saw them both, Fronnie. A little dried-up, thin, yellowish copper-head, a-layin squirmin back and forth, with Bollie Beaver's head onto it. And over agin it I saw a big viper snake. It was a bull viper snake. It had a big rough body and the skin was scalin from its body. It had Boliver Tussie's head on it. I saw a viper snake beside him, and its body was smaller and its skin was a lot slicker—it looked like a cow snake. It had Crissie's head on it. Their forked tongues hissed at me as I passed 'em— and they had six little snakes beside 'em—and the little snakes had the heads of Boliver's and Crissie's children on 'em. I didn't see Subrinea there. She was not in this den of viper snakes. They all hissed at me when I walked by 'em and looked over the Lake of Fire and brimstone."

2.

"Did you see yourself there, Anse?" Fronnie asks.

"I hate to tell you," says Anse, "but I did. That is why I'm a changed man. You'll never hear Anse Bushman takin the Lord's name in vain agin. You'll never see 'im usin a two-year-old club on anybody agin. You'll never see 'im tryin to git every loose dollar. I am too old to be lookin fer sicha foolishness and worldly goods to lose my soul. I saw myself there. I was swimmin in the Lake of Fire and brimstone. I can see myself now. Stout a man as I am—good a swimmer as I am—I wasn't swimmin at all. I was jest workin myself to death to stay on top and not gittin any place. I was doin what I like to do—work—work in the hottest place—and my beard was filled with the hot molten dirt and rock and ore, and I was prayin and hollerin fer the rocks to fall on me—and I was cryin fer water but I didn't git it. I was gittin my punishment for the way I treated my wife, my children and my neighbors here on earth. Boliver was a blowin viper snake and he was watchin me on the Lake of Fire and brimstone from the bank. He was stickin out his forked tongue at me. It's awful to think about; I wasn't dreamin and I aint crazy. I jest had a token and I aim to make things right the rest of my life. I aim to git rid of my two jolt-wagon loads of sin."

"Oh Glory! I'm glad," says Fronnie. "I'm so glad, Anse, that I feel like shoutin. I've let the breakfast burn and day-light will soon be here. I'll put another fire in the stove and git breakfast all over agin. I'll haf to scratch the burnt bacon from the skillet on the stove and burnt hard biscuits from the pan in the oven and dig the stuck coffee grounds out'n the bottom of the pot. But it's worth it, Anse, if I had to do it a hundred times. Oh, Glory!"

3.

THREE WEEKS later, and Anse is able to be sitting in the split-bottom chair set out in the sunshine by the barn. His right arm is limp at his side, and his right leg is no longer the pillar of strength that it has been. The bandage is gone from his head, and only the raw red scar remains to show where it had been.

"What do we aim to do about Boliver, Pa?" Tarvin asks. "How do you aim to make up fer all the wrong you have done to 'im?"

"If he wants to come back here," says Anse, "bring 'im back here when you go atter Subrinea. Bring 'im back and put 'im on the land. He loves this land. He will never do anything more to me. We'll git along now. There won't be all this fightin between us that there has been. I'm a different Anse Bushman now. This is the new Anse Bushman. The old Anse Bushman is dead. He was buried three weeks ago. Bring Boliver back to the shack he left. Let 'im have his crop that stands in the field. It belongs to him. He earnt it by the sweat of his brow. That is one fulfillment of the Lord's Word."

"You air doin' right, Pa," says Tarvin. "I'll be tickled to death that you air lettin Boliver move back to the shack. He'll be at home there. He ought to be there instid of town. He aint happy cooped up like a turkey in town."

"Lawsuits never settled anything in Greenwood," says Anse. "When the suit is over the fight is jest beginnin. Atter the suit is over, the guns begin to crack. Our trouble won't be over with the Tussies, but I aint afeared now. I know that I aint treated 'em right and if I treat 'em right then it won't be long until they'll be goin all the way with me. That is the new Anse Bushman. The new Anse Bushman is a happy man and he knows that he is happy. It took him so long to find out how to live. Now he has larned how to live on earth, when he is about ready to kick the bucket and go to the next world to meet his loved ones gone on before."

"Then I'll go and bring 'em home," says Tarvin. "I'll gear the mules and bring 'em back to the shack. We'll all try to live in peace."

"What hast Boliver been doin since he moved to Greenwood?" Anse asks.

"When I saw 'im the other day, Pa," says Tarvin, "he was layin on the porch with his big bare feet stuck over the edge. He was hollerin that he was fallin. People come along the street and stopped. There was a whole crowd gathered in front of Boliver's house. People jest laughed and talked when they looked at the bottoms of his feet. They looked big as fire-shovels and the skin on the bottoms of his feet looked thick as clapboards. Boliver was drunk as a biled owl."

"Town aint no place fer Boliver," says Anse. "Boliver belongs on the land. He belongs on this farm. I've jest been thinkin it over. Boliver hast his faults but he belongs to the dirt same as I belong to the dirt and same as you belong to the dirt—same as the grass, weeds, corn, cane and terbacker belong to the dirt. And Boliver belongs to this dirt. He belongs to these rough slopes—these rocks and these deep hollers. Be shore, Tarvin, that you bring 'im back."

"The Tussie children don't git along in town," says Tarvin. "They aint enough room fer 'em on a little lot. They git out in the road and play. They play on the street and git in other people's yards to play. They don't go dressed like the other children in town and people don't want 'em playin with their children. They play too rough. People git out and shoo 'em away. They air too much fer the children in town. You can tell a Tussie when you see 'im by his dirty face, hands and legs and the big bare feet. Boliver's boys have had several fights and Snail and Big Aaron hast been in jail a couple of times fer fightin."

"How do they live, Tarvin?" Anse asks.

"It's been hard fer 'em to live," says Tarvin. "Subrinea and Crissie have been takin in washins and cleanin people's kitchens. Big Aaron and Snail git a day's work now and then fer fifty cents apiece. Boliver finds work now and then fer a dollar a day. But Boliver gits on a drunk with his money. He buys that old cheap hooch. If it wasn't fer Subrinea I don't know what they'd do. Soon as I move them back to their home and to their crops I'll take Subrinea out'n the family. She jest can't leave 'em now, Pa."

"Son, from now on," says Anse, "the new Anse Bushman aint goin to be a hog and try to take everything. If there is a bushel of corn left over atter the corn hast been divided there aint goin to be no drawin fer the longest straw any more with my friend fixin the long straw fer me so I can git the extra bushel. There aint goin to be no more swindlin. I'd ruther give my renter ten barrels of corn as to take a ear of corn from 'im. That's what the Lord hast done fer me. I'm throwin my pistols and my knucks away. I've put my cigars away—my chawin home twist away—not that terbacker is vile to the spirit but I jest don't crave it any more. The Lord hast taken that taste out'n my mouth."

"I believe you *air* a changed man, Pa." says Tarvin.

"Changed," Anse repeats. "I'm a made-over man. I'm made over in and out. Son, I know people will think I'm batty. My mind is good even if I am gittin a little along up in years. But look among these hills—we don't care fer the laws of man! We play tricks with 'em. We can joke with 'em. If you got the money as I've allus had—you can git your way with the Law. That is man-made laws. The people that git cheated know that they have been cheated and they take to their own laws—their way of settlin disputes. They settle their troubles with powder and lead, rocks, clubs, fists and knives. Look at the fights we have had in Greenwood County—troubles that will never be settled until the Lord makes peace fer 'em. Look at the killin trials that never git to court here. They know trouble will start in the courthouse. Look at the people that follow the Lord; they don't have this trouble. It is the only way out. I know it. Let others do as they will. I know the path I aim to follow. I'm jest sorry that I've waited so long. Yit I'm not near as old as my Pappie was. He was eighty-two when he laid down his gun and quit fightin—put away his whiskey jug and was baptized in a stream of runnin water. I remember Pappie got sick and fell in the cornfield. He promised the Lord that if he got all right that he'd be a different man. All the time Pappie was sick he saw Devils and he fit Devils—Pappie had lived a wild weaked life. I'm like Pappie was and you'll be like I am. You air young and kickin up your heels now. You air eatin your yaller corn bread. Wait until later and you'll see the light and you'll give your heart."

Tarvin does not speak to Anse. He looks at the hills across Ragweed Hollow. He looks at the August sunlight on the buff-coloring full-maturing corn. He sniffs the scent of maturing corn on the morning wind into his nostrils. It is good to smell. Tarvin looks at Boliver's immense newground tobacco patch. He can see the light green under side of the tobacco leaves turn windwise when the August wind molests the leaves. Tarvin can see life about him—life among the growing and maturing crops—life among the green growing things, life among the trees, life and the quick pulse-beating of everything that grows, crawls, flies and walks. Tarvin feels the strong surge of life beating from his own heart—the surge of red blood against his ribs, strength in his body, strength to turn over mountains and see what is under them.

"I'm takin the mules this mornin, Pa," says Tarvin. "I'm goin atter Boliver. I want Subrinea back with me. I aint got a shack yit but I want Subrinea if I haf to live in the sheep shanty until I can git my house done."

"Take the mules and go, Son," says Anse. "The mules air there in the barn and the harness is bright and shiny. The wagon is settin there in the barn entry and the axles air greased. Bring Subrinea here if you want to."

"One house," says Tarvin, "no matter how big the house is, it aint big enough fer two families. I'll take Subrinea to the sheep shanty. We got the baby there. It can be born there."

"Subrinea might not want to go," says Anse.

"Subrinea won't care," says Tarvin. "She'll be happy there with me until we can git our shack built."

"Then you can have our old furniture," says Anse. "Your Ma will jest be glad to let you have it. And we can have a house raisin and throw you up a house jest any day this month. It would be better to cut the logs next month when the sap goes down in the trees."

"All right, Pa," says Tarvin. "That will be fine."

"Somethin more I want to say to you, Son," says Anse. "I think you air gittin a real gal. She'll be good to stick by you in the time of need. Subrinea belongs to the hills. She can work in the fields. She can hep you with the lambs in lambin time. She's a real gal."

"I know it, Pa," says Tarvin. "There ain't a better gal among the hills than Subrinea."

"I didn't think so at first," says Anse. "When I saw that purty gal, I jest thought about all the squatters I'd seen. One day last winter when I come down Cat's Fork, I found her buryin the dead lambs under the trees of Heaven. I thought she was a little off 'n the head. She was preachin their funerals and singin hymns. I can't fergit that, Tarvin. The longer I think about, the more I like Subrinea. She hast to be a good gal to do this. She aint got a hard heart in her bosom. She's a good gal 'r she wouldn't a-done that."

Tarvin puts the harness on Murt. Anse puts the harness on Dick.

"I'll tell you, Tarvin," says Anse, "I'll haf to larn Boliver how to plow. He don't understand it. But I believe he can larn. Boliver is a good worker and a good farmer. His fields air clean as a hound dog's tooth. There aint a weed in any row. He cuts the sprouts from around the rocks and stumps. Not many farmers do that. They let sicha places grow up and they become hidin places fer the copperheads."

Tarvin hitches the mules to the wagon. He drives the team from the barn entry, circles to his left around the barn and through the barn-lot gate to the jolt-wagon road that leads over the yellow clay bank and deep down into Ragweed Hollow. Anse watches him stand in the wagon bed with one foot on the brake beam, holding it down as the prancing mules hold back on the wagon tongue with their breastyokes. Tarvin has the leather check lines in his hands. The red tassels on the mules' bridles are waving in the bright August wind.

Anse stands and watches Tarvin until the wagon rolls out of sight around the bluff where the rock cliffs edge out. The last that he can see is Tarvin's shoulders and then Tarvin's head as he disappears from sight and Anse hears the rumble of the wagon over the rocks. Anse walks from the yard pine toward the house.

4.

"GOLDENROD is bloomin on the lazy pasture fields now," thinks Tarvin, "and Subrinea will go wild when she gits back to the hills. I can see her goin over the bluffs smellin the fingers of the goldenrod. And the farewell-to-summers have started to bloom on the bluffs. Subrinea is heavy with child but she will run out among the flowers like a bumblebee."

Tarvin looks at the goldenrod on the hill slopes. He looks at the farewell-to-summers on the steep bluffs. Their purple tops are intermingled with their white blossoms. Honeybees and bumblebees buzz lazily over their blossoms gathering sweets to make wild honey. They buzz as lazily over the wild flowers as the yellowish rays of sunlight fall on the warm moist productive earth. Crows fly over from the pine grove on the hill. They wing across the blue air in Ragweed Hollow by twos. Tarvin looks at them as they fly over.

"All things marry," thinks Tarvin, "and they don't marry by man's laws. I wonder if they have laws of their own or if they marry by their own God's laws. Look at the crows buildin their nests in the pine groves. Look at the birds buildin their nests in the thickets. Look as the snakes layin their eggs in the warm loamy earth by the rock cliffs. Look at the turtles and the terrapins layin their eggs in the warm sandbanks by the mountain streams.

"If all life could jest git along togither," thinks Tarvin. "There is where the rub of life is. We can't git along among our own kinds. The Tussies and the Bushmans never got along together. But now, somehow, seems as if we'd have to."

Tarvin drives the mules down the road past the Cat's Fork that turns to his left. He stops his mules and puts his foot on the brake beam. He looks at a green cloud of leaves that seem to form a part of the sky. The sky around the green quivering cloud is a high mountain of white rolling cloud. Tarvin can see the quiver of the green cloud and Tarvin can remember the trees of Heaven. He can remember the wild flowers, the brush and briars and the copperheads beneath the trees of Heaven—and he remembers the fine white hair-roots that go down downward, downward and downward to the eternal dust of her people. He can remember the dreams that are enclosed in that eternal dust whose way of life he loved—and whose eternal dust left a flower of living dust, beautiful to behold and full of life, love and living dreams.

"Not a nickel, not a penny, not a quarter, and not a dollar," thinks Tarvin, "and they lived life and they loved life. They hunted over the land and they lived and loved and they enjoyed the comin springs with the burst of herbs, flowers and leaves—and the thin blood in the veins of the trees and the sounds of the insects that was music to their ears—the hoot of the owl and the chicken-hawks callin from the skies—and the bull-bat screamin—and the sound of the wind—and life was about them. And they loved the sight of plants and the white petals on the bloodroot. They loved the earth and the smells of spring earth—wind, clean and sweet to smell with the flowers of spring. They loved the growth of the hot summer season with its rains and the moist loamy earth—and the crawl of the snake, the turtle and the terrapin. What were laws to them? The laws of Nature were their laws. They lived hard and they loved it because life was sweet to them. Now they are dust under the trees of Heaven and the strings on their fiddles air mute and cold and the toes that stepped briskly on the puncheon floor do not dance and the guitar strings and the banjo strings air silent as the dust.

"And the trees that fed 'em nuts and the vines that fed 'em berries air gone, and the land where their stock and hogs run free has been fenced by ugly wire fences. And the game that they hunted has gone—gone as they have gone, and my Pa has hepped to destroy all of this.

"But there's a whole lot left—the seasons of spring, summer and autumn that Subrinea loves, and her love to work with growin plants and livin things, and her love to work with her hands. The smell of the fall and the colorin of the leaves, turnin from green to brown and red. And the coolin wind that tastes to the lungs of frost, and makes the lungs feel deep and cold—good wind to breathe; and the ferns on the bluff above the cold blue streams of dwindlin autumn water—Subrinea loves them, and I love them, and I am married to Subrinea. When I married her in the sheep shanty, I married all of this."

The wagon creaks over the dark Kentucky earth. The high hills loom up on each side as barriers fighting against the sun. The water trickles down a channel that is infested with water moccasins, frogs, turtles, terrapins, willows and ferns. The wagon is slowly creaking over the twisted road and the mules are pawing deeply into the earth with steel-shod feet. Tarvin is riding with his hand on the brake beam now and the leather check lines in his other hand.

"Not a dollar," thinks Tarvin, "not a penny, but love and life in my heart. The bright August wind is good to breathe from the green growing life that covers the earth—this earth among the hills where life stirs at night and where there is music, work, fight, growth, sleep and dark, and where there will be the winy sunlight coming again tomorrow."

THE END